YEAR OF NIGHT

YEAR OF NIGHT

KATE BESWICK

Cover design by Fiona Bell Currie
Author photograph by Bee Gilbert

Matador
9 Priory Business Park
Kibworth Beauchamp
Leicestershire LE8 0RX, UK
Tel: (+44) 116 279 2299
Fax: (+44) 116 279 2277
Email: books@troubador.co.uk
Web: www.troubador.co.uk/matador

ISBN 978 1780885 513

British Library Cataloguing in Publication Data.
A catalogue record for this book is available from the British Library.

Typeset in StempelGaramond Roman by Troubador Publishing Ltd
Printed and bound in the UK by TJ International, Padstow, Cornwall

Matador is an imprint of Troubador Publishing Ltd

For Gerry and Kefi

CHARACTERS

Nadezhda Mikhailovna Serova (Nadyushka, Nadia)

Igor Fyedorovich Rozanov (Igoryoshka, Igoryok)

Dmitri Sergeevich Arensky (Mitya, Dima)

Eugenia Kirillovna Arenskaya (Zhenia)

Olga Nikolayevna Sherbatyeva (Olya)

Gregory Benediktovich Cherkansky (Gyorgy)

Vladimir Ladinsky

Nina Ladinskaya

Nikolai Stassov

Alexei Semyonovich Mordvinov (Alyosha)

Larissa Borisovna Mordvinova

Grisha Bobrov

Kyra Alexandrovna Orokhova

Leonid Emanuelovitch Lewitsky

Isidor Emanuelovitch Lewitsky

Boris Chengarov (Borya)

Pavel

Beate

Tanya

CHAPTER ONE

1915

I sat on a bench under the willow trees, behind the summer house on the lake, reading Pushkin and listening to the sounds of argument that came from the open windows of the dacha a few yards away. The air was sultry with the scent of jasmine, the cherries hung heavy and purple on the trees. I had planned to memorise the whole of "The Gypsies" before the end of the summer, and recite it to Uncle Igor; I could picture how impressed he would be by my accomplishment. He wasn't really my uncle, but I had always called him "Uncle Igor." I hadn't realised how long the poem actually was until I had begun, but I was determined to do it, although I was daunted by my slow progress. Today I was also distracted by the heat and by the argument on the veranda of our dacha.

Uncle Igor said something I couldn't hear, and then Dyedushka bellowed, 'You refuse to toast the tsar!'

I strained forward as Uncle Igor said something too low for me to hear and then raised his voice again. 'A useless war.' Then he added, 'That idiot is under Rasputin's spell. A drunken lecher runs the country! Let the workers strike for everything they can get! Your Russia is finished.'

'Get out! Get out right now!' I heard Dyedushka roar. 'None of that revolutionary filth in my house.'

I forgot about Pushkin. Would Uncle Igor be shot? Revolutionaries were shot. Was he a revolutionary? I prayed that he wasn't. They were joined by a deep, slow voice, which I knew was Papa. He never raised his voice and I could

1

only catch a few phrases: 'left wing university circles... bad influence...'

I heard our housekeeper Dunya calling me, but I didn't answer. I wasn't ready to give up the day and go in to supper. The air was still sultry but the sky had deepened to the gold of sunset. The book fell to the ground as I squeezed my eyes tight shut and prayed for God to forgive Uncle Igor for being a revolutionary.

There was a rustle of footsteps, a crack of a willow branch and Uncle Igor said my name. 'Nadia. Nadyushka. You have been listening all this time.'

I opened my eyes and scrambled to my feet, feeling embarrassed for looking silly.

He laughed. 'Don't be frightened. I won't corrupt you.'

He was tall and handsome in his cadet uniform and he carried his kitbag.

'I'm leaving,' he said. 'I have been told not to pollute the general's share of Holy Russian land. But I was looking for you.' He bent down and picked up my book from the grass.

'I'm going to learn it all by heart,' I told him, but it didn't seem so important any more. I asked immediately, 'Why didn't you toast the tsar? Because of Rasputin?'

'No, because he has betrayed the people he was sworn to protect. You don't have to think about it yet.'

'I think about everything,' I said. 'If he swore to protect the people, then he must protect them.'

He laughed, not in the teasing way most adults did, but in a way that made me feel as if we were collaborators. 'Good for you. Don't let anyone stop you thinking. Come, I'll get Simeon to take me to the station in his cart.'

'Dyedushka has the Victoria,' I said. I liked the idea of riding with Uncle Igor in the Victoria, behind the smart little horses with their blue harness.

'I don't want his damned Victoria.'

We walked down the road hand in hand. Uncle Igor's jaw was set and he took such long strides I skipped to keep up with him. His face relaxed, he grinned down at me and, idiotically, we both laughed.

As we reached the edge of the field, where the izbas were clumped together, we met a group of boys carrying something in a willow basket. I could hear scratching and see how the basket swayed so hard that the boy had trouble holding it.

'Good day, Baryn. Good day, little miss,' said the boy. His friends touched their forelocks.

'What have you got there?' Uncle Igor asked. Still holding my hand, he went to look.

'The rat, Baryn,' said one of the boys. He indicated a bigger boy. 'Shura caught it this morning.'

Uncle Igor nodded. 'Go on then, don't mind us.'

One of the boys raised the lid of the basket and another lifted out the huge rat, its teeth bared, its eyes slit with panic. He held it away from him, gripped it around its fat body.

'Look at that belly Nadyushka,' said Uncle Igor. 'Bloated with garbage.'

The rat clawed the air, and gnashed its teeth as a third boy poured a bucket of paraffin over its head. Within seconds, it was soaked in the stinking liquid and the air smelt of oil, the way it smelt when our dvornik, old Simeon, cleaned the wheels of the lineika. The boy who had carried the basket struck a match and touched it to the animal, which made a bloodcurdling noise, neither human nor animal. They managed to drop it onto the road, just before it was haloed by a ring of flame. Everyone pressed forward to watch.

I wanted to look away but I was hypnotised by the beauty of the fire, its heat burning within the heat of the day. The waxy smell of paraffin mingled with the sickly, sour smell of burning fur, scorched skin, heat and dust. The rat twisted in all directions, trying to escape itself. When the flames reached its face it began another screech, which was immediately smothered by fire.

The boys shouted and clapped and I could sense Uncle Igor breathing more heavily beside me. The rat's tortured body

3

became the blackened centre of the blaze; its belly burst open and I gagged as I imagined I could see the maggots from the rotting meat it took from our garbage. The animal desperately writhed in the dust accompanied by the background of shouting and laughter, which rose to a climax as fire and animal flared in one final moment of hideous, doomed beauty. Gradually its contractions slowed, and it twitched weakly before it lay still. The flames died down, leaving only a small heap of ash and glowing embers in the dust, beneath a bit of skull.

There was an awkward moment of hesitation, followed by a sense of anti-climax, as if something more should happen. But there was only the summer evening and the last pale stink of oil and smoke. The boys looked at each other and at the dusty road; they picked up their basket and left without a backward glance.

I was almost unaware of Uncle Igor as he took my hand again. 'I'll take you back as far as the summer house,' he said. 'Then they won't see me.'

We walked back slowly. I was consumed by the image of the rat writhing in its last moment when life met death. It didn't seem like the right sort of time to say anything. It was only a rat, but even so, I thought, it was something alive that had just died and it deserved the respect of at least a brief silence.

The burnt orange sky was touched with deeper red and purple. Behind me I could hear a splash in the lake, as a fish leapt and dived into the water.

'Well, Nadia, what did you think? Tell me.'

I fumbled for words. The truth was I didn't know. 'It was horrible,' I said. 'It was cruel and vile. How could they do it?' There was a tiny smile at the corners of his mouth. I had to admit the rest; Mama and Papa had taught me never to lie. 'But when it was in the middle of the fire,' I said, 'it was beautiful in a way. But it had such a horrible smell.'

'Yes, beautiful and stinking. Interesting.'

'Is that what happens when soldiers die?' I whispered, not

sure if I really wanted to know. One of our servants had joined up as soon as war was declared and had been killed within three months. Now my cousin Sergei was an officer fighting in Moldavia.

'Not exactly,' he said. 'It takes longer.'

Dunya was still calling from the veranda steps. 'Nadezhda Mikhailovna! Come in at once!'

Uncle Igor picked up the book, which I had left on the ground. 'But you watched. You didn't want to run away from it, did you? You weren't frightened.'

'No,' I said, surprised by the question.

'No. I saw you.' He nodded toward the dacha. 'You can imagine what the rest of them would do. But not you. You and I,' he said carefully, 'we're not like the rest of them. We are alike.' He looked at the book. 'Ah, yes, we were talking about "The Gypsies." Poor Aleko. He comes from the city and thinks he can join the tribe and be free without sacrifice. The old man warns him, remember?'

'But Aleko loves that girl,' I pointed out. 'It isn't fair,' I said. 'The gypsies are all supposed to be free, but they keep their bear on a chain. And when Aleko joins them, he doesn't say anything about that.' I struggled to explain something that I had worried about and that was still unclear to me. 'They say they're free, but they're cruel.'

'But Aleko is worse. He murders.'

'No, he isn't worse. He is jealous and he kills because of them.' I tried to defend Aleko. 'It isn't fair.'

'Fair. How old are you Nadia? Seventeen? Eighteen?'

'Uncle Igor! I'm fifteen.'

'Fifteen already!' he said, as if he was surprised. He handed me the book. 'If you learn this poem by heart by the time I come to see you in Petersburg, I will take you to a place where everyone knows lots of poetry.' He laughed and added in a dramatic voice, 'They read poetry all night, and for that night you will be sixteen at least. I promise.' He laughed again, gave an elegant bow and kissed my hand.

That night I lay in bed, breathing in the cool air and looking at the night sky flooded with stars. Dunya had left the windows open. It was such a hot night that the servants had dragged their mattresses outside and were sleeping on the balcony by the hayloft. Mama's parents, my Dyedushka and Babyshka had strolled round the flowerbeds, admiring the scented stock and stiff beds of heliotrope before they retired early, following their usual summer routine. Mama and Papa sat on the veranda.

'He does these things...' said Mama. 'He's always so difficult – so at odds – '

'Well, what do you expect?' said Papa, rustling his newspaper. 'We have to remember...'

'Sshhh ... '

Of course, I knew they were talking about Uncle Igor. It was puzzling: he wasn't exactly a relative but he was somehow part of our family.

'Remember he's not really your uncle,' Mama told me when I was little and began to call him Uncle Igor.

'Why not?' I had asked but she had said nothing. I decided not to tell anyone about the rat. But I would learn all of "The Gypsies" and lots of other poems as well. I was suddenly inspired to write a poem myself. I got out of bed and jotted down the title in my diary: "Burning Rat."

* * *

In October, it was too cold to stay at the dacha, and the carts were loaded again with trunks and furniture as we went home to St. Petersburg: to school, dancing classes, strikes and bread riots. I managed to memorise the opening stanzas of "The Gypsies" and struggled to write my own poem. After many failed attempts I abandoned the effort, and only the title "Burning Rat" was still in my notebook.

CHAPTER TWO

OCTOBER, 1916

My name day was on the thirtieth of September. Two weeks later, someone pulled hard on the bell at the front door and the *dvornik* appeared, announcing Uncle Igor. It had been a year since his summer promise, but I didn't have to remind him of it. He asked, as if he had not been gone for over a year, 'And did you learn all of that long poem? And are you still 15?'

'Uncle Igor,' I protested, 'I haven't been fifteen for a long time. Months.'

'And do you still like poetry?'

'Of course I do.'

'Then it's time to go to the Brodyachaya Sabaka together.' He said to Mama, 'My promise.'

'You shouldn't have promised such a thing. You can keep it when she's older.'

'If I can't go, I'll run into the street and die!' I said fiercely. 'I'll throw myself in front of the Chirinsky's horses. I'll jump in the canal.'

'A name day present,' said Uncle Igor. 'After all, at sixteen ...'

We were in the small drawing room that overlooked Lityini Prospekt. I could hear the Chirinsky's carriage passing beneath the windows and fading into the distance. They no longer had their troika. Horses had been requisitioned for the war and they had only their small carriage with the single black mare. It was dusk, and Dunya had started to light the lamps, which hissed their announcement of evening. Behind her, the parlour-maid drew the curtains. I knew that tonight the lamps, the heavy drapes, the heavily-embroidered cushions on the small sofas, would simply choke me.

'Sixteen is nothing – '

'Oh Mama, people are different now. It's 1916.'

'No they are not different,' she said. 'People are always the same, and young girls do not go running about in the evening. That will always be the same.'

She had spent the afternoon rolling bandages with the empress and the other lady aides at the Winter Palace, and she was tired. She had not been pleased when Uncle Igor arrived unexpectedly. The parlour maid brought her a glass of tea from the samovar and she leaned back in the armchair and sipped it delicately. The deep green wool of her afternoon dress fell around her legs in soft folds; her ears, her wrists and her fingers sparkled with small diamonds. I wanted to rush away from all of this. While I was going to school and doing homework and practicing the piano, the world was turning upside down. Uncle Igor was offering me a chance to be part of it. I waited for him to argue with her, to persuade her, but he stood back with his arms folded. He looked at the painting of the Caucasus that hung over the mantelpiece.

'It isn't fair!' I cried.

'*Brodyachaya Sabaka*. Stray Dog. What sort of name is that? It is obviously not an appropriate place for children,' said Mama, and added to Uncle Igor, 'How could you suggest such a thing?'

'Sofya,' Uncle Igor said to her, opening his arms wide, as if to display his offer for her approval, 'it is only an evening of poetry. Why are you making such a fuss?'

'It isn't safe on the streets any more, Igoryok, you know that.' Dunya finished drawing the curtains. Mama waited until she had closed the door behind her. Then she leaned forward and said in a low voice, 'There are riots, demonstrations, anything could happen. People are going wild.'

'I will throw myself in the canal!' I cried, and I knew I could not go on living in this overheated house, when everyone else in the world was breaking free.

Papa appeared in the doorway. 'What is this shouting?' he asked. 'Ah, Igor, hello, hello. Why are you here?'

'Misha,' Mama appealed to him, 'please, this terrible Igor wants to take little Nadia to a cabaret. He has made her some foolish promise.'

'The "*Brodyachaya Sabaka*," Igor said. 'For her name day.'

Papa gave me one of his mock-serious looks over his glasses. 'Her name day – is it her name day? How time flies. It seems only last month. It was last month.'

'I am leaving to join my regiment tomorrow, in Poland,' said Igor formally, as if to a superior officer. 'I might not be here for Nadia's next name day.' He paused and Papa bowed his head. 'I would prefer not to die for Russia, naturally, but one must be realistic – we are at war.'

'Yes,' said Papa. 'Things are very bad in Poland. The tsar has dug his grave. Dug his grave at Mogilev.' He gave a short laugh. 'Now it's only a matter of time.'

'Is Uncle Igor going to die?' I asked.

'Don't even say it.' Mama put up her hand as if to ward off fate. 'But if God wills... for Russia...' She put down her glass and closed her eyes for a moment.

'It isn't the officers who die,' said Uncle Igor. 'It's the men. You know they have nothing out there. No boots, no coats, no food. They are fighting with their bare hands because supplies don't arrive.'

'The late tsar said it,' said Papa. 'On his deathbed, he told Nicholas, 'Never go to war. War must be avoided at all costs'.'

'Yes, you see Sofya, this is my last opportunity to give a gift, so why not?'

'It will be interesting for her to go,' said Papa. 'Why not? The end of an era. She can remember it. Who knows what is coming?' He broke off, and I knew he was already thinking about the speech he would make at the Lawyers' Club.

After Papa left, Mama continued to object, but with less force. Finally, I began to cry. 'What if Uncle Igor dies? You'll be sorry.' And then she too began to cry.

'So,' said Uncle Igor. 'I'll take her and bring her back early and very safely.'

'Be sure you do,' said Mama. 'Don't let her out of your sight.'

'Mama,' I protested.

'Wait.' She rang the bell. When Dunya appeared she told her, 'My small box. The wooden one.' Dunya went upstairs and we sat in silence until she came back.

'Now.' Mama looked through the box. 'Wear these,' she said. She took out her diamond and pearl earrings.

'No Mama, they are too heavy. I will look silly, and people will think…'

'Never mind what people think. Why can't a young girl wear a bit of jewellery?' she said, as if she was angry. 'They will be yours one day anyway, so you might as well wear them now.'

'Thank you,' I said a bit uncomfortably. She fastened the earrings firmly on my ears and I felt as if she had sent her eyes to watch me. Suddenly, I threw myself into her arms and we embraced. When I kissed her, I saw she had tears in her eyes. There were still tears in her eyes as she made the sign of the cross over Uncle Igor.

It was a cold November night. As we crossed the bridge over the Ekaterinsky canal, I had to force myself to walk sedately beside Uncle Igor and not to twirl among the first gentle drifting snowflakes of winter, lacy bits of white in the navy-blue Petersburg evening. I felt very grown-up in my new white fur schuba and my matching hat. In the distance I could hear some workmen singing:

'At night I strut around
and rich men don't get in my way.
Just let some rich guy try
and I'll screw his head on upside down.'

Another snowflake floated slowly past in front of my face. I was tempted to stick my tongue out and catch it as my friend Lidia and I did on the way home from school, but I thought

Uncle Igor might be offended. He hadn't spoken. Perhaps I ought to say something? Maybe he was sorry he had invited me. What should I say? What did he expect from me?

'I love poetry,' I said now. 'I know more poetry by heart than anyone in my class.'

'Do you?' he said. 'Then you will enjoy yourself. tonight.'

I felt I should say more. 'Especially Lermontov.' We had begun to read him this term at school. I quoted:

'I want to live; I crave for sadness…
Against my bliss and love, in truth;
They sank my mind in idle gladness
And made my brow so very smooth.

There was another silence. I wasn't sure if I should go on. Perhaps I should have mentioned something more modern. Finally I said, as we turned into Kirochnaya street, 'I like Blok. I don't think Mama understands Blok. He's too contemporary for her.' I waited for his approval.

'You mustn't make your mama unhappy,' Igor said.

'I can't help it. We are in a new world. Everything is different now. Russia is changing every day. Don't you feel it, Uncle Igor?' He was not much older than I, and I was sure he would take my part.

'She's a good woman, your mama,' he said. 'As good as she can be. I hope you will be like her. Maybe a little bit better.'

'There's going to be a revolution,' I said. 'Everything is going to be different isn't it?'

'There will certainly be a revolution.' He lapsed into silence.

'Lidia and I cried when Beilis was acquitted,' I said, and added, 'with happiness.' I felt I had to show how well we had followed the case.

'Did you?' There was another silence. A few young people in student uniform lounged against a building. Coachmen waited with their horses. It was getting colder. I felt the weight of Mama's earrings. The diamond and pearl earrings did look well against the fur, I had to admit. And very European. Papa had bought them for Mama in Paris the year before the war. 'But it is so extravagant,' she had said.

He answered, 'Money is useless these days, the only thing to do is spend it.'

I pointed. 'Look!' There was a small upright piano lying in the gutter. Its music holder had been wrenched off, the wood scratched and defaced, and some of the keys were smashed. It looked like an old man who had been attacked by Cossacks. 'What is that?'

Uncle Igor looked at it. 'It's a German piano,' he said. 'Someone's contribution to the war effort.'

'But it is only a piano,' I said. 'The piano hasn't done anything.'

'It might play German music,' he said, but his face had darkened, and his cheekbones and beaky nose stood out like knives.

He put his arm around my shoulders in a friendly way, as if we were two lads together, two young men, although he was twenty-seven and I was not a boy but a young woman of almost sixteen and frightened to admit that the gesture excited me.

The Wandering Dog was in the basement of a building on a narrow alley off Kirochnaya Street and we picked our way carefully down an unlit flight of stairs. The room was dark; faces flickered in and out of light from the dim wall sconces and the spill from the brightly lit performing area at the centre. There was a man speaking. Was this poetry? I wasn't sure. He scooped the words in great arcs, up and down the scale. I felt that he must be saying something important, but then the audience laughed.

Groups of men sat at tables by the door. They noticed our entrance and raised a hand or nodded a greeting. Some were dressed in peasant shirts or embroidered waistcoats. They smoked pipes. The room was stuffy and thick with smoke. They sprawled on their chairs and nodded as the poet continued, or else gave each other knowing looks.

One of them greeted Uncle Igor, saying, 'Tonight, no politics, no war.'

Uncle Igor raised an imaginary glass, and peered around the room as if looking for someone.

'She's getting ready,' said the man. 'Does she know you're here?'

'Yes,' said Igor. 'Give her a message. Say I'm here with a young lady.'

I was puzzled. What message? What young lady? Me? I was confused by all of it: the darkness, the intent faces, the booming tones of the speaker, the heavy smell of smoke and the curling grey wisps that caught the light from so many pipes and cigarettes.

Then I saw a woman sitting at the front and I caught my breath. 'Who is she?'

'Anna Ahkmatova,' Igor murmured.

The light from the stage was partially thrown onto her face; she sat like a statue, all in purple, with a deep white collar that plunged against her waxen skin. A large, orange shawl was looped with casual perfection around her arms.

Igor saw me staring. 'She will read later on,' he whispered. 'Almost certainly she will, because look, Larissa is here from Moscow.' Someone was waving wildly to Uncle Igor. The light picked up the silver bracelets she wore on both arms, forcing us to see her as she shone in the darkness. Uncle Igor took me by the elbow and steered me on a careful path between the tables.

'Larissa Borisovna,' said Igor. 'You have come. How wonderful. And where is Alyosha? I must see him.'

'Well you can't,' she said. She clasped his hand with both of hers. Her hands were large, like a man's hands I thought, and her fingers were covered with silver rings. Uncle Igor had been whispering, but Larissa Borisovna made no attempt to keep her voice down and several people frowned. 'Didn't you hear?' she said. 'He was called up. He is at the Alexandrovsky Barracks. His health will never stand it,' she went on. 'But he is so noble, his own life means nothing. He thinks only of Russia. It is such a

13

beautiful, pure thing, but how can I live without him?' The man reading poetry raised his voice slightly. Several people turned to look at us and a very young woman said sternly, 'Shhh.'

Larissa Borisovna ignored her.

'War,' she said. 'We are taught that wars are terrible, but if all wars are terrible, what is not terrible about this one?'

Uncle Igor cut in quickly. 'We will speak later,' he said.

She stroked my coat. 'Who is this beautiful child, Igoryok? Not your daughter?'

Uncle Igor shook his head. 'Certainly not.' He added formally, 'Nadezhda Mikhailovna Serova, this is Larissa Borisovna Mordvinova. ' He smiled and said as if asking a riddle, 'I am Uncle Igor, but Nadezhda Mikhailovna is not my niece.'

'No one is a niece.' Larissa Mordvinova dismissed the idea. 'A niece is not a possible thing to be. She is Persephone come down into our dark world.'

I didn't know what to say. In my book of Greek myths, Persephone was small and delicate with long blonde curls and a flowery gown. I was short with heavy eyebrows and thick, dark hair, which was difficult to comb; Mama and I had rows over it. I had large, slightly oriental dark eyes, my nose was small and straight, and my mouth curved sweetly, I had studied myself in the mirror and made careful note of these things. I also knew that my legs were thick, like Papa's family, strong and sturdy but without elegance. I was not Persephone. I examined Larissa Mordvinova. She was small and boyishly slight. Her hair was light and cut short. Besides her rings and bracelets, she wore a large strand of amber beads. Her eyes were green and almost circular. I felt as if she was looking through me at something on the other side.

'Have you read yet?' Uncle Igor asked.

She shook her head. 'Not yet. Later. After Osip.' She clasped her hands and exclaimed to me, 'Osip is going to read! And he will read something new! Wait until you hear!'

She spoke as if I knew who this Osip was and felt about him as she did.

'Mandelstam,' Uncle Igor said to me. 'You are a lucky girl.'

'Come, Persephone.' She turned to me. 'Sit here.'

I sat between them, feeling like a large, overdressed schoolgirl.

A thin young man with curly red hair and a slight stoop began to read:

'I'm cold. And everywhere transparent Spring
Clothes all Persepolis with fluffy green,
But these waves of the Neva only sting
Me with disgust – like jellyfish I've seen.'

Larissa Mordvinova was shining in a new way: a light had been turned on behind her face, and it was transparent with happiness. I could hardly bear to sit beside such happiness. I didn't know what Persepolis was, or why the Neva seemed to fill the poet with disgust, but the words clashed in my ears with sounds that made me shiver and want him to go on and on.

Uncle Igor nodded and when everyone clapped, he half rose and raised his hands to applaud.

There were more readings mingled with songs and music, one after another. I seemed to understand less and less. After a while I stopped trying. The darkness and the smoke, the flickering sconces, sent me into a dreamy state, where the unintelligible verses had music beyond meaning. I seemed to be floating between the figures of Ahkmatova and Larissa Mordvinova beside me, who whispered after one poem, 'What did you think of that?'

'I … I don't know,' I said.

'Good,' she said, and stroked my face. 'Good.'

There were so many people. So much poetry. I tried, but soon I was ashamed to feel my eyelids grow heavy.

'You didn't understand a word of that, did you?' Uncle Igor said, after another poet had read.

'I understood some of it.'

All the lights suddenly went out. In the dark, a violin began to play. It played something romantic and repetitive, a phrase repeated over and over with only a slight variation.

'Scriabin,' Larissa whispered.

A light came up. There was a pier glass frame on the stage and standing in front of it was a woman in a long black cloak, her face covered by a white mask. The only part of her that was visible was the long, fair hair piled in high curls on her head. Beside me, Uncle Igor cried, 'Ah! Olya!' and leaned forward as if he could not believe what he saw.

'Who is it?' I whispered.

'Olga Sherbyateva,' he said, but I knew he was not paying attention to me. He said her name as if finally the evening had become important.

I thought, The "Wandering Dog" *is not a suitable place, Mama was right.* I didn't know why Uncle Igor wanted me to come with him. I hoped we might go home soon.

Olga Sherbyateva held herself absolutely still, and then as the final notes of music died away, she began to speak. She spoke to the mirror, as if she played with her own image, but then she reached through the space, and drew out another female figure, dressed in a white cloak and wearing a black mask. Back and forth the two moved through the mirror, and seemed to exchange roles as one woman drowned in the mirror and the other rose out of it, like a wave, interchangeable, yet never meeting. Sometimes the two women embraced or danced, but always something pulled them apart, the phrases they spoke and the phrases they heard.

'What does it mean?' I asked Uncle Igor. He did not reply. I knew he had eyes and ears only for Olga Sherbyateva.

I sensed that it was about love, that there was a ballroom and death. The two women echoed each other. The words rose and fell, sang and tolled like bells.

At school, our teacher had made us learn Turgenev's lines: '*Oh mighty, true, free Russian language!...It is inconceivable that such a language should not belong to a great people.*' We had giggled because our teacher had watery eyes and a thin voice and didn't look at all like a great person. But now I thrilled to those words.'...*Such a language... must belong to a great people.*'

Larissa touched my face gently, and lifted a tear from my cheek. She held it on the tip of her finger and smiled at me. Uncle Igor had not taken his eyes off Olga Sherbyateva.

The two women met on either side of the glass, if the mirror had had glass. They drew closer and closer together. The silence thickened. The room was as still as midnight. Then, from offstage, there was a shot. It was as if it had gone off inside my head, as if everything had exploded. I screamed, 'Help! Help!' and continued to scream, while as if from a great distance I heard the audience laugh. Some people applauded.

'You fool,' Uncle Igor said harshly. 'You stupid little fool. Idiot! It's a stage effect.' I covered my face, but he pulled my hands away, and I saw that he was furious. I shrank back from his glare. 'Someone must be dead!' I said. 'Someone has been shot.'

'Something is ruined thanks to you,' he said. 'You have ruined it.'

The masked figures had fled the stage. There was a hum of voices around my head, from which I gathered that people were trying to decide if there should be more readings. 'Of course there will be more readings!' cried Larissa, in her harsh voice. 'I have come from Moscow for poetry.' There would certainly be more readings if she wanted them.

'Come,' Uncle Igor said. 'It's late. This is not a place for children.' He said it as if it was my idea that he brought me here.

When we were outside, I sobbed, 'I didn't mean to spoil it … it scared me. Someone was killed. I was sure someone had been killed. Murdered.'

'That's all right, never mind, *golybushka*,' he said. 'Don't cry. It wasn't your fault. You couldn't help it. I forgot. It isn't a place for children.'

'Will you take me again?' I pleaded. It had nothing to do

with being a child. In there, that sort of thing didn't matter, I could see that. I wanted to go there over and over until I understood.

'Another time,' he said. 'And now, come on, or your mama will be angry.' He hailed a hansom cab for us. 'It is late and you are tired,' he said, as he helped me into it, and I felt relieved to be very young.

We went back to the house, so overheated, so safe, but afterwards I always believed I had heard a real shot and had seen a man's face, unrecognisable, behind a veil of blood.

CHAPTER THREE

FEBRUARY 1917

'The flowers finally arrived!' Countess Doudoukova greeted us after we had been announced. 'At the very last minute! I was afraid they weren't going to arrive at all. The florist said the delivery boys had run off to see the marchers on Nevsky. Can you imagine! Of course she won't have them back tomorrow, but what good does that do today?'

'Lityini Bridge is completely blocked,' Mama answered, adjusting her pale green chiffon stole. 'Strikers from the Vyborg district. And there are still queues at the bakery! Since early this morning.'

Papa spoke: 'People have no bread, their children will starve, and they know there is food, they see it in shops they can't afford, they blame the government. If something isn't done quickly…'

'It's all because of the Jews.' Count Doudoukov had joined us. Other guests heard him and stopped to listen. 'Jews and speculators,' he explained. 'They push the prices up, you see, by holding back flour supplies.'

'And Nicholas answers by sending in the military!' Papa had been deeply disturbed by the strikes and riots. 'Fifty people shot dead! Fifty people! And he calls it a *disorder*! If he doesn't listen to the people, no one will be able to stop them.'

'I heard there was trouble at Znamenskaya Square this afternoon,' said the countess. 'The police were actually helping those people to smash into shops. The police!' With a gracious gesture, she moved us into the party.

'Yes, and all the Cossacks were out,' I put in, eager to contribute.

'Not all,' said Papa. 'They sent the reserves out, and forgot to issue whips. How do they expect to control a mob like that?'

'It's dreadful,' the countess went on. 'It's put everyone in a terrible state. Ivanov's only just managed to deliver the ice cream, on time ...' She left the sentence hanging.

The Doudoukovs were having their annual party despite food shortages, strikes, and the recent riots. Huge bouquets and arrangements of flowers lined the blue and gold panelled walls, and were banked at one end of the ballroom. A trio of piano, violin and cello, played a medley of French songs.

Mama wore her diamonds, Papa wore his tsar's medal. My best friend Natasha and I had had lengthy discussion about what we would wear. As we had planned, I wore my raspberry velvet dress and my white cape, and Natasha wore her blue velvet dress.

Her two little sisters chased each other up and down the entrance hall, joined by Ilya Perkov's red haired sister Liuba and a very small boy of four or five who simply ran round in circles.

The rooms were crowded with people, many of the men in regimental uniform and epaulettes, the women, like Mama, in evening dress and dazzling jewels. As we entered I could see how we fit into the magnificent display, as if part of me watched and admired us from a distance. *How handsome everyone looks*, I thought.

After a short pause, the musicians struck up a mazurka and Ilya Perkov asked me to dance. He pumped my arm vigorously up and down and his fat cheeks were flushed. When he stepped on my foot, he said, 'That was your mistake. You are behind the music.' I knew he was wrong but I thought it would be impolite to contradict him, so I bit my lip.

It was a relief when Grisha Bobrov asked me for the next dance, a waltz. He was a bit shorter than I, which made me self-conscious, but he danced well and after a minute I began to enjoy myself. We waltzed silently around the outskirts of the room. Finally, he asked, 'Are you f-fond of dancing?'

'Yes,' I said, 'very. Are you?'

'Yes,' he said, with his slight stammer. 'S-sometimes.'

We continued to waltz in silence. People seemed to be gliding around us with the music, a melted rainbow of colour. The two little girls were now trying to dance together, taking huge steps and bumping into other dancers, who laughed, unperturbed. The little boy had fallen down and was borne off, howling, by one of the maids. Natasha danced past with her extremely tall cousin Nicholas, of the Preobrajensky Regiment. His epaulettes just framed the top of her head..

When the dance ended Grisha asked, 'W-would you like an ice cream?' I accepted gratefully.

He beckoned to a footman for two dishes of ice cream. I had just taken my first spoonful when the butler rang a small bell and Count Doudoukov raised his hand. A silence fell, as sudden and complete as if it had been expected. Not a chair creaked. I held onto my dish of ice cream, not wanting the spoon to make any chink against the china.

'My dear friends,' Count Doudoukov announced, 'I have just had word from the Tauride Palace. This morning at ten o'clock, in his railway carriage at Malaya Vishera, Tsar Nicholas the Second abdicated. He said that if his abdication was necessary for the good of Russia, then he was ready for it. We pray for him and his family,' the count concluded.

Everyone bowed their heads. Some people wept, others crossed themselves.

The silence that followed felt eternal. The orchestra did not resume.

'What will it mean?' Grisha finally asked.

'We will find out soon enough,' said Papa, 'but it had to happen. The country was about to explode. It was the only way to end the war.'

'At least Kerensky and Lvov will bring the men back,'

added Count Doudoukov. 'If not, the country will be full of deserters and bandits.'

'And now we will have a democracy. At last,' said another man.

'And with a bloodless revolution, thank God,' said Countess Doudoukova.

I looked down at the dish of melting stuff I was still holding. It seemed strange that ice cream still existed, a relic of another world. It looked inappropriate, and I put it down on the nearest table.

The party had ended, but we stayed at the Doudoukov's for a long time, wondering if it was safe to drive home. Those who lived nearby slipped out to go home on foot, without waiting for their carriages.

Countess Doudoukova said, 'Perhaps everyone should stay here until we know what is going to happen.'

'And go home in evening dress in daylight?' Papa exclaimed. 'Madness!'

'It is safe enough on the streets,' said Ilya Perkov's father. 'The revolutionaries have taken over only the centre. That's best avoided, especially in a car or a carriage.'

On the way home, I could hear shouting and singing. Bonfires cast a hot light on faces, banners and red flags. Some people banged on the window of the carriage, crying 'freedom!' and shouting the slogans: 'Bread and Land!' and, 'Russia has risen!'

A small bonfire burned on the corner of our street; a group of people warmed their hands. It was only when I saw them that I realised it was very cold.

Mama shivered and drew her fur coat closer around her shoulders.

'Why are you cold, Mama?' I asked, 'I'm not cold at all.'

'Even so, put your cape on,' she said. 'It's a cold night.'

'But a different kind of cold,' I insisted. 'It's new cold.'

She laughed. 'Nadia, you are too imaginative. Cold is cold.'

'There has never been a cold revolution,' Papa said. 'Even a bloodless revolution is for the hot-blooded.'

In the drawing room, Mama sank onto a chair and looked around in disbelief. 'What will happen now?' she asked, and began to weep. 'Nothing will be the same again.'

I put my arms around her. 'Don't cry Mama,' I said. 'There will be a new world, the war will end.' *And*, I thought to myself, *Uncle Igor will come back, he won't be killed in the war after all*

'I know.' She wiped her eyes with the tiny lace-trimmed handkerchief she used at parties. 'But the family? The empress, and the girls, and that poor little boy.'

Papa had been staring down at the crowds massed in the street. 'Yes, poor child. He is innocent. But it was his illness that brought Rasputin to court. Destiny works in strange ways,' he shook his head and added, 'The empress ... ' He stopped. 'No one will hurt the family. They will probably go abroad.'

'The English will offer sanctuary,' Mama agreed. 'After all, they are his cousins.'

Dunya stood in the doorway, waiting as always to see if we needed anything before she finally retired. We hadn't noticed her until she spoke. 'And when the war is over,' she said, 'they will come back and he will be the tsar again in a democracy.'

* * *

The song could be heard all over the city:
> *We renounce the old world*
> *We shake its dust from our feet*
> *We don't need a golden idol*
> *And we despise the tsarist devil*

I stood in the crowd with my friends and we all sang the next day, as the Red Flag was raised above the Stroganov Palace. People waved red banners, and we all wore red armbands. Celebrations ran through the streets like flame. Bonfires burned day and night. Everywhere crowds shouted and sang, people made speeches in every square. There was a perpetual carnival of celebration throughout Petrograd.

At school, we didn't even pretend to have lessons. Teachers and students joined in argument and discussion all day. I announced that I was a liberal and my friend Natasha sneered at me. 'They talk, that's all liberals do.' She was a social revolutionary, while my other friend Lidia was a bolshevik.

'They're going to take everything away,' she said. 'The workers will own everything. The rest of you will starve.' Another girl burst into tears. Lidia laughed. 'You can't laugh at her,' I said. 'If we are a democracy, then everyone is equal.'

Cars filled with soldiers and girls drove wildly around the streets. I saw the older sister of Lidia the Bolshevik in the back of a car, sitting on a soldier's lap.

'Where did you get the car?' I called as she waved to me.

'Reclaimed from Grand Duke Constantine for the people!' she shouted back as the car swerved onto the pavement and swung around the corner.

'Nadia, stay off the streets!' Despite Mama's warnings, I couldn't keep away from the meetings, the demonstrations, the excitement. I watched as armfuls of official documents were burnt; Natasha and I followed the revolutionaries from prison to prison and cheered as the doors were thrown open and thousands of prisoners were freed. 'No, comrades!' shouted one commandant. 'These are common criminals, not political prisoners! There are no politicals here!' But he was dragged away while inmates poured onto the streets.

The bonfires burst into higher and higher flames as buildings were set alight. I watched with Mama and Papa as fire devoured the Palace of Justice, leaving only the skeleton which finally collapsed with a mighty crash that sent a million sparks into the night sky.

'They talk about a miracle?' Papa said bitterly. 'This is a peasant riot. To burn justice...'

I thought of the men erupting onto the street from the prisons. "If the country is prisonless and crimeless," I quoted, "then police and courts won't be necessary."

He interrupted me, enraged. 'Slogans! This is an excuse for

destruction, merciless senseless violence! This is not a revolution!' His anger made me shrink back. He sounded like a different person. He went on more calmly. 'We Russians are a great people, Nadia. Noble, strong, brave and patient. We are also cruel and brutal and stupid. No revolution will change that. What's out there …' he gestured toward the still smoking building, 'must be controlled by a strong leader. Then Russia will be the greatest country on earth.' He looked at me. 'Kerensky is all talk,' he said.

Suddenly, no one was allowed to take more than ten roubles per day from the bank. When Papa went to get our safe deposit box, Mr. Martynsky, the manager, had gone, and a government official told him, 'All savings and securities have been confiscated.'

'My savings,' Papa said when he came home empty handed. 'Your savings, Sofya my dear. Nadia's future. Gone.'

'What will we do?' Mama asked. We began to sell things: the crystal wine glasses, Mama's best silver, a pair of candlesticks that had been a wedding present. We managed to get some money, but there was less and less food to buy with it and as the revolution burned on, we found ourselves living on a diet of kasha and potatoes.

I discovered that after a while, one doesn't feel hunger so much. Mama was afraid to go out now that the coachman had left and so Dunya and I, wearing Dunya's clothes, searched the market for food.

One day among the crowds I came upon a boy of about ten, waving a large butcher's knife above his head.

'Don't do that,' I said 'You'll hurt someone.' He grinned and continued to wave it so wildly I was afraid he might slice his own head open.

'It's the revolution!' he cried. 'I'm a revolutionary!' Suddenly he pointed the knife at me. In that instant I knew he would run me through. A group of young men came behind him, drunk and singing, *Ye tyrants quake, your day is over/Detested now by friend and foe.* The child turned to look at them, and I seized the opportunity to make my escape. I heard the sounds of breaking glass and I knew that another shop was about to be looted.

A scribbled note came from Uncle Igor in May: *I got away before my men could shoot me. I am with your parents at the dacha. The news is not good. All land is confiscated. I will do what I can.*

'What does he mean?' Mama cried. 'Do what?'

'What he can,' Papa said.

'But my family!' Mama insisted. 'Will he look after them?' She re-read the note. 'Confiscated. That's all. He says nothing about them. Misha,' she said to Papa, 'we should get to them somehow.'

'How?' Papa asked. Then he considered. 'People have left. But it's dangerous. The roads are full of deserters.'

One of our teachers said. 'A government is supposed to govern. Equality is not God's will.'

I stared at the blank space on the wall where the portrait of the tsar had hung and wondered what would replace it.

* * *

Count Doudoukov was arrested in August. His house was taken over by the Red Guards.

'Why? What did he do?' I asked

'No one needs a reason anymore,' said Papa. 'The Countess and the children got away, thank God, although the girls are both very ill.'

The heat that summer was suffocating. It lined the city in thick, motionless layers. You can get used to anything, I learned: to the baking heat, to the foul smell everywhere, to people collapsed in the street, ill, dying or dead. At first I lingered beside the bodies, wondering if I should do something to help, but it was no use, and after a while like everyone else, I walked on. You can get used to anything.

Then Papa came home one day, helped by a colleague. His

face was grey and there was a large wound on his head. He had said he felt unwell and had to go home. He had collapsed on the steps of the ministry.

'I called for help. Someone in the street yelled, "Bourgeois exploiter",' the colleague added bitterly. 'They knocked him down and tried to get hold of the briefcase. He held onto it. You might say he defended it with his life. They got his watch.'

We helped him to the bedroom. 'Get a doctor, Nadia,' said Mama. The telephone had stopped working weeks ago.

I went to our doctor, but he was gone. 'They went south,' said a neighbour. 'Kiev.'

I made my way through street after street. Finally, I found a sign for a Dr Isaacs. At first he refused, but I begged him and when he heard me speak, he agreed to come, first putting on a dusty workman's jacket and a red armband.

At Kammeny Ostrov Prospekt, a man was making yet another speech from the balcony of one of the noble mansions. This crowd was bigger and much quieter than the others, and as Dr Isaacs hurried us past I heard the speaker say, 'Take it all. it's yours. Take the houses, the jewels, the securities, take the gold, the silver, the furniture, the palaces. They belong to you. It all belongs to you.'

'Lenin. The provisional government is finished,' said Dr Issacs. He shook his head without slackening his pace. Afterwards, I couldn't get Lenin's voice out of my head, like a tune that gets caught in the mind: *It belongs to you. Take it all... it belongs to you.*

Papa lay struggling for breath. Occasionally a cry of pain escaped him, in spite of his efforts. He even tried to smile at me, but gradually his eyes were clouded. Dr Issacs came every day, although he told us there was little he could do. 'Typhus,' he said. 'It's spreading everywhere. Try to keep the fever down. That's all anyone can do.'

Mama spoke without moving her lips, as if she had been turned to stone. 'God's will be done,' she said.

Papa's face became almost unrecognisable. His skin was

yellowed and his eyes had sunk deep into the sockets. His features seemed to have collapsed, making his teeth huge and helpless at the same time. His long, thin nose stood out from his face like an old metal spike. He shook and burned alternately. 'Ice,' he croaked. 'Ice.'

All the servants had left except the cook and Dunya, who stood beside Papa and slowly waved a pillowslip above his head, as was the custom in her village.

The Ukranian grocer nearby had ice. 'Your mother was a good customer and a lovely lady,' he said. He gave me some sugar and flour from his private store. 'If you need more, come back,' he said. He gave me a bowl of ice, but when I brought it to Papa, he struggled. 'No! Ice,' he gasped. I rubbed it against his lips, but it was no use. He turned his head away.

I sat beside him while Mama sat on the other side, and I held his hand although he didn't know any longer who I was. I told him over and over how much I loved him, what a good man he was. I recalled events from my childhood: when he picked me up and swung me in the air and pretended to throw me away; when he took me to look for mushrooms; how excited I was when he lit the candles on the Christmas tree. I recited the poems he had taught me, over and over. As I talked, more and more, my love poured out, as if my heart had overturned. When I stopped, thinking he was asleep, he said, in a voice that grew weaker by the day, 'Yes... yes...' I talked on and wept and begged him to try to live. When I left the room, I could hear Mama's voice, so filled with love and sorrow that although the words were inaudible, I felt that even to listen to the sound was an intrusion into a private depth.

Mama and I were both with him on the morning that he looked at us and his eyes suddenly cleared. 'The damned people,' he said clearly. 'The damned rotten people.' He closed his eyes, and his head fell back on the pillow. I had a sense that we were all suspended, as if we were listening for something.

Dunya opened a window but there was no air outside, only the stink of the streets, and she closed it again. On the following afternoon, Papa opened his eyes again, smiled at us and tried to speak. Instead he gave a deep sigh, nodded once as if in response to something, and I felt his hand relax in mine as he lay at peace at last.

CHAPTER FOUR

DECEMBER 1920

I thought I had been awake all night, shivering, waiting for the footsteps, but to my surprise I woke up, still shivering, my body aching and frozen in the icy room. There was ice on the walls. A long icicle had formed inside the window. In the dark, Mama said, 'Nadia, it's almost light.'

That meant it was nearly nine o'clock. Mama could always sense the time. There was no point getting up earlier; the house electricity was off. Maybe it would go on later. I didn't answer Mama. The only way to live with the cold, I found, was to stay motionless at the core of it.

I thought, *Now it's today.* We were alive. The Cheka had not come for us in the night. We would have to find food and fuel somehow. I would go work in the office in the Ministry of Education, file papers and try to type documents judged safe for the eyes of 'former people'. It was too much to grasp. My mind closed.

'Nadia,' Mama repeated more urgently, 'We must start to queue or the canteen will run out of rations.'

Rations. My job allowed us rations. Slowly, reluctantly, my thoughts stirred.

From Papa's study, the Trofimov's baby set up its wail and Mrs. Trofimova screamed at it, 'Shut up, you shitty little bastard.'

Mama said, 'She's at it already?'

The other children started their clamour. A family of five had been moved into Papa's study. Mr Trofimov swore at his wife, 'Whore! Shut your mouth.' There was a crash as something heavy was thrown at the wall. Something else had broken. There wasn't much left to break. Most of Papa's furniture had been confiscated and we had sold his books at the Persepolis bookshop over a year ago.

Another day. As usual, Mama got up before me. It was still dark, but she made no move to light the nyedyshalka, the bottle of fat that served as a lamp. It made a light of sorts but it filled the room with smoke and went out at the slightest motion.

'There is some bread left,' Mama said. We had managed to buy a loaf of bread two weeks ago, for 1500 roubles. We had eked it out and there was still a small end left. I held my piece in my mouth to soften it.

'I will get some money at work today,' I said. It was a reason to stand up. I kept myself wrapped in the worn, filthy blanket. 'Perhaps we can find something to buy.'

There was no answer. What was there to buy? If there was something, my salary wouldn't be enough to buy it. A friend of Papa's had found me the job during the terrible winter after Papa died. I heard the man had been arrested a few weeks ago. I was fortunate no one at the ministry realised yet how I had come to work there.

I felt my way across the room and stumbled over the books I had kept. Russian fairy tales, Hans Christian Anderson and a volume of Pushkin, inscribed *To my beloved Nadia from Papa*. The covers had softened with mildew, but as I rearranged them I was grateful once again to Mama. I had offered to sell them, burn them, anything to give us money or fuel, but Mama refused. 'Hope,' she said. 'Keep something for hope.' When I saw my small pile of books, I felt the comfort of hope.

Mama had sold or bartered everything except her diamonds: the necklace, bracelet and the earrings that had been gifts from Papa. 'It's his hope as well. And ours, too. If we can find a way to get false papers,' she added, in her practical way, 'we will have the bribe ready.'

Outside, in the courtyard there was a storeroom where we used to keep bottles of wine. The wine had been confiscated and in later searches the officials were busy ripping mattresses and upholstery, looking for hidden valuables. No one was interested in an empty storeroom. Under a loose stone, we scraped the earth and made a hiding place for Mama's jewellery. We covered it up and fitted the stone tightly on top. Hope.

As we slowly ate our bread, Mama took out Uncle Igor's last note again. It had been sent from Moscow, but because the trains had broken down, it had taken nearly five months to arrive. Uncle Igor was in the Lyubianka prison. *There are twenty of us in this cell. Conditions indescribable. Ex-tsarists and Bolsheviks with ideas. Wait for me. I will be with you soon. Signed, Captain Igor Fyedorovitch Rozanov, of the Red Army.*

'What does he mean?' she asked. 'Has he deserted?'

'He is alive at least.'

She shook her head. 'I don't understand. How could he be in the Red Army?'

In the communal kitchen, Mrs Trofimova had lit the samovar and the Trofimovs were all shouting at each other.

'Shut up!' bellowed Mr Semenov from our drawing room, where he lived with his terrified wife and two grown sons. There was always a pile of empty bottles outside their door and the house smelt of their urine and vomit. I could see that Mr Semenov was already drunk. Or perhaps he was still drunk.

'Pipes frozen.' Mrs Trofimova's tone always carried general accusation, whatever she said. She picked the baby's dirty nappy off the floor and tossed it into the hall. 'The pipes are frozen,' she repeated. 'I had to use the pump out in the street.'

Mama put her cup down. 'You have boiled the water first, I hope,' she said, with a trace of the imperious manner she had once used with incompetent servants.

Mrs Trofimova shrugged and made a face.

The front door slammed. Oleg Malkin was back. He lived in the library with several women he claimed were his wives, as well as his elderly mother, two male cousins, their "wives" and other relatives who appeared from time to time. Everyone knew he was a bagman, involved in speculation or worse, and I steered as clear of him as I could.

'Where's your book?' Mrs Trofimova hit her older son across the head. She shouted over his wails, 'They said you should read. Now read!'

The child began to practice his reading from the Bolshevik-issued schoolbook. He read with difficulty, pointing to each word as he went: 'We. Are. Not. Slaves. Slaves. We. Are. Not.'

Outside, we passed the spot where the Ukranian grocery shop had been. There was nothing left of it now, except part of a wall and the cracked stone, floor. The grocer and his family had disappeared a long time ago. When Mama and I had struggled to prise loose the window frames for our stove, she said, 'He was such a kind man, Nadia. Remember the sugar?'

A body lay in the snow. How easy it would be to sit beside it, let my eyes close. Drift away.

'I'm too tired, Mama,' I said.

Mama put her arm around me and I leaned against her as we slowly moved on. 'Nadyushka, Dysha, Nadyushenka, Golybushka, come … another step. One hour. One day. Until our time comes. You remember what you read in Pushkin?

'I forget.'

'*Endurance is a gift from heaven*,' she quoted. '*It is given instead of happiness.*'

'*Endurance is a gift from heaven*,' I repeated.

We walked slowly on. Mama carried the container for our ration of thin soup and gristle.

'One day. Only one day.' She said again.

The city lay in a deathly silence. There were no cars, trams or horses. No one spoke. The quiet was broken by a shot in the distance. The yellow winter mists had rolled in and stained the uncleared snow. Two skeletal ghosts joined us on the filthy streets. It was my friend Natasha and her little brother. The round-faced child had turned into a bent, silent old man.

'Remember Lidia?' Natasha whispered. 'She's a party member

33

now. With a gun.' Natasha's aunt appeared, like a tiny shadow. She was almost transparent. 'The railway canteen has run out of soup,' she said. 'I've queued there since seven and they ran out just as I came in sight of the kitchen. If you're registered at the workers canteen, they still have something. There's another canteen near Smolney that has supplies, but over there the canteen workers steal everything right away.'

Mama said, 'Best to queue at the workers' canteen I think.' She looked at our food container. 'Our coupons are good over there.'

'People have been waiting there for three hours,' said Natasha's aunt.

'The Bobrianovs are registered as well,' Mama said. 'They might have a place in the queue already.'

'Didn't you hear?' The Bobrianovs were arrested two days ago.' The aunt's voice had dropped to the whisper used for any mention of cheka activities.

'God's will be done.' Mama crossed herself. I crossed myself too. What else could one do?

Mama went with Natasha's little brother and her aunt to queue at the workers canteen. Natasha went to the Third Petrograd university canteen where she was registered, although the university had now closed. They would still be in the queue when I finished work. Then we would have to find some wood.

I made my way through grey, silent streets; occasionally I passed more skeletons who mutely held out their possessions begging for custom.: an old pair of gloves, a child's bonnet, a small drawing of a sailboat,

I passed what had been my school. Everything that could be burnt had been ripped out. But the big front door was still standing, sealed with the cheka's red wax as it had been the day the headmaster was arrested. Maybe the wax could be eaten. I stood indecisively. If I managed to break it off and eat a piece. I wondered if I would be seen. If I was caught I would be arrested. The cheka wouldn't arrest me openly; arrests were always at night.

After the struggle to get through the day, there was always the possibility of the knock. I looked around but the street was empty. No one was visible except a rat who darted under the foundation. Wax could be chewed for a long time. The red colour would give it a certain taste. I overcame my longing and turned my back. It was too dangerous.

In the office, I greeted the Armenian woman manager and tried to ignore the stink of her breath and unwashed clothes. *I too probably smell like that,* I thought with disgust.

There were communist banners on the walls, and a photograph of Lenin with his arms upraised as if in blessing.. Above him was the slogan "Lenin: the Workers' Christ!"

Although I wanted to rip the poster off the wall and tear it to bits, it was a relief to spend a couple of hours a day in this room, which had some heat and where I could earn extra food coupons. Here I felt a sense of order in things, in the files, and in the typing Mrs Agajanian had taught me.

There was a copy of *Izvyestiya* on Mrs Agajanian's desk. The headline read: "Gorki says Culture is in Danger."

My friend Nina was not here. Instead there was a new girl in the office who I didn't recognise.

'Where is Nina?' I asked Mrs Agajanian.

The Armenian women handed me some papers. 'These go in the file over there,' she said loudly and then in a lower voice, 'The cheka took the family off last night. All of them.'

I buried my head in the files blinking hard to keep back my tears. Nina and I had stood together outside what had once been St Issac's Cathedral, held hands and wept, when we heard about the tsar's assassination. St Issac's was now named "The Museum of Atheism." The great icon of the Virgin had been destroyed, and we felt that our tears were not only expressions of grief, but a shared counter-revolutionary act.

The new girl, whose name was Svetlana, hovered close to me, asking for help with everything. She was younger than I, only sixteen, and her fear of making a mistake made her clumsy. I helped her pick up files and papers, although every extra move was almost too much effort.

Finally, as we stood side by side at the files, she whispered, 'Did you hear? They shot Bim Bam.'

'Bim Bam?' The clown from the Moscow Circus who made funny faces and sang nonsense songs. 'Why did they shoot Bim Bam?' I asked.

'A Chekist thought his song was counter-revolutionary. They shot him as he left the stage.'

Bim Bam. He came to St Petersburg every Christmas and I used to believe he had come just for me.

Another family had been moved into the morning room: the Iushkins and Mrs Iushkin's parents. The morning room was too small for all of them and their large linen chest, which scraped the hall floor and knocked against the wall as they dragged it in.

'Who is that?' Oleg Malkin peered out of his door. 'Is that Iushkin? From the Novgorod factory?' He went back into his room. Mama and I began to go upstairs with the pieces of wood we had managed to find near the garrison. We stopped at the sound of a shot and loud female screams: Oleg Malkin came out of his room, carrying a gun and followed by his elderly mother, in hysterics.

'Iushkin, come out of there!' he shouted. 'I'm ready for you, you bastard!'

Mr Iushkin emerged from the morning room, wielding a long narrow bladed knife. He rushed at Oleg Malkin, but Oleg fired another shot, which hit the wall above Mr Iushkin's head. Suddenly, Mama was between them.

She faced Oleg Malkin. 'Put that down!' Mama ordered. 'Put it down now!' Instead, he pointed the gun toward me. I screamed, but Mama, with a sudden and astonishing burst of energy, pushed him away. The man groaned and fell, more from surprise, I thought, than from Mama's action. Mama stepped over him, took the gun from his hand and gave it to the hysterical old woman, saying, 'Put it where he can't get it.'

She glared and growled at Mama in a fury, 'Some folks

think they can give orders to people who don't have to take them any more.'

I said. 'They'll kill each other some day. Maybe soon.'

'I hope so.' said Mama fervently.

'Sshhh,' I said. 'People are listening.'

We returned to our room. As if in recognition, the lights suddenly went on. We had lights and our ration. We had two potatoes. Mama had kept peace in the house. We had got through the day.

I was awakened by the knock on the door. Not a loud knock, but firm, calm and insistent. Mama and I immediately sat up, as if we had been waiting for it. The knock came again. It was a black, starless midnight, but I sensed Mama as strongly as if she was visible. I shook my head: *Don't answer. Run. Jump out the window. Fly away.* The knock came a third time. It was no louder, no harder. It had plenty of time. I could hear Mama breathing as she stood up and went to the door.

There were two men, one young, one middle aged. The younger man stayed back. The older man spoke Mama's name. 'Only a few questions, Comrade Serova,' he said. Without speaking, still with her blanket round her shoulders, she reached for her coat.

'It's only a few questions, you won't need your boots. We have the car.'

I knew what he meant. They always came at night when no one could see. No one we knew had come back yet.

'Wait,' I said to the man. He was round faced and grey haired; *he's probably got a family,* I thought, *maybe a daughter.* His expression was not unkind. Then I became aware of his uniform, his leather boots. 'You can wait,' I repeated and I handed Mama her boots. 'Mama, take them.'

She put her arms around me and as we embraced, I felt the strength in her arms and smelt her skin, still scented with sleep. 'Don't cry,' she whispered. 'Never cry.'

The younger man went down the stairs first. Mama went

next and the older policeman walked behind her. I started to follow them, but he motioned me back. They seemed to go so slowly, it was as if the moment would be suspended forever. *Maybe this isn't happening*, I thought, *maybe this is a dream*, even as I knew it wasn't.

'Mama! Mama!' The cry felt as if it had been torn from my throat; there must have been something in my voice that made them stop. Mama looked at me and raised her hand. I made the sign of the cross over her. Then they continued silently down the stairs.

A light flickered on from somewhere. It cast a pale gleam across the space on the wall where one of our pictures used to hang. The mark of the frame was still visible around it. For a moment, Mama was a shadow who moved across the empty space and out of the frame as they continued down through the hall and out the front door. I heard the sound of a car door shutting and a motor starting up. I listened to the sound fade as they drove away.

When they had gone, I listened to the silence they had left behind. Then, from somewhere in the house, I heard a door softly close.

CHAPTER FIVE

DECEMBER 1922

At the Nicolaevsky Station, people jostled and pushed and shouted as they struggled to get on the train to the provinces. It pulled out unsteadily, overloaded with passengers; some hung on from the outside, others lay across the roof. 'Pass the bag up here, comrade,' a man shouted.

His friend shouted back, 'This isn't for you, comrade,' and he pushed his way into a carriage. One leg and half his sack hung out. They wouldn't be able to close the door. The crowd stood packed in, pale and patient, waiting to trade their last possessions for food, for fuel, for whatever will keep them alive. Other people carried huge sacks to be filled with anything they could get their hands on, to sell at a huge profit in the little stalls that had recently opened in the Apraksin Market.

Bagmen. I watched them as if I was already standing behind a pane of glass. Mama and I had been on that train many times, taking china, glass, picture frames, Papa's watch and Babushka's crystal wine glasses, the dining room chandelier, clothes, silver, whatever was left after the Bolsheviks had ransacked the house and removed "state property."

The platform where Uncle Igor and I waited for the train for Berlin via Riga was also crowded, but it was quiet. I felt people pressing around me on all sides. They spoke in murmurs, or just sat on their suitcases, waiting. I wanted to hear Uncle Igor's voice, but I was afraid to break the silence. Uncle Igor said something to me, but despite the silence, I couldn't hear him, so I simply nodded in agreement. He called me 'Katya.' When I heard that and it reminded me that he was 'Viktor' now. Viktor and Katya Filatov. The names on our documents. On the other platform, the shouting continued, mixed with curses and laughter as the train pulled out. Near the end of our platform, I suddenly saw Papa's friends, the Bobrovs. They came to see us after Papa died. I barely recognised them. Mr Bobrov was almost transparent and his eyes were sunk back in his skull. Old Mrs Bobrova was sobbing. 'The last of their family is on the train,' Uncle Igor said. Vaguely, I remembered Grisha Bobrov, two years older than I, who had danced with me at the Doudoukov's party, on the last evening of the old world. He used to kick a ball with his friends in the Tavrichesky Gardens. Or was it his younger brother? I forgot, and then I forgot the Bobrovs altogether. I must remember only "Katya" and "Viktor" until we crossed the border.

The train was late. But everything was late now or didn't come at all. I thought, 'Something has gone wrong. It won't come.' Mama's friend Princess Volynska, was sitting on top of a large steamer trunk, weeping. Her husband, Prince Sergei, was with her. Uncle Igor frowned and I knew we couldn't speak to anyone or call attention to ourselves because of our forged papers. I stayed close to Uncle Igor, no …"Uncle Viktor" … and let him take care of everything. Someone pushed from the back of the crowd and we all leaned forward, I clutched my food parcel and worried again about Mama.

'What if the train has been cancelled?' I asked Uncle Igor. 'What will we do?' There was nowhere in Petersburg where we could go now. Another family had been about to move into our room as we left.

'It won't be cancelled,' said Uncle Igor. 'It will be here eventually.'

'But how do you know?' I asked, shifting my food parcel from one arm to the other.

'I don't know,' he said. 'But fate has brought us here, and for what, unless the train will come?' He sounded so certain. I believed that fate could easily abandon us at the station, but I must trust Uncle Igor. 'I trust fate,' he said, as he had said last night. 'And you must trust me. We must trust each other. The train will come.'

Fate. Uncle Igor is my fate. Of course I trusted him. Of course I did. I didn't have to understand what he said, only to trust him. I thought the names again: *Uncle Viktor. Viktor and Katya Filatov.* So far he had been right. But still, the Bolsheviks might have cancelled the train. Perhaps it was an excuse to collect all the "former people" in one place, all of us that are left, and then shoot us all at once. Why not?

My coat was thin, but that wasn't why I was shivering. I finally managed to sit crouched on the end of my suitcase. People made a cave around me in their dark, worn coats. There was a smell of unwashed bodies, a smell of sadness and hunger. I was awkward and uncomfortable on my case, but there was nowhere else to sit down. The benches were long ago burnt for firewood, the station clock had stopped and its glass was cracked. Weeds grew on the tracks. All down the line I could see idle engines and rusty machinery. The station smelt of chlorine. I thought about Mama again, and worried: *How can we tell her what we have done?*

The crowd around us parted, muttering as they shifted boxes and baskets to make a narrow passageway. Someone was making his way in our direction. Among the shabby, tired crowd on the platform, the man stood out in his new and splendid overcoat. When he reached us, he leaned toward Uncle Igor, embraced him on both cheeks and said quietly, 'Don't say anything superfluous.' Then he turned and left without another word and I still remember his back, broad as a shadow, in a heavy black overcoat and black fur hat, as he worked his way back, against the tide of passengers.

'Who was that man?' I asked Uncle Igor.

He shook his head. 'No one,' he said. 'Just someone. Don't drop your parcel. Hold onto it or it will get lost.' I held my parcel tightly. Uncle Igor had one too. We packed them last night with our provisions for the journey. They were bulky and some of the grease threatened to break through the slogans printed on the flimsy newspaper. But they were securely fastened with string, which Uncle Igor had found somewhere and wouldn't spill. I didn't want the parcel to touch my coat and stain it, but I held it tightly anyway, because he told me to.

'We're going to Riga,' he had told me. 'We have to leave quickly, and the train that leaves soonest stops first at Riga. So. We go to Riga. And then we change. There is a train from Riga to Paris. But if anyone questions you, we are going to Riga. That's all.'

Uncle Igor told me he had planned to go to Prague, where he had friends, but his "special contacts" had got us visas for Riga so we could leave immediately.

My friend Natasha's family had been planning to go to Berlin. Their visas would come any day, she told me. I had envied her. But then they were arrested.

'You must know that man,' I said now. 'You must know his name.'

'What?' Uncle Igor said. 'I don't remember. Someone's brother. Don't be an idiot with your questions.'

I hadn't really believed that he would call me an idiot and get angry now. I sniffed and blinked back tears. Still, he had stayed with me after Mama was taken away. If he had arrived sooner, perhaps she would have been released. He had been caught up with a group of Greens, he told me, and he had to escape. But he had come at last and he had saved my life. He had got us the visas. We were alone together; I should have felt even closer to him but instead I felt uncomfortable. Being alone with Uncle Igor reminded me that the title "uncle" was my invention. Without my family, he suddenly seemed like a stranger. I pushed the thought away. I couldn't allow thoughts like that now.

The train finally arrived. 'You see?' Uncle Igor said, and helped me lift our luggage into the carriage.

The Bolsheviks ransacked our house in the riots of 1917. What was left had been burnt for firewood, or traded for food, or simply worn out. I packed my icon, that had hung over my bed all my life. I took a few clothes and Mama's jewellery box, empty now, with its faint smell of lilac. I added the kaleidoscope Papa gave me for my name day when I was eight, and the battered book of fairy tales that had been with me all my life. When I was three, I had drawn inside the front covers with a green wax crayon.

I packed the photograph of Mama and Papa, forever frozen in the tarnished silver frame that I had refused to let Mama sell or trade, and finally the family photograph album. Before I tucked it into my case, I leafed through the pictures: Mama in a schoolgirl's pinafore, myself at seven gathering mushrooms with Cousin Yuri, photographed by Uncle Igor, Babyshka as a young woman in her pearl-encrusted Boyaryshna dress, ready for a costume ball. How they loved to dress up: so many photographs of family and friends dressed up in costumes of Mordva, Oryol, Tula, never smiling, always standing rigid, unsmiling, to show off the clothes, as if all our lives before the revolution had been a series of celebrations.

Uncle Igor loved to take those photographs; it was the one thing he did that pleased everyone. There were no photographs of him. When I pointed this out, he shrugged. 'I take the photographs. So I am in all of them. I'm merely invisible.'

It is like a stage set, I thought, looking at the photographs, *and then the set fell down and the stagehands set fire to the theatre.*

Finally, Uncle Igor had slipped his pistol under an old embroidered shawl... his pistol and his Rexo camera, which had been so expensive when he bought it that Mama and Papa wondered later where he had got the money.

The only thing I wanted to take with me was Russia. I wanted to take the whole country with me. My country, my family, my friends. They were all gone and I never said goodbye. I decided to say goodbye now. I was seventeen and already merely a former person, "human dust", but at least I was living dust, and before I blew away I would leave my farewell.

I took a piece of charcoal and wrote all the names on the wall of the room, across the empty spaces where our paintings used to be: Natasha, Sonya, Alyssia, Seriozha, Nina, Zenaida, Evgenia, Pyotr. Last, I wrote Papa's name: Mikhail Alexandrovich Serov. I wrote them all in the largest letters I could, over all the rest. And I wrote their epitaphs: "Murdered." I wrote it again, over and over, right down the wall, pressing as hard as I could: "Murdered". When I stood back I could barely make out the names by the fading winter light; there had been no electricity now for months or it was unreliable, and we had stopped trying to use it. Mama had been so proud when we were the first to have electricity installed. Now, in what had been the servants' room on the top floor, the light bulbs were black with dust and had rusted into the sockets.

'Goodbye,' I said. I thought I ought to say more than that. Something important. But what? 'I won't forget you,' I said. 'Never. Not for the rest of my life.' That was all there was. I was only speaking to my own writing, to childishly scribbled names on a wall. The new tenants would wipe it off immediately, or scribble over it. 'Goodbye,' I said again. The names looked down on me in living letters through the whole of that final night.

CHAPTER SIX

The heavy wooden benches in our third-class carriage were already full. With smiles and bows, and a wink for the ladies, Uncle Igor (Uncle Viktor, I reminded myself) managed to edge us and our cases across a small hunchbacked lady and the very large blonde lady next to her.

'So crowded, so crowded,' he murmured pleasantly to the businessman in the balding fur hat by the window, and before anyone realised it, he managed to dislodge the man and install me in the window seat, smoothing my coat around me and tucking our suitcases under the bench, before he settled himself close beside me. I felt very small, and grateful for his protection.

After a moment, the businessman changed places with the young boy next to him, so that the boy was sitting by the window opposite me, while the businessman sat opposite Uncle Igor. Next to him, an old man leaned on his cane with his eyes closed, lost in his thoughts.

The boy was younger than I, about fourteen, in an outgrown school uniform, the jacket riding above his skinny wrists and large bony hands. We faced each other, our knees almost touching. He took a book out of his scuffed and battered satchel. He didn't read, but clutched it tightly in his lap. More people arrived; a family with two children, a boy and a girl. The mother was terribly thin with fair hair pulled tightly back to reveal her domed, shiny forehead. The father was short and plump, and wore glasses with such thick lenses that his eyes were distorted and looked as if they were swimming behind the glass. The little boy's head was shaven, and he had a racking, moist cough, as if he was recovering from an illness. The girl sprawled on her father's lap and sucked her thumb. They crowded in next to the old man, who turned his head away when the child coughed. I was relieved they were sitting near the door, away from us. Also, the father's thick glasses made me uneasy.

'And there are people in the freight car as well,' remarked the businessman. His voice was educated and outraged, but the sole had come loose from one of his boots. The soles of my boots had worn out a year ago, but they were firmly tied on with string and had never fallen off entirely. I was proud of my boots, even though they were badly worn. Babyshka had made them out of an old piece of carpet from Dyedushka's study. The best broadloom. Mama had a pair as well. She had them now. We put them in the first parcel we were allowed to hand in. She would need another pair.

'All the way to Berlin?' asked the large blonde woman next to Uncle Igor.

'All the way to Berlin,' the businessman repeated.

'Did you hear that, Anya?' she said to the hunchback sitting on the other side of her.

'I heard. Unless they get off in Riga,' said the hunchback.

People continued to board, heaving suitcases and bags. Children called, 'Mama, mama!' babies cried. Carriage doors slammed shut. 'Here we are, Afansey, over here!' a woman called. The corridor was packed with travellers, kneeling on their possessions, waving their last farewells to relatives. The train was almost as crowded as the other one but here, voices were muffled, and as soon as people climbed on, they pressed their faces to the window as if they couldn't bear to let go.

The train stood in the station for a long time. A tightened string of fear shot through the carriage. I worried *Will we really leave? Will they stop us at the last minute, even with our visas? What if they look at our visas? Will they spot our false identity papers? My name is Katya Filyatova. Who is she? She is me. But who is that now?* Questions and fear whirled around in my head. And now I was afraid the train might not go to Riga at all. *Maybe it would be better to get off now,* I thought, and, as if he could read my mind, Uncle Igor said, 'It's only three days and we will be in Riga.' *Riga*, I thought. *Then where? Berlin? Paris? Prague? No. It is too far from Mama.*

Mama had said, 'Even if we could cross the border with false papers, how could I leave my husband to lie forgotten in his grave? And the others? Who will remember them in their own country?' And I was leaving her. We were doing the wrong thing. I turned to Uncle Igor, but he gently pressed me back into my seat and said, 'Trust me, *milaya* Katya.' I knew I must trust him. He knew how to manage everything that had to be arranged quickly. Otherwise, where would I be now? I thought of our house, with the washing line in the communal kitchen, our cold and dirty rooms under the leaky roof, the smashed banisters and the dirt-rimmed spaces on the walls where the pictures and mirrors used to be.

Finally the bell rang three times. The engine started to rumble softly, then louder. Cries grew louder as more people rushed to the windows. Relatives on the platform waved, weeping, making the sign of the cross over and over, mouthing unheard blessings. Everyone in our carriage rose as the train began to move slowly out of the station. Parents held their children up so they could see. The large woman next to Uncle Igor craned her neck as if she could not look hard enough, although her eyes were filled with tears. The hunchback, Anya, crossed herself. I could see her deformed, swollen hands. There was a loud, honking noise as the old man blew his nose. Then I forgot them as I watched my city falling away behind us.

It was mid-afternoon, cold and bright. The blue and gold top of St Nicholas Cathedral and the tip of the bell-tower gleamed on the horizon until they were out of sight. *This is the last time I will look at this*, I thought. *I will never run in the Tavrishevsky Park again. This isn't my place any more. Where is my place now?* A huge fear rose within me, a pain so great that it would devour me if I let it out.

The train finally moved off. It was a very old train, much battered, with scratched paint and a smell of coal and sawdust and wood shavings. It moved slowly, in uneven jerks. After less than an hour, it ground to a halt just outside Pavlovsk, as if it couldn't bear to leave Russia behind. It had been snowing and it would snow again. The chill ate into the carriage as afternoon darkened outside.

The large lady beside Uncle Igor said to the compartment in general, 'Such limits on luggage! I packed nothing for the summer.'

'We will be back by then,' said the hunchback, Anya, without taking her gaze from the window. 'This will all be over soon. There was no point taking too much.'

'Quite right, madam,' said the businessman, looking at Uncle Igor for agreement. 'Well before then,' Uncle Igor murmured.

The large lady looked like Mrs Kurilova next door. Where was Mrs Kurilova now? The Kurilovs vanished. People went into their house and stole everything they could use. Finally, it had no door, no windows or window frames. It was like an open tomb. Mama and I managed to prise up some of the half - rotted floorboards. The railings had been pulled up and piled on the street corner, where they lay rusting.

Someone was playing a guitar and I could hear the voices singing *Khorosh' Malchuk*.

I remembered what Uncle's Igor's friend had said: 'Say nothing superfluous.'

Among the people who had been moved into our house, I knew there was a spy. I knew there was a spy in the office where I filed papers. Everywhere there was someone, set to watch. And now there was one on this train. That's what Uncle Igor's friend had meant. There was the large blonde lady herself, who was still talking about Bolshevik disorder. The old man with the cane was surprisingly well dressed and his cane had a gold top. I was uneasy about that cane. No one had canes like that any more. And why was the large lady so free and loud in her speech? Was she hoping to draw us out?

Uncle Igor said, 'Katya, give me your food parcel. We should keep them together.' He used the name on my papers so

I would get accustomed to it. I tried. I thought, *Katya, Katya, Katya, and Uncle Viktor. I have memorised so many poems, why are these two simple names so difficult?*

The others watched us as I handed him my parcel, and he put it with his own. I watched him tuck them down between us, where no one could take them while we slept. The paper made a slight rustling noise. In my mind's eye, I saw through the layers of flimsy paper to our rolls made of the usual boiled moss, bark, who knows what, mixed with poor quality flour and a bit of herring. In my mind I lifted the top of a roll, and saw Mama's diamonds sparkling among the crumbs. Earrings and a necklace were all that was left after Uncle Igor had bribed "the right people" to get our visas so quickly. If they were in a basket, they might have aroused suspicion, but no one would pay attention to a couple of paper parcels of food, wrapped in old newspapers with Bolshevik slogans on them: "Death to World Imperialism!" "The Workers Triumph!" And beneath these were the rolls and in them among the crumbs, Mama's jewellery.

The boy looked at our parcels. 'It's a long journey,' he said. 'It's good you have brought food. I have brought nothing. My brother gave me some roubles, though.'

'There will be food at the stations,' said the large lady. 'The peasants come and sell produce. They have plenty. And they charge enough for it.'

'They are the "Workers,"' said Anya. Her voice capitalised the word and made it sound like something ludicrous. 'To the "Workers" now everything is permitted.'

I said nothing superfluous. I remembered Mrs Trofimova holding her baby over the communal kitchen sink, with its dirty nappy lying in the basin. Mama had explained about using the toilet but Mrs Trofimova had never seen one before and said, 'If you don't like it, comrade, complain to the house committee. This is state housing now. We do as we do.' And later, how I sensed someone watching Mama go down the stairs after the policeman, and the door softly closing.

We finally left the city and passed through small towns and forests. Everything was covered with snow. Silver birches were frozen white, ridges of snow iced along their branches. The window had icicles inside, small needles of ice. The train stopped again in the midst of a snowy nowhere, and a deeper chill spread through the carriage.

The father held his little girl in the crook of his arm, letting her head rest against his chest. His wife held the boy on her lap and rocked him. He coughed, and she held him closer. *Why won't the man take off his glasses? Why won't he let us see him properly?* I thought. *Katya, Katya,* I repeated to myself, *say nothing superfluous.*

I leant against Uncle Igor (no, Uncle Viktor) and felt the rough material of his coat. His eyes were closed, but his fingers played a nervous scale in his lap. His fingers were long and broad at the tips; his nails were, as always, immaculately clean and filed to perfect arcs. I covered his hands with mine, to still them. He opened his eyes, looked at me, smiled, pushed the parcels deeper between us so he could move a bit closer, and put an arm around me. I would have liked to fall asleep against him, like the child opposite, but I must not do that. To touch him made me uneasy, as if I would lose my balance, fall, and never stop.

Out of the silence, the young boy spoke to me. 'My auntie lives in Marburg,' he said. 'I am going to Berlin. My parents ... ' He shrugged. His face was small and pinched. 'My brother said I would be better there. He's a priest.'

Everyone looked at him. Anya said softly, 'They destroyed our church. All the ornaments, the icons, the lamps, everything – and then they smashed the windows.' She wiped her eyes.

'So far to go, all alone,' said the large lady.

I thought, *He has said too much. What did that woman mean?*

'What book have you got?' Uncle Igor asked softly, so he wouldn't disturb the children or the old man, who also seemed to be asleep.

Eugene Onegin, said the boy 'It was a prize. The headmaster gave it to me himself.'

'A prize indeed,' said Uncle Igor. 'You are taking Russia with you.'

The father shifted the child on his lap and recited:

'Will freedom come – and cut my tether?
It's time, it's time! I bid her hail;
I roam the shore, await fair weather
And beckon to each passing sail.'

He fell silent. The guitar still played in the next carriage, but quietly now, no one singing. Uncle Igor (no, Uncle Viktor) chimed in:

'There where southern waves break high
Beneath my Africa's warm sky
To sigh for Russia's sombre spaces.'

The hunchback Anya, in a surprisingly musical voice added:

'Where first I loved, where first I wept,
And where my buried heart is kept.'

The old man was not asleep after all. He said to the boy, 'Whenever you open that book, you will remember this time. So we will be with you somehow for as long as you live.' He looked down at his cane. 'That's good.'

There was a long silence. The businessman made notes in a small notebook. *What is he writing?*

It was getting dark now and the late afternoon light was steely dark blue on the snow. There were no lights in the towns we passed through, only the shadowy outlines of izbas and frosted trees.

The businessman finished writing, looked at his notes, and nodded. He showed them to the stout lady. 'Every woman I have ever loved,' he said. She glanced at the page, raised her eyebrows. 'Ah,' she said. Again there was a silence. I thought about fate. If fate has brought me to this place, I thought, then fate must intend that I survive. No. That I do more than survive. Only to survive after the past five years is not enough. I am sure fate intends more than that. I will do more than that, for Mama, Papa and all the rest.

The silence thickened. The lights suddenly went on, pale and greasy. They stayed on for a moment, casting a sickly yellow light that made everyone look ill.

I looked out the window, where there was nothing to see now but my own reflection. The blue-black night had swallowed the country. *I am going to Europe. Uncle Igor has saved my life. Perhaps I will go back to school, go to university and study, just as Mama and Papa wished. I will stop being Katya Filyatova.* 'Mama has her shawl,' I whispered to Uncle Igor. 'It was in the parcel they accepted.' The others looked at me, wondering, I was sure, what I was whispering. Uncle Igor nodded, but said nothing.

The guitar in the next carriage started again, slow and tentative, as if the player was trying to master a new song note by note. A baby began to wail.

The train picked up speed. *Someone in this carriage has heard everything and will report it somewhere.* I thought. *Who? What did we say that would be of interest? One never knows.* I tried to watch everyone as my eyelids grew heavy and tiredness dropped upon me like a stone cloak in spite of the cold and the hard seats. As the train relentlessly bore us further and further away, I heard the wheels lift their voice against the track and repeat their demanding gibberish. I felt Russia slipping away and embracing me at the same time as the wheels pulled the rhythm round and round... the embrace widened as it was blown back further and further behind me.

CHAPTER SEVEN

The journey was meant to take three days, but for three days the train stopped and started, in empty frozen fields or at small wooden country stations. It would clearly take longer than three days, but how much longer was impossible to guess.

'Perhaps they won't stop anywhere now, to make up the time,' said Anya.

'Perhaps.' Her sister sighed and looked out the window into the vast distance.

The carriage reeked of rotting food, vomit, urine and unwashed bodies. At night we arranged the suitcases between the benches so that we could stretch out to sleep. The little boy began to moan between coughs, and nothing his mother could do seemed to comfort him. His sister chanted endlessly to herself in a high-pitched, little monotone. In the corridor, people sat pressed tightly together against both walls all the way to the toilet, which was broken, had overflowed, and now gave off a stench that made me gag from several feet away, and turned back to our carriage, determined to hold out until it was no longer possible. The wailing of babies and children continued night and day.

During the day I watched the wide icy fields and small clusters of village huts go by. Wherever the train stopped, skeletons tapped on the windows, begging. At Tver, a sign announced "Hot water for sale." Passengers poured out of the train to fill bottles with hot water for tea. Uncle Igor-Viktor counted out a couple of roubles and said, 'Go, Katya. I'll watch the bags.'

The boy, Misha, still gripped his book as we waited in the queue for the water. 'Look,' he said. It was a horse lying in the snow. 'It starved to death,' I said. Misha shook his head. 'Frozen,' he said, and added, 'They will take it away to eat later.' I climbed back onto the train with relief. Even its noise and filth felt like shelter.

'We will be back, I think by the autumn at the latest,' said Nina Petrovna.

The businessman looked up. 'When Lenin finally goes, the tsar will return.'

'The tsar!' cried Anya. 'But ... ' She stopped. 'The greatest crime,' she said.

'They are alive,' said the man. 'I have it from a good source.' Everyone leant forward and he lowered his voice. 'The deaths? Bolshevik propaganda. They are in hiding. In England, all of them. The Allies are waiting for the right moment to mobilise and restore the Romanovs.'

Uncle Igor agreed.

As the train stopped again, further down the line, Misha and I saw more beggars, and more dead animals as we waited in another queue for water. We began to compete as we counted them. 'I've seen the most,' he said, as we paid for the water and started back to the train. 'You lost because you kept looking back at the train. It won't leave without us.'

At the next station, Uncle Igor-Viktor stood up. 'I'll go for the water. Wait here.' I watched him go into the station and I knew he wouldn't come back.

Anya, or as I called her to myself, Anya Hunchback said, 'You know, in Europe, they are wearing skirts above the ankle.'

'Are they?' I said. My dress had been made from one of mama's good blankets and my sweater was an old one of my cousin Yuri's. *We will look like beggars,* I thought. In the rush to leave, I hadn't asked "Uncle Viktor" what we would do in Paris. Now I wondered. Would we wander the streets and would people turn away from us in our old, worn-out clothes? How would we live? And if he doesn't return? I will have to stay in Riga.

'Yes, everyone is doing it. I have seen photographs of ladies in Deauville,' Anya Hunchback went on enthusiastically. 'It's shocking – ankles everywhere.'

I fixed my eyes on the station door until I felt someone tap my knee. It was Misha. 'You can come to my Auntie in Marburg,' he said. 'She will look after you.' I nodded. If Uncle Igor is gone it doesn't matter where I go. And then I remembered that he had our documents.

I was so sure Uncle Igor wouldn't come back that when he did, he looked unfamiliar for a second, a tall, lean man with a broad, bony face, narrow eyes and wide mouth, all framed by his fur *shapka*. How handsome he is, I realised, as if I had never seen him before, and his looks burnt through me.

'But you are not going to Berlin,' said Nina

'No,' Uncle Igor answered. 'Katya and I are going to Riga. We have relatives there.'

Why had he said that? He didn't want anyone to know we are going to change for Paris in Riga. I wondered why. But it might be superfluous. Uncle Igor was mysterious. He had been unable to shave and his face was bristled, but he was still handsome. Now I had seen him so clearly, I knew that no one in the world was as handsome as he was.

As we neared the border, guards came through at intervals, checking visas and papers. Close beside Uncle Igor, I dozed, or slept fitfully, waking when the light unexpectedly went on with its greasy yellow glare, and lying awake when it went off again, listening to snores, murmurs, loud breathing, and, late into the night, the soft sound of the guitar. I waited for our false papers to be discovered, but the guards asked no questions, merely glanced at them and passed on. I dreamed of Mama going down the stairs with the policeman, over and over and over, while doors softly closed on soft whispers. 'Come back,' I called in my sleep, but no one heard me. My voice made no sound. When I awakened, the dream seemed to go on, as if the wheels of the train played it over and over.

At the border, the train stopped again. From down the line there were shouts and laughter. 'Soldiers,' said the businessman.

We all froze. The little girl whimpered. Her father stroked her and whispered reassurance. We could hear them come closer. 'Papers, papers!' they shouted, and, 'Declare all state property!' There was a distant female cry and the sound of protest. I saw two young men as they were pushed off the train and marched off. There were a lot of soldiers. 'What goods are you carrying?' they shouted over and over, pushing people into the corridor. There seemed to be no sense to it. Some people had to open their cases, others were ignored. In our carriage we avoided each other's eyes.

Now there were two officers in the doorway. They looked around.

'What's in here?' said one of them. I could smell the fumes of drink they breathed into the carriage. Once more they looked at all the documents, and then one of the soldiers said, 'Do I smell state property? Yes. Do you smell it, Ivan?'

'Oh yes,' laughed the other. 'Can't mistake it. Property of the state.' They were so drunk they had trouble pronouncing the words. I saw more people, including several women, being pushed off the train and marched away. The grease from the parcel felt as if it would explode in front of everyone. The little girl whimpered again, and pressed her legs tightly together. Our documents, when Igor-Viktor handed them over, looked incompetent, obviously false. I stared down at my lap so no one could see my face. I couldn't see anyone else either, but I felt the silence throughout the train, heard the boots and shouts of other soldiers. I thought: *I will not be frightened.*

'I know where the stink comes from,' said the one called Ivan and then they lunged forwards. I cringed and I felt Uncle Igor tense but instead, they seized the old man, and pulled the cane from his hands. They unscrewed the top. It came away easily, and everything fell onto the floor of the carriage: roubles, rings, watches, and diamonds. The little girl wailed, 'Mama!' and a stream of urine flowed down her legs onto the scattered coins. The soldiers lifted the old man, who dangled between them like a large doll. His face had turned a terrible blotched red. They carried him off the train, while another soldier stood guard at the carriage door.

'It was as if they knew,' I said later, in Riga.

'They did,' Uncle Igor said.

'But how did they know? He said nothing.'

'There were people on the train. In every carriage. They know what they are doing. That's why I let them think we were going only to Riga.'

'Were they watching us?' I asked.

'Always,' he answered.

'Who was it?' I recalled everyone in the carriage, even the children.

Uncle Igor shrugged. 'We'll never know.'

They dragged the old man across the snow to join the others. After a moment there was a volley of rifle fire followed by silence.

Nina Andreyevna burst into tears and threw herself on her sister's lap. The hunchback cradled her head, whispering, 'Shhh, shhh.'

The officers stayed in the carriage, uncertain. They wanted more, I could tell, but there was no more. I made my mind blank so that my expression would give nothing away. Once more, they looked at everyone's documents. They examined our documents for a long time, but they were tired of the game now and thrust the documents back at us. Then an officer spotted Misha's book.

'What's this then? What have you got?' He turned the book upside down and gave it a hard shake.

'From my school…' Misha stammered, his voice thin and very young. 'My Auntie… Marburg.'

'My Auntie Marburg,' the officer mocked. 'Well, *Barin*, you won't need this then. State property.' He laughed and carelessly flung the book out the window. We looked at it lying in the snow as the train started and moved slowly across the border, toward Riga.

CHAPTER EIGHT

We weren't the only people who got off at Riga. We hung back as the other passengers dragged their things onto the street. Some were met by relatives, and the voices sounded very loud and bright after the quiet of Petersburg. The station still showed ravages of war in the scarred doors and cracked tiles, but it was very clean and the winter sun gleamed through the tall, glass windows.

Uncle Igor sank down and sat with his back against the wall. 'Oh my God,' he said. 'Oh my God.' To my surprise he was trembling. 'What have I done, Nadyushka, tell me.'

I squatted beside him. 'Uncle Igor are you ill?'

'No,' he said. 'I am a coward. You had to know. A coward.'

'You're not a coward,' I said. 'We're here. And they never noticed the parcels.'

'An accident,' he said. 'If it hadn't been for that old man, who knows?'

I didn't want to think about the old man. 'You're brave,' I said. 'Brave and clever and strong, and … '

He interrupted. 'For you, Nadezhda Mikhailovna. You made me brave.' I saw his eyes, red-rimmed from lack of sleep and full of tears. He looked as if he would say more, but instead he looked at the station clock. 'Pavel will meet us at the Livu Square. Come.' With an effort, he stood up and held out his hand to me. 'To the Livu Square. The station side.'

The light on the snow when we came into the big square, was almost too bright and the square seemed enormous. There was even an ice rink, with people skating. I looked around, bewildered. People strolled in the winter sun and they made me dizzy and confused. I was aware of how crumpled and travel-stained we were. My plait had come loose and strands of hair hung limply around my face. Our cases felt heavier. My body was stiff and aching and my eyes felt heavy. It was the first time I had seen Uncle Igor unshaven, and he smelt unwashed. I knew I did too. I thought we must look like something that had been washed up on the shore.

'Viktor! Viktor!' a deep voice called, and there was a man coming toward us, with a huge smile and outstretched arms. 'Pavel!' Uncle Igor cried.

Pavel embraced Uncle Igor formally on both cheeks, and shook my hand. He was short, much shorter than Uncle Igor, and heavier. His eyebrows were black and so thick that they made a straight line across the bridge of his nose. He looked as if he might have been a weightlifter, judging from the bulging muscles of his neck, and the ease with which he lifted our bags and swept us away with him.

He talked all the way, pointing out the great clock tower, the Blackhead's house, St. Peter's church, interrupting himself with bursts of laughter. I stumbled to keep up, dazed by the speed at which everyone seemed to walk. All the streets seemed to be narrow and cobbled, winding this way and that, lined with small houses, neatly painted in cream and blue and faded pink.

'You haven't changed. It's ridiculous,' Pavel said, looking at Uncle Igor.

'You have changed,' said Uncle Igor. 'I almost didn't recognise you.'

'I know. I'm an old man. But that's what happens when you're married.' Now he looked at me. 'With marriage, you grow old fast.' He laughed again. Pavel pointed out the Swedish Gate as we passed, and made us pause briefly to admire it.

'Not far now,' he said. 'Beate has everything ready for you, comrades. You must be tired, yes?' He smiled down at me. Then he turned back to Uncle Igor and became business-like. 'You can get the train to Paris in a few days. Some things are better done from here. The arrangements about Chengarov. We are waiting to hear from Lewitsky. Meanwhile, you'll stay with us.' Chengarov, Lewitsky. The strange names hummed around my head.

'But you are always crowded. How do you make space?' asked Uncle Igor.

'Igor Fyedorovitch,' Pavel laughed. 'For you? We always have space.'

He led us to a small, low-ceilinged house in a steep cobbled back street. The house was filled with other people, refugees like ourselves, waiting for trains. All the rooms had old mattresses and blankets spread on the floor, and the house was smoky and warm. When we arrived, there was a riot of welcome. Everyone seemed to know Uncle Igor. Still, they called us Viktor and Katya. Pavel's wife, Beate had set out a meal of fresh bread, cheese, sausage and tomatoes.

'Come, eat,' she urged, helping me to soup; real soup, thick with vegetables.

Uncle Igor gulped down the soup, wiped the bowl with a piece of bread, and rolled himself a cigarette with Pavel's tobacco.

'So, comrade,' said one of the men to Uncle Igor, 'You are going to work on Chengarov. He's a tricky customer. Who knows where he really stands?'

'We'll soon find out, eh, "Viktor?"' said Pavel.

Uncle Igor inhaled deeply, and blew the smoke out in a long narrow stream. 'And what about Alyosha?' he asked. 'I thought I would meet him in Prague, but "Katya's" mother ...' He made a gesture, and there were sympathetic murmurs.

'Fanatics,' said a man

'But understandable,' said another.

'Enough,' said Uncle Igor firmly, and they were silent. I began to feel uneasy. 'So who is in Prague now?'

'Good people,' said Pavel, and rolled a cigarette. 'But not Alyosha. That's the news. He has gone to Paris.'

'Alyosha in Paris?' Uncle Igor was delighted. 'Nadia, you remember Larissa Mordvinova? His wife.'

'Alyosha is well-intentioned, but that's all, in my opinion,' said someone.

There were too many names. The room was warm, it was the warmest room I had ever been in. I felt my head droop.

'Come, Katya,' said Beate, 'Let's find you a place to sleep.' She took me to a small room where several women and children were already sprawled on cots and mattresses. I fell sleep immediately.

Skeletal figures danced through my dreams: Misha, The Trofimovs, Mama, cousin Yuri, then Misha again, and the officer at the police station who told us the news about Mama. It was a dream full of parcels, trains, and rifle shots. I woke suddenly, wondering where I was. Then I remembered. Through the uncurtained window in this room, I saw that the darkness was starting to dissolve. I was still wearing my thin, filthy coat, but someone had taken the parcel. I vaguely recalled Beate taking it away 'to give to Igor Fyedorovich.' Suddenly, I knew what I had to do. Uncle Igor was going to Paris, but I had to go back to Mama. Even if I too was sent away, it would be better.

I got up very quietly and found my way through the dark rooms, instinctively feeling for the front door, remembering how to get back to the station. I opened the door and was about to slip out, when someone took my arm.

'Nadia, where are you going?' Uncle Igor whispered.

'I'm going home,' I said.

'What are you talking about?' He took my arm, led me outside and closed the door softly behind us. 'Let's walk,' he said. The night's darkness was transparent now, and there were pale clouds behind it. An early morning delivery cart rattled past us. A woman, muffled in a coat and shawl, came out of the house opposite and trudged to the corner where she turned and disappeared. Igor linked his arm in mine and led me in the same direction as if we were friends, strolling.

'The station is the other way,' I said. I stopped walking and faced him. 'I have to go back. I have to find Mama. She wouldn't understand this. She didn't leave. She talked about suffering with one's people. That's what she said.'

'You can't go back now.'

'Mama is alone. How could we do that? She'll get the parcels we gave in at the police station,' I said, 'and then she'll get nothing. She won't understand. She'll ...' There was a lump in my throat. I could hardly speak. 'She'll think I'm dead.'

He took me in his arms. 'No, Nadia, she won't. Trust me,' he said. 'You know it was dangerous for you to stay.'

'It doesn't matter,' I said. 'I don't care.'

'Yes, you do. You will be glad later. You'll be glad for your mama because this way you can help her more.' He turned me around and we walked back a few steps. Then he spoke in a sharp voice that told me he was angry. 'You have no money, no papers, no documents. You will certainly be arrested as soon as you cross the border. You would have been arrested anyway if I hadn't got the visas. Your papa is dead,' he said, enunciating each word. 'Your mama is in a camp. Where would you go?'

I pulled away from him and started back toward the station.

'Nadia, Nadia, stop!' He caught me again. 'Let's sit down for a minute,' he said. 'I have to talk to you.' We sat on the kerb, in a scattering of snow.

'It was my fault,' I said. 'It was all my fault. I didn't help mama enough. I wasn't brave enough for her.' I made my voice steady and reasonable, but when I said that, I began to cry again. He sat quietly and held me while I wept. I thought that now I would surely weep for the rest of my life, for all the loss, for everything I had not done. But after a while my tears ran dry and I lay, exhausted, in Uncle Igor's arms. We sat for a long time in silence. I could feel the steady beat of his heart.

'You know how much I love your mama,' he said quietly. 'When I was small, she was like my own little mother. Without her, I would have been nothing. You are very much like her. You know I would never do anything to harm you or your mama. How could I? I owe her everything good in my life. Including you. Especially you.'

'She wouldn't have left *me* alone in a prison camp. We have to go back,' I insisted and started to cry again. 'How will we send parcels?' I asked, 'if we are not there.'

'We will be able to do that. I have something to tell you – can you listen to what I'm saying?'

I didn't answer, but lay against him without moving.

'The visas – we got them so quickly didn't we? And the documents. There is a plan,' he went on. 'And I have agreed to be a part of it. It is a huge plan, with many people in many countries. We don't know them all and we never will, but still we are all fighting for a cause. You want to be part of our cause, don't you?'

'What cause?' I asked.

'Russia,' he said.

'But what will we do?' I asked.

He seemed to darken, as he always did when he was unhappy, and I was afraid for him. 'Uncle Igor,' I asked. 'What is it?'

'Why are you sitting in the snow?' Pavel was standing behind us.

'We didn't notice.' Uncle Igor brushed some snow off the kerb. 'Nadia is torn about leaving.' he said. 'I am trying to explain it to her.'

'Ah.' Pavel lowered himself beside us. He had his fur hat on, and a pair of heavy walking boots. He carried a small rucksack. 'I have to take Anton to Jurmala today,' he said, noticing my look. He put the rucksack between his feet. His voice was low and intense, in contrast to his usual joviality. 'Now you have crossed the border, we can be open together. Nadezhda Mikhailovna, you have been given papers, visa, passport, tickets, everything you need. You are asked to do something in return. Not a great deal, only to help us in a small way. Small but important. And it is the only way you can help your mother. Simple. Life is very simple. Really. There is a path with an end ...' he pointed straight ahead... 'and a path without an end.' His finger made a curve. 'You take the path with the end. That's all you need to know.'

He scrambled up and brushed snow off his coat. 'Don't think, Nadia. Do.' The door opened and Anton emerged, with one of the women who had shared the room with me. She carried a baby. 'Anton!' Pavel cried, 'All ready? Good.' He said to us, 'We have to leave now, but I will be back later.' He turned to Uncle Igor. 'And with news about Chengarov.'

The lights went on in the front of the bakery. A smell of fresh bread warmed the cold air, as a woman brought a tray of rolls from the back and set them in the window.

'You see?' Uncle Igor said. 'There are people everywhere. I don't know who they are, and I never will, and they might never know me. But at the centre of this plan there are powerful people and while we fight with them, your mama will be alive. Do you understand?'

'I think so,' I said, and struggled to show that I had made sense of it. 'We are going to fight the Bolsheviks.'

He looked at me blankly, as if I was a stranger and then his face brightened. 'Nadia, you are the most clever person I know. You and I will be perfect partners.' He took my hand, and I could feel the chill of his skin. 'I need you to work with me, Nadia. I will look after everything, I promise.'

'Anything could happen,' I said. 'Promises mean nothing.'

'Let's swear an oath. Wait.' he smiled and took out his pocket-knife. 'What if I said I will swear to you in blood – shall we do that? A blood oath.'

Solemnly, he pricked his finger and then mine. *It's a children's game*, I thought, but when we pressed our fingers together and I felt the drops of blood sliding together, I knew it was not a children's game. It was something that would truly bind us forever. 'Come on,' he said. 'We swear to be together as one person for whatever may come.'

'I swear,' I said.

He got up, wiped the knife on his sleeve and put it away. 'Damn the snow. My coat is soaked through. And yours.'

We went back to the house. Before he opened the door, he said, 'We must never speak of this to other people. Do you promise? If the leaders discover that anyone has talked about this, it will be bad for your mama.'

The next day Beate found me an old, warm coat and a dress. It had belonged to her sister, she told me, and the dark blue suited me "exactly the same." I had forgotten how patched my own dress was. I had stopped thinking about things like that. Beate also gave me a pair of thick-soled shoes. 'In Paris these are better than those felt boots,' she said tactfully. She offered to take my old boots and dress but I refused. Tenderly, I tucked them into my case.

That evening, Pavel, Igor and the others told me how pretty I was, how I must be careful, because such a pretty girl could get into trouble in the west. 'Frenchmen are not honourable with women,' they said. Uncle Igor said he would take care of all that. Then they talked again about Chengarov and Lewitsky, and the address we must go to, near the Champ de Mars. This time I remembered the names.

The next night Pavel said, 'You have your camera? Let me see.' Uncle Igor brought out his camera, which he had managed to hide, despite its weight, in a compartment inside the lining of his suitcase. He snapped open the front of the camera and as usual I admired the way the shutter could expand and contract like a little accordion.

'Mm.' Pavel looked at it. 'Not bad, but not the latest. You need more than that. You are no longer an amateur.' And he gave Uncle Igor a new camera, 'This is what they use for news photography,' he said.

'Nadia, look!' Uncle Igor exclaimed. 'This is a Graphex Speed Graphic! See how one can adjust the exposures? This camera can do everything. You have film or you change the back...' he demonstrated 'and you can use the shutter.' His hands caressed the camera as if it was alive.

Pavel also gave him a tripod, a portrait lens attachment, a long focus lens attachment, and a box of film, twenty rolls of it. Everyone applauded and exclaimed; *he must be doing something of great importance*, I thought, *to be given such equipment*.

65

Early the next morning, Pavel walked with us back to the station and put us on the train to Paris. He stood on the platform and waved goodbye. I waved back for as long as I could see him standing there in his collarless shirt, with his coat open and his fur hat pushed back, waving and laughing.

CHAPTER NINE

JANUARY, 1922

Two days later, Riga was something that happened so long ago I could barely remember it. From the moment of our arrival at the Gare de Lyon, Paris exploded around me. I stood on the pavement, dazed.

'Come on,' said Uncle Igor impatiently, and then he saw my amazement and smiled. 'Ah yes, the air of Paris.' We walked slowly, laden with our photographic equipment.

The day was cold and slightly overcast, but there was light coming from somewhere behind the clouds. People passed to and fro, talking loudly, as if it didn't matter who heard them. A woman laughed. All the speech sounded bewilderingly rapid. I had got "fours" regularly in French at school, but after my school had closed during the chaotic months following the revolution, French, along with so many other things, had got lost in the struggle to exist. Now the sounds were familiar and I thought I could almost understand them, before I realised that I didn't. *I will have to learn what they are saying* I thought, hurrying to keep up with Uncle Igor, who strode forward, his head up, his face alight with pleasure.

'Smell it!' he exclaimed. 'It's Paris! Paris can swallow you up. Just the smell.' It was a smell of bread, of chestnuts, flowers, drains, and something else that seemed like the smell of air and light. A girl sliced ham in a butcher's window. I watched her cut slice after slice of pink meat, ringed with shiny white fat. Next to the butcher there was a patisserie, with rows of bright iced cakes in the window. Someone called loudly to a child,

'*Içi, Michel. Içi!*' I felt dizzy surrounded by so much of everything everywhere, as if a basket had been overturned from the sky.

People carried string bags full of food casually, not held tightly to their chests like something infinitely precious. They carried it as if they knew that when it was finished, there would be more. Whole loaves of bread. Uncle Igor set a fast pace and as we hurried along, all the contents of shops caught my eye, one after the other. Some shops had exciting-looking beaded silk dresses in the window. (The woman on the train – what was her name? – had been right about skirts.) Hats and shoes flashed by. We hurried past stalls banked with fruit, flowers and vegetables. I wanted to stare at the people, but everything frightened and excited me at the same time. Uncle Igor was right: this place would swallow you up.

'Look!' I pointed.

A woman was walking a small dog. She and the dog wore identical red and black checked coats.

'Even the dogs have coats!' I said. There was too much of everything.

Uncle Igor laughed.

* * *

The Chengarovs lived in a large apartment house near the Champ de Mars, on a wide, quiet street, lined with trees and imposing stone buildings. They all had similar large windows, wrought iron balconies, and heavy, arched oak doors with iron grilles. Uncle Igor found the number and paused in front of the door with his hand raised. 'Well,' he said, 'now we begin.' He hesitated and I thought he looked uncertain.

'Did you forget something?' I asked.

He kissed me lightly on the forehead. 'No. Thank God you're here,' he said. Then he pressed a large button, and I heard the distant clang of a bell.

The concierge informed us that Monsieur Chengarov lived

on what turned out to be the second floor. A small, noisy lift took us upstairs and a maid led us into the drawing-room.

I thought I had been transported back to Russia, before the revolution. There were the same panelled walls, the heavy mahogany furniture, large potted plants, embroidered cushions and shawls, little tables with lace cloths, covered in photographs of people in court dress, photographs of estates, children and dogs. There were paintings, icons, ornate mirrors as well, everything overlaid with the sweetly rich vinegar smell of borscht.

There were a number of people, reading newspapers, writing, or talking quietly in small groups. Uncle Igor and I hovered in the doorway. *What do we do now?* I wondered. A group of people were playing bridge at a table near us – three men and a woman. The woman looked up when we entered and stared at us openly. I stared back at her. She had a sharp face and a pink velvet bow in her bright red hair. After a moment, she went back to the game.

'Igor Fyedorovich!' said a man with bright eyes and curly fair hair.

'Georgei Benediktovich!' Igor said. 'Yuri!' They embraced.

'And when did you arrive in Paris?' Georgei Benediktovich enquired.

The woman at the bridge table looked up again, obviously listening.

'We have just arrived,' Uncle Igor said, indicating our bags, which looked particularly old and shabby on the splendid red patterned carpet. 'As you see.'

'And you came first to Chengarov, like everyone else?'

Uncle Igor lowered his voice. 'They told us to come here. Pavel sent an introduction.'

Gyorgei said, 'If you need anything, Chengarov knows everyone. But after that, contact Leonid.' They both laughed.

The red-haired woman and I were openly staring at each other now. The man next to her, a handsome man with a shock of white hair and a white moustache, also looked up and said, 'Zhenia, your bid. *Fais attention!*'

'And what about Olga Nikolayevna?' Uncle Igor asked.

'Oh, she hasn't forgotten you,' and they laughed again.

An old man began to play the violin, softly and badly.

A few people drifted toward the windows, or greeted friends. *What is this place?* I wondered. *Is it really someone's house?* It seemed like a place that would always be warm and rich-smelling, that everything here, including the people, had always been here like this and would stay unchanged forever. The Chengarov's drawing-room felt unreal.

A short, broad man with enormous shoulders hurried toward us, beaming. 'Igor Fyedorovitch Rozanov isn't it!' he exclaimed, 'Welcome! Thank God you have arrived safely.'

Uncle Igor introduced me. Boris Chengarov bent over my hand in an old-fashioned way that made me feel like a girl from a past era. He was a balding, red-faced man with a natural ebullience, checked by an anxiety that he wore like an ill-fitting coat.

'Come,' he said. 'Come and eat something and my wife will show you ... you will stay here of course?'

'Yes,' said Uncle Igor. 'With pleasure. It will make everything easier.'

Chengarov spoke to the room at large: 'Igor Fyedorovitch Rozanov, a great photographer, is going to photograph my little collection.'

Collection? I wondered. Igor had said nothing about a collection. *Collection of what? Does he mean these people?*

Gyorgei turned away as Mr Chengarov escorted us to the dining-room opposite.

'You must stay as long ... a day, two days ... three, four days even ... as long as... Evgenia, my dear.'

Madame Chengarova was tall and, I thought, wonderfully elegant, with a diamond watch pinned to her breast. She greeted us cordially, and said, 'You must have something to eat. Fortunately, our cook is of the aristocracy and can manage anything at any time.' She rang a little bell and a woman appeared holding a cigarette. Madame Chengarova said, 'Would you mind, Your Excellency, if it's no trouble, our friends have just arrived.' Without speaking, the woman put down the cigarette, and vanished.

Madame Chengarova smiled. 'She's a wonderful housekeeper and she's glad of the job but she does like us to use her title. And why not?'

'She will take her time,' said Mr Chengarov. 'Come first, and see.' He turned to me, 'You don't mind my dear? I have been so thrilled about the article, and you will enjoy this, I know you will. It is something ...something very... yes.' He laughed and rubbed his hands together. 'Come and look, or ...' his face fell slightly, 'perhaps you want to, you know...? Perhaps later?'

He looked so sad at the prospect that I said quickly, 'No. We want to see the collection now, please Uncle Igor.' I hadn't known anything about this collection, whatever it was, and I was determined to see it immediately.

'But you have guests,' Uncle Igor gestured toward the drawing-room.

'Please,' I insisted, and Chengarov beamed at me. 'Not guests,' he said. 'A few people, that's all – as always.'

This was true. I discovered later that at the Chengarovs' there were always a few people who were not exactly guests. The Chengarovs' home was an open house for every Russian who arrived in Paris or even passed through. There were people who came for lunch or dinner, people who came in the morning and stayed all day. In the front hall there was a large glass bowl that was always filled with tickets for the theatre, the ballet, concerts or cabarets. His guests were expected to help themselves. Writers, painters, drunks, students, professors, veterans of Wrangel's army, or Kornilov's campaign. People sometimes played the piano or recited poetry or sang, but more often they talked. There was no end to the talk. They thronged his large drawing-rooms, ate food prepared by Madame Chengarova and the countess, argued and gossiped, but they all had one thing in common: they wanted Boris Chengarov to help them in some way.

'Borya,' said Madame Chengarova. 'Please. Let them eat something for God's sake. Look, here it is.'

The countess came in with a fresh cigarette in one hand, and a plate in the other. She put it down in front of me and, unexpectedly, smiled.

While she brought in the rest of the food Mr Chengarov poured three glasses of wine. 'This is a great moment, a great day altogether,' he said. 'My little collection in *Das Artes* and not only that, but my business has taken an exciting new turn: this week I have bought manuscripts from Tsvetayeva and Remizov. I now own one hundred manuscripts.' He poured wine and raised his glass. 'To The Return,' he said.

'The Return,' we murmured.

It was the most delicious chicken I had ever eaten, each piece succulent with butter. After a few mouthfuls, however, I had to stop. I put down my fork and looked around. The walls were covered with large landscape paintings in elaborate frames, and on the sideboard there was a pair of decanters and a set of crystal glasses on a silver tray. How had they managed to bring all these things out with them? I wondered.

Mr Chengarov had been talking without pause. He was flushed now, and his little eyes darted here and there as if there was a crowd listening. 'Everything,' he said. 'So you see, I am ready. Everything is printed, ready for distribution.'

Uncle Igor nodded. 'This is a huge undertaking, Boris Leonidovitch.'

'Yes!' he cried, 'Yes! It is enormous! All of *émigré* Russian literature! And I tell you,' he leaned forward, 'I am the only one who can do it. It takes vision and money. Money and vision! That is to say… yes… faith!

'And courage,' said Uncle Igor.

'Well,' Mr Chengarov looked down into his wine glass, 'I am not a brave man. But with the vision and the money… it's all there!' he said. 'In the warehouse! The warehouse is full! Everything printed. Ready.'

'What is in the warehouse?' I asked. The room, Boris Chengarov, the heat, the food, all felt like a dream.

He began to explain, while Uncle Igor tackled the chicken,

how he had bought the rights and manuscripts of *émigré* writers, 'all of them,' and had printed them, ready to publish in Russia when the Bolsheviks were gone. 'Which they say will be by the summer.' He had plans for the future: editions of all the Russian classics, a magazine, annual poetry collections. 'I have had all the manuscripts printed. They are in my warehouse, ready. You must come and see them. Over one hundred writers. I tell you, it's beautiful. When the world sees this, they will be amazed. Every *émigré* writer will return, dead or alive.'

We finished eating and he led us to his study, which was at the end of a short, dark passage.

'Wait,' he said. He opened the door, switched on the light, and ushered us in with a flourish. 'My little hobby.'

At first I thought we were in a nursery or a toyshop. The wall in front of us was lined with shelves full of music boxes. He stood aside to let us examine them, all the time watching our faces and beaming with pride.

The boxes were intricate and beautiful. Some were in the shape of houses, or churches, small escritoires, tiny consoles. There were figures of animals and caged birds, there were dancing girls, and there were large, elaborately inlaid boxes with glass fronts, through which one could see scenes from some other, miniature world, waiting for the key that would wind them back to life.

'You will like this one,' he said to me. It was a ballroom complete with a chandelier, and couples in evening dress. At the first tiny note of the Strauss waltz, they began to move elegantly round and round in time with the tiny figures of the orchestra. He wound up another box: on the little ice rink, to the sounds of Mozart, small figures gracefully twirled on the ice, below a small wooden chalet and a snowy path through tiny birch trees. In another box, a coach and horses went up and down a mountain, to Mussorgsky. He wound up another and then another, until the room was filled with the tiny tunes, as the figures went round and round in their beautiful boxes. Children danced, bears turned round and birds sang in golden cages.

Boris Leonidovitch watched them, his eyes bright and clear as a child's. 'These have been my love since childhood. The publishing, the manuscripts, yes, that's a huge project, but that's only business. These are for me only, for my heart. All my life, since my godmother gave me a small music box, so small, like *that*,' he measured a space with his thumb and forefinger, 'and it spoke to me only of happiness.'

'Extraordinary,' said Uncle Igor. 'What a collection.'

'And you?' Boris Leonidovitch asked me. 'Have you seen anything like this before?'

'No,' I said. 'Never. Not even – ' I stopped. I couldn't take my eyes off the boxes, taking in each tiny, perfect detail. The tunes clashed together like little bells. It was a world of the past, before my own memories began, a world that had been taken away and reduced to a mechanical miniature of itself. At the same time, I wanted to burst into hysterical laughter. With an effort, I controlled myself.

'This is not my original collection,' he said. 'My Russian collection was much better than this. Although these,' he added, 'are very good of their kind. After the return, I will get them all back. Perhaps I will open a museum. Yes. A private museum. When I have the complete collection.'

'But this one is a Reuge,' Uncle Igor said, impressed. We all watched it in silence as Mr Chengarov wound it up and pressed a button. It was a tiny gramophone that played "Haiti." There were six other little discs in the rack beside it.

'I think,' said Uncle Igor, 'I'll do a photograph of the whole collection, and then in several small groups.

There was a pause. Boris Chengarov narrowed his little eyes. 'You say these photographs are for *Das Artes*?'

'That's right,' Uncle Igor said. 'But this is of such enormous interest and importance, I think *Europa* might be interested as well.'

'Exactly what I thought. Yes. *Europa*. I had thought, if it will be for *Europa*,' he said in a different tone, 'do you think they might pay?'

No one spoke. The ballroom dancers began to turn more slowly, as if they were tired.

'You mean you want them to pay you for printing them?' asked Uncle Igor.

I thought, *Was this what we have been told to do? Photograph the music boxes? How could this be part of the counter-revolutionary plan Uncle Igor had told me about?*

Boris Leonidovitch began to speak in partial sentences again. 'Because, you see... the manuscripts... the warehouse is full. I have it all ready to go. As soon as the government falls... yes? But I have invested my own money in it. All of it entirely my own. And to keep my business active, here, in Paris, there is only a small business,' he said quickly. 'I print a few little things, everything is invested in the return, and we must keep building on that. It costs a great deal of money.'

'You have no partners?'

'How can I have a partner? The people out there ...' He raised his eyebrows in the direction of the door. 'Here in Paris there is everyone,' he said. He sat at his desk, and suddenly he looked serious, businesslike. 'Left wing, right wing, social revolutionaries, mensheviks, monarchists, eurasians, everything. And they are at each other's throats. And there are people who are none of those things, who are here in nests, to settle and watch. I can tell immediately. No, I have to protect my interests, and the interests of Russian literature.'

'And how do you know which is which?' I asked, avoiding Uncle Igor's look. I stared into Boris Chengarov's small blue eyes.

'I am a businessman my dear, I can judge people in an instant. I know immediately.'

'I can see that,' said Uncle Igor. 'So you have financed this entirely with your own money.'

All the music boxes were silenced now, except the little gramophone, which still played "Haiti."

'I have had to take loans, naturally, and there is a large mortgage on my estate.'

'Your estate?' asked Uncle Igor.

'I borrowed on my property,' he said. He paused, looked from one of us to the other and added 'in Russia.'

'But no one owns property any more.' Said Uncle Igor.

'When this is over,' he said, 'everything will be returned. That's the law. The estate belongs legally to my family. The lender understands this. He allowed me to take out a large mortgage, admittedly, at a very high rate of interest, but that will all be put right.'

'How can you do that, at a very high rate of interest?' Uncle Igor asked. He sounded casual. As he spoke, he leant over one of the boxes to inspect the scene within. 'You are a very brave man.'

'But they will have to pay damages. I understand the place is in terrible condition.' He squeezed his eyes shut for a moment. Then he opened them and said, as if each word gave him pain, 'They stabled their horses in the house... imagine.'

'Afterwards, everything will be returned,' said Uncle Igor.

'Plus damages,' said Mr Chengarov. 'It will all be put right, the books will sell, business will expand, everything will be paid off. But for the moment, I need money. There's still a great deal to do. There are young writers here who must be encouraged, who must believe that their work has a place in Russia.'

'You would not, say, accommodate the Bolsheviks in some small ways, perhaps the photographs ...?'

Boris Leonidovitch stood up and banged the desk so hard that I jumped. 'Are you mad? I don't accommodate in any way whatsoever. Let the others do that! Let them abase themselves before the enemy. I've heard them! They say, "We must go to Canossa" and admit our mistake,' he spat out the phrase. 'I will not "go to Canossa!" Not one photograph of this collection will ever be seen in Soviet Russia!'

* * *

Madame Chengarova showed us to a room on the top floor, with a double bed and a divan. There was a bathroom next door and she said, 'Use everything. There is plenty of hot water, as much as you like.' I stared at her, thinking I must have misunderstood. She laughed and patted my cheek. 'Oh, yes,' she said, 'we have plenty of everything. There is everything here for our friends,' she opened her arms in an inclusive gesture, as if hundreds of friends stood by the gleaming basin, '...for anyone who comes.'

The bath water was beautifully hot. It rushed in full flow out of the tap, and didn't stop until I turned it off. I lay back in the bath and tried not to feel angry with Uncle Igor. After all, he had said I wasn't to do anything. He didn't have to tell me. Still, I felt like a child shut out of adult concerns. I remembered being a very small child in a bathroom that smelt of roses, like this one. He should have told me about the music boxes. When we swore our oath, I thought it meant we would have no secrets. I ought to have known. He should have explained it all to me. That was what it meant to swear an oath. I didn't understand. It would have been pleasant to think about the music boxes. I watched the water turn grey, with dirty flecks of soap. I got out and then on impulse, filled the bath again. The water was still hot; I got back in and washed again with the rose-scented soap. I wrapped a towel around my head and looked at myself. I saw a girl who looked a bit like me, with heavy eyebrows, a thin, pale face, and shadowed eyes. I unwrapped the towel and let my hair fall to my shoulders, framing my face in lank, wet strands. I piled my wet hair up and held it with one hand while I turned my face this way and that. Not pretty at all, I decided.

When I returned to our room, Uncle Igor was standing at the window, staring out at the night. When I stood beside him, I could see an outline of the roofs of Paris against the night sky, and a spread of hundreds of lights.

'You never told me about the music boxes,' I said. 'Why didn't you tell me?'

'Didn't I tell you? Well it isn't important. They're wonderful, aren't they?' He was looking out the window, smoking. He blew a stream of smoke against the glass. 'Poor man.'

'Why didn't you tell me?' I asked again.

'I didn't think of it,' he said impatiently. 'It doesn't matter. Look at the lights, Nadia. See the tiny blue light? All by itself in the sky? That's the top of the Eiffel Tower.'

We looked at it together. 'Was that what you really came for? The photographs?'

'No, no. It was an introduction. I told you before. I came for information. About his business,' he added, 'not his heart.'

'And did you get your information?' I imitated the mockery of his voice.

'I got some information. I'll get more tomorrow. It has nothing to do with you. I'll take care of everything.'

'We swore an oath,' I insisted. 'So we should both know everything.'

'That's enough,' he had dropped his voice. 'Don't keep talking about it.'

'But I thought we were together,' I said. My voice quivered.

'Nadia, we are, but you don't need to know everything. Now don't talk about it any more. You understand me?'

* * *

I dreamt we were still on the train, and Mama waited at every station, waving and smiling. 'I'm coming,' I called. 'I'll bring you the music box.' But she shook her head and waved again, and I held out my arms as the train rushed on to where she waited at the next station. 'I'm coming,' I called, and she smiled, and said, 'Leave it to Igor, leave it to Igor.' And in the dream I was suddenly at peace and I knew everything would be all right.

CHAPTER TEN

I was awakened by the sound of rain. A featureless curtain of raindrops streamed down the window and blurred everything beyond it. This was Paris, shrouded in mist. I smelt tobacco. Uncle Igor was dressed and sitting on the edge of the divan smoking.

'Uncle Igor?' I asked. He was so lost in thought he didn't hear me. 'Uncle Igor.' I raised my voice.

He looked up at me blankly. Then he smiled. 'Nadyushka,' he said. 'Let's do this as quickly as possible and make Chengarov happy. But not too quickly,' he added. He put out his cigarette in a saucer, and picked up his camera and his new portrait lens.

In the bathroom, I was tempted to run the bathwater again, but there was no time. Instead, I picked up the soap and inhaled the heavy sweet scent of roses, as if I could drink the aroma with my skin.

I dressed hurriedly, while Uncle Igor opened the back of his new camera, broke the seal of the film roll and began carefully threading it through the spool. 'Very important, these photographs.'

'What do you want me to do?' I asked. I felt confused and stupid. I still wondered why he hadn't told me about the music boxes. He had said it didn't matter, but the question wouldn't go away. Had we really been sent here on a complicated railway journey with false papers to take photographs of music boxes? It felt absurd, and also frighteningly unreal. I knew Uncle Igor kept things from me and I didn't want to imagine what they were. When I was small I had been taken to a puppet play of *Hansel and Gretel*. I remembered the gingerbread house and how the witch had suddenly appeared from behind the garishly-coloured sweets. I had been so terrified that I had hidden under the seat and had to be carried from the theatre, a source of amusement to the adults. I was frightened now of the music boxes, as if they were sweets with a witch about to leap out from behind them.

'You? Do nothing. Not yet. Just hold the light steady, stay close to Chengarov.' Igor seemed nervous. When he turned the winding key to the first number, his hand trembled slightly.

'It will be all right, Uncle Igor,' I said. 'The photographs will be wonderful. All your photographs are wonderful. They'll be like the pictures you took at Papa's –' My voice caught on the word. 'At Papa's name day party. The ones Babyshka put on her dressing table.' I remembered the photograph in the cut crystal frame on Babyshka's rosewood table.

'You're quite sure?' he said.

'I am positive,' I assured him. Then I asked again, 'Why didn't you tell me about the collection?'

'I told you, I don't know,' he said. 'And I said it doesn't matter.' His face shut down again, shut me out. He got up. 'Come,' he said.

Downstairs I could smell coffee and hear the chatter of children followed by Boris Chengarov's huge laugh. The Chengarovs were both at breakfast at one end of the large table. Three little girls and their nanny sat opposite. Boris Leonidovitch looked up as we hovered in the doorway. 'Ah, Igor Fyodorovitch and Nadia Mikhaelovna. Good morning. You have slept well? Good,' he said without waiting for an answer. 'Sit down, sit down and meet my three naughty little tsaritsas'. The two older girls giggled, and put their hands over their mouths.

The youngest child dipped her small finger into the glass dish of jam.

'Irina, no, that's naughty,' said Madame Chengarova and the nanny reached out to take the child's hand. The little girl pulled away and sucked the jam from her finger, watching her father all the time.

'Oh let her have it. She likes it,' said Mr Chengarov.

The children were introduced to us. 'And perhaps if you're very good Igor Fyedorovitch will take your photograph,' he said, adding to Uncle Igor, 'A family portrait, the children and Evgenia, yes?'

Madame Chengarova smiled. 'Are you going to show our guests how you can recite?' she prompted her daughters.

Boris Chengarov beamed at the children. They looked down. 'Come on, just a few lines that you do so nicely.' Still giggling, all three girls slid off their chairs and stood in a row, the smallest one holding her sister's skirt. At a sign from the nanny, they recited in a high, toneless chant:

'*Lyublyu tyebya, Petra tvorenye,*
Lyublyu tvou ctrogu, ctrounu vud,
Nevu derzhavnou tyechenye...'

The two eldest stopped and looked at each other and then at the floor.

Without thinking, I prompted: '*Bererovoyu yeyo granut* '

All three looked at me, waiting.

I stopped. Boris Leonidovtch applauded. 'You see, tsaritsas, how she knows it? Every Russian who is not a barbarian knows this poem. In Russia, it is shameful not to know it, isn't that right?' he asked me.

We had to memorise that at school,' I said. I had been a bit older than Chengarov's eldest daughter. I had liked to whisper the passage from "The Bronze Horseman" to myself for the sheer glory of the words: *The transparent twilight and the moonless gleam...*

'So, when we go home, you will know it too,' said Chengarov. They nodded, not giggling now.

Madame Chengarova made a sign to the nanny, who shepherded the little girls from the room. Chengarov blew kisses after them. 'My most precious ones,' he said. 'And they speak beautiful Russian don't you think? We never speak

French here. So already they know that Russia is their real home.'

Madame Chengarova poured me a cup of coffee. There seemed to be so much of everything. No one could ever finish eating all this. Bread, butter, honey, jam, cheese, toast, milk. What would they do with it? There was a basket of rolls in front of me. I automatically thought, *Take one for later*. My hand reached out almost of its own volition, but I caught sight of Uncle Igor, who frowned and shook his head. I felt ashamed that I had had such a thought.

Mr Chengarov drank another cup of coffee while we ate. Then he wiped his mouth, raised his eyebrows, looked at Uncle Igor with his unexpectedly hard little eyes, and rose, saying 'Well, shall we begin?' Uncle Igor rose with him almost immediately and I followed.

'If that man comes …you know who I mean? Let me know,' he said to his wife. Then he ushered us once more to the back room, and switched on the light. He seemed about to leave us then, but instead he lingered.

'If I may suggest,' he said diffidently, 'Perhaps the smaller boxes could be grouped over there on the desk, where the light is better? To catch the details.' He began clearing things off the desk: a brass paperweight, a large inkwell, a leather container with pens, a blotter. He lifted a musical shepherdess and set her down delicately. 'But not alone,' he said. 'Perhaps next to the little ballroom. If you agree,' he added, as if making an apology.

The rain had eased to a light drizzle, but the patch of sky I could see from the window was heavy and overcast. I looked down and saw that this room overlooked a side street, with a shop that displayed a large painting on an easel and another next to it, where I could see a lavish swathe of fabric draped across a chair. I was intrigued by the painting, which was a vivid contrast of red and deep blue. What was it? It looked like splashes of colour, but it wasn't just splashes, it was a painting of something. At an upper window directly across from us, a man opened his curtains as a large dog stood on its hind legs and looked at me.

'Nadia, Nadia !' said Uncle Igor. 'Help Boris Leonidovitch, don't just stand there gawping.' He took out the camera. 'Boris, you have a wonderful eye. Well, I should have known, with such rare items. Museum pieces,' he added. He set up his tripod, adding casually, 'They must be worth a great deal.'

'Yes, yes,' said Boris. 'See that? Priceless.' He indicated a gold-faced clock, with porcelain Spanish dancers on each side. 'It is a loan, from a firm in Germany. A kind of loan.' Again he looked as if he was wearing a jacket that was too small. 'I wanted to consider first – but what a beauty it is.' He contemplated it. 'I am a weak man,' he said. 'I must have things when they are beautiful. Money will come from somewhere.'

Uncle Igor adjusted his camera and shifted from one foot to the other, leaning forward to get the right angle. 'Money can always be found,' he said.

'You are right! It's what I have always believed.' Chengarov said the words like a solemn oath. Uncle Igor had clicked the shutter, and Chengarov stepped forward and touched the clock lightly. 'Igor Fyodorovitch,' he said, 'Would you mind, would it be possible to take one with…'

'With you?' asked Uncle Igor. 'But of course. It's essential for the article.'

Boris Chengarov straightened his tie, smoothed his hair, and stood rigid as a general In the profound quiet of the room, the snap of the shutter sounded like a pistol shot.

After that, the photographs went smoothly, although setting up each one took a lot of time. Boris Leonidovitch ('Borya, please, I am Borya,') made more suggestions. He and I carried boxes back and forth from the shelves to the desk. Then he changed his mind, and we did it all over again. Uncle Igor agreed with everything Borya said. 'However you want it, it looks right,' he said, 'it's impossible to disagree. Much as I would like to,' he added, and they both laughed. He advanced and retreated from under his cloth, adjusted camera angles, and kept up a rhythmic murmur, 'Yes, that's excellent, Borya, you are right.'

A distant bell clanged. 'Ah,' said Borya. 'I know who that will be, you must excuse me. My wife can't be disturbed. I must deal with it.' He slipped from the room.

Uncle Igor motioned me to be quiet, while he listened to Borya go down the hall. Then he put down his camera. 'Enough,' he said. He went to the desk, and began to open the drawers carefully, easing them out one at a time, and going through the contents, scanning letters, newspaper cuttings, and scribbled notes. 'What are you doing?' I asked. Why was he going through the desk? Then I remembered with a shock: information. "They" wanted information.

'Those are Borya's papers,' I said.

He ignored me. He was looking through a file from the bottom drawer, nodding at the contents.

'What a lot of bills,' he said. 'Some of these go back two years. More.' He saw the expression on my face. 'Nadia, they want to know about him. There are some things people won't tell you.'

He took papers out of the file, listened as if he heard a sound. 'No,' he said. He opened another drawer and leafed through some thin papers. 'Look at this one. And this. All these loans, payments – now these are debts!' He put everything back and closed the drawers.

'All unpaid. What a gambler.'

'Uncle Igor!' I exclaimed. I put out my hand, as if the gesture would stop him.

'Come,' he said, with one of his lightening changes of mood, 'I have one more thing to do. Pick up the box,' he pointed, 'that one.'

It was the little ballroom. Something about its miniature splendour suddenly repelled me.

'Go on,' he said, 'just hold it up.'

'I can't,' I said. 'I can't touch it.'

'Why not? What's wrong?' he raised his eyebrows and I was shocked to see that he looked as if he was about to laugh.

'I don't know,' I said, 'But I can't. Please Uncle Igor, don't take any more photographs.'

'One more,' he said. 'One more, just for me.' He left the camera and loosened my hair, which fell around my face. He gently brushed it back, and held out the music box to me. Still with the feel of his fingers on my hair, I took it from him.

He went back to his camera and began to adjust the lens. 'Yes...Yeees...' Hypnotised by his voice, I stared at the tiny room with the striped red and cream wallpaper and the little chandelier, ready to shine down on the waltzing figures.

'And turn your face a bit toward me. Yeees.' He went under the cloth. 'A little smile.' His voice was muffled. 'You look enchanted,' he said, and when I saw the picture much, much later, I could see what he meant: that transfixed gaze upward. A girl under a spell.

Then the shutter clicked.

'I didn't smile,' I said.

'No.' He carefully put the camera away. 'But it was perfect. Did you enjoy that? You do it very well,' he said. 'I must do more. Because you enjoy posing, don't you?'

I looked away, embarrassed. Despite myself I *had* enjoyed it. Just before the shutter clicked, I had felt a sense of pleasure that had nothing to do with me, and was something I didn't want him to know.

'Go on, you can say yes if you like. Because I know, it *is* yes, isn't it?'

I shrugged, half nodded, with an awkward laugh, like one of the Chengarov children.

'I shall take more then.' He tensed, listening. 'Pin your hair up. He's coming back.'

CHAPTER ELEVEN

Uncle Igor and I were sitting on a small red-brocade-covered sofa, opposite two women who were deep in gossip. '...and all night she was there,' one of them said to the other, who nodded, looking at Uncle Igor out of the corner of her eye. He seemed to ignore her, and instead showed me how to roll a cigarette. I was displaying my skill under his direction, when suddenly he looked over my head. 'Ah!' he exclaimed, and the two women looked up, startled. 'There is Alyosha! But where is Larissa?'

The women followed his look and one of them said to the other, 'It's Alexei Mordvinov. I knew his sister. The family was of the left, but after the revolution, he suddenly joined Wrangel and the white volunteers. They say he is very clever.'

'A handsome man,' said her friend.

'Hmm,' she replied.

He had been standing in the doorway for some time, unnoticed. Later, I understood that he was like that. He knew everyone and everyone liked him, but no one paid much attention to him. He didn't seem to mind. The lock of thick fair hair that fell across his forehead looked as if it was asking someone to smooth it back. He looked around the room like a child at a party. Then he saw us.

'Igor Fyedorovitch! My old friend!. I heard you were in Paris!' He had a strong, warm voice. It was the most memorable thing about him and I learned later that he had trained as an actor before the war.

'Alexei Semyonovitch! Alyosha!! I heard you left Prague.' The two men embraced. 'Does everyone come to Chengarov?'

'Oh yes,' he said casually, 'everyone. Even him.' He nodded towards the man I had seen the evening before at the bridge table. He was still at the bridge table, with the same woman and two other men. The man with the white moustache suddenly threw down his cards, banged his hand on the table and said, 'How can you defend such a thing! How can the French ever forget Kronstadt! It's impossible for them to recognise the Bolsheviks after that.'

A slight hush fell on the room while some people paused to listen. The other man leant forward and began to argue, with gestures, in a low voice. The red-haired woman tapped her cards and the game resumed.

'An important person,' said Uncle Igor, presenting me. 'Nadezhda Mikhaelovna Serova.'

'I am Alyosha,' he responded, and bowed over my hand. 'Larissa told me about you long ago. I remember the word 'Persephone'. And she was right, as always.'

I laughed. 'I don't know why she called me that. I don't think I am.'

'Ah ! Larissa is not like you and me. In her world we have different characters. She sees us in a splendour.' But when he said that, he looked sad.

'Isn't that good?' I asked. 'To be splendid?'

'Yes,' he said, but he didn't sound convinced. 'But splendour has its price, like everything else.'

He perched on the end of our sofa and smiled at the two women opposite. They nodded to him, and resumed their conversation.

Someone had begun to play the piano.

'So,' said Uncle Igor, 'I hear you had an interesting time in Prague.'

Alyosha began to speak very quickly. 'Yes, yes, interesting, a lot of thinking, but Paris at the moment is the capital of Russia. One cannot do anything important if one is not in Paris. There are great things happening here: a new political group.'

The two women opposite had stopped talking and were openly listening to us.

'A way of looking at the revolution, why it happened, who we are, what we will become at The Return. Many questions. None of these people...' he indicated the other guests, '...ask these questions. They wait for the Bolshevik collapse and while they wait, they stagnate.'

A group of women came in and greeted the pianist with delighted little cries.

'I can't talk here,' said Alyosha. 'The place is full of fanatics. Come to the Eurasian society meeting – you will meet the only interesting people in Paris. We have talks, discussions, and a journal. Here,' he said to me, 'may I present you with the first issue?' He had been carrying some rolled up papers under his arm. He carefully unfolded one. The cover had a large sketch of a horse leaping over a mountain.

'Thank you,' I said, impressed. 'Shall we go to a meeting, Uncle Igor?'

'Everyone must come,' Alyosha said. He offered one of the journals to the women opposite. They turned away ostentatiously and shook their heads.

'Alyosha, you're at it again,' said Uncle Igor. 'Always another new answer. What happened to your theatre group in Prague?'

Alyosha's face fell. 'It was just some play readings. But this is different. It is a new vision. Not mine. You know Troubetskoy? Karsavin? Mirsky? These are serious people. Read the journal. I know Paris is full of journals, but this is different. It's about our spiritual leadership...' He had begun to stammer. Then he saw someone across the room and raised his arm. 'Seriozha!' He started to go, but turned back to us and added quickly, in a rush of words, 'You know the Garikovs are going back. They are in a pension on the Rue Rouvet at the moment. It's a reasonable pension and there are many Russians there. In case you are looking.' He broke off and called, 'Seriozha! I must speak to you I have the journal!' And he was gone.

'He didn't say anything about Larissa,' Uncle Igor remarked. He handed me my cigarette, which I had put down in a small ashtray. 'You made a good impression on him.'

'Did I?' I had forgotten what he looked like. The woman opposite was now eyeing Uncle Igor with a look of open admiration. I sat up straighter, and raised my cigarette to my lips. Of course women would look at Uncle Igor. He leant back against the sofa with his arms outstretched, like a conqueror, and returned her glance with his lazy, amused smile. Next to Igor, Alyosha had looked like a boy of my own age, or even younger. It was hard to believe that he and Igor had both fought in the tsar's army.

CHAPTER TWELVE

Bon Bon Dubonnet, read the advertisement on the kiosk on the corner of the Rue D'Éperon and the Boulevard St Germain. It stood out among the advertisements for *Byrrh, Gitanes,* and *Dr. Mabuse* at the Cinema Christine. *Bon Bon Dubonnet.* I had been sitting in the Café Danton waiting for Uncle Igor for a long time and it was as if Dr. Mabuse and the yellow and black Dubonnet poster had come to sit opposite me, with only the window between us.

'Wait here,' Uncle Igor had said. He ordered me a *café crème* and gave me a copy of *Poslednaya Novosti.* 'I'll be back before you've finished reading. "The very latest news," he joked. 'So recent, I'll be back before it happens.' He added more seriously, 'Read it carefully. *The Latest News* is the most important paper in Paris.'

Chengarov was going to take him to the fabled warehouse. I was curious to see the hundreds of manuscripts he had described, but Uncle Igor was firm. 'I don't want you any more involved. It's not necessary.'

'What are you going to do?' I asked. 'Why is it a secret from me?'

'I am going to do ...' he waited as the waiter, the *garcon* as Uncle Igor called him, put the coffee in front of me. 'Nothing at all,' he added, as the man turned away, 'But I need you to say you weren't there.'

'Igor,' I said, 'did they tell you to do something dangerous?' I deliberately called him just Igor, not Uncle Igor. It assured me we were real partners.

'Don't be absurd,' he said, and once again, stroked my hair. This time, he let his hand linger gently as he said, 'I am only going to have a look. You know, in an experiment, there is a control? You are the control. I am not going to leave you behind.'

At first I was self-conscious about sitting here alone, at one of the unsteady round tables, but I noticed there were other people sitting alone as well. They looked as if they had been planted here, to play chess, read, or write in small notebooks like Uncle Igor's. Unlike Uncle Igor, I sensed they would be here forever. They had nothing else to do.

I opened the *Latest News* and turned to the "Help Wanted" pages. Tricycle deliverymen. Night-watchmen. Chauffeurs. Taxi drivers, I noted, could make two thousand francs a month. No other job seemed to pay that much. What could we do? The Chengarovs had already explained to us that we would have "grey cards" which only allowed us to take menial employment. I scanned the pages: seamstresses, music hall dancers, waitresses, blacksmith's helpers, sign painters. I looked down the next column: jobs for butlers, gardeners and chambermaids. I didn't know how to do any of these things. As a child, I had learned to do cross stitch. What could I do? And Uncle Igor? We couldn't count on money from these "jobs" that Uncle Igor was asked to do, and even if we sold Mama's jewellery, the money wouldn't last forever. There were no advertisements for photographers. My mind began to work in a feverish but logical way, as it had when Mama and I had counted out our coupons and the profits from the sale of our possessions.

Fortune-tellers, palmists, astrologers. Cheap meals at the Russian canteen. There were also invitations to use the services of money lenders, or firms wanting to buy "jewellery on commission." I turned the page and read more: "Used men's suits." "Worn gowns from fine dressmakers: 150 francs." On the next page was the church calendar and a list of services in Orthodox churches across Paris, beginning with the Alexander Nevsky Cathedral on the Rue Daru. Uncle Igor had showed it to me already, and I thought fondly of its golden domes and imposing spire.

"Packages to Russia for seventy francs," I read. I could send Mama one hundred grams of tea, four hundred grams of coffee, two hundred grams of rice and one thousand grams of tapioca. If only I could do that. Could I? Even as I read the advertisement, I knew it was impossible. How could someone in a labour camp be allowed to receive a parcel from abroad? What a ridiculous idea. And anyway, where would I find seventy francs? Still, I thought, maybe there was a way. Uncle Igor's friends, after all, were highly placed. That was why they could carry out their international plan. Surely they could manage to smuggle one small package. My throat tightened. I was finding it difficult to breathe. It was a new experience and an unpleasant one. Why hadn't Uncle Igor come back yet?

The *Latest News* had poetry as well. The names were familiar: Khodasavitch, Gippius. They must be very old now, I thought.

I read: *It is good there is no tsar./It is good there is no Russia./ It is good there is no God.* The poem was by someone called Ivanov. *Life could not be more dead – ever/ There could be no blacker day/And no one will help us. Never/But who needs help anyway?* I understood what he was saying. But could it be true? I thought it might be true. But I didn't want it to be true.

Without Uncle Igor, everything seemed to have been diminished and drained of colour. I tried to comfort myself by remembering how Uncle Igor and I had sat in front of Pavel's house in Riga and mixed our blood, but all I could think of was the feel of his hand on my hair, how he had said, 'You enjoyed that, didn't you?' *Yes*, I thought. *Yes, yes, I did. Yes.* I hoped he would take more photographs of me.

The smell of damp seemed to get stronger, the sky was the colour of tin, and people hunched into dark, grey coats hurried past the cafe window. My new coat was grey as well; Madame Chengarova had found it for me. 'Your coat is too thin,' she had said. 'You need something warm.' Mama's old coat had been warm once, but when Madame Chengarova said that, I realised that now it was so old, that it had split under the arms and parts of the sleeve were bare where the fur had worn away. Here in Paris, no one looked like that. The new grey coat was warmer and only a little bit too big.

Uncle Igor hadn't left me any money, and I wasn't sure if he would be able to pay for another coffee or a roll. We had spent almost all the francs he had brought with him. When he gave The Trust, which he referred to always as "Moscow," the information they wanted, we would have some money at least. And I would know if Mama was still alive. Uncle Igor said this was the only way to be sure.

Although there were many customers, the Café Danton was very quiet. No one raised their voices or made gestures. When they spoke, they spoke in polite, even- tempered, short syllables, which sounded as if one syllable implied a sentence, suggested an opinion, like a code. Even the three Frenchmen at the next table only muttered politely as they passed documents to each other, and, I thought, debated the contents. I stared at them, fascinated: They nodded, scribbled on the documents and muttered again. They were doing it all far too openly; anyone might see them. They were almost too well-dressed as well, in high-collared shirts and dark waistcoats.

I took another sip of *café crème* and watched people as they hurried by outside, trying to guess if they would come into the café or not. How strange it was that this was a passing moment in their progress through their lives, a moment they would never remember, whereas I would never forget it.

Why does everyone think Paris is so beautiful? I thought. Why do they never say that everywhere smells of damp and drains, that the winter is simply dull and wet? I longed for a proper winter with real cold snow, and even the icicles that had formed on the inside of our window. I ached for the frozen banks of grimy snow on the Nevsky Prospekt, the icy white sky of St. Petersburg in January. I longed to be back at the Chengarov's, where everyone spoke Russian.

I opened the journal again. I skimmed an essay by Miliukov on the imminent collapse of the Bolshevik government, due to

93

their betrayal of the peasantry, and turned to the announcements of a veterans society meeting, a lecture on Pushkin in a café in Billancourt and a forthcoming "Miss Russia" competition. I yawned. Then I was alerted by an announcement of the new Eurasian Society programme. There would be a discussion about "the spiritual mission of the Russian emigration" and a talk on "Eurasian roots and the Turanian future." It was similar to what Alyosha had said the night before in the Chengarov's drawing room.

I finished reading *Poslednaya Novoctu*. Looking around, I noticed a rack of French journals by the door. I decided I would take one and try to read it. I pushed my chair back awkwardly, and dropped the Russian newspaper. As it fell, it brushed against the table top. The table wobbled, the cup tilted and fell to the floor followed by the saucer which slid after it. They both lay beside the journal. Bits of muddy liquid dripped into the thin cover. I froze where I stood, unsure what to do next, afraid to move. Suddenly the waiter was there with a cloth. 'Mademoiselle,' he said with a slight smirk, as he collected the cup and saucer, fortunately unbroken, put them back on the table, and wiped the drops of coffee off the table top.

The three Frenchmen at the next table had watched it all happen. One of them said, '*Ils sont tous pareils, ces saletés d'étrangers,*' and they ostentatiously looked away from me. I sat down, feeling the flush of embarrassment spread through my body. I didn't want to move again. I felt too clumsy to do anything but sit very still, and wait.

Bon Bon Dubonnet. I pretended to sip coffee from my empty cup, almost hearing the sluggish dregs slide across the bottom. Igor might never come back. I couldn't predict what he would do. I tried to make a plan. I have come so far, I must keep going. Should I ask the café owner for a job? There was something I could do after all. I could wash up. I would have to tell him the truth, that I had no money and nowhere to go, that I had been sitting here all afternoon, pretending to be like everyone else, and had even created a disturbance. I couldn't ask him. I decided to go from one café to another until I found someone who would let me earn a few sous for a meal and a room somewhere. It felt like a forlorn and impossible situation. But I wouldn't beg. I would never, never beg. The grey of the city seemed to close in.

Then suddenly, Uncle Igor stood in front of me. The air lightened, the café expanded and colour flowed back.

'It took a long time,' he said, raising a finger to the waiter to indicate to him to bring two more café *crèmes*. 'Did you think I wasn't coming back?'

'Yes, I did. I was making plans,' I told him. 'How I would go on by myself.'

He raised his cup to me in a toast. 'Good for you, Nadyushka! A strong woman. But I will never leave you. We swore an oath.' He patted his camera case. 'I have enough to send them – plenty. What a man he is. You know, I like him. He's crazy of course but he's generous. And my God he knows a lot of poetry – he loves literature, all literature. He told me it's like a religion. Do you know he met Turgenev once? Really. When he was young.'

Uncle Igor drank his *café crème* in two gulps. 'Now we can go and finish the job and we'll have some money.' He counted out three sous and put them on the table. 'And what did you think of the journal? Did you like the Ivanov?'

It is good there is no tsar, I quoted.

'That's the one.' He pushed his chair back. 'Khodasavich was furious that he was in the same issue. But they printed it anyway.'

We walked and walked, to a long street crowded with what seemed like hundreds of elderly people. We walked past an anonymous string of tailoring shops, laundries, shabby cafés, rooming- houses and small hotels. There were signs in Russian and in Hebrew, and a strong smell of fried food, and unwashed humanity.

We stopped at a *tabac*, with dusty boxes of cigars stacked in the window next to a small humidor. An elderly man with shaggy eyebrows and a small grey beard sat behind the counter, crouched over a newspaper. He didn't look up until Uncle Igor said, 'Do you have two stamps? I want to send a letter to my grandmother.'

'Already?' the old man asked. Uncle Igor opened his camera case and quickly handed the man a roll of film and a notebook. The old man nodded, and was momentarily invisible as he put them away somewhere underneath the counter. When he straightened up, he had an envelope, which he gave to Uncle Igor who put it in his camera case.

'I heard from my old grandmother recently,' he told us. 'She is well and sends her greetings. She hopes you will find somewhere to stay immediately.'

'Tell her we are looking, Monsieur Lewitsky,' said Igor.

Monsieur Lewitsky gave Uncle Igor two stamps. 'She wants you to move immediately. For your safety.' He went back to his newspaper.

'What did he mean by safety?' I asked when we had left.

Uncle Igor took my arm. 'He meant that our business is finished, that's all. How fortunate that we met Alyosha, don't you think? We'll go to that pension in the Rue Rouvet. Now we have money.'

'Uncle Igor, what will happen to your information?'

He shrugged. 'Who knows? It will go into a file somewhere and they will forget about it until they need it.'

CHAPTER THIRTEEN

MARCH, 1922

The news came like a bolt of ice through the rush and bewilderment of the following weeks.

'He's dead,' Uncle Igor said the words as he opened the door in our pension. 'A terrible accident. He fell off a bus.'

A lorry went by outside, and our windows rattled

The room smelt of benzine. I had been sitting on my bed waiting for Uncle Igor and trying to clean a stain off my dress with lighter-fluid. My new friend, Kyra Orokhova, had told me about that. She lived in the room across the hall with her parents, Count and Countess Orokhov and her younger sister, Sonia. Count Orokhov worked as a doorman at the *Café Cossaque*. The countess worked in the glove department of the *Galeries Lafayette*. She and Kyra also made a bit of money doing embroidery to order. Kyra, it seemed to me, knew all there was to know about how to get by in Paris.

'Fell off a bus?' I asked. 'Who?' But I knew right away who he meant.

'Boris Leonidovich.' Uncle Igor said the name evenly, without emotion, as if it was a name he had read in the newspaper. 'He must have slipped on the step.'

I tried to imagine Chengarov's solid body arching backward from the bus onto the street.

'How could that happen?'

Igor continued to stare at me. 'I don't know,' he said. 'Only God knows how these things happen.'

We continued to look at each other. He arched his

eyebrows, and I knew he was waiting for me to say something. I tried to read his thoughts, but I could only think of his long eyelashes, his strong, square face and full mouth. His expression was inscrutable.

Igor said, 'Do you feel sad? Do you want me to comfort you?'

I shook my head. I had liked Boris Chengarov and he had been generous to us; I wished I could cry, but I had no tears, only a vague pain at the base of my throat, the kind of pain that comes when a story has the wrong ending. 'It feels as if it was so long ago,' I said. I meant the days we spent there only three weeks ago. 'It feels like a story, only it wasn't supposed to end this way.'

The news ran through our pension like an electrical current. At all hours there were people gathered in doorways, exchanging news on the landings, or at the entrance on the Rue Rouvet.

Zhenia Arenska lit a cigarette. Her face was crumpled and powdery, and she held her cigarette holder stiffly in her wrinkled fingers, their nails red with varnish. 'I had such a sense something was going to happen to him.'

'He had a heart attack,' said Kyra's sister Sonia, her mean, pretty little face screwed up with tragedy. Uncle Igor refused to call her Sonia. He said, 'Sonia is a name only for an angel.' He called her "Koshka". 'A heart attack, that's what it was. He had an attack and fell over, dead.' Koshka said the word "dead" as if it was the first tone of the funeral bell.

'It was a heart attack most certainly,' said Mama's friend, Madame Bobrova. I had last seen her on the platform at the Nicolaevsky station. Now she and her family made soft toys in their room upstairs. Her husband, Capitan Bobrov, nodded in agreement.

'I am not so sure,' said their son, Grisha, softly. They ignored him.

'He had a terrible argument with the conductress,' said Zhenia Arenska. The pink net bow trembled on her red hair. 'She told him he had not paid enough fare. He said she had made the mistake, she insisted, he insisted, and of course, he became excited, and flung his arms open, like this ... ' she demonstrated, scattering ash on the stairs, 'and he overbalanced backwards. Poor man.'

'How do you know this?' asked her husband, General Arensky.

'I know,' she said, and inhaled.

'He might have stumbled on the steps,' Grisha Bobrov stammered.

'Listen to how they talk,' said Igor later. We had bought two rolls and two slices of ham. I had arranged them on a plate on the table between our two beds. He picked up one of the rolls, eyed it and put it down. The air was pierced by the regular whistles as trains went by. The smell of smoke, oil and charcoal seeped in through the window. He quoted from Krylov's fable: 'People willingly believe what they are willing to believe.'

I sat on the bed, thinking again about Chengarov falling backward off the bus. I could picture the blood oozing around his head like a pillow as he lay in the street. A piece of wallpaper was loose. I started to pick at it.

'Stop that,' said Igor. 'If the landlady sees that, she'll complain. Look what happened to Alyosha and Larissa. They had a little argument, broke the leg of one chair and the landlady took them to court.'

I tried to smooth the paper back so it wouldn't be noticed, but it flaked from the damp patch underneath.

CHAPTER FOURTEEN

The cathedral was crowded. People were clustered in the open doorway and inside, the cold winter air mixed with the smell of incense and wool coats. I recognised many of the people I had seen at the Chengarovs', their faces sombre and remote. The Perkov family brushed past us; Ilya's hair was gleaming with pomade, and he supported his mother, who patted his arm continuously as if he had been personally bereaved. His father and sister followed behind. Count and Countess Orokhov stood close together, their heads bowed. Their daughters, Kyra and Sonia-Koshka, were a few feet away. Koshka's little face was a tragic mask, as she dabbed at her eyes with a tiny handkerchief. Kyra embraced us both. People made their way through the crowd to exchange embraces, greetings or condolences. Then the congregation was gripped in a sudden hush like an intake of breath, as the triple peal of bells announced the start of the service.

People drew back to make way for the open coffin, borne by junior priests and followed by the priest himself, all in their ceremonial, silver embroidered robes and black hats Novices lit the long thin tapers. When the coffin had been set on the altar, the bells began to toll the life of Boris Leonidovich Chengarov, the smallest bell first, gradually ascending, the bells getting larger, their sound deeper, as they passed through his youth, manhood, maturity, and adult life to the final, single bell when mortal life was severed by death. We are all the same, I thought, only the last bell comes at different times. Around me there was soft sobbing, and the rustle as the congregation crossed themselves. I crossed myself as well, although I noticed that Uncle Igor stood rigidly beside me, staring at the coffin as if he couldn't believe it. As the bells tolled, all the weeks since we arrived in Paris seemed to be gathered into the sound and disappear with the last echo of the bell, as if it was something I had dreamed. Boris Leonidovich had no more reality and neither did I. I thought of Mama's pale shadow going down the stairs, across the empty spaces where the pictures had been. I bowed my head.

The priest blessed the deceased with holy water, read the absolution prayer and pressed the paper into the coffin, into Chengarov's hand. The choir sang: "*All mortal things are vanity; they do not endure after death. Riches do not last, and glory is left behind. For when death comes, all these things are destroyed.*"

Old women in faded black, men in worn jackets, bowed their heads, crossed themselves and murmured, 'Amen.' Behind me, someone moaned. It was Larissa. She was trembling. Alyosha put his arm around her as she crossed herself over and over.

The service was very long; the choir sang, chanted, and the congregation began to shift forward and back. People made their way out, crossing themselves, while others moved forward. The smell of incense grew heavier. The tapers flickered.

I felt Mama's arms, remembered the scent of her skin. I heard her say. 'Don't cry, Nadia. Never cry.' *I won't cry, I thought. She's still alive, somewhere. The shadow was only a shadow. Someday we will return.* And I prayed for "Someday."

The choir sang: "*In but a single moment death overtakes them...*" and then, "*Give rest to the soul of Your servant fallen asleep.*" I closed my eyes, reached for Uncle Igor's hand and prayed for the soul of Boris Leonidovich and for my own soul, for Papa's soul and Mama's and for Uncle Igor; then my thoughts grew soft and muddled, and, 'Please,' I prayed, 'let us stay together forever. Please don't ever take Uncle Igor away.' There was no point asking God for anything else because as long as Uncle Igor was with me, he would take care of everything, and without him I wouldn't be able to live anyway.

The priest said the last blessing and the mourners began to move forward to give the final kiss to the departed. Chengarov lay in his white-satin-lined coffin, his waxen face unnaturally smooth, ageless and expressionless. He looked like an anonymous doll in a black suit. It was like saying farewell to one of his music-box figures. Madame Chengarova and the children were clasped together at the other end of the coffin, so still they too might have been a mourning group, moulded from wax. I bent over the doll and the crowd moved us on, in a gentle tremor of motion.

'Let's wait here until they come out.' Uncle Igor guided me to the side of one of the lower steps, while people streamed out of the cathedral and waited. The bells rang another triple peal, and the coffin was slowly carried out.

'Igor. You son of a bitch,' said a woman's voice.

'Olya,' Uncle Igor said, 'I heard you were here. I have been thinking of you constantly.'

'Liar!' she said. She was blonde, her hair fashionably waved; she wore an unusual beaded coat and a large-brimmed hat trimmed with matching beads. She looked fleetingly familiar, and the way she looked at Uncle Igor would have been intimate, if she hadn't turned away immediately and cried, 'Kolya, wait!' to someone in the forecourt.

'No, really,' Uncle Igor called after her. 'You know I think about you.'

I wondered why he suddenly sounded anxious.

People were moving away from the cathedral now. The steps were almost clear.

She stopped, flashed another smile at Uncle Igor and said again, 'You son of a bitch.'

'Uncle Igor, who was that?' I asked.

'Oh,' he said it the way he had spoken about the stranger at the Nikolayevsky station. 'Someone I used to know. A difficult person.'

* * *

At the Chengarovs the next day, the windows were shut and the curtains were drawn. We rang the bell. After a long wait we heard footsteps, and a man opened the door. He was short, only an inch or so taller than I, with an official look despite his pale, unhealthy face.

'Repossession order,' he said in French. He showed us the official paper. Igor translated for me. 'Fraud. Tax evasion.'

'The police and the bailiffs came two days ago.' The official informed us. 'I am just here to post the notice. No one can come in.'

I represent the Russian Security Service,' said Igor. 'This young lady,' he pushed me gently forward, 'is a distant connection.'

'The family have gone,' said the man. 'There is no one here.'

I could see past him into the empty foyer, stripped of its furniture, carpets and chandelier. Even the plants were gone.

'But there is a legal matter,' Uncle Igor said, his voice soft, 'concerning the Russian Nationals in France documents...' I listened in awe as he spoke rapidly, in a tone that declared his official importance '... documents essential to inspect the premises particularly involving Russian Nationals who have broken the laws of France. We take this very seriously.' I watched the man's expression change as Uncle Igor continued his invention. 'It will only take a minute.'

The man frowned, hesitated, then said, 'One minute only.'

We walked around the empty apartment. A faint smell of borsht still hovered somewhere in the background. Everything was gone. Slowly we went from room to room. Our footsteps were too loud. They sounded like nails on the bare floors. There were marks on the wallpaper where pictures had hung. In a corner of what had been Boris Leonidovich's study, there was a crumpled pile of papers. Uncle Igor rustled through them.

'Nothing there,' said the official, who had followed us. 'They cleared the place. And the warehouse. They took everything.'

Igor looked at him. 'I left some photographs with him,' he said.

'Well, you won't see them again,' he said. 'Everything's gone. The warehouse is shut as well. And it's been sealed. Another one of your people has already been there.'

CHAPTER FIFTEEN

NOVEMBER 1922

Fog rolled across the Seine. After another grey, overcast day. Towards the evening, a cloudburst brought a sudden explosion of rain.

'I need to walk,' Uncle Igor said. We walked restlessly from Notre Dame around and around the small streets near the Sorbonne.

I didn't linger at the shops, with their displays of books by people with names like Gide and Breton. We couldn't afford to buy books anyway, not yet. When Igor needed to walk like this, I could almost see the darkness fold around him and knew better than to speak. I also knew that he didn't want to be alone in that darkness, that he had to know I was there. So I said nothing as we walked down the Quai des Augustins, past the booksellers' stalls, across the Pont Neuf where barges appeared on the river out of the mist, and back across the Pont au Change to the Ile de la Cité. There was a deep rumble of thunder; Igor threw back his head, spread out his arms and shouted back at the heavens. Then as the rain began, 'It's you,' he said. 'I can do it with you.' In the following downpour he walked faster, laughing as if suddenly exalted. I almost had to run through huge glistening puddles to keep up.

'Do what?' I cried, but he strode on. Water splashed over my shoes and onto my stockings.

When we returned to our room he didn't bother to take off his damp coat, but picked up his camera and pointed it toward me as if it was a weapon.

He set our new chair in the middle of the room, just clear of where our mattresses lay, end to end along the wall. As soon as I had taken off my wet coat and shoes and settled myself, he began to focus.

My feet were still damp to the bone. I wriggled my toes against our thin carpet.

'Sit still, Nadia.' He adjusted the angle of his camera and crouched behind it. Despite his promise, this was the first time he had photographed me since the morning at the Chengarovs' and as soon as I saw him with his camera, I knew that part of my mind had been waiting for this, but had been afraid to ask. It didn't matter about my wet feet. What did wet feet matter? I was ashamed that I had even thought about it.

From where I sat, I could see the drying prints, pinned to a string over the deep basin, with its odd chips and rust stains. After we could no longer afford the pension, we had been lucky to find this room with a basin and a single-burner *flamme bleue* on the Rue du Regard, near La Rotonde and La Coupole, the cafes where "everyone" went to argue into the night.

The shelf by the basin was overflowing with things: Igor's developing trays, his chemicals, and, slightly apart from them, carefully covered with newspaper, the basket of unsold vegetables we bought cheaply at the end of the day. Our table was covered with the objects Igor found for a few *centimes* at the Marché aux Puces: a spectacle case, an old leather tobacco pouch, a woman's glove and an artificial flower. These were for what he called "pictures for myself." While he worked I sat on the divan and watched him, trying to be invisible. I had even helped him develop the film, after he had showed me how to wash the negatives. Those photographs were completely unlike the prints drying over the sink, which all looked identical: wedding groups, a bride and groom on the steps of the Alexander Nevksy cathedral or the smaller churches in Passy or Auteuil, each couple in the same pose surrounded by similar-looking dark-suited relatives and solemn children.

'They all look alike,' I said. Igor agreed.

'They are all alike. They all think the same thing.' He made three copies of each photograph: one for the family, one for the newspaper, and one, with all the names on the back, to send to The Trust, via Lewitsky. The Trust paid for the photographs, which made it possible for Igor to charge the low prices that had begun to bring him more work.

'Keep your head still.' I wished I knew what he wanted. What had he seen in my face the first time? It seemed so long ago, although it was only six weeks. Like almost forgotten Riga, it was faded and unreal. There was nothing, it seemed, that was *now* and also *then*.

Uncle Igor's friend, the short, curly-haired Georgei, whom we had met on our first evening at the Chengarovs, had turned up at our pension shortly after the funeral.

'What a scandal,' he said. 'I heard he was actually dealing in pornography.' He lowered his voice. 'That could be true, actually.'

We went to the Russian Canteen, a subterranean room at the bottom of steep, winding stone steps, where we sat under portraits of the imperial family and announcements of concerts by the Don Cossack choir and the imminent arrival of the Moscow Art Theatre. Gyorgei waved greetings to several acquaintances and then began to gossip about Alyosha and Larissa.

'Of course she is tremendously difficult actually, so why does he put up with it? And now she has lost her head over Grisha Bobrov of all people. That stammer!' My surprise had nothing to do with Grisha's stammer. I wondered how someone like Larissa Mordvinova could lose her head over an ordinary, pleasant young man like Grisha. It would be more plausible if she had lost her head over someone like Uncle Igor. Grisha wasn't even as handsome as her husband Alyosha.

Gyorgei had spoken normally but now he lowered his voice again. 'Better to meet in the Tuileries next time,' he said. 'One can't speak freely here.' He flicked his eyes from one table to another. 'Those three people are Eurasianists, the two people at the next table are socialists, the woman with the notebook is a friend of Kerensky. There are even some followers of Burtsev actually. So you see. And everyone will immediately want your opinion so they can decide who you are.'

'So what is my opinion?' asked Igor, eyeing the woman with the notebook. Gyorgei smirked and I made patterns on the table with my finger, while Uncle Igor caught her eye and smiled slowly, until she smiled back. Then he turned back to us with an air of having scored a small triumph.

'The usual opinions,' Gyorgei said. After some more inconsequential chat about mutual friends over strong tea and a plate of *pelmeni*, Gyorgei said, 'It is difficult, isn't it, in Paris? But there are places where one can earn enough to get by.' He and Uncle Igor stared at each other for a moment. 'It's not much money, but who has money?' He looked around. 'Something to establish credentials for the moment. Naturally it will lead to something else.'

'I understand,' said Igor. 'Unskilled work. It's not what I expected.'

Gyorgei shrugged. 'What else? Without the papers.' He quoted: 'A man is born with a body, a soul and a passport. Without a passport, it's hard to keep the body and soul in one piece.'

* * *

'Sit still, Nadia. Look out of the window.'

The window of our new room faced the brick wall of the next building. Our shutters were open and a flat, grey light filtered through the grimy gauze curtains. They held dust like a reminder of all the previous tenants. I thought perhaps I would wash them until they were crisp and white. It meant lighting the gas jets under the bath. How much would it cost to heat that much water? Four francs at least. I would need a bar of laundry soap as well. Another four *sous*. Everything had its cost attached like a shadow.

'Sit further back in the chair.'

I sat back. It was a small low-backed armchair covered in a faded, heavy, red linen that was starting to split at the top. I could feel horsehair against my neck as I pressed myself against it.

'It has years of life, Mademoiselle. Years of life,' said the bald, young stallholder at the Marché aux Puces. Igor had paid for it with the last of the "Chengarov money," and together we carried it back to the Rue du Regard. I hoped that buying it was a sign that I, too, would have years of life.

'Damn,' said Uncle Igor. 'Turn the chair around.'

I turned the chair around, sat back again and stared across the room, where our clothes hung from nails that the landlord had banged into the wall. I had finally been able to unpack my icon and when I looked at it now, by the door, I felt protected, with some promise of a future. The familiar Parisian smell of damp and drains seeped through the walls. I sniffed; the people downstairs were frying something. A sound from the communal lavatory on the landing gushed through the building. It happened so often I hardly noticed it, only wondered idly if the landlord would ever fix the chain, which had been replaced by a rope.

I wanted to rub my eyes but I didn't dare. The job Gyorgei had found for us was in the *Atelier Grenier*, painting signs. *"Interdit de Fumer," "Salon de thé," "WC."* I filled in the letters, over and over. After a few hours my eyes itched and burnt from the enamel paint and varnish. Uncle Igor worked there as well, when there were no weddings to photograph. Many Russians worked there, because the pay was low and we were hired by the day. We had no choice. We had the grey cards of the unemployed: we could only do unskilled jobs and we were not "entitled" to anything. Thanks to a connection of Boris Chengarov, we had got a decent price for Mama's jewellery, but the money was dwindling.

Underneath the icon, I had arranged my books. The blue and gold binding on the *Collected Fairy Tales* was torn. *If I knew how to repair that,* I thought, I could get *a job as a bookbinder.* But that was skilled work. I did not have the right papers. I let my thoughts wander. I would need new shoes soon. Rent, food, shoes, baths, fares, underwear, stockings, soap, towels. Francs and *sous* subtracted, multiplied and divided, went round and round in chaotic circles. Someday, I was sure, I would be able to buy one of the books I saw in shop windows, Gide or Breton. But it would take a long time. Still, I had faith.

'No!' Uncle Igor exclaimed. 'It's nothing! It's just a face. It's not right!' He picked up the film canister. 'I can't...' he began, and then suddenly hurled the canister across the room. Instinctively I ducked, but he had thrown it to one side of me and I heard the crack as it hit the window. There was only a small chip in the lower pane, but it would make trouble with the landlord, I knew. It would cost money to repair. We might even be evicted. The French could do what they liked. Their landlady had evicted Alyosha and Larissa for quarrelling too loudly.

I touched Uncle Igor's shoulder. He picked up the container, tossed it to one side, and cupped his hands on either side of my head. I closed my eyes. I could smell the damp wool of his coat. He brushed his finger lightly across my eyelashes and whispered, 'Don't let me frighten you.'

'You don't frighten me,' I said. Saying it made it somehow true.

He took his hands away and stepped back.

'Open your eyes.'

I opened my eyes. I saw him suddenly as if a stranger had appeared in front of me: his slightly oriental eyes, his long lean body, the long curve of his mouth, his lips now pressed tightly together.

'Such a lie. A pretty girl in a chair.' He gripped my arm and stared at me, not seeing me, thinking. I reminded him of something he had said to me several times: 'You said photography should say something that cannot be spoken. What didn't you want to speak about?'

I was afraid I had made him angrier by repeating his own words. After all, I wasn't sure what he meant. But he became calmer.

'You're right,' he nodded and almost smiled. 'You are right.'

He pulled me across the room, pushed me down into one of the small chairs at the table and swept the clutter of objects onto the floor, leaving a half packet of *papyrosi* and a saucer full of ash. He overturned the saucer, stretched my arm across the table, turning my body sideways and setting the angle of my head awkwardly against my arm, manipulating me like a doll. I made my mind blank while he snapped the picture. But still, behind the blank I felt a kind of excitement when I heard the sound, as if in that instant a secret would be revealed that only he could know. He closed the camera.

'That's it,' he said. I raised my head and waited. 'Death. It's a photograph of death.'

'Igor...' I began.

"No more "Uncle?" he asked. He put his camera away carefully, took one of the last cigarettes out of the packet, lit it, took a puff and passed it to me. 'Ah well.'

'Why was it death?' I inhaled slowly, returned it to him and helped him off with his coat, which was still wet.

'The truth? I don't know. But why make it look otherwise?' He started to take down the dry prints. 'You know, we could go on like this forever, waiting until we are needed for something else.'

'Uncle Igor, I mean... Igor, please...' I spoke out of a cloud of confusion. 'What are we doing? What will they need you ... us ... for?' I made myself go on. 'Why was it a photograph of death?' I asked again.

'Because death is always waiting around the corner and on certain days, it stands in front of you and won't let you pass. You've seen it, haven't you?'

'Yes,' I admitted. 'But The Trust ? Who are they, Uncle Igor? Really, who are they? And how can they exist in Russia?'

'They can exist, Nadia, because they are working within

111

the Kremlin. One of our members is very close to Lenin himself.' He looked into my eyes. 'I've told you. We help The Trust and your mama stays alive. You understood all that in Riga.' He sat down in our new chair, leaned back and spoke carefully, as if explaining to a child. 'All the *émigré* political groups hate each other. You've seen that yourself. The Trust wants to unite every *émigré* counter-revolutionary group to restore the monarchy. There is no more for you to know.' He lowered his voice. 'And nothing for you to talk about to anyone.'

There was a sound on the stairs outside. We both tensed, and I imagined I heard once again that knock on the door, that repeated itself at any approaching sound at night. The steps went past us to the floor above. A door opened. A voice called out in French. The door closed.

'I don't understand what they're doing,' I said. 'Do you mean they're planning another revolution?'

'God forbid. But there are many ways to draw a sword.'

* * *

I woke up from an uneasy sleep in which Chengarov, Larissa, Gyorgei and my school friend, Natasha appeared and vanished, lost in a fog, or running up the steps of a menacing-looking building that might have been a prison or a church.

Uncle Igor was lying on the other mattress, spread-eagled on his back, his eyes wide open, struggling for breath. In the dim light I could make out the sweat on his face. Instantly I was fully awake and at his side.

'Uncle Igor,' I cried. 'What's wrong?' *Oh God, don't let him die*, I prayed. *'Keep him alive.*

He turned his head to me, then rolled over the other way. His voice was muffled. 'I can't sleep,' he said. 'It's no good. I have such nightmares, I don't want to sleep.'

'What is your nightmare?' I said. 'Tell me.'

'Nothing,' he said. He rolled over and sat up with his back

to me. He was crouched over and I could hardly hear him. He was still trembling.

'Terrible things. I can't tell you.'

'It was a dream.' I wiped his face. 'I have bad dreams too.'

'Not like this.' He sat up and began to pull on his trousers.

'Uncle Igor!' I cried. 'Where are you going? Shall I read to you?' Igor often asked me to read to him from

'It's no good, Nadia, not now.' He spoke as he put on his jacket. 'I have dreams about my mother. I thought all that was over. I thought this would finish it.' The icon looked down on him, as he lit the end of a half-smoked cigarette. His hand was shaking, and he put the cigarette on the saucer where it continued to release a thin stream of smoke.

'Oh God,' he said.

'What was the dream?' I asked.

'About my mother.'

'But you said you didn't know her.'

He banged his head against the wall and the icon seemed to tremble.

'It's no good. I can't talk. I have to walk.' And he was gone. I started to go after him, but I was afraid. This time he needed no one. I wandered around the room, collecting the things he had swept off the table and putting them back. What does he mean? I wondered. I knew I would have to collect whatever he let escape and put the pieces together until I answered my own question, because he would never tell me. He is dark and he is light, I thought, he is hard and soft, he is heavy and he is weightless. He is something greater than I could ever be. The knowledge swelled around me until I fell asleep in spite of myself.

When I woke up, he was sitting on my bed, still wearing his coat.

'I had to walk,' he said. 'I was going to walk forever, but I came back because I didn't want you to worry.' He lay down beside me and stroked my arm. 'I've never been good at waiting. I need to take action. Something has to happen or I will make it happen.'

113

CHAPTER SIXTEEN

JANUARY 1923

I dipped my brush in the black enamel and carefully filled in the outline of the letter *O* in *ROBES*.

'Work from the outside toward the centre,' my friend Kyra Orokhova instructed me. 'So it will be even.'

I worked the brush round and round. The monotony of the work made it difficult. It easily became hypnotic, demanding attention but providing no stimulus. Occasional conversations ebbed and flowed around me, but one couldn't afford to be distracted or the hand would slip and the sign would be spoilt. There was a one-franc fine for every mistake, not to mention the wrath of M. Grenier. Next to me, Kyra put her brush down for a moment and gave me a sly half-smile. As usual, I noticed she managed to make even old clothes look chic. Today she had twisted a long, soft bit of green and rose silk around her neck and knotted it low at the front of her mended shirt-waist blouse. She reminded me of the illustrations in *"La Vie Parisienne,"* where ladies were drawn posed on staircases or beside small, smart cars. Even without the scarf, she would be elegant. Because I envied her, her friendship flattered me.

'By the way,' she said, 'Alexei Mordvinov thinks you are so interesting.'

I caught a small drip from my brush with the sponge.

'Does he really?' Kyra and I had gone to hear Prince Svyatopolk-Mirsky give a talk on Tolstoy in a room on the Rue Denfert-Rochereau. To my surprise, Ilya Perkov was there, standing to one side looking down at everyone, as if he still wore his little fur coat and gloves. I pointed him out to Kyra and we were making our way towards him when we had accidentally come face to face with Alyosha.

'Wasn't it inspiring!' he exclaimed. I only had time to say 'Yes' before he rushed to where Zhenia Arenska, her red hair like a lantern at night, beckoned him. 'He must write something on this for the Eurasian!' he called out over his shoulder before he vanished.

'I only agreed with him,' I said to Kyra.

'Well, he said you were interesting. He also said he heard you can type.'

'Only a bit.' I wondered where he had heard that. Before Mama was arrested, when I was a file clerk at the roads ministry, I sometimes had to type a timetable when there was no one else to do it. How could Alyosha have heard about that?

M. Grenier was at my shoulder. He pointed at my sign.

'A sharper line, mademoiselle. Pay attention! You are both doing too much talking. Remember, this sign is for Chanel!'

Kyra rolled her eyes as he walked away.

* * *

'Kyra said that Alyosha thinks I'm interesting,' I told Igor as we climbed up the steep cobbles of the Butte Montmartre towards Lewitsky's shop on the little Rue Houdon.

'Why?' Igor had waited so impatiently for this meeting and now that Lewitsky had summoned him, he was alternately tense and morose. 'Probably because I told him you could type,' he added.

The shop was closed, the windows shuttered. Uncle Igor hesitated before he knocked, as he had when we arrived at the Chengarov's. There was no answer. He licked his lips and banged harder. A small light went on at the back of the shop, and a silhouette appeared. It moved to the door, opened it a crack and peered out at us.

It wasn't a face. It was a crumpled mass of smashed features squashed into each other: one eye bulged and the other had sunk back into the skull, half the nose had been hacked away. I thought I was looking at a corpse risen from an unmarked grave, and wanted to run, but horror kept me frozen to the spot.

Uncle Igor said in his usual courteous manner, 'Good evening, sir. Will you kindly inform Monsieur Lewitsky that Viktor and Katya Filatov have come from Pavel in Riga?' Without a word, the creature opened the door just wide enough far us to enter and waved us toward the slice of light at the back.

'Who's there, Isidor?' asked Lewitsky, and then he saw us. 'Ah, Viktor and Katya. They are expected.'

The back room was unusually warm and smelt of the coal fire that burned in the grate. I had imagined that Lewitsky would receive us in an office with a desk, files and even a typewriter, but we were in an ordinary sitting room distinguished only by the size of the four chairs grouped around the fire, and the large radiogram on a table beside it. Despite the lamps, the sideboard, the bookcase, the cigarette boxes and the ashtrays, there was something uncomfortable about the room; after a moment I realised there were none of the usual family photographs or objects salvaged from the past. The walls were bare except for a map of Europe above the radiogram and one of Russia on the other wall. The two maps and the heavy armchairs seemed to completely fill the space.

Two men were bent over a low table. One of them looked away and got up with his back to us as we entered. The other was Gyorgei, curly-haired and rosy as ever, who raised his hand in salute to Igor.

'Igor! We meet everywhere.'

'You are acquainted?' said Lewitsky.

'Old friends,' said Gyorgei.

'Good,' said Lewitsky. 'That makes it easier.'

The other man kept his head lowered and shrugged on an overcoat. Lewitsky ushered him out. Isidor remained with us. I was both revolted and fascinated by him; I wanted to stare, but at the same time I was afraid to look at those mashed and twisted features. I kept my gaze on the worn, green carpet and admired Uncle Igor's ease, sprawled in his chair with his legs outstretched, talking to Gyorgei.

'That's Simonov,' Gyorgei explained, indicating the man who had just left. 'He only arrived from Moscow this morning. He means well but he has Soviet manners.' Then Gyorgei began to talk about the Diaghilev company and their new season at the *Théâtre des Champs Elysées*.

'Nemnitchovna, what a performer!' he exclaimed. 'I was completely drained by her *Giselle* ! A perfect performance. And the new ballet will be a sensation! *Les Fâcheux!* Diaghilev has persuaded Braque to do the designs.'

From where he stood behind Gyorgei, Isidor looked at each of us as if committing us to memory. I wondered if he could hear, or speak.

Gyorgei chattered on. 'And I hear the costumes and the scenery are the identical print! Nijinska saw them and said to Kochno…'

'Gyorgei,' Lewitsky had returned, 'I think we have concluded our business for now.' Gyorgei stopped talking as if he had been switched off, nodded and hurried out with a quick farewell wave.

'You have met Isidor,' Lewitsky said, 'My brother.' He watched me as I forced myself to look directly at the man's face and say, '*Ochen priyatno.*

'So,' Lewitsky said. 'How would you say you have been getting along?'

'To be frank,' Igor said carefully, 'It's slow, somewhat disappointing, I'm sure you understand.' Lewitsky had not asked us to sit down, and we stood together by the door. As if he hadn't heard, he poked the fire and little sparks danced round the poker.

'Waiting is always difficult,' he said, 'But you have been making contacts, I understand, and establishing your cover.

You are just in time. The Trust is ready, and they need credible people.' He motioned us to two of the armchairs and sat between us. He offered us cigarettes and waited until Isidor had lit them and withdrawn into the corner.

'There is a man here in Paris,' Lewitsky began, as if telling an old folk tale. 'He was a general who led an elite regiment, but despite his oath of allegiance, he was opposed to the old regime. He fought bravely nonetheless and after October he briefly attempted a monarchist takeover. When it failed he fled the country, in order to make propaganda in Europe. Like Kerensky, he is a Mason, but in one of the "right wing" orders. He is also connected with former members of the White Guard. We know all this.' Lewitsky spoke rapidly, as if repeating an old, dull story. Now his voice slowed. 'Recently, we suspect that he has gone further.' He fell silent, and raised his eyebrows slightly, waiting.

'How much further?' asked Igor.

Lewitsky's tone grew clipped. 'Underground activities. Destabilisation. Terrorism. Counter-revolution. Anarchy.'

'Who is this man?' asked Uncle Igor.

Lewitsky looked hurt. 'In a minute,' he said. 'Wait.'

I thought, *'He's enjoying himself.'*

'If this is true, we want this man'. Moscow finds you both ideal for the job.

So here is the plan: we must first of all make sure that he is genuine. What exactly is he doing? Where does he go? Who does he see? What does he say? Has he sent associates to Russia?' Lewitsky made his way around his questions as if they were trees in a forest. Uncle Igor sat forward, tense, smoking.

Lewitsky raised his voice. 'When we are certain of him and his activities, then we must approach him and persuade him that *we* are genuine: we must create mutual "trust".' He smiled briefly at his joke and touched his palms together. 'After that, there will be a joint meeting between his organisation and ours.' He nodded as if he saw something in the distance.

'And after the meeting?' Uncle Igor prompted.

'Moscow will handle it from there,' Lewitsky said with indifference. He pointed at me. 'Nadezhda Mikhaelovna,' he said, 'You will first of all gain his friendship. Make note of his conversations and encourage his confidences. You will pass this information to your uncle who, along with Gyorgei, will contact him as our representatives from Russia, and persuade him to ally himself with us.' He gave another brief smile. 'It will not be so very difficult. He is very fond of young women.'

What had he said? Had I heard him correctly? I couldn't believe it. I must have imagined it.

'Confidences?' I asked as if I didn't know the meaning of the word.

Lewitsky said, 'You will have a job as a waitress in the restaurant this man uses regularly. The owner is Tanya Katseva. She's an old friend of his. Tanya is not one of us, she is not interested in politics, but, like you, she has family in Russia and she is also concerned for them. He paused and closed the cigarette box. 'There will be no questions asked.' He leant towards me. 'Would you like a glass of water?'

'No thank you,' I whispered, but he said 'Isidor,' and it seemed that almost immediately Isidor was handing me a glass of water. I made myself look into his one bulging, bloodshot eye and said, '*Spasibo*.' I touched the glass to my lips, and set it down immediately. I plucked a question out of the many that crowded my mind. 'Why would this man confide in me?'

The possible answers choked me. I picked up the glass of water, but I knew I would be unable to swallow.

Uncle Igor said, 'And may we know this man's name?'

Lewitsky smiled. 'General Dmitry Sergeevitch Arensky. I thought you might have guessed. He has a most devoted wife, but he is charmed by young people, especially, as I said, by young women. He misses his own youth. So an intelligent, sincere young girl like yourself, particularly with your liberal family background, will be able to catch him off guard. It will not be difficult for you. I believe he is charming,' he added with

119

a touch of contempt. 'Igor Fyedorovitch,' Lewitsky continued, 'we want you to continue with your present work. Little photographs of daily events. It will look odd if you both suddenly have new employment. But you will have more opportunities to work for the various émigré journals here in Paris. Apparently.' He stopped and gave me a quick look of what seemed to be displeasure. Then he repeated, 'Various journals. And naturally there will be more than weddings and baptisms.' He half smiled. 'We will send you a list of the people and events that you are to record.'

'I see.' Uncle Igor put out his cigarette and nodded. 'I see,' he repeated. 'And what about Gyorgy? Isn't he somewhat lightweight?'

'That is his strength. Who ever suspected Gyorgei of anything? Gyorgei will use his fertile imagination to bring Arensky word of his own destabilising activities.' Lewitsky stood up, the interview was over. Igor and I also stood. 'Is this agreeable?' he added, as an afterthought.

'How much?' Igor asked.

Lewitsky flinched as if Igor had thrown something at him. 'This isn't about money,' he said. 'There will be of course a payment according to the quality of information and the final success of the task. And there will be a small advance. Not enough to make anyone question your cover. You understand all your work will be for The Trust or organs of The Trust. You are not free to show or sell any photographs privately. None whatsoever. No photographs of anything. Agreed?' It wasn't a question.

After a moment, Igor nodded. 'Agreed.'

'Good. Excellent.' Isidor poured three glasses of cognac. 'To the cause!' said Lewitsky.

'The cause,' Igor echoed, and I in turn repeated softly, 'The cause.'

Outside, the night was coming to an end, but the darkness was still heavy, with a few pale stars. I followed Uncle Igor up the narrow street, through the equally dark silence that lay around us. Paris is never silent, I thought, this is some other place. Then a cat darted across the street and down a shadowed alleyway. There was a loud hiss and another cat screeched.

Uncle Igor said, 'It was a bad bargain, but at least there will be some money, and our job is clear. And who knows what I will be able to manage when they aren't looking. Now you must get to work on General Arensky, so that we can do the job quickly.'

At the words "a bad bargain" I suddenly felt my legs give way, refusing to take another step. I had to lean for support against the nearest wall.

'Uncle Igor, are you sure this is right? Why do they want us to do this?'

He came close to me. 'Are you all right?' he asked. 'You're not ill are you? Shall I carry you home? The way I did at Christmas when you were five? All the way from Borodinskaya! Do you remember?'

'I'm not five,' I snapped. But still my legs refused to move. 'Uncle Igor, how can I do this? They know already that Dmitri Arensky is anti-Bolshevik. Why don't they simply approach him?'

'You only have to make a friend and tell me about him. After that, you are not involved. I do my job and after that I am not involved. That's the truth.' He added, 'At least we are together in this.'

He raised his chin, and I felt the fear and fire of a man going to battle. But the memory of the alien warmth of Lewitsky's room, and Isidor's mutilated face made me hesitate. 'What would Papa have said if he had been there?'

Uncle Igor looked deep into my eyes. His breath was deep and even. 'Nadia,' he said, 'please believe me. You can do this. You must do it. On our oath I promise: your mama and papa would be so very proud of you.'

Would they? Uncle Igor held my gaze steadily, while I trembled in the moment. I had such a strong sense of danger that it was an almost tangible space between us. Then I remembered how he had come to me in Russia, just in time, and I decided: I pushed my hesitation away and flung myself into his arms, holding onto him as if he would carry me to safety again.

CHAPTER SEVENTEEN

MARCH, 1923

'Overcoming the revolution,' Uncle Igor read the notice aloud from *Contemporary Notes*. He said, without looking up from the paper, 'It should be interesting. And our friend will be there. He goes to all the meetings, right or left. Very clever. You can get a better view of him there, and who knows? Talk to him at last.'

His voice had the expressionless tone that I had come to recognise. In turn, I inhaled my cigarette and stared at him as I exhaled a cloud of smoke. He beckoned to the barman for two more glasses of their cheap, raw tasting *vin rouge*.

'Our other friends will be pleased.' He looked up. 'Our "Moscow" friends. We don't want them to get restless.'

I had been a waitress at Tanya's for almost six months and still hadn't managed to collect any useful information about Dmitri Arensky, except that he had a fanatical love of card games, had seen the film 'Doctor Mabuse' twice and intended to go again, although his wife, Zhenia, preferred "Way Down East."

'When Lillian Gish sits in that rooming house with the baby – oh my God! That poor woman! Tragic!'

'None of these people can touch Mosjoukine,' General Arensky pronounced.

'Well, no, naturally not,' his wife agreed. "House of Mystery," now that is a film!'

They and their regular companions, the Ladinskys and the Stassovs, played bridge until the cafe closed. When they spoke, they spoke almost entirely about the food, comparing Tanya's *pozharsky* cutlets unfavourably to those served at the Strelna in Moscow, at Cubats or Old Donon in "Pitr," as they still called it, ignoring the new name, "Leningrad."

'Old Donon!' Zhenia exclaimed, 'With the wonderful Romanian band! Do you remember, Mitya?'

Arensky said, 'Not Old Donon. They never had music. *New* Donon had the band. Gulesco's band. I remember better than you do.'

'Old Donon,' his wife insisted. 'I was there often.'

'But Tatania Gregorievna does what she can,' Madame Ladinska always went back to the subject of food. 'After all, she can't get the same ingredients.' Their conversation, as I described it to Uncle Igor, was more like a pause, as they waited to resume the real conversation when I had left.

'That's all information for 'Moscow.' It means they have something private to say. But The Trust knows that already.'

'They talk about recognition,' I volunteered. 'General Arensky says that France will never recognise an illegal government like the Soviets. He knows Poincaré and he says he's sound.'

'Well, he's wrong there,' said Uncle Igor. 'France will recognise a government they can trade with. It's all about money Nadyushka, legal or not.'

'It would be easier for you to go to this talk,' I said. 'You can talk to anyone.' He laughed. We had gone to a bar he liked near the Rue de Lappe. The waitresses were naked from the waist up and their breasts either swung or bounced as they served. When they went upstairs with a customer, they casually picked up a towel from the table by the bar. Our waitress had rolls of fat beneath her heavy breasts with their brown nipples. Uncle Igor eyed her casually and gave me a grin that embarrassed me. I scowled at him.

'It's only flesh,' he said. He picked up *Contemporary Notes* again. 'This meeting is part of the Eurasian idea; all the most interesting people in Paris are involved: Svyatopolk-Mirsky,

Karsavin, Suvschinsky, Troubetskoy. Even if you don't speak to our friend, it is a point of contact for later.' His eyes wandered to the waitress again. She was leaning on the bar. 'She's glorious, Nadia, really. Look.'

'Are you going to photograph her? You are, I know.' She looked greasy and unclean to me. The thought that he might photograph her made me flinch, as if it would get his camera dirty.

As usual, he read my thoughts. 'It's not like *our* photographs,' he said, and raised his glass. 'She might be useful, that's all. If I can make a private arrangement. Not that I will be able to do anything with the pictures. A bad bargain.' He muttered to himself.

'Don't they want you to record the meeting?' I asked.

The Trust often sent him to public meetings, charity balls, even boxing clubs, for which they paid a few francs. Otherwise, we scraped by on the money he earned from photographing weddings, baptisms and the like, as well as my wages at the restaurant. The extra francs from The Trust were important.

'Not this time.' He swallowed his wine. 'It's better for you to go alone. Anyway, I have a small private assignment: the Torgov's ugly baby. It looks like a pig in a bonnet.' He pushed his chair back and I followed. 'But they will pay twenty francs.' And I knew "Moscow" would get a copy of the photograph for which they too would pay twenty francs. Why would "Moscow" want a photograph of the Torgov's baby I wondered? Or the photograph of the pastry chef Doulgov, or the Krocheine's anniversary, of Dr Marchak eyeing a rack of magazines at a kiosk in the Rue de l'Eperon? But I reasoned, of course, The Trust would want to know about everyone, every possible ally. Allies were essential to achieve The Return.

Spring had clearly arrived, I noticed, as I arrived at the Rue Denfert-Rochereau to hear *Overcoming The Revolution*. The street was off a neat little square with cream-coloured villas set behind chestnut trees, their swelling, upright buds looked like festival candles. It was late afternoon, falling into dusk and although the air was cool, the sky was clear. In Petersburg, this was the time of the spring winds but this was a French season; without the wind it wasn't spring.

I stood uncertainly on the pavement, looking up at the tall windows on the third floor of number seventy-nine. The curtains were not fully drawn and people passed slowly back and forth across the narrow band of light. Dusk was darkening now; lights went on here and there in other windows. Someone pulled the curtains completely shut. I rang the bell. The concierge unlocked the iron grill, let me into a large courtyard and without speaking, pointed me to a staircase on one side. In the shadows nearby, someone leant with his face against the brick wall. I hesitated and then saw it was Alyosha. As I stepped towards him, his whole body clenched as if he had been seized by some terrible pain. I wondered if he had had an accident, if I should call the concierge, but he didn't move. I waited for a moment; then I walked slowly around the courtyard, examining the small trees in big clay pots, and reading the French names on the other entrance doors. By the time I returned, Alyosha had gone.

Upstairs, the room was crowded. Light wove through the smoke that drifted above the circles of conversation and greeting. Kyra caught sight of me and waved me wildly to a seat beside her.

'Everyone is here,' she said. 'Look, there are the Remizovs.' She indicated a small, neat man, almost doll-like. His huge wife waddled solemnly behind him. Kyra continued to point out people: 'Khodasevich, his wife, Berberova, Merzhkovsky, Gippius, Berdayev, Tatischev... and there's Poplavsky, the one with the dark glasses. He never takes them off. And there's Mirsky of course.'

'Is Mirsky going to speak?' I asked. I had heard his talk on Tolstoy at the Brasserie Steinbach. Since then I had loved Tolstoy above all other writers.

'No, tonight only Professor Karsavin will speak. See him?' She pointed out an older man, ravaged but still handsome, with a long straggling beard. A young girl clung to his arm.

'His new wife,' Kyra whispered. 'His third. And you saw Larissa Mordvinova, didn't you?' I hadn't. Kyra rolled her eyes to the right and I saw them: Larissa and Grisha. She was speaking to him, saying something so intense that just to watch her was to feel its heat. Although they didn't touch, they were wrapped in an invisible intimacy. It seemed almost improper to watch. Then Alyosha was making his way towards us.

'Nadezhda Mikhailovna!' he cried. 'I'm so glad you came.' He sat in the empty seat next to me, showing no trace of the agony I had witnessed. Kyra nudged me. I noticed, as I had at the Chengarov's, how boyish he was, despite his pallor and the dark circles under his eyes. A sense of sadness hung about him, at odds with the slight smile that seemed to linger permanently at the corners of his mouth.

Alyosha seemed to know everyone and to be overjoyed to see everyone. A stream of people stopped to greet him. I thought I might have imagined the figure downstairs hunched in despair, if it weren't for something in those greetings that suggested comfort or reassurance of some kind.

'You know Gregory Benediktovich,' Alyosha introduced me.

'We are old friends,' Gyorgei said. He ostentatiously lifted my hand to his lips, gazing at me with his twinkling eyes. He clapped Alyosha on the shoulder. 'Stay strong, old chap.'

There was a rustle at the door and the sound of a familiar voice: Zhenia and Dmitri Arensky had arrived; I watched their slow procession to the front row. He was tall, still erect, with a white shock of hair and a neatly trimmed white goatee. Zhenia Arenska's red hair had been piled into a high spray of curls. She had draped a pink, embroidered shawl round her shoulders, and she acknowledged acquaintances with a wave of her cigarette holder as she marched towards us.

'Alyosha, *golybchuk!*' she cried. Arensky stopped to wait for her. For a moment his eyes met mine and he looked as if he were about to speak to me. *He knows I'm Igor's informer*, I thought, and he's about to announce it, but he only inclined his head in polite recognition and looked back at his wife.

'Believe me, we are your friends,' she assured Alyosha. 'We respect you, we love you.' She dropped her voice to an emphatic whisper. 'And as a friend, I tell you, you must take a stand.'

'How can I?' he answered. 'She is a genius.'

'There are many Russian geniuses,' she retorted. 'It's nothing new.' Her whisper grew louder and more emphatic. 'Don't retreat! You're no coward, we all know that.'

Her husband looked uncomfortable. 'She's right,' he said. 'No surrender. You understand.'

They made their way to the front row. Alyosha, who had risen to greet them, sat down again, sighed and looked at his feet. The room was full now; people shared seats or stood at the back.

At a signal from Karsavin, Alyosha went to the front, raised his hand for silence and introduced the evening. When he spoke, his spine straightened, his voice sounded deeper. He had an air of confidence and passion that added something dramatic to the atmosphere. He spoke of his own search, 'which I know we all share,' for a way to reconcile 'my own truth even in defeat' with the need to 'serve Russia, the motherland, which lives inside us until the end of our days. We all ask questions. This evening we will hear a possible answer.' He sat next to me again, as Professor Karsavin rose.

He spoke for a long time, and from his first words I felt as if he were speaking directly to me.

'Who are we and where do we belong?' he asked. 'Do we find our roots here in Europe? No. So is our place in Asia? No. We are from a new continent: neither Europe nor Asia. We are Eurasians, with a unique culture which is alien to the foreign cultures which have tried to corrupt it. We are all agreed that communism is an evil and atheistic movement. But at the same time we are not proposing a violent counter-revolution. The revolution was an inevitable stage of our history, which Marxism, like other foreign invaders, has usurped for itself.'

There was some applause, led by Alyosha. After a moment, Kyra and I joined in. Karsavin raised his hand for silence and continued. 'But we will never realise ourselves in a culture warped and diseased by foreign values. Our home is not here.' He took a sip of water, still looking at the audience.

He's right, I thought. Now I understood clearly why it felt at times as if I was at the end of the world, unable to find my way back.

'The revolution was not in itself an alien event,' he explained. 'But in communism we have once more been taken over by foreign and alien ideas.' He spoke of materialism, atheism, the replacement of spirituality with technology, the blasphemous worship of the individual.

Alyosha was leaning forward slightly, his face totally absorbed. In the front row, Dmitri Arensky sat upright, still military, as if reviewing troops, his expression neutral, but missing nothing. Beside him, Zhenia Arenska nodded her head and her cigarette holder simultaneously.

Karsavin continued: 'We are considered, in the eyes of the western cultures, to be barbarians, held back by the Mongol invasion. I say: may I remain a barbarian!'

There was a soft ripple of laughter. He raised his voice like a battle cry. 'The privilege to be irrational! To reject the science of the Marxist God! To say no to western corruption!'

There were so many things to understand. I felt as if I were back at school, dreaming of the future in which I would do something important for the world. I sensed Alyosha looking sideways at me, watching. I turned back to Karsavin quickly, feeling the blush warm on my face.

'The communists have substituted temporal power for the spiritual leadership of orthodoxy. We must fight against this blasphemy,' he said, 'but not against our own people. We will not shed the blood of our brothers.'

Alyosha bent his head and put his hand to his eyes. Now the speech was rising to a climax.

'The communists, who deny God, who persecute priests

and believers, cannot prevail. The darkness of materialism will destroy them as the same darkness will destroy Western Europe with its worn-out ideas of individualism and democracy. And I for one hope for this destruction, for only by destruction can there be rebirth. And in the rebirth of that new world we will find our true home. Eurasia will arise to shine its light as a moral example to the world.'

Kyra raised her face to the light as she applauded and I saw the tears shine in her eyes. I wiped a tear from my own cheek. Under the sound of the applause, Alyosha whispered, 'We are going to print this in *Evrasia*.' He added something about "Spalding money" that was lost in the general hubbub.

Alyosha stood, raised his hand for quiet, and announced: 'At our next meeting Prince Svyatopolk-Mirsky will give a talk on Avaakum, and there will be a performance of new work by Stravinsky. We will also have details of our coming programme of debate and discussion, and at that time the next issue of *Evrasia* will definitely be available. We apologise for the absence of the current issue, but this will all be put right in the near future.'

There was another burst of enthusiastic applause. People began to get up and move slowly towards the exit. I got up as well, so that Alyosha and I were facing each other.

'Who is Avaakum?' I asked.

'Ah, a long story,' Alyosha said. 'He was the first of the Old Believers, a martyr for the Russian church. His autobiography is fascinating... he exorcised demons.' He was flushed with enthusiasm. 'His story is important for us. Perhaps we might go for a walk and discuss it one day, if you are free?'

Kyra gave me a sly smile and moved away.

'Interesting.' Gyorgei appeared behind Alyosha's shoulder. 'But you should leave that Chosen People stuff to the Yids, they do it better.'

Alyosha started to answer, but instead he stared, frozen, as Larissa and Grisha got up. Now Grisha was speaking and her face was raised to him with an expression of rapture. They left the room still enclosed in that invisible space. Alyosha stared after them with a terrible look of hurt and humiliation. I felt I had to do something, I couldn't turn away this time.

'Much to think about.' It was Dmitri Arensky. Beside him his wife nodded thoughtfully, 'It is a beautiful idea, a vision of some ideal future Russia,' Arensky went on. 'But still there is the old question of what is to be *done*? Always the question: '*Shto Dyelat?*' He raised a finger in emphasis. 'What is to be done? I will watch with interest.' They moved slowly away.

'He's right,' Alyosha said. He was still looking at the place where Larissa and Grisha had sat. His face had become pinched and shrunken.

'Is there anything I can do to help you?' I asked. He looked at me blankly, and suddenly took my hand.

'Thank you,' he said. 'We need clever people.'

I didn't understand what he meant. Then I realised he thought I meant the Eurasian movement. Did he really think I could be useful to such a thing? What use could I possibly be? I remembered what Uncle Igor had said.

'I'm not clever,' I told him. 'I only type a bit.'

His face lit up. 'Can you really type? But of course I heard you could type. But that is clever! It's exactly what we need. If you would be interested?'

'Yes,' I said. 'Oh yes, if there is anything I can do.'

He took my hand.

'Then you must come to the office and join us.'

CHAPTER EIGHTEEN

'I want to give you something,' Igor said a few days later. It was a cold, bright Sunday and after church we went to the Parc Monceau, where we walked under the trees on the slope above the path, where people held lively group conversations on the double sided benches. We stopped under a large tree. The day was suddenly warm, golden and shining. He took a box out of his pocket, opened it and held up the necklace to the light. I exclaimed 'Igor! How beautiful!'

'You like it?' he asked.

'Like it!' The sun caught the dark green glass beads and turned them into multi- shaded green shots of light. 'Oh Igor,' I breathed.

'You really like them?' But he knew I did; when he smiled he looked young; he looked gentle and happy. 'Here, put them on.' He fastened the clasp himself, and I felt his breath against my ear. 'Let me see,' he said, and when I turned around his eyes gleamed with an almost savage delight.

'It is beautiful,' I said. 'I will wear it forever.'

'It is worth nothing,' he frowned. 'Not like your mama's diamonds.'

'Then I will have it forever,' I said, 'Because I will be the only one who knows that it's beyond price.'

'Nadyushka,' he said, and kissed me. 'You know you are my good fortune.'

'But,' I hesitated. 'Why ...?'

'Why not?' he said. 'You have given me so much, Nadia, and I wanted to tell you so with some small thing.'

I wore the beads when he photographed me, a solitary figure with my head down, sitting on an empty double-sided bench in the Parc Monceau. It is one of my favourite photographs: the dripping trees, the pale mist around the girl waiting on the bench. Where is she? Who is she? What is she thinking?

Afterwards, as we crossed the Boulevard Haussmann with its shuttered Sunday silence, he said, 'These photographs are only for us. I'll never show them to anyone else, even if I starve.'

CHAPTER NINETEEN

'Alexei Semyonovitch,' I stood in the doorway of the office and spoke in my most severe tone, 'is this the work you meant?'

Alyosha made a vague gesture with one hand. 'It is various things,' he said.

The office of *Evrasia* was in a house off the Rue Lazare Carnot, one of a row of rundown villas, with small patches of overgrown weeds, on the edge of Clamart. The other rooms were all let to Russian families. The building was deserted during the day and, as I heard the stairs creak under my feet, I felt as if someone was hiding behind every door. The office itself was the front half of a shabby room on the second floor. The back contained a studio couch, a basin and some rough pegs along the wall: someone lived here as well.

The room was chilled with age and smelt of French drains and Russian tobacco. I imagined I could also smell something like library paste, which reminded me of Mr Bargevsky's classroom at school. Alyosha stood and held his hands out to greet me from behind the desk which was strewn with papers. A number of handwritten, scrawled pages had slipped to the floor and lay around the desk like snowflakes. The cracked leather sofa held more stacks of paper and untidy piles of newspapers: at a glance I could see titles in Italian and German as well as Russian. A copy of *Pravda* lay on top of the pile near me. "Workers Meet Production Target," the headline announced over a photograph of a joyous crowd. There were papers and books everywhere I looked, but the room itself was dominated by a large painting on the wall: a horse galloping at full stretch across the steppes.

'Wonderful, isn't it?' Alyosha said, as he followed my gaze. 'I thought of it the other night when Karsavin spoke about the spirit of Russia. To me the horse is Turania.'

I stared at it. 'It looks as if it will run just like that forever.'

'You're right! It will run and devour all the space in the world!'

He turned away to cough; I looked around the room. On the other side of the desk there was a typewriter like the machine I had used at the department of railways in St Petersburg; at the sight of it my fingers stiffened and I felt a reminiscent chill in my hands. It was set on a wobbly little table with a Paris telephone directory under one leg.

'It isn't necessary,' Alyosha said. 'There are only six people in Paris to telephone anyway.'

Alyosha didn't look well today. His skin was almost transparent, his long fair hair limp and unwashed. The only colour in his face was the slight feverish glow on his cheekbones. He was wearing a Russian peasant shirt with a wide belt, too big for his slight, boyish body. Nevertheless, I thought, he was really handsome after all. His face had a purity that was saved from prettiness by an arched, aquiline nose and deep-set green eyes.

'But where do all these papers go?' I didn't see a filing cabinet, only a small bookshelf, already crammed with documents, books and copies of *Evrasia*. I couldn't imagine what he expected me to do with them.

'That's the problem,' he explained. 'I don't know. I have a good system for my thoughts and my ideas because they are up here,' he tapped his head, 'but when things are on paper I don't know where they go. I thought you would know how to do these things.' He added apologetically, 'They've made me the secretary, I don't know why. I've always found it impossible to keep things in order.'

'Order is essential,' I said firmly. 'Uncle Igor says so. He and I label all his photographs and negatives and put them in a special order.' A long time ago I had been an untidy child who dropped things on the floor and rushed into the next moment. *Life teaches you*, I thought, *to take care of things, to stack crumbs neatly.*

'Where would you put this for instance?' Alyosha picked up a sheaf of notes. 'This is a report from Savitsky about a talk given by Klepnin on Alexander Nevsky at St. Sulpice. Now, does it go under "Talk," "Savitsky," "Klepnin," "Alexander Nevsky" or "St. Sulpice?" Where?' With every name, his voice and manner changed. He became gaunt like Savitsky, then had an anxious smile like Klepnin. When he said "St Sulpice", I could almost smell the incense.

'You see,' he announced, raising his hands and his voice, 'It's exactly like life.'

After a short, dramatic pause he lifted Savitsky's letter with two fingers and dropped it on the typewriter, where it slid slowly to the floor. I automatically applauded.

'You liked that?' he asked. 'I was going to be an actor once. I even trained with Kommisarjevsky for a year.' Uncle Igor had told me Alyosha did odd jobs as a film extra, and it seemed to me that he could be a great actor. I said so.

'Oh, it's all well enough,' he dismissed the idea. 'But one must have a greater purpose in life.'

'In that case, you must put things in order.' I returned to the matter at hand, feeling I must prove my worth as a helper. 'Uncle Igor says everything should be at your fingertips.'

'That's not like life.'

'No,' I agreed, 'but it's how Uncle Igor does it.' I began to pick up and separate the papers. Alyosha sat beside me, brushed away a lock of hair that hung over his forehead and lit a cigarette. He seemed as youthful as Grisha Bobrov and it was only when he was seized by a long bout of coughing, that he suddenly looked like a man of thirty. It was a dry cough that rattled his entire body, leaving his face covered by a light film of sweat. When he wiped his upper lip, I saw that his handkerchief was clean; this told me that he was being looked after by someone, somewhere and I felt relieved.

'I'm so sorry. It's damp today,' he excused himself, 'And so I am not so well.'

Indeed, after a few days of sun it had begun to rain again, lightly but steadily.

He smiled at me. 'What a pretty necklace,' he said. 'Lovely beads. They sing. And the colour speaks your name. Maybe I should buy something like that for Larissa. Was it from the *Marché aux Puces*?' He spoke as if thinking aloud. 'But even so there is no money. Anyway she knows I adore her.' He brought his attention back to me. 'And she adores me. That is the problem. I make her so happy that she is not inspired. But that is how it is with genius.' There was a sad silence. 'Genius needs new inspiration. Always. A young poet like Grisha Bobrov is necessary for her work.'

The horse galloping across the steppe seemed to be Larissa's spirit, running with the wind that bent the trees painted on the horizon. As Alyosha looked at it, I wondered if we had had the same thought.

'But really she can't live without me. I couldn't say that to those people the other night. They wouldn't understand.' His eyes narrowed and he put out his cigarette. 'You saw me downstairs didn't you?' I nodded. 'I thought so. It was good of you to say nothing.' He took a breath. 'I must explain.' He lit another cigarette, inhaled and offered it to me. 'You see, the thing is,' he repeated, 'Larissa needs me. I need her.' He paused. I waited politely for him to continue.

'No,' he said, 'That's not true. She doesn't need me. She won't leave me, but she doesn't need me. I feel I can talk to you. You understand.' There was another sad silence. I bowed my head.

'Alexei Semyonovitch,' I said, 'Where are your shoes?'

He looked down and then back at me in surprise. 'I don't know. Now that is extraordinary.' We both stared at his long, pale toes.

'Alyosha, we must find your shoes.'

We both began to search, stepping over and around piles of papers and files. There was a heavy notice board leaning against the wall. Behind it I found a strangely shaped object that felt like snakeskin. It was thick with dust.

'It's a charm!' Alysoha cried and began to talk about shamans who beat their drums and flew away, about the use of totems by peasants in Siberia, how the Komu tribes believed the stars were nailed to the sky. 'What a heritage we have!' he exclaimed.

'Go on,' I said. 'Tell me more.'

'Oh, it will take weeks. There are so many stories.' He took the cigarette I offered and inhaled again. 'I was ill as a child,' he told me, 'I had to stay in bed for days at a time. So I read the *bylini* and the *ckazki* over and over all day, and then I would lie awake at night and picture Prince Igor riding into my room and the Firebird sitting on the end of my bed. And I always thought how fortunate I was to be Russian.' He handed me the cigarette and went on almost as if it were another story, 'If I leave her, she will kill herself. This Grisha Bobrov is not the first young poet in our lives.'

'Grisha must have been hypnotised,' I said. 'He never wrote poetry.'

'When she cares for someone, she discovers that they are a poet. She thought I was a poet for a while. She calls Grisha her eagle. But soon he will fall to Earth like the rest.' I put my hand on his shoulder. He went on, 'How can I leave her? She is free to suffer and produce great work because she knows I will be there.'

I struggled to follow his thought. He picked up the snakeskin charm and shifted it from one hand to the other, and set it down carefully on the desk in front of him.

I finally said, 'But if she needs to suffer, why does she need you to suffer?'

He had kept his hand on the snakeskin.

'It's complicated,' he said.

'Doesn't it make you angry?'

'Yes. Frequently. But what can one do? It seems to be a problem only death can solve.'

I suddenly thought of something. 'There was a story in *Paris Soir* last week,' I said. 'A man burst into a room and found his wife with her lover and he stabbed the lover right in the heart. There was a drawing of all three of them. She was on the floor screaming and you could see by the husband's face that he had gone mad. Poor man.'

He almost smiled. 'And don't you think that was a terrible thing to do?'

'Yes, but when I looked at the drawing, I could understand. I think the Judge should have let him off. He only did it because she *betrayed* him!'

'Nadia,' Alyosha sat down, leant back in the chair, and looked up at me with a theatrical frown, 'you are a savage! You are descended directly from Genghis Khan!'

He started to cough again, a paroxysm this time. His whole body heaved as he choked and gasped for breath. 'You … are … a barbarian … good … for you.' He just managed to say the words. I could barely make out what he was saying.

'Alyosha, shall I get you some water?'

'No.' And once again he was wracked by a fit of coughing. 'Yes, yes,' he gasped. 'Please.' He lowered himself to the little chair at the typewriter.

I poured some water from a china pitcher on the desk into a thick glass tumbler beside it. He sipped gratefully and took a few breaths.

'That's better,' he said. He was shaking. 'I won't die in Paris. I know that.' He got the words out with difficulty. 'Larissa saw it in the cards. They said I am going to die for my country.' He seemed to breathe more easily. 'Oh, my God! How wonderful that would be! To die for Russia!' His voice was strong now. 'Even if I died the moment my feet touched Russian earth, I would be happy, because I would see my soul. How could I see my soul here in this place? How could it find me?'

I put the glass back on the table. I had heard of the soul that shadows your life and only appears at your death.

'But how could you lose your soul?' I argued. 'Even in Paris your soul must know where you are all the time, because surely it has been with you always, waiting to be born?'

While I was speaking, he had slid from the chair to his knees. He crouched fumbling among some papers. I wondered if he was having some new attack of illness, but when he looked up he was smiling.

'See,' he said, 'I have found my shoes.'

He lifted one long, thin leg and then the other as he put them on.

'But they are on the wrong feet,' I said.

'Yes. It is the beginning of spring. The *leshii* have come out of their trees to create havoc everywhere. This is the only way to protect oneself against them. I advise you to do the same.'

He pointed at my shoes and criss-crossed his fingers. I laughed, and criss-crossed my fingers in imitation. For a second I thought I should do the same with my shoes, but the shoes made my feet look so clumsy I didn't want him to notice them.

I left the office carrying announcements of the next meeting that had to be put everywhere in emigré Paris. I would walk from Billancourt to Montparnasse, from the Renault factory to the tearooms around the Rue Daru, to the Russian Canteen, and of course at Tanya's. It was getting dark; Uncle Igor would be at the *Rotonde* along with everyone else.

The evening had begun. I looked down at the Seine where the lights were reflected in the water; sounds of music came from a café, and through the open doorway I could see people dancing. A young couple danced out on the pavement, laughing and singing Maurice Chevalier's new song "Boom…boom – da dada dada da – boom!" She was wearing a green, pleated dress with layers of organza at the neck and shoulders. As I walked past them, the young man called out to me in French. I didn't understand what he was saying, but he smiled and waved. I looked up and saw the stars nailed to the sky.

I thought, I must tell Uncle Igor. And when I approached the *Rotonde,* I saw him sitting at a table with his arms around a woman.

CHAPTER TWENTY

I could just make out a magazine on the table in front of them; their heads touched as they bent over it. The woman had her back to me, but I could see Uncle Igor laugh and whisper something in her ear that made the bird on her hat quiver. Her handbag lay on the table: it had a glittering silver chain and a silver buckle. I was sure that her shoes would match it exactly. Clusters of people shifted around them, moving conversations from table to table, while waiters threaded their way through, carrying trays, collecting cups and glasses.

There was a strange hum in my ears. I seemed to be watching a distant, silent world moving behind that pane of glass. Why had Igor said nothing to me? This was not how I felt when he interrupted me to follow a woman with his eyes. Then, I knew he was teasing me, showing off. This was different. This was something he didn't want me to know.

Inside the Rotonde, there was a general low hum of conversation punctuated by silent spaces where people read, or played chess. The air smelt heavily of smoke. Uncle Igor didn't see me come in. As I made my way towards him, I passed the Arensky's friends, Vladimir and Nina Ladinsky, who sat at a table with three men I had not seen before. The men had the dazed look of the recent émigré, taking in the lights and the noise as if they couldn't believe their eyes. I wondered if the Ladinksys would come to Tanya's later and if they would bring these people with them.

I stood beside Igor for a moment before he saw me. Then he blinked and gave me a sleepy smile, still with his hand lightly touching the back of the woman's neck. She looked at me with a mixture of curiosity and vague recognition. As soon as I saw her face, I knew who she was. She was the woman at Boris Chengarov's funeral, the woman who had called Uncle Igor a son of a bitch. I saw now that she was older than Igor, and not exactly beautiful. Her cheeks were a bit full and her chin was an elfin point just starting to soften. Her lips were painted a bright red that was bleeding slightly over the cupid's bow. For all that, something about the way she held herself insisted that she was a beauty. Her blonde hair, beneath her little hat, was fashionably waved and a small fox lay around her neck with its tail nipped in its mouth, clashing oddly with the bird on her hat. She cocked her head to one side and gave me a bright smile.

'Olga Nikolayevna Sherbyateva, you remember my friend Nadezhda Mikhailovna Serova,' said Uncle Igor formally, raising his eyebrows at me. Why are you standing there like that, Nadyushka?'

'Your little Nadia,' the woman, Olga Sherbyateva, cried. 'But I assumed she was a child! That's why I said the necklace was too grown-up when you showed me. And you said nothing.' She seemed to melt even closer to him. He still had his arm around her, but he was looking at me. I thought he seemed uneasy.

'You were right,' Olga went on, 'Your taste, as always, is impeccable. You don't need my opinion.'

'I didn't ask you for your opinion.' He took his arm from around her. 'For heavens sake, sit down Nadia.' I sat down slowly. Olga Nikolayevna's smile seemed fixed to her face.

Uncle Igor added to me, 'No one needs to give me advice. I had already chosen it.'

'You have perfect taste in everything,' Olga Nikolayevna laughed. 'You remember how particular you used to be about *certain things*.' She raised her eyebrows and watched me when she said it.

He looked uneasy again, and turned back to her.

'I still am, when possible,' he grinned.

She seemed pleased by that, as if she had scored a point.

'Anyway, you two are old friends,' he added.

'Are we? Really? And how do I know this very young old friend?' Her voice was musical, light tones in a minor key, with an undertone of mockery. I heard Mama's voice in my ear: *'At her age hair that colour is dyed.'*

'From *there*, of course. Where else? When she was a real child.'

She patted his hand. 'Oh Igoryoshka, you are naughty, you love your secrets! Doesn't he?' she asked me.

'Yes,' I said. 'He is a secretive person.'

Uncle Igor and I glared at each other. Igor said coldly. 'And why not? Everyone has secrets. Paris is not the interrogation centre.'

'There are many steps between secrets and police interrogation,' I said.

'It is too late for a philosophical discussion,' he answered. We continued to glare at each other.

'Igoryoshka, who are the people with the Ladinskys, do we know them?' Olga asked. She took a cigarette and craned her neck to see. She had an unusually long neck, and a memory stirred. Igor ignored her.

'You had a dramatic encounter,' he looked from one of us to the other. 'Am I the only one who remembers?'

'But how can it be?' She tilted her head back. The bird on her hat quivered again.

'The *Brodyachaya Sobaka*,' and he banged his hand sharply on the table. The coffee cups made little jumps.

She opened her mouth in a sign of astonishment. 'My God!' she cried, throwing up her hands in a dramatic gesture. That gesture and her long neck brought it all back: the strange and fearful excitement of that evening, the masked woman in the looking glass.

She breathed out a long 'Aaah, yes! And this is that little girl?' She leant forward, as if telling me a story about myself. 'I remember how you screamed, you were so frightened by the play. The revolver shot offstage... well, we are no longer startled

143

by such things, are we?' She sighed and smiled. The sigh and the smile were both artificial, I thought, but there was an emotional counterpoint under her theatricality that wouldn't let me despise her.

'Ah, you have become such a beauty!' she exclaimed. 'You make me feel so old, yes, completely ancient.' She looked me up and down in one quick, expert flick as she smiled. Her eyes were an unusually deep blue, set off by beads of mascara on the tips of her lashes.

'Nadia, that's a serious compliment,' Uncle Igor said. 'Wherever Olya goes, everyone looks at her.' The way he said her name made me wonder how long they had been together in Paris. Did he know she was here before Boris Chengarov's funeral? Was it planned before we arrived?

'Oh no longer,' she sighed. 'But at least one has the comfort that one's friends remember.'

Uncle Igor gave me a sideways look, lifted Olga's hand and touched his lips to her wrist as she began to recite, just loudly enough to draw the attention of people at surrounding tables: *'At the feast of light/looking in the pattern of a diamond ring/at the burning octagons' reflections/the diamond sparks an everlasting thing…'* Her listeners applauded.

'Magnificent', said a man.

'A magnificent poem,' Olga agreed. 'The divine Balmont.'

I was sure I hadn't heard that poem before, but the way she spoke brought back my memory of the long ago evening: the darkness, the voices and the sense that I shouldn't be here.

Uncle Igor continued to kiss her wrist lightly as she finished: *'Thunder and lightning lie in the gem/fires burn. Lights stream forth and all these cry; let's go! Let's run! Let's shine!'* she choked off the final words with a little "Oh!" of pain and pleasure. She drew her hand away, and I saw the tiny marks on the underside of her wrist. I waited for her anger, but to my shock, she smiled.

Uncle Igor sat back. He gave me another uneasy glance and turned his attention back to Olga Nikolayevna.

Olga began to speak rapidly, as if the poem or the bite had suddenly excited her. 'But you must photograph your beautiful niece. Photographs like that would certainly sell.'

'I hate being photographed,' I said. My throat felt tight.

'Oh, but I can see it so clearly, that wonderful strong face, that...' She made an arc with her hands, 'That intense look, imagine it framed with a marvellous piece of velvet.' She had put down her cigarette, now she picked it up again, and regarded me. 'I have a feeling for these things...'

Uncle Igor said, 'I don't like posed photographs. They are always propaganda.'

'Propaganda,' she spread out her hands, and again people at nearby tables looked at us. 'I am not interested in propaganda – dreadful word, so ugly. I only want to see the beauty in everything. I am not at all interested in politics, only in life.'

'They are the same thing,' I said. 'It's obvious.' I took the last swallow of Igor's coffee. 'This coffee is politics,' I added. I quoted: '*The evening cold is terrible/ the wind anxiously blasting, twisting.../the anguished shuffling of footsteps/ Upon the road, steps non-existing.* That's politics,' I said.

'Nadia loves poetry,' said Uncle Igor. 'Like you, Olya, she memorises as she reads.' But there was something in his smile that told me to stop.

'Oh I see you are clever,' she said. 'I'm afraid I am not clever like you,' she made the word "clever" sound like a deficiency of charm or attraction.

'Olya my dear,' it was Nina Ladinska. She bent over and the two women embraced. Ladinsky stood just behind her, but their three friends had gone.

'Did you see those men?' Ladinsky muttered, in such a low voice that we all had to lean forward in order to hear. 'They are from a Soviet trade delegation and they were told to contact me when they arrived. They say the economy is growing, there is more housing, more prosperity. They wanted to give me information on the latest trade figures from there. All lies, naturally. They want me to print it.'

145

'As if it were true?' Olga asked.

'Of course. In a paper like mine, they think it must be considered accurate. And I *will* print the information. But,' he smiled grimly, 'On the next page I will print another article that will tell our readers the truth.'

'Wonderful!' said his wife.

'Where are they now?' Uncle Igor asked.

'They were expected at a meeting back at their hotel. The Soviets like to have their meetings at night.'

'What a terrible time we live in, who would have believed it?' said Madame Ladinska. Then she looked at me. 'But this is our little friend who makes us so comfortable at Tanya's.'

'But she would, of course!' cried Olga. 'This is my dearest Nadia Serova. I've known her since she was a child.' She put her arm around me and briefly pressed her cheek to mine. I could smell her powder, and feel the satiny texture of her flesh. 'Don't wear her out running back and forth – look after her!'

I pulled away. 'I can look after myself,' I said. Igor and I looked at each other steadily for a moment. I could read an appeal in his face, which I resisted. There was an awkward pause, and Olga Nikolayevna gave a musical little laugh.

Uncle Igor said, 'Olya means the best for you. You know how she is.'

'I don't know,' I said and he darkened, but Ladinsky said at the same time 'Olya means so well for everyone; she makes the world into a family.'

'Family?' Madame Ladinska looked around, 'There are people here that one would never dine with at home, and now we are like one terrible family. We have no choice. Fate has thrown us all together.'

'But Nadia is more than that, isn't that so, my dear?' Olga asked Uncle Igor. 'We are like a real family.'

'And every family has a black sheep,' said Uncle Igor. 'Like me.' There was a tense silence.

Madame Ladinska pursed her lips. He added, 'Nadia is the

family angel. She makes even a black sheep like me a little bit white.'

'So you must be sure to tell Mitya and Zhenia,' Olga trilled.

Ladinsky said, 'I will be sure to tell him. In fact, Mitya has already noticed her. You know how Mitya is about young women. And as well, he is always careful.'

'But now he knows this is Nadia Mikhailovna, my dear friend.' Both Ladinskys smiled at me and Madame Ladinksa embraced Olga again. As they left, they stopped by a group at another table, and Madame Ladinska said something that made them turn and look at us. But I noticed it was actually Uncle Igor they were looking at.

'Nadia,' Igor said as the Ladinskys left, 'What is all that paper you're holding?'

I had almost forgotten about the flimsy packet I still clutched.

'They're announcements of a Eurasian meeting.' I read the heading. 'There will be a talk on Glinka. Alyosha had them ready but he can't distribute them. He hasn't got the time and besides it's bad for his health.'

'Oh, how interesting,' Olga said. 'A great idealist, Alyosha. Like a child.'

'He is the secretary,' I said.

'Yes, he gets paid a bit for that, it's a way of getting money to Larissa of course; she would never accept a gift. He is delightful,' she cooed. 'We were extra revolutionaries in that film about Marie Antoinette and he was as charming as ever.' She turned to Igor. 'Alyosha played a prisoner of the bastille and he looked absolutely the part! I almost didn't recognise him.' She inspected her bruised wrist 'And do you know they haven't paid us yet, and I have been to the office four times already.'

'Nadia, don't sulk.' Uncle Igor picked up his coffee cup, saw it was empty, and pointed at me in admonishment.

I noticed once again how long his fingers were. I also noticed that his nails were bitten to the quick. When had that happened? I had never seen him bite his nails.

'I haven't got time to play your games,' I said.

'No one is playing games,' he said. 'Please, Nadia.'

I stood up. 'I have to go now,' I said.

'But we will meet again soon,' Olga held out her hand to me, but Igor took it. He pressed it lightly as she said, 'I want to see you often.' She smiled and looked into my eyes. 'Very often.'

'Like family,' said Uncle Igor.

I had nothing more to say. Without a word, I turned away and left with my head held as high and proud as I could manage.

CHAPTER TWENTY-ONE

Igor likes danger, I thought, as I unfolded a tablecloth and smoothed it neatly across the table. *He likes to know that people talk about him.* I collected a knife and a slightly bent fork from the wooden box in the kitchen. *Olga Nikolayevna likes it too. She likes people to notice her,* I thought scornfully. *But Igor is part of something greater than that.* The fork was not quite clean. I wiped it on my apron.

Tanya's voice interrupted me: 'Nadia, why are you standing there like that? You have done enough with that fork. People are waiting and this is getting cold.' I hurriedly collected the bowls of borscht and a plate of herring and cucumber and settled into the long night of greasy plates, dirty glasses, hastily wiped down tables and the high rising tension of people all talking at the same time. The same sounds and smells as the cafe I had just left, where Uncle Igor pressed Olga's wrist to his lips, and left the bruise later, as if a wolf had drunk her blood.

At the back of the café, I pressed my foot against the door to steady myself while I balanced the tray. Like all the trays at Tanya's, it was a lightweight black tin decorated with bright enamelled red flowers. It felt too light for the thick blue and gold crockery Tanya favoured and sometimes I was afraid it would simply fold up in the middle.

Behind me was the murmur of French and Russian voices. Tanya's had been discovered recently by the French set who had discovered Chagall and Bakst and adored the Russian ballet. For these new arrivals, Tanya had raised her prices. Maria Dimitrieva sang *Raskinylos Morye Shiroko,* "How Wide the Sea, on the gramophone. The smell of hot butter and frying meat wafted into the dining room whenever the kitchen door opened. In front of me was the smaller room Tanya reserved for private meetings, discussion groups or occasional poetry readings. I cradled the tray carefully with one arm and felt my run-down heel throw me slightly off balance as I fumbled for the doorknob. The shoes Beate had given me in Riga were sturdy, but a year of daily walking on damp pavements had almost worn them through. I calculated that, by saving a few centimes a week, it would take a total of four weeks' wages for a new pair of shoes. I needed those shoes badly. I told myself to stop thinking about it, but still I saw shoes in every plate of *pelmeni* and every glass of vodka.

The front room of the restaurant featured an old samovar on a special table with an embroidered cloth. There were starched white tablecloths on the dining tables, pink-shaded lamps, gilt mirrors, tapestries, a large photograph of the Imperial Family and paintings of hunting scenes in Old Russia. In the back room there was no décor at all. An overhead light was shaded with a stained peach cloth. The tables were bare. Tanya said she was going to do something with it someday, but she never would, as long as there were Russian émigrés with no money. There was a small bar and an ice chest that didn't work. The only decoration was a large mirror behind the bar.

After three months, I knew the names of everyone who came to Tanya's regularly, the ones who sat in the front room all night, joining in any and all conversations, occasionally singing or walking out in fury, part of the "evening theatre," who were, as my friend Kyra called it, "permanently temporary," and the ones who came to the back room every week like clockwork. On Mondays, the Young Poets Group, on Tuesdays, The Brotherhood of The Russian Truth, who discussed political philosophy. The handsome film actor, Ivan Moujskine entertained colleagues on Fridays. Tonight, Thursday, was the Arensky's regular evening where they met friends, talked and played bridge until the small hours. Where else did they go, I wondered. What else did they do, what else could they do?

Lewitsky's instructions throbbed endlessly in my mind: 'Get close to Dmitry Arensky, find out everything you can about him.' I knew more about Dmitry Arensky now: he had been a military aide to the tsar; after the October revolution he had led a battalion in the Ukraine until the collapse of Kiev, when he had fled the country and finally arrived in Paris via Constantinople and Belgrade. His wife Evgenia Kirillova, was a member of an old Moscow family, known for the beauty of its women. She had managed to get out of Russia after the civil war, disguised as her maid and (it was rumoured), helped by a Bolshevik official who was in love with her. She had been detained by officials along the way, and had been arrested and almost deported when she finally arrived in Finland. Somehow she had been spared and had made her way to join her husband in Constantinople, where she arrived penniless and burning with fever. Her face, although ravaged by poverty and illness, was still striking, with clear, chiselled features, set off by her untidy red hair, and there was something pure in her profile, always wreathed in cigarette smoke, that left me slightly in awe of her. I had never heard her speak of her escape except occasionally, to say 'We are here by the mercy of God.' Despite her charm, I sensed that her knowing eye took in more than she let on, and I was sure she would use her long cigarette holder to fend off any attempt to get close to Dmitri Arensky without her consent.

The Arenskys, after moving from one pension to another, now lived in a small hotel in Billancourt. He spoke four languages and did some translation for a firm that imported machine tools; Evgenia Kirillovna hemmed scarves or trimmed hats. When they were not at work, they made the rounds of cafés and played bridge. When they could, they went to the cinema.

General Arensky was a prominent member of émigré groups: the General Military Union, the Supreme Monarchist Council, and the Russian Central Association, regardless of their differences. He took every opportunity to protest at anything even vaguely pro-Soviet. All this information was available to anyone. But "Moscow" suspected that there was more than protest, that Arensky had secrets. When "Moscow" was sure of these secrets, Igor and Gyorgei would 'liaise', as Uncle Igor put it, between Arensky and "Moscow." Igor depended on me. Lewitsky depended on me. "Moscow" depended on me. And most of all, Mama depended on me. I prayed every night that Mama was alive and well. But I knew my prayers would only be answered with the help of "Moscow." And with news of Mama, Lewitsky would pass along the envelope of francs that would buy me the shoes I needed, that would finally fit. Images revolved in my mind, like scenes in a film: I could hear Uncle Igor murmur, 'Our friends are getting restless.' I knew that if something were useless to him he cast it aside. I had seen his eyes go blank at the mention of a former friend. 'Who?' he would say. 'Oh, him.' Why should I be any different? How terrible it would be to be cast into Igor's outer darkness. It would be like being dead.

Silence fell as I came through the door. Dmitri Arensky, in his worn dark suit, stiff-collared shirt and dark tie, never raised his eyes from his cards while Zhenia Arenska ostentatiously waited for me to leave, holding her cards in one hand and her cigarette in the other, its holder like a narrow banner between her thin fingers. I held the door open with my foot and edged into the room, gripping the tray which seemed to get heavier with each step. The chairs at Tanya's were small and Nina Ladinska needed two. She continually arranged and rearranged her hand as soon as it was dealt, while her husband Vladimir, large, round-faced and reassuring, would give me a small, courteous nod.

Suddenly Arensky looked up and gave me a sharp look from under his thick, grey brows. I had the absurd thought that his brows were like two mice, and then my heel betrayed me. My ankle twisted, pain shot through my foot and I cried out involuntarily as I clutched at the tray. It tilted and suddenly Zhenia Arenska was holding the tray steady. She took it from me with a surprisingly strong grasp.

'Never mind, never mind, nothing is broken,' she said, and set the tray on the bar. I limped after her.

'Nothing has even spilled,' said Nina Ladinska. 'At least not too much.' She remained seated; her chins quivered as she stretched her neck to see.

'Are you hurt?' Ladinsky asked.

I tested my weight on my ankle.

'No, no I only stumbled. I'm so sorry.' I tried to smooth back the hair which had come loose and straggled around my face. Tanya was particular about neatness.

'Put some ice on it,' said Nina Ladinska. 'Ice is excellent for sprains. '

Arensky interrupted her. 'I hear you are a protégé of our friend Olga Nikolayevna.' He was a man who commanded attention without raising his voice and even Vladimir Ladinsky turned to face him.

There was a silence. I stared at him, frozen with surprise, conscious of my stained apron and untidy ends of hair.

'That she has known you from childhood,' he went on.

'And what a surprise this is!' Zhenia Arenska cried. 'We had no idea.'

They all regarded me with benign smiles, as if I had been given to them as a gift.

'She is your guardian until we go home. Olga is fortunate to have a child here,' Nina Ladinska pronounced. 'Someone to care for.'

I was going to say, 'No, not a child,' when she added, 'To be without family... our daughter chose to stay in Moscow.' She sighed and shook her head, giving off waves of stale perfume.

'Olya always kept *certain things* to herself.' Nina Ladinska's puffy cheeks quivered. She turned to her husband 'Isn't that so Volodya?'

'She has always been personally very discreet.' He agreed.

It was suddenly so simple. I was where "Moscow" wanted me to be, in exchange for a small lie. I couldn't do it. I would not become Olga's accomplice. The silence continued. Arensky frowned.

'Yes,' I said, 'She has been like a mother. Dear Auntie Olya.' I thought I might choke. I sounded breathy and unconvincing even to myself. Later, I learnt that when one tells a lie, it is better to say too little than too much. Now, I continued to babble. 'I used to think she looked like an angel, with her blonde hair, and I wanted blonde hair just like hers.' What made me say that? Mama was like me, with dark thick hair which hung to her waist when she let it down. I mustn't think of that or I would become emotional and make a mistake. I couldn't seem to stop talking. 'And she taught me so much about poetry,' I said. I couldn't stop. 'She introduced me to Pushkin. When she read it to me, I learnt to love poetry as she does.' The reality of my private discoveries which I shared with Papa, melted into this lie.

The air became close and stale, as if the memory of all the people who had planned and argued in here had seeped into the worn green wallpaper. Arensky put his cards down, leant forward and inspected me. 'You know we are all your Auntie's friends here,' he said. 'We have seen how she tends to be...' he scowled at me ... 'flamboyant with people. She has a great maternal instinct. She draws people in very quickly.'

'I understand your mother was a Rozanov,' Zhenia informed me. She closed her eyes briefly and said the name again. 'Rozanov. There was a Tatyana Rozanova who married Count Yurikov.' She turned to Ladinsky. 'Volodya, you remember? We didn't know them well,' she said, 'but I know the name.'

'She was my mama's oldest sister,' I lied. 'My aunt.'

'So your Uncle Igor is Tatyana Yurikova's brother,' she said, working it out. 'He's very young to be her brother. A late child presumably. I know of the family,' she said, in a satisfied way.

'So how do you know Olga so well?' Zhenia Arenska

pursued. 'How did you meet? Not through your family, of course.' She waited. I shook my head, wondering what to say. She concluded, 'It must have been through poor Sergei.'

Now I would have to lie again. Who was Sergei – her father? Her brother? Why hadn't Uncle Igor said anything about him?

I repeated her words, 'Yes, I met her through Sergei. Poor Sergei. He was a great friend of Uncle Igor.'

'Oh really?' Zhenia leant forward slightly and peered at me. Her look made me realise for the first time that she was short sighted. 'You met through your Uncle? How interesting – most unusual.'

Arensky chuckled. 'You are a very sophisticated young lady for your age.'

'Am I?' I asked. I had made a mistake, I knew. I added again, 'Poor Sergei.' *I have said that too often*, I thought.

Arensky was still looking at me. He raised his eyebrows and smiled. 'And are you also fond of birds?' he enquired.

I hesitated for a moment until I sensed agreement was necessary.

'I feel the same as Auntie Olya.'

'But not as strongly, I hope,' said Nina Ladinska. 'It's a great mistake for her to keep birds in Paris. We will be leaving soon and what will she do with them?'

In that moment I instinctively learnt something else about lying: always include the truth when you can.

'I don't keep birds. I never have.' The small truth was a great relief. 'But I think birds are so beautiful.' Another small truth. It fed the lie. 'I used to watch them with Auntie Olya for hours.' A picture formed in my mind to illustrate the lie: a small child holding "Auntie Olya's" hand, in a park watching birds.

'So there is some family connection,' Ladinsky spoke slowly as if working it out. He seemed to be watching himself think and nodding agreement with himself.

'And this means that she and your Uncle Igor have been

acquainted for a long time,' Zhenia blew out a stream of smoke. 'How very interesting.'

'But why have you never mentioned this to us?' Arensky asked.

'I didn't want to interrupt you,' I stammered. My voice wavered childishly and I looked away from him at the cards scattered in the middle of the table. Zhenia had handed the plates round while I had been talking and Vladimir Ladinsky was crunching on two pieces of cucumber at once. 'Interrupt us? Interrupt what?'

'If you were talking about important things,' I said weakly.

'And what could be more important than one's family? If you are like family to Olga Nikolaevna, then you are like family to us. You must remember that.'

I felt reprimanded. 'I'm sorry,' I said.

'But now we know all about you!' Ladinsky pronounced through a mouthful of cucumber. He swallowed. 'So you needn't be shy. And by the way, thank Tatiana Andreevna for this gift.' He lifted a herring.

Dmitri Arensky spoke and again they all turned to him.

'I noticed you were at the Eurasian talk last week,' he said 'What was your reaction?'

What would he like me to say? I remembered how Zhenia had assured Alyosha they were his friends.

'I thought it was thrilling,' I said, 'A new ideal. It was – it made me feel that all of this!' I made a gesture indicating Paris in general at which they all sighed their agreement, 'That it might mean something after all.'

'You are an idealist, I see,' Arensky said. The way he said it made me feel we had become friends and I was able to look directly into his eyes. They seemed to pierce through me, knowing everything, but I held his gaze and went on.

'If that means believing that there will be a place for us in the future as Russians, not the way we are now, then yes, I think I'm an idealist.'

'Bravo!' said Zhenia Arenska.

'You see? The appeal to the young,' General Arensky addressed his friends. 'What did I say?' He turned back to me. 'But did it occur to you that there is no way to bring this about without including the Soviet idea? You all left Russia too soon. You were unfinished, without enough knowledge.'

'Your generation is lost,' Nina Ladinska murmured. 'Soviet products.'

'I didn't understand everything Karsavin said,' I admitted. 'Alyosha is going to explain it.'

'I will explain it,' said Arensky. 'I too am an idealist, and I will make it all clear.'

He spoke as if making a public announcement.

'Young Russians mustn't be swayed by fine words and so-called ideals. Be very careful about where certain ideals will lead. I will explain everything. Not here, but at Le Petit Vavin, where you will find me during most afternoons. I look forward to an interesting discussion.'

I closed the door and leant against it, taking stock of what I had done. Behind me I heard Madame Ladinska's raised voice, shrill with excitement: 'So that's the man! Olya would never tell us ...'

'Yes,' Zhenia said. 'Remember she was completely out of her mind with love.'

Their voices dropped. Out of her mind with love... I remembered something else about that strange night of poetry. 'Tell Olga Nikolayevna I am busy this evening,' Uncle Igor had said. Nothing was what it seemed, I thought. Things were going on around me and I never knew. And now, again, I had agreed to do something he didn't want me to understand. It was like the music boxes and his beautiful old friend, Olga. *After our oath*, I thought, *how could he do something like this without telling me?*

Galina passed me, carrying two carafes of vodka, frozen into their buckets.

'Why are you standing there?' she asked. 'People are waiting.' She hurried away. Now Maria Dimitrievna was singing

"Moya Milaya." It was the last record in the album. I had been in the back room for the space of six songs.

What am I doing? I thought. *Who is Igor really?* I felt I had stepped away from something delicate and precious, something I would be unable to return to without shame.

CHAPTER TWENTY-TWO

He spoke as soon as I opened the door. 'Why were you so rude to Olga Nikolayevna?'

'Rude?' The accusation made me catch my breath with shock.

'We both found it extremely embarrassing. I thought you had better manners.'

The room was dark, dominated by the smell of chemicals, stale food and drains; a black curtain was nailed across the corner where negatives soaked in the basin and drying prints dangled above it, pinned on their string. The subjects made ghostly white shapes against backgrounds that melted into the darkness of the room. At the far window, the shutter was open a crack. Igor stood beside it, his profile touched by the pale flicker of a streetlamp.

'*Rude* is from another kind of world,' I said. I raised my voice. 'I don't care if you were embarrassed. Why did she do that?'

He ignored me. 'I think you should apologise to both of us.' He closed the shutter with a sharp bang. Now I could only sense his presence in the dark.

I pressed on, 'You let her lie. And then I had to lie again later. I've told so many lies tonight. Is that what you wanted? Why?' I couldn't keep the words unspoken 'Are you doing something you won't tell me?'

'Don't talk to me like that.' I sensed him coil as if he were about to spring. I moved to one side and a chair rattled as I brushed against it. 'You behaved like a jealous woman.'

'I'm not jealous.'

'Yes you are, it's obvious. You made a fool of yourself.'

I was more accustomed to the darkness now. I hit out at his silhouette. 'I hate you! I hate you!'

He gripped my wrists. 'No you don't. Tell me, what did Arensky say?'

'They kept talking about poor Sergei. I said I was sorry for him, and I called him poor Sergei as well.'

Igor laughed. 'Arensky will find that intriguing. So young and yet such a woman of the world.'

'They asked me if he was alive,' I said. 'I said he was. Who is he?'

'Olga Nikolayevna's husband. He was very handsome and extremely rich. They moved in different circles. He had a number of male protégés. People talked but no one really knew anything. You were a great discovery for them this evening.'

'But you know it wasn't true! I said he was alive because I was afraid if I said he was dead, something would happen to Mama. Oh, Igor, how could you let me do it? You didn't contradict her at all. Did you and she arrange it?'

'You didn't contradict it either,' he said.

There was a sound outside the door. We stood still, waiting, listening to the footsteps coming up the stairs. We waited as they passed and stopped further down the corridor.

'The Frenchman.' Uncle Igor said, still holding my wrists. 'Tonight was a stroke of luck.' He went on. 'Olga speaks from her feelings. It's the way she is... spontaneous, a little mad, but don't you find it charming? I do. And useful. Everyone knows how she is. Come on, Nadia, don't be angry.'

I wrenched myself away from him. 'You never said I would have to lie about myself. Why do you want me to do that?'

He spoke as he went back to the window. 'I knew the Ladinskys would pass on the news. Which Nina Landinska would embellish. Whatever Arensky is involved with, they know about it, you can be sure. So, my darling "Katya," we move forward.'

'They wanted to know about us, who we were. How I knew Olga Nikolayevna so well. Arensky will find out,' I said.

'They will talk about it and find out, and then what? They will never believe anything I say again. And then what will happen to us?'

'They will believe you. They want to believe you.' He turned away and went to the row of dry prints. He took one down and examined it.

'And why *poor* Sergei?'

'He couldn't bear to leave the country. He had a young friend and he thought he could make an *accommodation*. He was wrong.'

Outside, the cesspool pumps had started down the street; steam rose from the pavement bringing a fetid stink into the room. Igor snapped the shutters closed, but the smell still lingered.

'You were quick-witted this evening,' he said.

I said bitterly. 'And now Arensky is going to explain Eurasianism and Russian politics to me. Because I am Olga Nikolayevna's "daughter" in Paris and a great friend of "poor Sergei." And they will keep talking about it.' Words weren't enough. I picked up one of our plates and smashed it on the floor.

We both stared at the smashed pieces in surprise and looked up at the same time.

'You are exactly like me, Nadia,' he said. 'I would have done the same.' He looked at the print he held. It was a photograph of a Russian boy scout troop in Meudon, cycling in formation. After a moment he ripped it viciously into a handful of scraps, which he scattered across the smashed crockery.

The action made me catch my breath. He brushed his hands together, kicked aside a bit of debris and spoke calmly. 'If he has plans you'll find out what they are and you'll tell me. It's so very simple.'

'Uncle Igor,' I said, 'it wasn't necessary to do that!' I wasn't sure if I meant the lie or the destruction. 'The Trust could go directly to Arensky and ask him if he has plans. He makes no secret of how much he hates everything Bolshevik. He would tell them everything.'

'It's not the way they do things,'Uncle Igor said. "Moscow" have to find out for themselves.' People here don't say openly what they do even if they say openly what they think. Words are a game. Whose side is he really on? Everyone is on one side or the other – nothing in the middle. There is no co-existence.'

He drew closer to me. 'If he does find out you have told a story, he will be so charmed by your sincerity and your innocence that it won't matter. But don't ever quarrel with my friends. They are my friends for a reason. You and I, we are one person,' he said. 'We have our oath, remember? So we must behave in the the same way.'

I could smell the harsh scent of tobacco mixed with faint sweat on his shirt. I was all at once acutely aware of the hollow at the base of his throat. He hesitated; for a moment I felt he was going to touch me, but then he seemed to change his mind.

'And I had to pretend I knew about her birds – birds!' I gave an hysterical little laugh. 'And there will be more lies because they will expect me to know more and more.'

'She has always kept birds,' he said, as if I should have known. 'Olya is a silly, charming woman,' he murmured. 'And except for those birds, she's alone. She's a perfect cover. She has no politics. With her, I have no politics. And besides, she's madly in love with me.'

'I don't want a cover,' The way he said it sounded as if he was offering a trap. 'Are you in love with her?' I asked.

'I don't know,' he said. 'I might be. I've been trying to decide ever since I met her.' He brushed the question aside and went on, 'Now Arensky will confide in you, you'll find out who he's working with, where, and how many people. You will get close to him. It shouldn't be difficult, after all you won't be the first. Only a young woman could get past his guard.'

I sank onto the mattress, curled over and covered my ears. *Let me disappear*, I prayed. *Let all this never have happened.* I heard him push his chair back and the floor creak under his feet.

'What are you crying about, Nadia? You see, I'm not lying to you. Everyone knows about him, even his wife will understand. There's nothing wrong with it. It's the company he likes. An adoring listener. No more.'

'What kind of man are you?' I cried.

'A fish,' he said, 'swimming through the shipwreck and so are you.' He sat beside me. 'The Trust wants us to help them fight for something. Do you want to have something to live for, or do you want to be like all the others, waiting here, where we're not wanted, getting by from day to day until you die? You are asked to do something for your country, Nadyusha, to be part of something your parents would be proud of – isn't that worth a silly little untruth? A typical young girl's pretence to start a conversation. Touching, really.'

When he said it like that, of course it was. I suppressed my doubts; I was making a fuss over a "silly little untruth." He bent down and peered into my face.

'Yes,' I said after a moment, and sniffed. I wiped my eyes with the back of my hand. 'But what you say I should do with Dmitri Arensky…'

'I say terrible things as they come into my head. I would never want you to do that. Forgive me please. Yes?'

I turned my head. He had to almost turn his face upside down to look at me. 'Please?'

I couldn't help it. I smiled.

He sat beside me. 'Your innocence is so beautiful, Nadia,' he said gently. 'I love your innocence. It's a precious thing. I want to keep it forever.'

Something in his voice made me tremble.

'No-one is innocent forever,' I said.

In reply, he raised my necklace with one finger. Then he let the necklace drop; the silence swelled around us as his lips pressed against mine. For the first time, I was alone without my powerful "Uncle Igor" as my protector, and I felt blind panic, such as I imagine an animal would have when instinct warns them of danger. His mouth pressed hard as his tongue forced my lips apart. I tried to scream but it came out as a strangled cry against his mouth. I pushed against him, he let go of me and I shouted, 'Don't! No!' I managed to push him away and screamed as loudly as I could, 'Stop it! Help!' and struck a wild blow at his face. It landed against his ear and he cried out in surprise.

There was a sharp knock on the wall. An irritated elderly voice said, '*S'il vous plaît!*'

Igor turned his back to me. 'Oh my God,' he whispered. 'What am I doing? God forgive me. I'm sorry. I'm so sorry.' He buried his face in his hands.

From a distance I could hear the whistle of the little Train d'Arpajon that brought its vegetables down the Boulevard St Michel punctually at two a.m.

'Nadezhda Mikhailovna,' he said, and the way he spoke was as if I was to blame, 'Maybe you should leave here. If you went away that would be the one good thing I could do for you.'

The floor seemed to open at my feet, as my secret fear suddenly became a reality. 'You're not a bad person,' I said. He still had his back to me. 'But if you're like this it would be better for me to leave.' The words I'd just spoken seemed to echo back to me. 'Where would I go? This is the only life I have.' I could see his shoulders tense. 'There is nothing else.'

'I know,' he said, then added, 'There is nothing else for me, either.'

'But you ruin it,' I said.

'I know!' he cried. 'I know that!' He turned back to the photographs. 'I can't help it. I destroy everything as soon as it's mine. And you are beautiful.'

'If Papa knew about this he would shoot you, and if Mama knew she would never allow you to come near me again. You might have thought this but you should never have done it. '

'You're too wise,' he said, his voice had a dead, hollow

sound. He echoed my words. 'I would never be allowed near you again if they knew. I should never have come near you at all. I have to tell you, I have always loved you so much. You have always been my only true family.' He got up and moved toward the string of prints.

'Then it's better for me to leave.' It was easier to say it now that he was not sitting next to me. *I have to go*, I thought, *go anywhere*. I burst out crying, but when he spoke his voice was flat and without emotion.

'Please believe me, I won't do it again.' He was looking at the photographs. 'In everything my desires become ruinous. Even this garbage. Nothing lets me forget my dreams. I want to tell you that now so you will understand better. I would never want to hurt you. It kills me when I do. Do you understand that?'

'No,' I said. 'I don't understand. I don't understand you at all.'

He spoke low and hard. 'When I look at you I see the photographs I have made with you and I want to – oh my God – I want to do terrible things. I can't control it.' He pulled one of the prints off the string; it made the other prints sway with alarming violence.

'Garbage,' he repeated. 'Nadia, this is hack work. Photographs for someone's file. Any fool could do it.' He spoke as if he addressed someone beyond me. 'Remember I showed you the work by Brassai, Atget, Steichen? Those people are artists, Nadia, because they say what they see. If I could speak the truth like that, to make people see ...' He pulled down a photograph of members of the Russian Student Christian Association, grouped around the Metropolitan Evoglu and again the other prints swayed. 'I can only see what I'm told to see.' He dropped the print and rubbed his fingers together as if to cleanse them. 'But this one, Nadia, look.' He carefully unpinned another. It was a study of a middle aged man sitting in his room wearing headphones, listening to the wireless with an expression of deep devotion. 'He's listening to a concert from Moscow,' said Igor. 'He invited me to join him. But he soon forgot I was there.'

We looked at it for a silent moment. The tiny room, the single chair, the upright posture and reverently bent head of the old man.

'I managed to make that one good,' said Igor, and no one will see it but a couple of émigrés and a file clerk in Moscow. This life is killing me, Nadia.' He began to pull photographs down at random. 'I can't go on like this – '

'No… no Igor, don't!' I seized the photographs. We struggled with them and I was afraid they would be crushed or torn, but I held on. Finally he let them go.

'Why did I agree to this?' he cried.

'Because they are your work for The Trust.' I quoted the words he had said to me. 'They want us to fight for an ideal. Do you want to be like all the others, getting by from day to day until you die? You are asked to sacrifice for your country.'

There was silence. He stood close to me and I could hear his breathing but I couldn't read his thoughts.

'Thank God for you.' His look burned into my face. 'Do you understand me a little now?'

He had become very thin; his eyes were deep-set and hollow, the skin drawn tightly over his cheekbones. His ragged nails made me want to take his hand and smooth them back to the elegance I remembered. But I would never touch him again.

'I am not a photograph,' I said

'To know that someone loves you, makes life possible. You do love me, don't you?'

'No,' I said.

'Yes. You do. You care. Tell me you care for me and we'll never speak of it again, I promise.'

I couldn't lie any more. 'Yes,' I admitted. 'I care for you. More than anything.'

'That's enough for me to know,' he said on a sigh. 'We must never say these things again.'

Outside it was just starting to get light. A small bell shrilled as a pair of policemen went by on their bicycles. One of them called out a question to someone passing by.

Dawn crept up as I lay in bed feeling strangely bitter and bereft. How could he have said that this was the end? Even I knew that if you admit you love, that is only the beginning. I had an image of the world full of people with feelings they didn't speak about. Millions of unspoken feelings making an invisible weight in the air. Unexpectedly, I felt caught in the memory of the little pulse at the base of Igor's throat. *What am I becoming*? I thought. Then I heard a soft, sound from the mattress which lay end to end with mine. I raised my head; Igor had wrapped his head in the blanket to muffle his sobs. I lay on my back and stared into the darkness. How can anyone leave a man who weeps? My eyes grew heavy and I fell asleep filled with doubt, and the knowledge that no matter what happened in my life, there would always be Igor... Igor... Igor...

CHAPTER TWENTY-THREE

OCTOBER 1923

'Alyosha says it's an extraordinary film,' I told the Arenskys as we walked down the Boulevard de la Republique. 'It's called. *Stachka.*'

Mitya said, 'The name is all you need to know. *Strike*? The film is blatant propaganda. Lenin himself commissioned it. This Eisenstein is young and Lenin knew he would do what he was told.'

I had met Mitya and Zhenia Arensky by chance on the Boulevard Jean Jaurès, and we strolled together to le Petit Vavin where I had begun to sit with them and play chess. The street had filled up with the day's business and it was crowded. I bumped into women with sacks and baskets who shook their heads at me impatiently as they scowled through the market, looking for bargains. Mitya greeted a couple of taxi drivers, formerly officers in his regiment. They greeted us, then checked their tyres, preparing to start work in the centre of Paris. A noisy group of people came round the corner, escorting a bewildered-looking man in a Russian shirt, carrying a battered suitcase, obviously a new arrival.

The café was on the Rue Traversière, where old men sat quietly on benches in front of the shoddy apartment blocks, waiting for time to pass. From behind a closed shop came the sound of a harmonica. Next door to the café, a shop sold fresh coffee. The bitter richness of the smell floated out of the door, giving the street a touch of leisure and well-being. The houses were mostly let as single rooms, and the small balconies were strung with washing and the occasional hopeful plant.

Inside, the room was already full of chess players and men reading the Russian newspaper and arguing loudly. I heard the familiar words: 'Perekop', 'Kolchak', 'Stolypin'.

Mitya dismissed Eisenstein and the film, and returned to the topic that constantly occupied him. 'I will write to Poincaré again,' he said. 'To recognise the Bolsheviks is to go to bed with a murderer. I explained this to him already. I gave him the facts.'

'Poincaré, Poincaré!' cried Zhenia, fitting a cigarette into the holder, 'He understands, but what can he do?' She offered me a cigarette. I saw she only had three left and shook my head, but she insisted, 'Take one, take one!'

'They don't listen.' Mitya went on. 'We are shabby émigrés. We have no rights, and the Communists sell them the new world – new freedom,' Mitya said bitterly. 'And they say "Oh, you émigrés, you don't want the workers' state – you don't love the workers."' He lit Zhenia's cigarette and then mine.

Zhenia returned to the film. 'Alyosha told you to see it? He is becoming a Communist sympathiser. He's a weak man, Nadia, and he is influenced by whoever has the loudest voice. If he wasn't so weak he would walk away from Larissa like that!' She snapped her fingers. 'She is a vampire. He lets her suck his blood.'

'She has made herself disliked by every émigré group,' Mitya agreed. 'And why? She's impossible.'

'I would feel sorry for Alyosha, but he does nothing about it. Poor man,' Zhenia added automatically.

Despite the overcast skies and the drizzle, the air had brightened. Some days, like today, brought sudden quick warmth, like a promise of the heat to come. I still wore the coat I had got from the Red Cross, a thick grey homespun. I had huddled in it gratefully all winter, and I realised with pleasure that it was starting to feel too heavy. Perhaps I might start to save enough to buy a new coat next winter. A woman walked past the window enveloped in a cape with a raccoon collar. Kyra had told me they were the highest fashion. They cost over a year's wages.

'Naturally this film will be more propaganda for the workers.' Zhenia tapped some ash into the saucer. 'And it will all be lies.'

'Strike? I remember that factory strike,' Mitya said. 'It was in 1913. Riots spread all over the city. The workers were egged on by anti-monarchist agents. Fortunately the police managed to put it down that time. But one could see how things were going to go. If the tsar had only understood.'

He turned to me and spoke firmly. 'If you go, don't sign anything.'

'I want to see the film,' I said. 'Everyone is talking about it, not just Alyosha.'

'At the entrance they will ask you to sign something, or to come to a meeting- don't do it.'

'It won't be better than "The Last Laugh," Mitya assured me. 'Murneau. He is the greatest genius.'

Zhenia said. 'No. D.W. Griffith. He is unsurpassable.'

They began to quarrel about films.

* * *

The cinema was in a basement of a building off the Boulevard Sebastopol. As I followed Alyosha down the narrow, uneven stone stairs, I was momentarily reminded of St. Petersburg and the Wandering Dog. There were notices stuck to the walls: protests, petitions, a talk at the Eurasians, a concert, lectures, and a visit by Mayakovsy who would give a reading to the workers at the Renault factory. There were stills from films I didn't recognise, and a photograph of Lenin at the Goskino no.1 Film Factory. At the bottom of the stairs, an unshaven young Frenchman in a shabby sweater, with a starved face and big red hands, put down his cigarette, narrowed his eyes and said, 'Membership?'

'I am a member,' said Alyosha. 'The young lady is my comrade.' He added to me, 'This is a film club. They don't sell tickets.'

The Frenchman pulled out a piece of paper, with a coffee cup stain across the top.

I turned my back on him. 'Alyosha,' I whispered, 'We can't do this. These people are French Communists.'

Alyosha whispered back, 'I know, but if you want to see the film you must join. It's the only place one can see it.'

The Frenchman said sullenly, 'Membership costs one franc as a donation for Russian Relief.' He pushed the grimy form towards me.

'You only need to sign a name.' Alyosha whispered. 'Any name.'

After a moment's hesitation, I signed 'Anna Karenina.' The young man gave me a membership card without comment.

'How is it you already have a membership?' I asked as Alyosha opened the heavy door to the cinema.

'They have wonderful films here,' he said. 'All the best work from Russia. It's the only place in Paris that shows them.'

'Did you sign your real name when you joined?'

'I had to. I knew the manager already,' he said. 'We were working backstage at the Opera House and he invited me. But I used a different patronymic. Andreitch. No one will know. If they notice they will think it's a distant relative perhaps.'

'Alyosha you are foolish.' *No wonder people talk about him*, I thought.

The cinema itself was small and dirty, and smelt of garlic and urine. As at the Wandering Dog in St Petersburg, the air was heavy with smoke. A few other people were waiting for the film to begin: an elderly Frenchman with a woman who was either his twin sister, I thought, or his wife; a young Frenchman who kept his beret on while he slumped in his seat and inhaled thoughtfully on his cigarette; a few serious middle aged women; and a young couple locked in an embrace. Among the scattering of Russians, I recognised some film people I had seen at Tanya's. I noticed Aleksander Vertinsky, looking as handsome as he did on the covers of his record albums; he was with a small, plump woman who alternately chattered at him and waved to acquaintances as soon as they appeared in the entrance. I recognised the great film actor, Mosjoukine and shamelessly stared at him. He was with two other men, all in dark coats and scarves. They leaned back casually, spoke to each other almost without moving their mouths and blew out clouds of cigarette smoke between remarks. There were one or two other familiar faces: a teacher from the Russian High School in Boulogne, a girl who had been several years ahead of me at school; she had been a noted beauty and now I heard she did facial massage. She was with her husband who worked at the Renault factory. Had they too used false names?

An extremely thin woman of about fifty with a bony face and cropped grey hair, took her place at a small upright piano. She struck a few chords and then played *Dybynushk*a, softly. As the lights went down, a pair of latecomers slipped in and tiptoed past us. It was Grisha Bobrov, with Larissa.

The pianist continued to play: she had moved on to *Ja vstretul vas.*

Grisha and Larissa sat down. She flung her arms around him and pressed her face into his shoulder. He flinched and she drew back, only to bury her face in her hands. The couple in front of them lit cigarettes. Larissa clasped Grisha's hands in hers and raised them to her breast as if helping him pray; two streams of smoke curled lazily upward. Alyosha lowered his head.

'Never mind,' I said, touching his arm.

'Mind?' he asked in a dull tone. 'I have no right to mind.'

The pianist played *Stenka Razin*, the lights went down, the screen flickered for a moment, and the film began.

The images appeared: workers, factory stacks, more workers. Image overlapping image. Informers posed in frames and sprang to life: they sent a chill through me. 'One-eye', 'The Fox', 'The Bulldog'. Men with animal names. The camera cut from the man to animal. Face after face filled the screen with anger, revenge and cruelty. In the cinema, the audience booed. Scenes overlapped. A man took out his pocket watch, and opened the back to reveal film, which he dipped into developing solution. I thought of Igor. "*The Wolf,*" I thought. In this film Igor would be called "The Wolf." But he wasn't in this film. It was nothing to do with him. Scenes unrolled before us in an endless montage. 'Eisenstein says montage is the nerve of cinema,' Alyosha whispered to me, but he wasn't watching the film.

I watched with horror and recognition. Crowds threw rocks, a man was smashed under a plank. Rain hit the pavements. Mounted police dispersed the crowds with hoses. The laughing face of a commissar. A shot of hands, hands and more hands.

Under cover of the noise, Grisha got up and hurried out. Larissa followed him, arms outstretched, weeping.

The informer recovered his soul. His eyes blazed as he said, 'Back to my cell,' and tipped a bottle of ink over the manager's desk. The audience cheered, A woman shouted, 'Workers unite!'

The pianist played loud minor chords. There was a long, slow shot of the dead lying in a field: men, women, and the tiny corpse of a child.

The final legend filled the screen in huge letters: REMEMBER, PROLETARIANS!

There was applause and a few boos. The lights came up. I was surprised to find myself still in Paris. Alyosha had his arm around my shoulders; it was the first time he had done that and I hadn't noticed.

Outside we lingered awkwardly. I wondered if I should make any reference to Larissa. Instead I tried to distract him by talking about the film. 'You were right,' I said, 'the montage was extraordinary. Did you say Eisenstein called it "the nerve of cinema?"

'Oh, Nadia, you don't know what you're talking about.'

I had never heard Alyosha speak in that tone.

'I mean it,' he went on. 'It's not just another film; it's a portrait of the savagery, the energy of the Russian people. The energy,' he repeated.

'Violence,' I said. 'I have never seen such a violent film.'

'That's right. Violence … passion!' He stabbed the air with his hand. 'God, where is it?' He looked at me and seemed to become calmer. 'In a hundred years no one will care what Larissa did or didn't do; we will be forgotten. They will only care about her poems.' But he sounded for the first time uncertain. He returned to the film. 'They were right, but they were strong because they were united. No one has power alone. United, the workers can defeat the greatest power. The film showed that.'

'They wanted courtesy and an eight hour day,' I said. 'Like here. They went on strike for that here as well. Remember that? But in Russia, when they didn't get it, they went mad.'

'But it was a wonderful film,' he insisted. 'They rose up against oppression. And they didn't give up! The tsar sent the army against them and still they were willing to die. For freedom! That's something one can die for.'

'Yes,' I said with a sigh, 'it was wonderful. But my Papa once said "The Russians are a great and noble people, on both sides. And on both sides they are stupid and violent and lazy. They will inform on each other and torture each other until everything is covered with blood." As I recalled his words, I could almost hear his voice, speaking from a distant past. 'The film was like that. He was right.'

'The film was what really happened. And they finally won. Soviet art will rule the world,' Alyosha said. 'What are we making? There's no unity here. Who said it? We are human dust.'

We had been walking down the Boulevard Montparnasse. We passed the YMCA correspondence school. 'You know that the YMCA gets its textbooks from the Soviet Union,' he said.

'They want us to return,' I said. 'But the French want us to assimilate. Become French.'

'We could live here for a hundred years and still we would never be French. He took my arm. There was a gallantry in his manner that charmed me and made me feel young and delicate.

He spoke again, out of his own thoughts. 'Grisha Bobrov has been offered a place in the People's University to study commerce at night. He doesn't want to be her poet anymore.'

'What made her think Grisha was a poet in the first place? Grisha was never interested in poetry.'

'He looked like a poet,' Alyosha answered in a lighter tone, as if mimicking Larissa. He dropped his voice. 'That's all she needs. In Russia, his family lived on the same street as Blok. So she found the poet within him. She says he has betrayed her. That to give up poetry is a betrayal. She overwhelmed him. I can understand him. She is like a wind that pounds and pounds at you. It exalts you at first, but then it is a tornado that will tear you in pieces,' adding softly, 'it's too strong.'

'Nadya! Alyosha! Come!' Kyra stood in front of La Coupole, beckoning to us. She looked radiant, wearing a rust coloured dress with black satin cuffs and black, white and rust embroidery. 'You must meet my genius!' She noticed my admiring look at her dress. 'Isn't it lovely? It's a sample. It's going to be the latest thing next season. Mama has got an important order from Paul Poiret.' She interrupted herself with the cry, 'Here he is!'

La Coupole was crowded. A wave of voices in several languages rose with the smoke.

Kyra's genius was heavyset, like a boxer, red-haired and painfully neat, with an old fashioned high collar and a jacket with frayed cuffs and a split under the arm.

He said without preamble, 'What do you think? If Christ came here today? What would He do?'

'What He liked,' said Kyra. 'He would be anonymous, and He would walk around Paris weeping at what He saw and no one would notice.'

'Oh, no!' I exclaimed, 'It would all happen exactly as before, and all the time people would say "This time we will know he is the Lord." But still it would turn out just like before.'

'Kyra never told me you were a cynic,' the genius said. 'But I think you are.'

'Where would He live?' Kyra speculated. 'In the 16th I suppose. Or do you think maybe He would prefer Meudon?'

I said, 'He would live in a single room in Belleville with St. Peter and St. John and St. Mathew. And there would be trouble with the landlady over bedbugs.'

Alyosha spoke, his voice unusually harsh, 'If Christ returned, He would start a club: The All-Russian Union of Former Believers in Christianity. He would never get a word in, because the Russians would all be arguing.' He sounded bitter.

'Yes,' with the Union of Old Believers Presently in Paris,' added Kyra. 'And the Union of Soviet Christians.'

'No!' cried the genius. He stood up and raised his arms in a gesture of blessing. He intoned, like a liturgical chant: 'Christ would be here at La Coupole. He would look around, throw up His hands, He would drink cognac and smoke cocaine. And dance to *Rhapsody in Blue*.'

The tsarist general at the table behind, who still wore his decorations, got up and ostentatiously walked out, followed by his wife. 'Outrageous,' she said as she stalked past.

'Madam, you are outrageous!' the genius called after them.

Kyra stroked his face. 'He feels very bad today.' She explained to us. 'He sees more deeply and so he sees more terrible things.'

'Oh God, why is life so complicated?' the genius asked. 'No one understands abstract thought. Without abstraction life is without soul. Abstraction is the truth.'

'We need our high-minded abstractions,' said Alyosha. 'Because our lives are pointless.'

When we left, Alyosha said, 'Kyra is very good at meeting geniuses. This is the third one. In my whole life I have met only one genius.'

I decided I had to be firm. 'Alyosha,' I said, 'Dmitri Arensky once said you should put your foot down. No really. I've heard other people say it. She does what she likes, the other émigrés dislike her and don't accept her.'

'It's not her, Nadia,' he said. 'It's not Larissa I love, it's her work. Her work is my ideal. She is part of the culture we are here to preserve. It seemed once as if that was an ideal to believe in. But it's hard to keep faith like this. And it's not enough.'

He paused and said, 'Will you walk with me for a bit?'

We walked slowly down the Boulevard Montparnasse, in the direction of l'Observatoire. As usual we passed other Russians, singly and in small groups, walking the evening away.

'Nadia, think of it,' Alyosha said. 'All over Europe there are Russians walking around strange cities where we can never be at home, walking and walking, sitting on benches by foreign canals, planning The Return. And if France recognises the Soviet government, there will be no return for us.'

'They won't,' I began. 'Dmitri Arensky says – '

He interrupted, 'We have no papers, no representation, no country. One million people with no country. It's tragic don't you think?'

'It's tragic when you say it like that,' I said, But I can't remember when everything wasn't tragic, so it doesn't seem tragic to me. I want things to be better, that's all.'

He took my arm again. 'Dear girl. There were such terrible things done then – inexcusable things. The workers went wild after the revolution, but it isn't like that now. The state is in control. They make certain everyone is treated fairly.'

'That's not what I hear at Tanya's,' I countered. 'People say their families tell them to write postcards, not letters, because anyone who gets a letter from abroad is suspect. They are reported immediately.'

'It's because there are so many wreckers,' Alyosha assured me. 'Internal émigrés, who want to destroy the ideal. When the Soviet state is fully constructed Lenin says there will be no need for a police force, because everyone will be in harmony, there will be no need for laws to break. "One symphonic mind."

I thought of the man who had come for Mama, Mama who had done nothing, had broken no laws.

Alyosha looked at me. 'It's a golden idea. And logical. The freest country in the world. That's what he said.' And he repeated: 'One symphonic mind.'

We walked on down the Rue d'Alésia, where the shop-fronts were shuttered for the night, and lights showed dimly behind drawn curtains. Through one window, whose curtains were open, could be seen a family sitting round a small table. Through another, I could see a young girl copying something from a book in front of her.

A few people walked slowly, aimlessly along the streets. Alyosha knew most of them and greeted them with a nod that told me this was one of his habitual routes. We continued to walk.

'Well,' he said finally, 'I have bared my soul, as usual, before you. You are not really a soul-barer are you? What is in your soul?'

'Oh, it feels as if my soul is so full of little things,' I said. I wanted to tell him about my sadness and doubt, but I didn't have the right words.

'Not little things – the tender roots of things,' he said gently. 'And where will your life grow from these roots?'

No one had asked me this question, not even Uncle Igor.

'I don't know where my life is,' I said, and my voice quavered with uncertainty.

'What were you going to do?' he asked.

'Before the revolution? I was a child,' I said. 'I wanted to learn everything there was in the world, everything, and then do something great and important.'

He laughed, 'I wanted to do that too.'

'And I wanted to write poetry.'

'I should have guessed. We are so much alike,' he said

"Burning Rat," I said. 'That's as far as I got.' I laughed to cover my shyness about it. 'I started to write a poem called "Burning Rat."

"Burning Rat?" What was it about? Can you remember it?'

I said, 'Oh, it wasn't about anything, and I do remember it. You just heard it.'

He looked puzzled and then laughed. 'You remind me of my own youth.' Still smiling, he said, 'And did you not try to write any more poetry?'

'I think I forgot about it. There was the war and the revolution and Papa...' I stopped.

Alyosha reached for my hand, but something made him pull back. I was grateful to him for that.

'Poor Nadia,' said Alyosha. 'You have suffered a great deal.'

'There is no use talking about it,' I said. 'Uncle Igor was there just after Mama was arrested. He managed to get to us, but they came for her first. He saved my life.' I tried to imagine how I would have got on, alone in St Petersburg. 'There is nothing to say about it. If we keep thinking, we will die of it. And I won't die of it. They will not make me die of it. Uncle Igor and I will keep each other alive. We swore to do that.'

'I envy you that,' he said.

'I still want to do something good,' I said. 'Not great and important maybe, but good.' I thought for a moment and tried to find the words. Could I tell him that I wanted to be happy?

He suddenly pointed. 'Look at that.'

At the bottom of the stone steps beyond our bench, a man lay across the dirty pavement. His legs were splayed open. His face was shadowed by ingrained grime and his dark shirt was missing the buttons. His hands, also filthy, lay across his body, the fingers curled around some phantom object.

Even at this distance I thought I could smell him. 'Is he dead?' I asked.

'Not yet.' Alyosha said. 'France. In this wonderful free country, he is free to be abandoned. Oh yes, everyone is so free! Free to sleep under bridges, to starve, to beg in the street. Decadence. The West is finished.'

I was confused. 'Should we do something?'

'What can we do? Every day we are here, we betray our country. For a Russian it is impossible to belong anywhere but Russia. Nothing we do here can change the world enough.'

'Homelessness is a country,' I quoted, almost without thinking. 'It's a place to live, so it's a kind of home.'

'Yes! You are right,' he said. 'We have discovered a new country called Loss. But still we look back at Russia. How can we help it?' he said. 'We will never be ourselves here. Not what we might have been.'

'But Alyosha, we will be something. We are changing, the world is changing. If we are here, we must be able to make something here.'

'The Bolsheviks have made a new world, and what are we? Shabby people in cheap cafes, protesting our superiority to a world that doesn't want to hear.' He cupped his hands around his mouth. 'Shouting up from a hole in history.' He lowered his head and looked into my eyes. 'Human dust. The Soviets are creating a paradise and we are putting on another cultural evening,with more songs, speakers, poetry, tears, more toska, dysha.'

Someone in the upper floor of a nearby house was playing the piano. A Chopin prelude fell softly into the night air, as we stood still and listened, hand in hand.

It finished and the pianist began again. Alyosha bent down and kissed me, very gently. He said, 'In a different life I would ask you to come back with me.'

I'll always remember that he said this, I thought. 'I'm glad you told me,' I said.

'It is one of the good things about Paris, being your friend.'
'And for me.' I answered.

CHAPTER TWENTY-FOUR

JANUARY, 1924

Mitya Arensky slowly moved his knight two squares down and one square to the left.

'Guard your queen,' he said.

'My queen!' I exclaimed. 'I didn't see it – oh!' I felt as if he'd fired a pistol at me. 'Look,' I touched the queen. 'I'm bleeding.'

He smiled. 'You are such a romantic.' I knew he saw me as a romantic now, as well as an idealist. And this evening he had said, 'You are loyal. It is a great quality, but your loyalty must not become romantic.'

'It won't,' I assured him.

'Ah, you are also young, so you don't see it. That is for others to see.'

'Mitya,' I said, 'I can see that you are a bit of a romantic as well.'

'She has found me out!' he said. 'You're right. Like you. We share many things, I think.'

'I hope so,' I said. 'Like loyalty.'

He gave me one of his sharp, appraising looks. 'Like loyalty.'

Thanks to him, I had acquired a passion for chess. It was during his instructions in the intricacies of the game that I began to call him 'Mitya.' Mitya loved all games, bridge, horse racing, backgammon, even *svaika*, but chess was his obsession. Papa had begun to teach me the year before the revolution, explaining the basic moves as if the pieces were children, but Mitya played chess as savagely, with as much cunning, as if it were a real war, and now I played that way as well. Romantic or not, I believed that I had been given a country and its people to protect. I would have to lose a bishop. I groaned and moved the piece. Like a gull diving for a fish, he plucked it up and put it with the crowd of black pieces he had already collected. The last few moves could only be a formality.

'You concede?' he asked.

'You know I won't,' I said.

'Good for you, Nadia, take him by surprise.' Zhenia had been watching the game and listening to the gossip at surrounding tables at the same time. She knew nothing about chess. She removed the tiny stub of her cigarette from the holder and put it out in the ashtray, careful not to get the crumbs of hot ash on her fingers.

'You take her side again, because you want to quarrel with me, but you are too late and anyway you don't know what you're talking about,' Mitya said.

Unperturbed, she said, 'Do you know, I just heard that Tanya read the cards this morning and saw that the Bolsheviks will be out by the summer. That's only three more months.'

He paused. 'The summer? It's possible,' he added, looking at me, 'If certain things fall into place.' He held my attention, in a way he had, as if somehow evaluating me. I thought: we are playing another kind of chess.

'In any case,' he said, 'How can they stay long, when you need fifty million roubles to feed one person bread and a potato, but workers receive only two-and-a-half million roubles?'

'Terrible,' Zhenia sighed. 'I told Lady Deterding today that I will take on some extra sewing for her, and then we will try to send another Red Cross parcel to Yuri.'

'Good,' he said. He turned back to me. 'I dreamt about my brother, Yuri last night, him and Sophia and the baby. They were alive, but very far away.' He took my knight with a rook, and my king was trapped. 'Yes,' he went on to Zhenia, carefully gathering up the pieces one by one. 'They were going further and further away; I wanted to call out, to run to them, but I couldn't move.'

'I have that dream sometimes,' I said. 'About Mama. She's on the other side of a frozen lake.'

'Always it's winter,' he said. I nodded and stroked his hand that was closed around the pawns.

'Well played,' Mitya said gallantly. 'No, really. You are improving. You need to play more often and you will see.'

The tables here at the Café Murat were set apart to allow for the grouping of left, right and centre, where each group could criticise the other without being overheard. Aside from chess, this was a place for politics, and I waited to hear the word that would let me tell Igor that there was indeed an "Arensky group" of counter-revolutionary recruits who would join with us. An international force made my heart beat faster, as if we were on a giant chessboard with real people. *Now*, I thought, *all the white players will meet.* At last I could see all the pieces of this dangerous game, from The Trust within the Kremlin itself down through Pavel, Lewitsky, Uncle Igor, Gyorgy and me. And surely Arensky as well. All of us quietly working to overturn the world yet again.

The Ladinskys joined us bringing with them a large, full-faced man with a small moustache, one of the many ex-officers who came to this café to see General Arensky. When the man said he had served with Kolchak, Mitya cried, 'A great man! One day he will be among the saints!' Vodka was served. We raised our glasses: 'To Kolchak!'

'To Kolchak,' I cried.

'To the tsar.' We all raised our glasses again.

'God rest his soul,' murmured Zhenia, fitting a fresh cigarette in the holder and extending it to the officer, who gallantly half-rose to light it.

'People are still loyal,' he said.

Mitya said, 'We know the Bolsheviks only control Moscow and Petersburg, isn't that so Volodya?'

Yes it's true,' Ladinsky agreed. 'Outside the cities people are starving, people are angry. Naturally the Bolsheviks have betrayed them and they would fight them if they could.'

The officer looked from one man to the other, and I knew that he would join them the next night in the back room at Tanya's. He glanced at me. There was a pause; then Mitya nodded, and I knew that now he trusted me. I would soon be able to tell him everything, maybe even tonight, and he would understand.

'Outside the cities, the people loathe Communism. They're only stopped from overthrowing it by force and their own weakness,' said the officer. 'But Lenin is in frail health…'

'In fact I hear that that isn't Lenin at all,' Nina Ladinska announced. 'Lenin died a long time ago, and they can't let anyone know, so they have an actor who looks exactly like him.'

'We all know that,' said Zhenia. 'You see how he always appears wrapped up – like this,' she mimed a blanket. 'But the French and the English don't want to admit the truth.'

'The left wing and the "great experiment,"' Ladinsky said grimly.

'Oh yes,' said Mitya. 'God, how they want to believe in this workers' paradise.' He spat the words. 'Communism will destroy the West.'

An argument broke out with people from other tables. Underneath the voices, I distinctly heard the officer say, in a low voice, 'Stassov is ready.'

Arensky glanced at me. 'Good,' he said to the officer. 'How much?'

'One million francs.'

'Impossible.'

'Impossible for less.'

He pushed his chair back. 'I have heard enough for one evening – why are we sitting here? Zhenia – I must have air! At once!'

Zhenia and I both hurried to get ready. Despite his eagerness to leave, Mitya formally held out Zhenia's balding fur coat and bowed as he helped her into it.

Ladinsky said, 'We will be at the café St Michel shortly, if you are passing.'

It was very late now, but along the Rue Traversière and the Place St. Michel, the little cafes were still full of music, shouting and steam. An impromptu group of men played popular songs which competed with the romantic ballads sung in a cracked, husky voice by an old woman who knitted shawls for a living and used to sing in the best nightclubs in Moscow. In another café a young man read poetry, and at the café next door, the inevitable argument had broken out. We lingered just inside the door while Mitya tried to follow it.

Unlike Tanya's, which was starting to attract European customers, these cafés had crumpled paper tablecloths, dirty napkins, and bent, dull cutlery. They served black bread, herring and pickled cucumbers in thick, cracked china dishes accompanied by ill-assorted glasses of cheap vodka.

People sat three-deep at the tables, standing up to make themselves heard. The Ladinskys shared a table with several men in worn army jackets, and their weary-looking wives. To my surprise, Grisha Bobrov was here as well, at a table with Boris Poplavsky (still in the dark glasses he had worn at the Eurasian meeting) and a severe-looking girl, who clung to Poplavsky's arm.

A pleasant, dark-haired young man kindly gave his chair to Zhenia.

'He is the son in fact of Professor Koliansky, and a friend of Princess Tatiana,' Zhenia whispered. She made room for me on the edge of the chair, but I remained standing beside Mitya.

A large man boomed: 'We, here in this room, are Russia out of Russia. That is the meaning of our life. We have been chosen by God to hold the light of Russia and keep it alive.'

'Bravo,' said Mitya. Zhenia rose to her feet to applaud with the rest.

Grisha stood and shouted, 'Mayakovsky says that the new Russia will shine a light on the world.'

Mitya pushed forward.

'Mayakovsky is a thug, a Soviet thug. Forget Mayakovsky. Read Dracula. That is our true story! They are Dracula and you should have a stake to put through their hearts.'

Grisha looked confused. He caught my eye, and stammered, 'But when Bely talks about throwing pineapples...'

'Hoodlums, all of them,' Mitya continued. 'The filth...'

Grisha looked as if he had more to say, but seeing that he was drowned out, sat down and began an intense conversation with Poplavsky and the woman.

'Breshkovskaya had the right idea, but who listened?' said one of the former officers.

'Nikolai Nikolaevitch says she was a traitor,' said the professor's son, 'And as he is the claimant to the Russian throne we must not argue.'

'He cannot claim the throne while the Royal Family are still alive.'

'They are alive and in hiding, I know it for a fact.'

'Breshkovskaya was a traitor, certainly,' said Ladinsky.

'And a stupid woman,' said Zhenia. She twisted around to see me. 'I remember her as a girl; always some bee in her bonnet, but she had a good heart.'

More vodka was drunk. Pelmeni and onion soup arrived.

'A Franco-Russian meal,' said Nina Ladinska. 'International.'

A very old man stood and, pulling a small book out of his pocket began to read his poetry, written long before the revolution; many people, including Zhenia, the Ladinskys, Poplavsky and his friend, murmured the well-loved words under their breath. When he dropped the book, Ladinsky picked it up and found his place for him, but the audience continued speaking the words without pause.

A woman at a nearby table interrupted suddenly in a loud, harsh voice.

'There was a dish that they used to serve on my dear sister's name day – it was made with rabbit and cream and juniper berries. It was simple but so delicious I cannot begin to describe it.'

'I have never killed a rabbit,' said a skeletally thin woman with a gap between her teeth, 'But I would certainly shoot Lenin on sight. On sight! I hope for his sake he never comes my way.'

The old man continued to recite a poem about love among the elegant courts and ballrooms of imperial Russia.

'Lenin?' asked Mitya. 'I would shoot Kerensky first – the betrayer.'

Loud voices disagreed with him:

'Not Kerensky... Lenin must go first.'

'No,' Arensky insisted. 'If you put Kerensky here,' he indicated and placed a glass of vodka, and Lenin there,' placing another glass of vodka, 'Kerensky would go first, no question.' He downed the glass. 'As they say in American films, he sold us down the river, he let the chariots roll over him and then said thank you.'

'In Berlin there is terrible unemployment. People are leaving,' said a man.

The very thin woman announced, 'I hear Bely has gone back.'

A cacophony of voices rose:

'Gorky went back.'

'Yes, Gorky. He cries all the time, I hear.'

'Too late. I could have told him.'

'Bely went to visit my Aunt just before he left Berlin,' said the thin woman. 'And he said he could not bear to live without Russia, not at any price.'

Nina Ladinska began to cry. 'He is a brave man. They will destroy him, and he knows it.'

'Chekhov?' A new arrival raised his voice. 'I'll tell you about Chekhov. I said to him "Anton Pavlovich, you need a metaphor for all this: a family estate? Or why not an orchard?" "That's it," he said, and he was so grateful to me. We discussed it and discussed it. I wrote The Cherry Orchard; line by line, I wrote it.'

'He was a terrible drinker when he was young. He drank and sat in taverns all night. But he knew how to attract women.'

'All the stagehands at the Moscow Art Theatre are Bolshevik spies.'

'Read Dracula!' Arensky shouted again. 'It explains everything. It's a true story of our time. Russia has sold her soul to the devil, and the nations of the world look on and nod. It is a horror.'

They began the litany of remorse and regret:

'If only we had educated the people...'

'If we had educated them, but without the land...'

'No, we should have given them the land.'

'We should have promised them the land if they were educated.'

'If only we had not spent so much time in discussion...'

'We never took action!'

'We took the wrong action.'

A stocky young man in a jacket without a shirt jumped on a table and cried,

'I love you all! I want you all to know how much I love you!'

'My darlings!' Olga Nikolayevna had arrived; she stood in the doorway and held out her arms to us, her face alight with hectic gaiety. 'Did you read *The Latest News* today? Don Aminado's poem? He says the Russians have taken over Paris – that everything in Paris is now Russian – no French are to be seen! It's too witty! They have begged me to recite it later!' She embraced me. 'Nadia, *golybushka*, how are you?' She embraced me again, and asked me quietly 'Where's Igor? Has he said anything about me? Is he ill?' Her gaiety gave way to anxiety, and her tone of voice to pleading.

'No, what made you think so?' I asked brightly. 'He is meeting Osorgin at the Home for the Aged at St. Genvième du Bois, to discuss photographs of the residents.

'Oh,' she cried softly, 'But I was expecting him here – he promised...' Once more she threw on her smile like a stole. 'Oh, that is exciting! But be sure to tell him my friend is here from Russia and wants to talk to him about a film.'

The Arenskys had discreetly withdrawn.

'I must go,' I said to Olga without answering her question.

It wasn't raining now, but the weather had settled into an indecisive mist. The damp crept around us like an insistent whisper.

Zhenia shivered and drew her coat closer around herself.

'It is so cold!' she said. 'One is always shivering in this city. In Russia we survive the cold easily.'

'France has a different kind of cold,' Mitya said. Zhenia shivered again.

'This was the most expensive coat one could buy before the Revolution. Without this coat I would have died in Constantinople,' she told me. 'It's true, it always pays to buy the best.'

'In Russia people are eating dirt,' Mitya said. 'They drown hungry children in the river.' We walked in silence, leaving the café noises behind us. His spirits had fallen abruptly. 'Another night full of spineless, miserable people, quarrelling.' He muttered, 'If they had only united against the Bolsheviks they could have driven stakes through their miserable hearts.'

'And you too, Mitya,' said his wife.

'Of course I include myself – you think I don't? What a vale of tears life is.'

But the message was *Stassov is ready*, I thought. It could only mean one thing. Now I will ask him and when he tells me about the "Arensky group,"I can tell him about Lewitsky and the Trust.

'Life is not only a vale of tears, Dmitri Sergeyevitch,' I took his arm. 'You are a man of battle, you have fought your way out of tears before.' His face was a blank. Had I made a mistake?

Zhenia interrupted, 'Dear Olga,' she said. 'The last time I saw her with your Uncle Igor, I thought what a handsome couple they were. Don't you agree, Mitya?'

He agreed. 'They are made for each other really.' He and his wife smiled at each other. Zhenia had planted herself on the pavement.

'But there always seem to be such problems.'

'She is married after all,' I reminded her.

'Oh, Sergei,' she shrugged him off. 'You know all about Sergei.'

Once again I had nearly given myself away. What was it I should know about Sergei? I had asked Igor, but he said, 'It doesn't matter. Don't mention it.'

'Yes,' I said, trying to sound as if it was a familiar story, 'But still...'

'Anyway, where is he? No one knows.'

'Yes,' I said again, happy to get back on a sure footing. 'Uncle Igor is a complicated man. People don't really understand him.' *Now*, I thought. 'But he would have so much to tell you if he thought...'

'She seemed so relieved to see you. Have she and Igor quarrelled again?' It seemed again as if Arensky hadn't heard me. 'Why does this happen?'

Why was he interested in Olga and Igor? I would have to wait.

'I don't know,' I said. 'But Mitya, there are more important things...'

Zhenia said, 'She is beautiful, she is intelligent, she would do anything for him. Tell me, Nadia, is there another woman perhaps?'

'No. Uncle Igor isn't like that. He has other interests. If you would meet with him...'

Now Arensky took my arm. 'Everyone is full of secrets, everyone has dreams. Especially Russians. And artists. And your uncle is both. Zhenia and I spoke about him with Zadkine at the Maison des Artistes. He finds him most original, doesn't he Zhenia?'

Zhenia put in enthusiastically, 'Oh, he says the ideas are most original and wonderfully strange. But he won't show them to anyone. Zadkine met him by chance at Maria Vassilievna's Canteen and they spoke for a while, but then he rushed away. Now Zadkine says he won't speak to him.'

'Uncle Igor doesn't like to talk about his work,' I said.

Perhaps, I thought, he suspects and wants to know more about Igor before we speak. As I began to talk about "Uncle Igor", the words tumbled out of me, about his fluency in French, about his charm, his knowledge of film, of poetry, of sport, how he had begun boxing with Georges Braque who had introduced him to Brassai, how he had new ideas about using light.

I realised I had been babbling and added, 'But most of all, he longs for Russia. Like everyone else. It is his only true passion.'

'But he is not like other émigrés,' Arensky said. 'He is well paid for his work?'

'No,' I told him. 'The Maison des Artistes doesn't pay him anything at all. He has only had one or two pictures there.' I was surprised that Mitya had noticed them.

'So how does he manage?' There was an edge to Mitya's voice. 'He must have an income from somewhere. You are surely not both living on your wages alone.'

'No, not at all,' I stammered. 'He is paid for portraits, and what news photographs he can sell to French magazines, that sort of thing. Between us we just manage.' This was the wrong time to let Mitya know that Igor was paid by "Moscow" for information.

'Like the rest of us. Scraping by.' Again Mitya fell into a heavy silence. At the Pont d'Issy, we leant on the parapet, staring at the Seine. The lights from the other bank danced briefly across the water like tiny jewels, each one dazzling for a moment before it was replaced by the next.

'Mitya,' I began, 'There is someone who wants to ask you a question.' I had put it awkwardly, and he frowned at me.

'Someone asks a question and three people give three answers and then we spend another night where we sit and eat onion soup and see the same terrible people,' he said. 'Again and yet again the same.' I started to speak but Zhenia signalled me sharply to be quiet. He wasn't going to listen to me. I felt as

191

if I was facing a locked door. This was not the Uncle Mitya I had come to know. This was a different sort of man. His vigour and command had drained away. He seemed to have aged and shrunk into himself.

'Dmitri Sergeyevitch,' I asked. 'Are you ill?'

He glanced at me, then stared back down into the depths of the Seine.

'I am never ill. I have never had a day's illness, thank God.' He shook his head. 'I cannot bear this life. I am too old. I have no strength.'

'You are not too old, you of all people,' I told him, and it was true, until tonight he had seemed to be ageless with wisdom and yet at the same time my contemporary. 'You will never be old.'

'She's right,' Zhenia said. 'You see, she knows who you are. If you become old we will all be long dead.'

'Please, Mitya, listen to me. I must ask you...' I desperately wanted to tell him about The Trust. But I had been instructed to discover his plans before telling him anything.

Again he interrupted. 'I cannot live here, I must not live there. I am facing nothing but the void.' He seemed to speak and listen to himself speak at the same time. He turned away from the water. 'I am so tired,' he said. 'I am old and tired. You are very good to spend time with me.'

I slipped my hand into his, and felt how strong it still was, under the soft flesh. Zhenia said, 'He is so fond of you. It's like the old days for him, to have young people to talk to; he said it the other night, the exact words. He said, being with Nadia is like the old days.'

There were a few people still wandering on the Boulevard de la République, near Pyshman's grocery store, or looking in the windows of the Librairie Russe.

'I despair of mankind, Nadia, can you understand that? I despair.' He gripped my hand. 'You know the French government will eventually recognise the Bolsheviks, and trade with them. They will raise millions for the Russian peasants, and for us – what? Nothing – we are worse than animals, the soul of Russia is dead.

'You mustn't despair,' I said. 'Believe me, you are not alone.' I could say no more. Would this allow him to reveal his information? I waited. 'Many people are with you.' I added.

'There are people everywhere who want to control, to infiltrate, to spread propaganda, and they are persuasive, believe me. You are young and you must be careful.'

The Arenskys had recently moved again, this time to a hotel on a small street behind the Immaculate Conception convent on the Rue de Dôme. The hotel was a small, narrow building, streaked and darkened with age, so much like our new hotel that it could have been the same place. A few yards away small fires burned where some gypsies had made a camp. There was one light on in a top floor window, and I could see a boy of perhaps twelve or thirteen staring out, huddled in a blanket.

'Poor child,' Zhenia remarked. 'He has TB. This climate will kill him. And he is a clever boy.' Mitya leant against me heavily, as if he had trouble holding himself upright.

'Come,' he said. 'Don't leave me now. Come and sit with us for a few minutes.'

'Yes, do come up,' said Zhenia. 'He used to have so many people all the time. It's lonely for him.'

'How can I be lonely?' he said sharply. 'I do nothing but sit in cafés all day talking.' Zhenia pressed the bell. 'Yes,' he said softly. 'It is lonely.'

We heard sounds within and the concierge shuffled to open the door, muttering to herself, while her fat dog growled around our feet.

'Leave the light off,' Mitya said as he unlocked the door. 'The curtains are open anyway. There is enough light to see.'

The window faced the convent garden across the street and there was indeed enough light to make the room visible. Mitya leant against the wall and looked out of the window in a way that reminded me of Uncle Igor.

'There is someone by the gate over there, watching this building. As usual.' He sat down in a large armchair and closed his eyes. After a moment he said in a weary voice, 'Now Nadia, what do you want?'

Zhenia stepped in front of the door, and the cold of the room shot through me as I realised they had planned this. But in spite of the chill, I had a sense of relief that we would all finally be able to speak freely.

He opened his eyes. 'I too have my informers. I know you have been watching me, and you report my actions to this Uncle Igor of yours.' There was a silence. He looked out the window. 'Is the man outside one of your people?'

'No,' I said, although I was no longer sure of anything.

Zhenia began to draw the curtain. He pulled it from her hand.

'Leave it alone! He is watching for a sign that there is someone in here. I've told you before.'

'He mustn't see Nadia.' Her voice was sharp. 'So far he's too busy warming his hands. I'm watching him.' She shut the curtains.

After a moment, Mitya said, 'All right,' and she switched on a small lamp. The pool of light seemed to warm the room and give significance to everything in it.

The room was the same size as ours, but more fully furnished, indeed crammed with chairs, including the armchair, a round table covered by an embroidered cloth, and a small, dark green sofa which looked to me very elegant; a sleeping alcove was screened off by a curtain. There were photographs on the wall of the tsar and his family, of Zhenia and her family on their estate in Usman, portraits of Kolchak, of Mitya in full dress uniform at Kolchak's requiem, of regiments of soldiers, young and smiling. There was a large icon over the door and a small work table in front of the window, with Zhenia's paints and a large stack of greeting cards to be filled in. Clothes, bedding, shawls, kitchen utensils, cushions, all spilled in a colourful jumble out of the half-closed suitcases, which were stacked in a corner next to a couple of packing cases supporting piles of books and periodicals as well as a bible and a samovar.

Zhenia said, 'We should unpack, but there's no point when we will be going back so soon.'

The carpet bore a faded pattern of birds of paradise, the tips of their wings worn to invisibility. Mitya said in an even tone,

'I know you and Igor Fyedorovitch are part of an organisation called The Trust. Tell me about The Trust.'

I said, 'Do you have plans? Is there an Arensky Group?'

We stared at each other. His look was steely and I saw clearly how it would be to face him in battle.

The silence continued.

'Is there an Arensky Group?' I finally repeated, trying to keep my voice steady. 'Are there many people involved?'

'Tell me about The Trust,' he repeated. 'Everything.' He would say nothing, I knew, no matter how long we sat like this.

'No one can tell you everything.' As I told him as little as possible about the monarchists within the Kremlin, I had the feeling that he knew about it already. I repeated exactly what Igor had explained to me so many times.

'No one knows the other members, even in Paris. It is too dangerous for one person to know too much, only "Moscow" knows everything.'

'This is also dangerous,' Mitya remarked to his wife. 'I know about these "Moscow" people.'

'Remember Belgrade,' she said and pressed her lips together.

'They can be found out at any moment. How can they stay underground? They are surrounded by informers. And when they are discovered and shot, everyone in the network will be shot, wherever they operate, in Paris, Berlin, Riga.' He looked at me. 'I also heard this from a friend who has been reporting to me.' He leant towards me. 'My friend allowed himself to be recruited by The Trust. He is experienced in these matters. It was foolish of them to send you,' he said. 'You are not experienced. You are easily read. Also your lie was foolish. It

195

announced itself. I am not a fool and we have known Olga Nikolayevna for many years.'

I wished fervently that I had never begun to play chess with Mitya. What would happen to me now? More important, what would happen to Igor? I spoke very quickly as if my words would keep a door open, 'You and The Trust are of one mind, they are looking for you and people like you – you are looking for them. They wanted to know if you actually had an organisation before they approached you, I was only told to make the connection. I tried to ask you earlier, but you're right, I am not experienced.' I trailed off and looked at the faded bird on the carpet.

'I knew what you were doing,' he said, 'But I wasn't ready to answer your question.' His voice grew warmer, and he confided, 'Your inept lies are more reassuring than a skilful lie. You are an honest person,' he smiled, 'and if I had a daughter I would wish her to be like you.'

'You would?' I stared at him, thinking I would never understand people like him, that he was right, everyone had secrets.

His voice was still reassuring. 'I want to know about you as much as you want to know about me. Your Igor should have thought of that.'

'Not Igor,' I said quickly, 'Lewitsky.'

Again he became the army man. 'Ah yes. Lewitsky. The yid with the smashed up brother. A clever man, Lewitsky. He worked for the Cheka after 1905. Why? And why now The Trust? With that brother? That is a mystery. But my informant also tells me it is true. And his connections with "Moscow" are genuine.'

Zhenia asked, 'What does Olga know about all this? Is she too making sure of us?'

'Olga Nikolayevna knows nothing,' I said. 'Uncle Igor would never let her know it all. Very few people are allowed to know these things. That's why he keeps his distance.' As I said it, I knew it was true, although Igor had said nothing of the kind.

'Poor Olya,' Zhenia murmured. 'She is so much in love. She has hopes.'

'Her hopes are her own affair,' I said more sharply than I had intended.

Mitya went on, 'I have made no secret of my opinions.' Without emotion, he ticked each point off on his fingers. 'The Bolsheviks have committed an unspeakable crime. Russia will pay in blood until the monarchy is restored and if it is my blood that pays, I will be proud and grateful to pay it. I will continue to say that until my last breath. There was no need to lie about being Olga Nikolayeva's goddaughter or about wanting to learn chess or anything else.'

'It wasn't a real lie,' I said, close to tears.

'But it wasn't the truth. So how can I trust you? What makes you think I have an Arensky Group?'

'Stassov is ready,' I went on boldly, trying to keep my voice as businesslike as his. 'I heard that tonight and you know I heard it. But he needs a million francs. A million francs is impossible. You said so. But if you can confirm the facts it might not be impossible.'

Mitya continued to look at me. He sat erect now. There was no sign of his earlier weakness. I thought I saw the beginnings of calculation in his eyes.

'What facts?' he asked.

'That Stassov is ready.' I said. 'That there are others. That you have associates. If you have the people, they have the money. I know they can pay. Believe me.'

He looked as if he was about to laugh. Then he pressed his lips together and became stern. 'Why should I believe you?' he demanded. 'You will say anything Igor or Lewitsky tell you to say. It might be true or a lie. It doesn't matter. My informant told me this.'

'If I tell him about Stassov,' now my voice was shaking badly, 'he will want to meet with you and you can decide if you want to tell him more, even if Stassov is the only one.'

Zhenia spoke for the first time. 'But how do we know that

"Moscow" is what they say they are? That is, will we unite or will we be shot in the back of the neck?'

I fixed my eyes on the faded bird.

'Igor Fyedorovitch will be able to prove it to you if you give him the information they want.'

'This story seems absurd. Why should we believe it?'

'Because it is absurd,' I said. 'Life is full of absurd things – in life nothing fits as it should. Things are only logical in stories.'

After a moment, Mitya said, 'I will meet with Igor Fyedorovitch, but under my conditions. He comes alone. I bring an associate. I will let you know the time and the place. There will be no time to inform or prepare. And you will not be present at the actual meeting.'

I agreed with relief. I felt I had failed everyone in some way, that I had been a blundering idiot. How could I have underestimated Mitya and Zhenia like that? I wished that I would never have to face them again. I looked from one to the other, trying to find a way to tell them of my affection, that was something apart from all of this.

Zhenia stepped aside and opened the door. To my surprise, she smiled at me. Mitya, too, stood up and took me by the shoulders.

'No one can be trusted,' he said. 'Dostoyevsky imagined a world where there would only be informers. Everyone would be an informer on everyone else. And it has come to pass. I am not surprised and you should not be surprised either.'

CHAPTER TWENTY-FIVE

'This one,' Kyra said, as she tugged the dress out from the middle of an untidy pile of clothes. 'This can be made chic.'

'No,' I interrupted. 'Not that one.' I spoke with a violence that made her blink. When I had asked Kyra to help me look for something at the Clingancourt market that could be made over into a dress for the spring, I knew she would be able to find the right thing out of the piles of worn out, frayed garments. And she had. 'I don't want it. It's ugly.'

She held it up. It was crumpled and limp, with a torn sleeve, but looking at it I thought of fresh butter, of late summer evening skies, of marigolds in full bloom, of everything warm and golden. Only Kyra, with her expert eye, could have extracted this from the used clothing stalls at the Marché aux Puces. It didn't have the deathbed look of most fleamarket bargains; it was out of date, but in good condition. Whoever let this go must have been rich.

'Like new,' said the stallholder, a stout Romanian woman with a few short black hairs springing from her chin. 'And only three francs eighty.'

'For that?' Kyra gave a light, contemptuous laugh. 'I might pay two francs.' She lifted her chin with all the hauteur of Prince Dolgorushkov's daughter. She sounded as if her offer was a kind of favour. The woman looked down and pawed through the limp garments on her table. Even her chin bristles seemed uncertain.

Kyra turned her back and muttered to me, 'There's plenty of material there. Mama can alter it to look as if it came from Paul Caret. Like mine.' Kyra was wearing a dress in the new style, a short, straight, waistless shift, deep blue, with rose clusters embroidered down the sleeves. She looked both chic and original. On the Champs Elysées, French women flicked their cold eyes towards her, noticing the details. She handed me the golden dress and I let the soft material flow across my hands. I longed to have that dress – I had four francs, and it was spring.

The days were still bitterly cold, but they were bright, sun-washed and green. Leaves burst from the trees in the Tuileries and the Bois de Boulogne. A few cafés had begun to put a table or two outside. Children ran freely in the Luxemburg Gardens. It would be Easter soon. This was a time of hope and I wanted to greet it with something new. *Contemporary Notes* ran advertisements for Easter food: kulich, paschka, ham, curds, Easter eggs. I had even begun to dream of sending something to Mama, maybe through Lewitsky and his complicated chain of connections to The Trust. I knew that such a thing could not happen, but merely to believe it might be possible made it possible to believe this would be over and that I would see Mama again.

'No,' I said. 'I don't want it. It's ugly.'

She looked at me as if I had committed an idiocy. 'It will look new when Mama has remade it.' Kyra was right. Her mother, Princess Dolgorushkova had become a skilled seamstress. She made dresses to order, and her name had begun to be mentioned among the Parisian women who decided on the latest fashion. She cut without a pattern, first holding the material to herself in front of a mirror, and followed her instinct with the embroidery. Each dress was unique and exquisite and took hours of labour. She received 250 francs for each dress, but they sold for four times that amount.

I felt a sharp wave of hunger that only this dress could satisfy. If Mama could see me, she would smile and raise her eyebrows with pleasure. Kyra's light, scornful, voice told me she had already started to haggle. I held it against me for a moment and then thrust it back at her. I couldn't have it.

Igor hated yellow. He turned away from yellow as if it smelled bad. 'Yellow makes all women look ill,' he said. 'It's the colour of disease.' The dress was impossible. 'It's awful,' I said. 'I hate yellow.' Kyra must have realised that wasn't true, but what would she think of me, a woman of twenty-two, dressing to please my "uncle?" Kyra experimented with clothes: a scarf, a buckle, oddly shaped beads, and when her mother said, 'Oh not that', she would say firmly, 'Yes that.' Looking at this golden dress with its possibilities, I envied her.

'I don't like it,' I repeated.

Igor was tense and agitated these days, waiting for Arensky's approach. Sitting and walking with him through his long sleepless nights, I understood the importance of what I had done. Now I had to be at Igor's side and worry about him constantly, until my worry became a sort of prayer. Not even Kyra's buoyant presence could pierce it. Igor and I had put our lives in danger. I had sensed it before, but now it was real and I walked in its shadow. 'No one can be trusted,' Dmitry Arensky had said, and since then I wondered who was watching my actions. It could be anyone. I even wondered for a moment if it could be Kyra. She had pressed her lips together as she did when something displeased her.

'There must be something else,' I said.

'Are you going to take it?' the stallholder asked. Her voice was insistent. 'It's good material, seldom worn. I can make you a price. Three francs.'

'No.' I snapped. I started to walk away. 'It's all wrong. I'd rather have nothing.'

Kyra tossed the dress aside.

'Two francs eighty,' the woman called after us.

'That was a bargain,' Kyra said. 'Really, if Mama embroidered the skirt, over the worn places... ' She gave up. 'Well, if you don't like it ...'

We made our way through the Marché aux Puces. We had all been here so often we recognised each stall and many of the elderly and destitute habitués, all trying to get by. Old, worn goods were laid out on dusty rugs, spread across boxes; a broken straw hat sat next to a pile of jackets, smudged with

201

something that wouldn't come out. All the worn out objects on earth, it seemed, found their way here, struggling for one final hour of use. Everything smelled of the stale air at the backs of drawers and cupboards. An old man shuffled over and picked up a pair of broken boots. He bent them, testing the soles; his own boots had one sole flapping.

I glanced at Kyra, hoping I hadn't made her too angry. At the same time I noticed how beautifully her dark hair had been bobbed. It came forward in little points that emphasised her straight, even features and oval face. For a moment I was swept away, ready to rush and shear off my long plaits without another thought, but my hair was important for Igor's photographs.

'There will be something else,' I reassured her. 'We always manage to find something.'

'Yes, there's always something else here.' She fell silent.

I was right; I had disappointed her. Now she would become bored with me. She began to walk more quickly. I tried to find something I could say or do to distract her.

There was rubbish underfoot. The smell fought against the sudden warmth of the day and won. The market people with their fleshy faces and cynical eyes called out the value of their goods: 'everything new', 'as good as new', 'best shirts'. There were household good as well: There was a cooking-pot that had only a small chip. My hand hovered over it as I thought I should buy this now that our new place had a real, if miniscule kitchen, but I turned back to the piles of garments. We hardly ever used the kitchen for cooking anyway. Igor stored equipment there and I kept my records of our expenses, his work and his sales.

'Are you going to buy this, mademoiselle? It is a work of art.' The man held out a crude drawing in a cracked frame, 'A bargain.' His tone was mocking.

'No,' I said.

He cursed me in a language I didn't need to know.

Kyra walked on, pausing at stalls aimlessly. I tried to say something to distract and amuse her. 'Grisha Bobrov bought a terrible yellow cravat here the other day,' I said. 'He wore it to la Coupole, with his old shirt. He looked like a monkey.'

She lifted her chin slightly and slid her eyes in my direction. 'What an unkind thing to say.' Her voice was indifferent, detached. 'Poor Grisha. He was trying to look smart. And the Bobrovs are completely destitute now that Professor Bobrov can no longer do factory work.'

I looked away. How could I have said that? I wished I could take it back. Of course it was unkind. The stupidity of it only served to remind me again of the shadows around me. I thought I saw Igor's friend, Valya, looking at spectacles, but it was someone else. French. A stranger.

I stopped at another stall. Kyra frowned as I took a piece of red material from the pile. 'Not so hard,' growled the stallholder.

It was a large, frayed shawl, a rich glowing raspberry. By some miracle it had only faded a little and its warmth told me exactly why Igor loved the colour. This shawl spoke his name.

I examined it carefully, keeping my face expressionless. It smelt stale with the must of its past life and the market, but when I gave it to Igor he would lift it to the light, and get the feel of it, as he did with things he might use. How he would use it I didn't know, but I knew it would become part of the world that belonged to us. It was Igor's favourite colour: that must be a good omen.

'How much?' I asked.

'It's useless,' Kyra said.

'Is it?' I turned it over.

'Look, it's got a stain down here' she pointed at it. And the material – you can't cut that.'

'How much?' I repeated.

This stallholder was a small man of uncertain age, with the fleshless hands of a skeleton. He took the shawl from me. 'Two francs fifty,' he said.

'Too much,' I said, trying to imitate Kyra's aristocratic contempt.

'That's the price,' he shrugged.

Kyra was silent. She looked around as if she had nothing to do with me. *She might help me a bit,* I thought. But I knew she wouldn't, not now. Still, I had asked her to come today and help me. I really wanted her to help me forget for a while, but how could she do that?

I thought of my precious four francs. If I could get this for one franc, I would have three francs left to put toward new shoes. I sighed and frowned at the shawl.

'Fifty centimes,' I told him. 'Look, it's stained.'

He looked at the shawl and looked at me. 'Mademoiselle, I am not a charity.'

He and I began to haggle in earnest. He was outraged, then despairing. He pleaded with me not to let his children starve. He insisted on the quality of his product, of its unique style, each time taking off a centime or two. I wouldn't budge. I sneered, gave the shawl back, turned to leave, and reluctantly turned back. As we made offers and counter offers, I felt myself harden. Finally, I got the shawl for one franc twenty.

'It isn't worth any more than that, but still you did well,' Kyra said. She looked at me with a new respect and added, 'You did really well. And the colour suits you.' Her good humour had returned. 'In that colour, with your hair undone you will look like Paraskeva Pyatnitsa.'

Really? Would I really resemble the powerful Saint with her long flowing hair, flying across the country to enforce observance? I wanted to look more modern, but it pleased me all the same.

'Oh, how sweet!' Kyra cried. 'How sad.' It was an old, worn out doll, bald, with a chipped nose and one leg missing. 'I loved dolls. So did Mama. She made such beautiful clothes for them.' Kyra picked up the doll, draped my shawl around it and arranged the folds. 'That's how she started to sew. She made me a Vasilitsa doll, a Baba Yaga doll, and dolls from each province. When we came to Paris, it was the only practical thing she knew she could do.'

She unwrapped the doll and put it back. 'It's strange. Last night, I dreamt I was back in Kharkov, and the dolls were all on their shelves. I was so happy to see them and I thought, how strange, they're not even dusty. And they all smiled. It was symbolic of course.'

'Why was it symbolic?' I asked. Now I knew we would have one of our long rambling discussions and I would learn about the latest fashions and ideas. 'Maybe it just meant you were dreaming about your dolls. Maybe it was a prophecy,' I added hopefully. 'A prophecy of The Return.'

'Ah, no. Sigmund Freud has discovered what our dreams really mean. He says everything we dream is a symbol,' she declared. 'And you know what everything is a symbol *of*.' She gave me a sly look and we both began to laugh.

'A doll? A symbol of *that*?'

'Everything is a symbol.' We laughed some more.

'I am the symbol of a symbol,' said a voice. Kyra and I both jumped, and my heart beat with an irrational fear. Then I saw it was Alyosha.

'What are you doing here?' I was shocked to see him. 'Were you following us?' I demanded. 'How long have you been here?'

He raised his eyebrows. 'Yes. Why do you look so fierce? I saw you haggling over that dress, so I followed you. Didn't you see me?' He pointed at me. 'And you didn't buy the dress. What have you bought instead?'

Somewhat abashed, I showed him the shawl. Kyra sighed.

'What is it for?' Alyosha asked.

'I don't know,' I said, fumbling for an answer. 'I like the colour.'

His lopsided smile widened. 'That is wonderful!' he said. 'To buy it only for the colour! Nadia, you are a woman who will survive.'

He linked arms with us, and we began to make our way through the market.

'So, Kyra, what is so new about Freud? There are symbols everywhere, from the beginning of mankind.'

'There's more to it than that.' She had grown cool again. I wondered if it was her beauty that gave her the right to become indifferent, withdraw, and have to be wooed back. 'Our outer lives are a dream. Our dreams tell us the truth. That's how everyone creates now.'

'But surely artists have always expressed their dreams.'

'Not like this,' Kyra said. 'And not just artists. Everyone.'

I was once again in awe of Kyra. She knew so much. What would she say about Igor's photographs? His close-ups of glistening wet pavements, of the slick of light on a figure, must be more than simple representation. When I looked at his photographs, I felt that they implied his idea that a photograph should show "the thing that cannot be spoken." And his photographs of me? They felt like dreams. The lights and shadows, the curve of my arm, my neck, my back: seated, standing, leaning against a window, my hair down, my reflection in a shop window; was it actually me or was I a symbol of something?

'You have to read Freud,' Kyra informed Alyosha. 'Our lives are symbols of our unconscious,' she began to sound uncertain. 'In a way. And our dreams ... ' She broke off, distracted by a wide-brimmed hat on a nearby stall.

'You mean,' Alyosha said, 'The revolution was a symbol of a dream. ' He picked up the hat. 'Maybe you're right. A Western idea. Marx. Freud. The pursuit of self-knowledge above all. How terrible.' For a moment his face was a sad mask. Then he put on the hat, tilted it at an angle and made a face. 'Now. Is that my unconscious?'

He smiled at me as he replaced the hat on the stall. 'I'm sure my fate speaks to me in dreams.'

'Yes, we know that, but now we know there is more,' Kyra cried. 'Freud says they are a new way to understand ourselves. What we really want. Who we really are. Savage. Elemental.'

I didn't want to think about my dreams: the snow, the cold, the trains which never stopped, the gunfire. In dreams I often found myself climbing the stairs of our house, which went nowhere and vanished as I stepped on them. When I woke, it would take me a moment of consciousness to push those dreams to the bottom of my mind, and when I did, I breathed more easily. But my friends were waiting for me to say something. I repeated what our maid Dunya had told me when I was small. 'If people come to us in dreams,' I said, 'it's because they want to tell us something and this is the only way. They comfort us, and they warn us. And they prophesy.'

We had stopped walking. I had raised my voice for emphasis and passers-by glanced at us. One woman laughed and said something to her young companion. An older couple looked frightened and hurried away.

'But there is no sense to things,' Kyra insisted. 'There is only the madness of life. Look at us. Our lives are absurd.'

Alyosha started to interrupt. 'But madness is a direct result of social upheaval. When we give ourselves to something greater than ourselves, we will no longer be mad. '

'No.' She cut him off. 'Life is simply insane. Once you see that it is all beyond reason, things make sense.' Then she conceded, 'People in dreams might be telling us about our past in *general*.' Our eyes met, and we couldn't repress a giggle.

Alyosha looked puzzled. 'Dreams remind us of our past. Our past guides us. Nadia is right. Freud, Cocteau, Breton: these people are talking about man as an individual isolated from everything around him. This is an unbearable state. And for people like us, it's not natural.'

'But we can all recognise this ...' Kyra began, but Alyosha interrupted. This was one of his favourite topics. He talked about Russia's tribal past, about the need for communal life. He said, 'In the West, they are obsessed with the self. To move forward we must get away from this.'

'We can't escape anything,' I said. 'It is all decided before we were born.' I spoke slowly, trying to work it out. 'Even if we think we struggle against our destiny, that struggle is how we are meant to work out our fate.' I wanted to believe that, but when I said it, I felt that Kyra's theory of insanity made more sense.

Alyosha looked at the ground, and hunched his shoulders. 'But,' he said, 'if it is our destiny to fail in the struggle? Perhaps,' he concluded, 'struggle itself is our destiny. The struggle to Return. Perhaps fate means us to find strength that way.'

We went to a small bar at the corner of the market. Working men and day labourers filled the place with the smell of sweat, tobacco and garlic breath. The coffee was heavily watered and had a thin, sour taste.

Alyosha bent his head over his coffee, and looked uncomfortable. 'There was a meeting of the Central Committee of the Eurasians today.' He began, and I knew that he had had a purpose in seeking us out after all.

Kyra and I waited. The bar was crowded. A thin man in an dark overcoat leant back with his elbows against the bar, and absently sipped a *fine*. Three Frenchman were arguing, interrupting each other with rough voices and gestures. An old man was shouting down the telephone behind the bar. He repeated over and over, '*C'était dans la valise. Dans la valise!*'

Alyosha ran his finger around the rim of his cup. 'We have had an extraordinary letter from Spalding.'

'Oh my God, the Spalding money?' Kyra leant forward. 'What happened?'

They want me to write an answer. I refused. Then I walked out.' He looked up; his face was even more drained of colour than usual, all angles and shadows. We were sitting by the window, and his fair hair was caught in a sudden ray of light. 'I couldn't live with myself if I stayed. It would be dishonest.'

'*J'irai à la gare*' the old man shouted. '*La gare!*'

I said, 'You walked out? You left *The Eurasian*?'

'Spalding's withdrawn his support?' Kyra repeated.

'No.' Alyosha sounded irritated. 'It was more important than that.' He paused again, to make sure of our attention. 'He wrote that he was proud to support the Eurasians as the spearhead of a bloody revolution in Europe which will lead to a war which will crush the Soviets.' His voice quivered as he spoke the words. 'How can he think we would consider such a thing?'

On the pavement outside, an old man wheezed out tuneless sounds on an old accordion. Another held up a sign advertising *La Loterie*.

'But that's not what the Eurasian is about,' I said. 'Is Spalding really the only patron?'

'Without his money, we would collapse. I can see that as well as anyone. But a counter-revolution!' Alyosha cried, clenching his fists. 'How can we take money from someone like that? It is against the basic ideal of the Eurasians. Starting a bloody revolution in *Europe* to crush the Bolsheviks?' He shook his head in disbelief. 'How could this Spalding believe such a thing?

'Is that what you told them?' I asked. 'What did they say?'

'They brushed me aside. Mirsky said Spalding was merely eccentric,' he added in disbelief. 'Karsavin said the English were all ignorant anyway and completely mad.' Alyosha was shaken by a cough. When he had got his breath back, he felt in the pocket of his jacket and mimed the action as he spoke. 'So I took out my money and threw it on the desk.' He slapped the small marble table top with his palm and the table trembled. 'And I got up and left.' He made a wry face. 'So now I can't pay for this coffee. Can you pay?' he asked me. 'I will return it, I promise.'

I had one franc eighty left. I pushed the coins into a small pile in front of him. 'Alyosha, I said, you must think this through.'

'Oh no,' he said, 'No. This is too much. Only for the coffee.'

'Alyosha, take it.' I insisted. He tried to push the money back to me, but I resisted. 'Please,' I said.

'What can I do but be grateful?' Alyosha took the money, and divided the coins equally between the two of us. He gave his little smile, and inclined his head in the boyish, but half-formal gesture that was characteristic of him.

'You're making a hasty judgement,' Kyra pointed out. 'You don't know that they agree with Spalding. How can they agree?

Ask yourself. The point of the Eurasians is that they are not European.'

Kyra had cigarettes. She passed them round and we lit up in silence. 'But Alyosha,' she said, flicking a stray bit of tobacco off her lower lip, 'does that mean you won't go back to the Eurasian Society? In the first place, what will you do for money? It would be mad. Or are you secretly English?'

'Are you laughing at me?' he asked.

'No.' But she was smiling.

'You like to laugh at me,' he said. 'I know people do.'

'Alyosha,' she said, but she was still smiling, 'don't be a child.'

'I am not a child! I'm a man of honour.'

I rose to his defence. 'Kyra, you're unfair.' Alyosha had half risen and I tugged at his arm. 'Alyosha, sit down.' Reluctantly, he sat, still scowling at her. 'It would be better to starve,' he said.

Kyra shook her head. 'Only those Americans at Les Deux Magots think it's wonderful to starve.'

'Because they don't starve,' I said. 'We could live for a week on what they spend on starvation in one day.'

'I learnt how to starve in Constantinople,' Alyosha said. 'If it's for something greater than one's self, it's not difficult. And it's better than betrayal.' He inhaled the cigarette and shook his head, 'I don't want to leave the Eurasian. It's what I believe in. But I must know where we stand.'

'Kyra said, 'Alyosha, you are the golden soul of the Eurasians. Even Mirsky says so. What you do stands for their ideals.'

He said, 'I am nobody. I am only the office boy.'

'That's not the point,' I said. 'You are the soul. You can't leave.'

'What exactly does Spalding want you to do?' Kyra asked.

'He hasn't made demands yet,' Alyosha admitted. 'But he will. And we will have to agree, because it is his money. Can't they see that? I can only protest by refusing the money.' He turned to me. 'Nadia, you understand how it is, don't you?'

It was common knowledge that Alyosha and Larissa were nearly penniless except for Alyosha's pittance from the Eurasian society and his work as a film extra. I could picture their debts piling up like a wall of stones: the scenes with the landlord, visits from creditors, the begging letters. The shapes of money and bills formed their weary, inevitable patterns in my mind. 'Yes, I understand,' I said, 'but what will you live on?'

'This isn't about money,' he exclaimed, leaning forward.

'Think of Larissa. That money was for her, really.' Kyra stopped. 'I'm sorry,' she said.

He suddenly buried his face in his hands, and I remembered his despair the night of the Eurasian talk. After a moment, he looked up, and, as on that night, he looked as if it hadn't happened. 'It's true,' he said. He even smiled. 'I know they only paid me to get money to her, but they will find a way to give it to her without me. I shall have to do more film extra work. What I can get. I can run errands, make deliveries, work in a shop…' He trailed off.

'Alyosha,' I had tears in my eyes, 'please! You must go back, you must keep working and fighting. It's you who leads the rest of us. I couldn't stay either, if you left. If you leave, you'll betray all of us.'

'But how can one not betray someone?' he cried. 'If I leave the Eurasian, I betray my beliefs. If I accept Spalding's money, I betray my beliefs.' He looked down and spoke in a voice so low I could barely hear him. 'I betrayed my own family, did you know that?'

I knew. Igor was fond of saying, 'Alyosha's mother was a Bolshevik and his wife is a Monarchist. It will keep him talking forever.'

Kyra touched my arm, nodded toward the door, and quickly slipped out. Alyosha and I watched her go, almost running when she was outside.

'Where is she going?' he asked. I shrugged. I wondered if

we had annoyed or even bored her, if we hadn't been interested enough in Freud. Alyosha returned to his subject. 'When I joined Wrangel's forces, my mother never forgave me. She never spoke to me again. Never in her life. At the end, my sisters told me, she cursed my name.'

'Why did you join?' I asked.

'I was in the army. I had trained as an officer. My mother had gone to jail as a revolutionary and now the revolution meant that Russia herself seemed to be crumbling into murder, famine, disease. I had to defend her.' He tapped some ash into his saucer, and stared at it as if it contained a message. 'And I had met Larissa. At that time I was her prince. Her noble warrior who was going to fight for an ideal.' He brushed his hand across his cheek. 'She was overwhelming, and so was her love for Russia. Our love.' He inhaled deeply on his cigarette and exhaled the musky perfumed smell of Gauloise. 'I dream about my comrades.' He went on. 'They walked with no boots, with disease and terror and death. School friends, people I had known from childhood. They died face down in the mud. You and your Freud!' he suddenly exclaimed. 'Those are not symbols, they are real people in a terrible place. I can't disown them. But my loyalty to them means I am guilty of turning my back on my country now.'

'Alyosha. Do you believe in people or ideals? I asked. 'Which one is worth dying for?'

'The ideal' he said firmly. 'What else can one believe in? The self alone is nothing. But an ideal is a way to change the world. Not only one or two heroes, Nadia, but to unite our strength for The Return.'

He inhaled his cigarette again, thinking, calmly watching me think. Suddenly I wanted to tell him everything, about Uncle Igor, about Dmitry, about Lewitsky, all of it. I wanted to say it out loud.

'Alyosha,' I said, 'you are the most honourable person I know.' I wondered how I could say that, and mean it, as I did at this moment. But I was only a visitor in the pure air of

Alyosha's vision. Igor was the flesh and blood of life itself.

I noticed two men in the doorway of the bar. They were obviously French bourgeois, well-dressed, clean. They were the sort of people, I knew, who liked to come to the Marché aux Puces for the thrill of seeing the underbelly of Paris. With shame, I saw one of them point us out to his companions.

Alyosha saw them too. 'This is not an authentic way to live, on the charity of foreigners. There is more for us to do than this.'

'Alyosha,' I urged him, 'please go back to the Eurasian. If there are people who want to corrupt your ideals, then you must stop them. Speak out! Don't just leave and close the door!'

He thought for a long time and we sat in silence again. His lips moved slightly as he put it to himself.

'*A cinq heures!*' the old man shouted. '*Cinq heures! Oui! Cinq heures!*'

The waiter approached us; we looked into our empty cups and raised the dregs to our lips. I stubbed out the remains of my cigarette in the saucer and wondered if Kyra would come back.

Alyosha took a deep breath and said slowly, 'Maybe I should go back but refuse the money.'

We were silent again. He looked at me anxiously, waiting for me to speak. 'What do you think?' he asked finally.

I couldn't laugh, as Kyra would have done. It seemed so pure, so right, and yet it was clearly impossible. I must tell him so I thought. 'Alyosha,' I said, 'if you do that ...'

He wasn't listening. His face had brightened, and he looked like a youth again. 'That's the best way. You're right – stay, and stand for the Eurasian ideals. But I won't take his money, and I will make sure everyone knows why. Even Spalding,' he added. And then I had to smile. 'Why not?' he demanded. He threw back his head and recited: "*In this life, to die is nothing hard. To live is harder and by far.*" He breathed deeply. 'Larissa is right. Mayakovsky is our greatest poet. He was his usual self now: hopeful, excited, inspired. He was about to outline more of his plans, when Kyra suddenly dashed through the door. She darted past the dour man at the bar, laughing. 'Nadia, Alyosha, look! I'm such a fool.' She held out the doll. 'I couldn't resist. I would never let myself think about all that, but she was like a message from the others. So worn and battered, but they want to be remembered!' She laughed. 'I'll clean her up and dress her as Vassilitsa the Beautiful, with a beaded headdress, so she won't be bald any more, poor thing, and she will be a symbol of all the others.' She sat down, and set the doll on the table, where it sagged against the coffee cup. She lit another cigarette. 'When I saw what you did, Nadia, I thought, why not buy something because you want to. Why not? You're right. It's been such a long time since I've bought anything just because I wanted to. Nadia, you're so strong!' She surveyed the doll, with its bald head and cracked nose. 'How ridiculous,' she said at last. 'How stupid.'

CHAPTER TWENTY-SIX

It had been a slow night at Tanya's. A handful of people in the front room lingered over borscht. Some people in the back room were reading short works by Chekhov which had been translated into Esperanto. 'The Sovpedia will trample the Russian language into the mud – for this!' they said, with shared outrage. I glanced at Tanya's kitchen clock when I thought an hour had passed, but it was never more than a few minutes.

When I turned into the Rue Offenbach, I was surprised to see a figure in the doorway of the *boulangerie* opposite our apartment house. At first I thought it was one of the whores who used the main streets by the bars, but there were no customers on this street and the figure didn't stand as if looking for trade. It stepped out from the doorway and then I recognised her. 'Olga Nikolayevna!' I exclaimed.

She turned, with a little cry. 'Oh, Nadezhda Mikhailovna, *rolybushka*.' She wore her fur, and a hat with a veil. She said brightly, 'My little Nadyushka. How unexpected.'

She sounded as if we had met by chance on the Boulevard Montparnasse at noon. Didn't she realise it was after midnight? Had she come to see us? At this hour? If she was in some kind of trouble, we would be forced to take her in. After all, she was "one of us." But she smiled happily and looked down at the bag in her arms.

'I had to buy birdseed for my darlings,' she said. 'There is a place in Clamart where one can buy it very cheaply. And then of course I met some friends as one always does and we walked together for such a long time, because they had to tell me about a wonderful young Russian poet from Berlin. He calls himself

Sirin, but he is the son of Vladimir Nabokov. I have a friend who was actually at the meeting when he was assassinated. They say the son's a genius. There will be a reading and a discussion at the Green Lamp. Gippius will naturally attack it. But Poplavsky will speak in favour.' She was speaking too quickly. 'Has Igor heard about this young man? He will be so interested.' She fluttered her eyelashes. 'I seem to have found myself on your doorstep! Yes? I have been walking all around, I was so filled with the poetry.' She fell silent and I noticed her rapid breathing.

'Is this where you are living now? Igoryok told me you had moved,' she exclaimed. She looked at our building with theatrical surprise as if she had just discovered it. 'But you are so fortunate! I am still in the same hotel. It's so cramped, but it's convenient, and where else could I stay with the birds? My darlings – one must make some sacrifices. Anyway, we won't be here much longer.' She shrugged up the collar of her shabby fur and poised her head prettily against it. 'I heard tonight from my friend. He has seen Kuprin in Moscow. My friend says he is alive and well. Not writing, but at least alive. And my friend also says the Soviets are about to collapse. I asked Ehrenburg directly, but Ehrenburg of course, is careful.' She smiled again, and her eyes went to the red shawl on my arm.

I said nothing. It was getting cold. Her smile trembled. 'I have to go,' I said. 'Igor will worry if I'm late.'

'Of course, of course, he is concerned for your welfare, he often tells me,' she cooed. 'But I always say, Mitya and Zhenia won't let her come to any harm.'

I felt her smiling after me as I turned away.

Our two tiny rooms in the Rue Offenbach had belonged to an elderly widow Gyorgei knew, who had moved to Zemgor, the Russian old age home at St. Geneviève des Bois. The old lady had left behind a torn raffia wastepaper basket, a few ticket stubs for long-past concerts, and a green glass paperweight. The place was shabby, but clean, and unlike our previous rooms, I had no desire to improve it. We had our chair, our mattresses, and we had acquired a saucepan, two plates, two forks, two cups and three glasses. Everything was part of our lives, but if we had to leave tomorrow, I thought, I could leave it all behind. There was the photograph of Mama and Papa still in their frame, now black with tarnish, there was my beloved icon, like a heart that beat silently, and the rest was a matter of indifference.

Igor was waiting. He jumped up when I came in and I saw he had his pistol beside him. I hadn't seen it since we left Russia.

'What's wrong? What are you doing?'

'Just in case,' he said. 'Was he there? Did he speak to you?'

'It's not his night,' I said. 'You know that. There was a reading. They say the Soviets will force everyone to speak Esperanto.'

He interrupted me. 'What the hell is wrong with Arensky? What's he playing at?'

'It's only been three days, Igor.' I said.

'Why not make contact immediately? What's he waiting for?'

'Olga Nikolayevna is downstairs,' I said. I put the shawl down next to his pistol. 'I think she's waiting for you.'

'For me? Why? I never told her to wait.'

'She's carrying some birdseed,' I said.

He gave a short laugh. 'Well let her go home and feed her birds.'

'Aren't you going to see her? Why is she waiting like that?'

'I told her I loved her. But that was all.'

'Igor!'

'What of it,' he said impatiently, 'One must say something. And anyway I meant it.'

'You didn't really mean it.'

'I meant it. She's a wonderful woman. How can one not love her? But I didn't tell her to wait down there. I left her at the *Dôme*.'

He parted the curtains an inch. The shutters were open.

'She's still there. How delightful! Let her wait, if that's what she wants to do.' He had shrugged her off with that indifference of his that always chilled me.

He lit a cigarette, and sat down heavily, the pistol and shawl on the table beside him. 'All right. All right. What do you think? No don't tell me what you think. It has to happen soon,' he said. 'Arensky understands that.' He picked up the shawl and dropped it. The end trailed across the pistol. 'He must have lied to you. Oh my God, Nadia, tell me again, what did he say? Never mind. I know what he said. So where is he?' he shouted. 'What is he waiting for?'

'Igor, I don't know,' I said. 'But I know Mitya will do exactly as he says. He's a man of honour.'

'Mitya,' he mocked. 'Did he tell you to call him Mitya? Such a good friend?'

'No,' I said. 'Not exactly. But others do and ...'

Still with the cigarette between his lips, he picked up the end of the shawl and twisted it slowly around his wrist. He flicked the cigarette away. I quickly picked it up, put it out with my thumb and forefinger, and laid it aside. He was still talking. 'You're very fond of Arensky aren't you? Your *dear* friend Mitya. And don't think he doesn't know it. You know what I think?' He was looking at me now with his long lipped, narrow smile. 'The longer he waits, the longer he keeps you with him. That sounds right, don't you think? This is all a trick. He won't want to give you up. But when "Moscow" takes over, you'll be unnecessary to everyone.'

I was standing near him. Suddenly, he picked up the other end of the shawl, looped it around my neck, and pulled me toward him.

'Stop it, Igor that hurts!' I cried.

He gave me his slow smile. 'Ah, so you are going to be like that.' He drew in his breath, and then relaxed. 'I'm sorry, my little *dysha*, I didn't mean to hurt you. See, it's all right.' He played with the shawl, draping it, arranging it around my neck and shoulders, the way Kyra had draped the doll. 'What does his wife think about you?' he asked. 'People always wonder about these girls. You're not the first. She puts up with it, smiles and prays. He needs her, he's used to her, but he always has to have a girl like you.'

'We are friends,' I said. 'Like family, Mitya says. After all, *Uncle Igor*,' I emphasised the word "Uncle" 'it has only been a few days.'

'If he refuses our offer, we will have failed The Trust. They don't like that. And they don't give a second chance.'

'What will happen?' I asked.

'Anything,' he said. 'We're not important to them. Arensky is important. Arensky, alive and willing.'

'Mitya … Dmitry Sergeevitch, is a good man. A beautiful man, and Eugenia Kirillovna … '

'Also beautiful?' He smiled.

'What will happen if Mitya doesn't – ' I paused.

'Take the bait?'

'Bait?' I felt the word rising, putting a face to a doubt that I hadn't seen until now. 'Bait is a bit of dead meat, Uncle Igor. It waits until a fish gets hungry. Mitya isn't a fish!' I shouted. 'And I am not dead meat on a hook.'

'You know I don't think you're dead meat. What do you want to call it? The lure. The invitation. The offer. If he doesn't take it,' and now his voice hardened again, 'we are finished.'

'Like Chengarov?' I asked abruptly. The name had come to me unbidden and it made a hard flat sound as it hit the air between us.

'Who knows about Chengarov?' Igor said. 'He had an accident. It was unfortunate.'

Unfortunate! I wanted to run to Mitya and bring him back here with me, Mitya and Zhenia both. Something was wrong, and more than anything I wanted to go back to a time when I could see the path in front of me, shining with an ideal. I wanted badly to talk to Alyosha.

'This was a terrible mistake,' Igor went on.

'What do you mean? What kind of mistake? Mitya wants to accept The Trust, of course he does. We are all of one mind.'

'Don't be so sure. He's not all he seems. I grew up with people like that. They are corrupt at heart – cruel and corrupt. Don't let him corrupt you with flattery.'

'Mitya isn't corrupt,' I said.

'They're all corrupt,' he answered.

'Who are? Not Mitya?' I asked.

'Why do you call him Mitya? He's not your equal, he's not like your girlfriend Kyra.'

'I know that.' I tried to think when it had begun. 'I told you, others called him Mitya, and soon I felt as if we'd known each other for a long time and it happened that way.'

'He has nothing to do with you,' Igor raised his voice. 'He's not your family.'

'Neither are you!' I shouted. The words escaped from my mouth of their own accord. 'Mitya … '

He slapped me. It was not a hard slap, but it was so unexpected that I screamed.

'Shhh.' He put his hand over my mouth, and even in the moment of shock and pain I was aware of the touch of his skin. 'Don't ever call him Mitya again. He's nothing to you.'

'Nothing,' I said.

He took his hand away. 'When I hear you say that I want to kill him,' he said.

He let me go and we stood slightly apart, both of us breathing heavily as if we had been dancing. My face still stung where he had hit me. 'I'm sorry,' he said. 'I would never have done that to you. I couldn't help myself. I'm mad. Think of me as a madman.'

'No Igor. You're not mad. You want to hit someone. You want to hit M…' I swallowed the word. 'Dmitri Arensky. I am not General Arensky.'

'I'm mad,' he said. 'I'm going mad. This is driving me mad. I didn't think it would be like this.'

'Igor…Uncle Igor what do you mean?' He relaxed a little

and I felt that he had needed me to call him 'Uncle' at this moment.

'Knowing he's there, watching, around a corner, walking a few steps behind, and when I turn, there's no one. And then I feel him watching again. You see,' he spoke calmly, 'I'm mad. All day, wherever I went, I felt him watching me. What does the man want! He was there, Nadia, I knew it, I sensed it. I almost saw him. I'm turning into a madman.'

He went into the other room. It was even smaller than this one, more of a cupboard. I heard his suitcase click open, and then I heard him murmur something to himself. I waited, trying to concentrate on the soft folds of the shawl. Then I wandered to the window, parted the curtains as he had, and peered out.

I see it in my mind now, like a photograph: a girl with long dark hair, her head bent, looking down at the street. She is half hidden by the curtain. The profile is so young, so sad, and with an air of anxiety. That imaginary photograph is as vivid to me as any of the others, because at that moment I saw Olga Nikolayevna again. She was in the same position, still looking up at the building. She didn't see me. It was still dark and she was half shadowed, half in a pool of gaslight. She clutched the bag of bird seed with one arm. She raised the other hand to her lips and blew a kiss toward our apartment.

Igor was suddenly in the room. 'Why are you standing there like that, wrapped up in the curtain?' he asked. 'Come away from there, you'll catch cold.'

I turned back to him.

'We'll go down to her together,' he said.

CHAPTER TWENTY-SEVEN

Olga had gone. 'It's not good for her to do things like that,' Igor said. 'Now I will have to go to her later.' I waited for him to explain, but after a quick look up and down the empty street, he set off toward the Luxemburg Gardens. After a moment he fell back and kept pace with me. We matched our footsteps deliberately in an identical rhythm and Uncle Igor glanced at me from time to time, in a way that made me uneasy. I heard a high, childish laugh coming from somewhere. A figure moved on the Rue Blondel. I went rigid, trying to find the source.

'A gull,' he said, and added, 'It won't be like that. They'll get rid of me very quietly.'

'Igor, please don't say that,' I begged him. 'Mit... General Arensky hasn't actually refused to meet you.'

Igor started to speak, but checked himself. After a moment he said gently, 'Nadia, you are a good person. I rely on you.'

There were still people walking through the night: the homeless, the beggars, the clochards. Also the pimps, the whores, the pickpockets, the people who swarmed onto the streets and quais at night, when Paris turned around and revealed the city beneath.

We crossed the pont d'Issy and walked toward Montparnasse. Near the *Closerie des Lilas*, the usual groups of Russians were walking the night away. Khodasevich and his wife passed by on the Boulevard Montparnasse with the Bunins. The Zaitsevs were walking toward them, but the couples elaborately ignored each other. Everyone knew the Bunins and the Zaitsevs were not speaking at the moment.

Igor said, 'If Arensky refuses, we will get no help from the

French. To them, it will be more Russians feuding among themselves. If they even notice.'

Igor turned sharply off to the left, and we were in an empty narrow street, with an open gutter curving through the cobblestones. One side was lined with trees, the other side was only a long, high stone wall. There was a metallic smell of still, dank water. It was silent, dark, shuttered, as if life had been cut off at the root. There was a faint light from an unidentifiable source: the moon perhaps, or a street lamp. Igor turned his head quickly and tensed as if he had seen something.

'There's nothing here Igor,' I reassured him. 'No one would be in this street.'

'In a city, even an empty space has people in it,' he said. 'No street is empty.'

'Mit... Arensky is accustomed to being careful,' I said. 'You understand that.'

'It's complicated,' he said, 'too complicated.' He began to open his camera, changed his mind and closed it. 'Maybe it's better to end like this. Fail and let "Moscow" finish it.'

We went into the Luxembourg Gardens, where he stopped a short distance from a couple on the bench by the Medici canal. They were in shadow, clasped passionately in each other's arms, pierced by lamplight, which also touched a bare tree, like an upright bone. They were unaware of us. I longed to know how it would feel to be in such an embrace. I watched for a second and imagined myself as that girl, in Igor's arms. We walked on through the swarming shadows. Even the chairs were set like couples in conversation. For some reason it all brought back his slap, which had set off a desire for him so unlike any of my childish affection, that I felt I had become someone recognisable, but at the same time different and embarrassing, as if part of me stood exposed. I wanted him passionately, not only his body, but more, the mystery of his very being. He was a story that had gripped me and made me want to read more and more. I shivered.

'Are you cold?' he asked.

'No,' I said. And indeed the clean spring air made my coat feel thicker than ever. He adjusted the collar around my throat, and I knew he could read my thoughts. But he said only, 'Now you are both beautiful and warm.'

He adjusted the time exposure and took a photograph of an old building, lit by one gas lamp. A policeman stood underneath, smoking. A black limousine de luxe waited for the light to change. Igor captured the face inside: a woman in a black evening dress. Her face in the light was blank as a corpse.

'It's the way the world will look after its death,' he remarked causally. 'These people are their own ghosts.'

On the Place d'Italie, the brash lights of a little street fair blazed wantonly into the night. Even at this hour it was crowded; masked girls stood around the little booths, and a few couples danced to *'C'est mon Gigolo'*. Igor stood behind me with his hands on my shoulders and moved us back and forth to the rhythm of the music. The Ferris wheel turned. A young couple stood in one of the cars with their arms around each other, laughing. I gasped as the car swung up, and tilted them dangerously to one side. 'They could be killed!' I cried.

'They would be fortunate,' said Igor. 'One moment of ecstasy and then: the end.'

At the top, the couple held their balance while the car swayed.

'Igor!' I exclaimed. I imagined us together in that car, bodies pressed tightly together, as the wheel went round and round. In my mind it went round forever.

He had managed to get a photograph of the couple just as the car swung them upward into the light. He closed his camera again. 'We have to go,' he said. 'It's almost time.'

'Time for what?'

He became serious. 'Something I have to do,' he said. 'You won't like it, but I want you to know.'

We went to a building on the Rue Bosquet, near the Ecole Militaire. Uncle Igor knocked on a door at the far end of a courtyard. It opened a crack.

'Philippe?' Igor said, and the door was opened.

'Come in, I am making some jam.' Philippe was tall, with long dark hair and a long pale face. He wore an elaborate Chinese kimono. There was a light, oily perfume around him as he ushered us into the tiny, dark foyer. He handed us each a kimono.

'To maintain the atmosphere.' He explained.

Igor looked like an oriental mandarin, while I struggled to get my arms through the correct parts of the sleeve: it was uneven and hung on me awkwardly. Then Philippe ushered us into a room which was completely dark, except for a few twinkling lights from small oil lamps.

'Are you looking for her? She's here. The usual couch,' said Philippe as he picked up a small black ball on a long needle and turned it around over one of the perfumed oil lamps. The oil and the opium created a perfume that was strangely sweet and thick, and seemed to close in on me.

Out of the darkness, shapes began to emerge. The walls were lined with divans, covered in velvet and brocade throws and large satin cushions. Beside each divan there was a metal tray which held a small collection of laquered boxes, ceramic bowls, and long pipes. The lamps twinkled. I could see bodies lying silently, immobile on the couches, as if paralyzed by dreams. The perfumed smoke curled around a large statue of the Buddha, which sat on a small raised platform in the centre of the room.

'Ah,' said Igor.

He led me quietly over to Olga. Her eyes were half open as she stared sightlessly at the ceiling. A pipe lay beside her. Someone nearby raised a pipe and sucked on it with a faint hiss.

Igor bent over Olga and kissed her lightly on the forehead. 'Olya,' he whispered.

She half turned her head, and murmured, 'Ah, yes... I knew it. The third pipe. You always come... the third...' She turned her head again to face the ceiling and her eyes closed.

'It's me,' Igor whispered. 'I have my camera. Will you be angry with me? May I, Olya?' he whispered. He was already

225

adjusting the light meter, getting the shot into focus. She opened her eyes and, to my astonishment, smiled vaguely. 'Why not?' she drawled. 'It's... beauty... They say it rots the body, but no, it doesn't rot beauty. It brings... after the third pipe.'

I couldn't tear my eyes away as he took the photograph. No one seemed to notice. Except for the click of the camera, we were wrapped in a deep, perfumed silence, broken only by the small hissing as someone sucked on a pipe.

Philippe had prepared his "jam." His pipe was old and exquisite, inlaid with delicate patterns of ivory and gold.

'How many pipes has she had?' Igor whispered.

Philippe sucked his pipe slowly, closed his eyes and exhaled. The smell made me feel unsteady, as if I too had had some "jam." He raised a languid arm to the small slate that hung on the wall beside him. 'Three,' he said.

Igor fumbled under his kimono and brought some coins out of his pockets. 'This is for the third pipe,' he said. 'Tell her I was here, won't you?'

Philippe nodded. 'Will you have some?' he asked. 'Oh no, you don't like to dream, do you? But perhaps your friend?' He smiled at me.

'Another time,' said Igor. 'Don't forget to tell her.'

'I never forget,' Philippe inhaled again. Igor wrote his initials on the slate, next to Olga's name.

Outside, I took deep breaths of cool air, trying to get the smell out of my lungs. My head was swimming and I leant against the wall. 'Why? How did you know?'

'I thought that's where she would go for comfort.'

'How can she do that?' I asked. My voice sounded odd, like a hard-edged intrusion into this blurred universe.

'She is romantic, she's sad, she wants to forget. There is only one way I can help her and it's impossible, so I help as I can.'

'How?' I asked.

'I would have to be with her always, that's all she wants. And if she can't have that, she will have –' He indicated the studio.

I thought of our careful budgets, how we just managed to get by, day by day: the old clothes, the cheap rooms and poor food, how we walked to save metro fares. 'You gave her money,' I said. 'You paid our money for her to do... that.'

'Yes,' he said. 'And why not? Her life is unbearable. She lost her home, her family, her child, everything. She isn't young. All she ever had was beauty and charm. To buy her one pipe occasionally? It's a small enough gift.'

'Have you been there with her?' I didn't say it, but what I meant was, how much of our money had paid for Olga Nikolayevna's "comfort."

'Once but never again. I won't allow myself to be captured by dreams.'

'I would never – never – pay for such a thing.'

'Oh, why not? It isn't so bad. She has to have someone else to give her dreams. It's sad,' he said.

'Stupid,' I replied. 'It's a stupid thing to do.'

'Don't be cruel,' he said.

'It's cruel to bring me here.' I said.

'I brought you because you had to know,' he said. 'I want to share everything with you.'

All the perfume and scented smoke seemed to have gathered in the pit of my stomach. 'I'm going to be sick,' I said.

He put an arm around me and helped me across the courtyard. 'No, you won't. Some people react like that to the smell at first. Don't worry, we won't go there again.'

We went out, back onto the Rue Bosquet. Someone blocked our way.

'Igor Fyedorovich.' Gyorgei was smiling, as always, 'I knew you would be here. We saw you earlier at the *Dôme*. Poor Olga Nikolayevna. Her little weakness. Understandable, but dangerous.' He spoke as if he was relaying another wonderful piece of gossip. 'Arensky is waiting to speak with you. And he is waiting with Stassov! He is at the *Bonne Goutte*, Rue Marie-Blanche.'

'Now?' asked Igor.

'This is a convenient time for him.' A breathless giggle escaped him. 'I'll take you there. It's best we go together.'

We began to stroll, apparently aimlessly, up the Rue Montparnasse. Gyorgei whistled *Mon homme*. 'The divine Mistinguett,' he said. 'Have you seen her? What a performer!'

'Do you ever go home?' Igor asked.

'You can ask!' he exclaimed. And then we said no more until we reached the Rue Marie-Blanche. The café was a place for market traders who ate huge rolls filled with greasy sausages. Arensky sat near the coffee urn with Stassov, a short man with unusually broad shoulders, like a wrestler. Igor went toward them. I started to follow, but Gyorgy stopped me, making graceful, meaningless gestures with his hands. 'Only Igor,' he said. 'You know General Arensky laid down his conditions.'

'Only Igor?' I asked. I was still in a dream of Olga Nikolayevna immobile, dreaming her opium dreams, waiting for Igor.

'Yes, you remember. We have it in hand. There will be no problem. Are you feeling well?' he asked.

'Feeling well?' I still felt dazed, and unreal.

'Take a nice breath of fresh air. On a night like this, one truly enjoys Paris. In fact,' Gyorgei said, 'I must go to the Robilevs now.' He hesitated. 'You ought to walk around a little. Just for a few minutes. You really are very pale.'

'It's the lamplight,' I said. 'Everyone is transformed.'

'True,' he said, as if struck by the thought. 'That's very true. How interesting. I must tell the Robilevs. But take my advice, walk around a bit. Get some fresh air.' He hurried away.

I stood alone on the street, waiting. What would happen? No one would tell me, I knew that. I was meant to be ignorant and innocent. I wanted to push all that innocence away. If Igor wanted us to share everything, then it must be so. *I am not Olga*, I thought, and went to the café door. Again, someone blocked the way. It was Isidor, Lewitsky's brother. He had come from some nearby shadow, and stood with his grotesque, smashed face, his bulging eye fixed on me, one finger raised in warning. Involuntarily, I shrank back, and after a moment, he withdrew into the shadow. I understood that he was Igor's guardian at this interview, and my disgust at his appearance gave way to gratitude at his presence. *They have it in hand,* I thought. *There will be no problem.*

I wandered to the corner, where there was a small brightly lit bar. The door swung open and angry voices broke out, as a red faced, drunken Englishman was pushed out onto the street. He staggered and swore as he fell almost at my feet. The whores shouted and laughed as his head hit the pavement. I heard the sound of bicycle bells: the police were coming. I went quickly up a side street.

The street was narrow, with small houses crushed together, broken by signs saying "Hotel." I walked aimlessly down another one, nearly identical. I mustn't go too far, I thought I must wait outside the cafe. I turned to go back, but I was suddenly disorientated, unable to remember which way I had come. There were tiny side streets, alleys, turnings... I went down one and then another until I was truly lost. 'Igor? Uncle Igor,' I called out helplessly, knowing that wherever he was he couldn't hear me.

A man spoke to me in French and suddenly I didn't understand anything he said. '*Non!*' I cried. '*Non!*'

'*Russe?*' he asked.

'*Non,*' I said like a fool, and ran the other way.

A sudden scent of hyacinth cut across the night. It must have come from one of the flower stalls that stayed open until dark and had only just closed. It brought back a forgotten moment: a table set with white linen and gleaming silver. I am sitting on someone's lap, holding a painted egg. I breathed in the scent until it dissolved in the misty air.

'*Mademoiselle, mademoiselle.*' A face grinned at me out of an archway. It was a dark-haired Algerian, who grinned and beckoned to me. '*Içi, içi,*' he said. '*Non,*' I said and backed away, but he was now surrounded by other men, all, to me, identical, also grinning. He grasped my arm. '*Içi,*' he whispered and drew me toward the arch. He held out an object and I saw it was the shrunken head of a woman, her skin stretched so tight it pulled her features sideways. A tuft of hair sprang from the top of her head. 'Real,' said one of the men, pointing it out to me. The Algerian held it closer for my inspection. '*Voulay?*' he said. '*Voulay?* Ten francs only.' The shrunken shrivelled head cried out to me for release. I backed away into something solid that said, 'What are you doing?' It was Igor.

He pulled me away from the Algerians, who gabbled shrilly and then vanished as if they had never existed.

'What were you doing with those people?' he asked, but he spoke in an abstracted way.

'Someone approached me,' I said, 'and I went this way to get rid of him. What happened?'

Igor said, 'We've got him. We're finished here. I want to get away.'

He gripped my wrist as if to make sure I wouldn't escape.

'Igor,' I gasped. 'You're hurting my arm.'

'Sorry,' he said, and kept walking, pulling me along.

'What happened?' I asked.

'He has Stassov. "Moscow" has the money. Don't talk about it.'

'Why not? Is something wrong?'

'No!' he shouted, and I was afraid to say any more.

Back in our rooms in the Rue Offenbach, Igor sank onto the couch, leaned back, and knocked his head against the wall. 'Oh, my God,' he said. 'He looks as I imagined my father. What I saw and what I imagined are so much alike. I hadn't noticed.' Unexpectedly, he laughed.

'I have to walk,' he said. 'I have to walk. I'm going to suffocate in here.'

'Do you want to walk again? I'll walk with you,' I said although my eyes were heavy, my legs felt like lead and it was almost daybreak.

He started to rise, then leant back and closed his eyes. 'Oh my God, it's all too complicated. Much too complicated.'

'Igor, please tell me what's wrong. What have you done?' I asked.

'What do you mean? Nothing! I've done nothing! Why do you keep asking that?'

I didn't answer.

Abruptly he said, 'Sonia. What a beautiful name.'

'Sonia?' I repeated, startled. 'You said that name once before. Remember? You wanted me to pray for her. Who is she?' Waves of tiredness soaked through my body, and my head was still dizzy from the evening, Someone called Sonia had now joined Olga and the couple on the Ferris wheel, Isidor and the Algerians. They floated back and forth slowly, all part of the night. 'Sonia?' I asked again. 'Which woman was Sonia?'

'No one,' he said. 'It's a name. Beautiful.'

'Yes.' I tried to placate him. 'Was it someone you knew?'

'Oh, my God, I have to walk.' But he didn't move. Instead, to my astonishment, he started to weep.

'Igor Fyedorovitch,' I said in my sternest tone 'what is it you're not telling me? Has something happened to Mit... to General Arensky?' My firmness dissolved and I begged, 'Please, please tell me.'

'No, no. It went exactly as it should,' he said. 'Nothing has happened to anyone.' His eyes were closed. He leant his head against the wall. Tears still oozed out of the corners of his eyes. 'It was so simple. He was ripe for it.'

'You can tell me.'

'It's up to "Moscow" now. For us, it's over.' He leaned back against the wall and looked at me with half-closed eyes. 'They didn't trust me you know. This was a test. I had to prove to them...'

'Igor,' I began, 'I know there's something ... '

He said, 'Don't say that any more.'

I sat beside him. I hadn't realised how thin he had become.

I took his hand, feeling his thin strong fingers and seeing his ragged bitten nails.

He opened his eyes, and I couldn't bear to see how red-rimmed they were, how sunken in his face. 'I can't live with wanting you the way I do.'

'Shhh,' I said. I held his hands with their unhappy, bitten nails.'

'Oh Nadia.' He gently and slowly stroked my neck with one finger. He drew me close and we lay silently together for a long time. I think those moments were the happiest I ever spent with "Uncle Igor".

Then he stirred against me. 'We mustn't,' he said. 'We promised not to do this.'

'I know.'

He took a deep breath. 'What can I do? You're not a child. You said it yourself.' He held me closer. 'There's nothing we can do.' His hands fumbled with my dress.

'No, Igor, no.' But my heart beat faster and I felt the excitement and fear sweep me out of myself.

'It doesn't matter now,' he said. 'None of it matters.' He said, 'I wont hurt you.' And he began to loosen my clothes.

I watched myself letting him do it, thinking that I should protest, that this was wrong, and then thinking oddly: this will ruin my life. And then I knew, I wanted my life to be ruined.

It was fast and hard and violent. There was pain and someone cried out in my voice and it was over.

I lay still, looking into the darkness. The room was filled with dead bodies, one piled on the other. One of the corpses raised its head: it was mama. She stared at me without expression and then returned to the pile of skeletons. Her photograph watched from its frame. Was I awake or asleep? If it was a dream, was it a symbol of something? Then I fell asleep again.

When I woke up, Igor lay on top of me, his head on my breast. My leg was was numb and starting to prickle painfully. I tried to move, but I couldn't shift his weight. He stirred, sighed. There was a dull ache somewhere between my legs and something sticky underneath me. I felt dirty and obscurely ashamed.

He opened his eyes. 'Are you all right?' he murmured.

He rolled off me. I immediately curled up tightly, staring at the opposite wall, where his photographs were pinned up. The Eiffel Tower at night, yes, and the photographs of me, half naked, lying on this bed, one hand across my breasts; lying on my side with my arm over my head; standing by the window, a sheet draped around me, exposing my shoulders and back. Pictures of a young girl full of romantic stories and fairy tales, particularly intimate because they were images no one would ever see.

'We couldn't stop it,' he said gently. 'It had to happen. Sooner or later.'

I didn't answer. I wanted to wash. I wanted to go to the public baths and scrub myself with very hot water. The ache between my legs seemed to spread to my heart.

'It was meant to be,' he said. 'And it was very, very beautiful. For me, truly. Was it good for you? Yes. You are so lovely, my Nadia.' He sounded young, uncertain, a note of pleading in his voice. 'To love you is something amazing. You felt that, didn't you.'

I didn't move. I lay curled up, and listened to him pleading with me to love him.

CHAPTER TWENTY-EIGHT

FEBRUARY, 1924

'But I look at every woman,' Igor said absently. He squinted through the viewfinder. 'Not just Olga Nikolayevna. I like to look at women. You know that.'

I did know it, but everything was different between us now. 'Even when they're ugly?' I was sitting on the edge of our chair, wearing only the red shawl, thrown lightly over one shoulder. The lights were out except for the lamp, which cast a shadow across me. I balanced myself with one arm on the back of the chair. My other arm felt stiff from holding up my hair. We had been working on this photograph all evening. I yawned.

'There are no ugly women.' Igor was squatting on his heels, angling the camera. "Moscow" (through Lewitsky as usual) had arranged for Uncle Igor to receive one of the new, fast Leica cameras. We were experimenting with it, trying different angles, and different kinds of light. Uncle Igor was right, I thought, formal portraits were definitely finished now that the Leica had made the tripod unnecessary. A photographer with a Leica was free to interpret, not just record. Lewitsky had said when Uncle Igor inquired, "Moscow" won't pay for it.' But they had.

'I look at people.' he said. 'I can't help myself.'

'Why don't you move the camera more sideways?' I said, and added in the same breath, 'Not people. Women.'

'No. This is what I want. You must lean more to the side.' I angled my upper body as best I could. The shawl slipped from my shoulder. 'That's right ... oh yes, yes.'

'But you look at Olga all the time,' I said. Even while I spoke I could imagine how my body, an out of focus shape against the dark background would become, through his lens, an abstract pearlised curve of flesh, would be a half-thought caught on the wing. It was cold now, but I could tell by the way the camera was poised that this would work and that warmed me. 'She thinks you're in love with her,' I said. 'And when she's with us, you don't look at other women.'

'I look at everyone,' he said. 'You don't notice, because you are so busy watching her. Silly girl.' He snapped the picture, got up and stretched. I sat up. The shawl fell to the floor. He picked it up and with a gallant bow, put it on my lap. As he did, his eyes lingered on my breasts with the expression I had seen whenever a woman passed by.

'We need Olga Nikolayevna,' he said. 'If we want to be together we have to be together with her. Otherwise, what would people say?'

This was the brief period of Igor's great photographs. Unlike his harsh photographs of the night people of Paris, these are both abstract and personal, reflections of light and water and glass. They are a carefully arranged and painstakingly created passion. A figure striped with shadow, a girl hazily lit, with her head turned. The face is always unclear. Over and over he photographed me and he experimented with foreshortenings and odd angles: from underneath, from above, standing, seated, lying down, reflected in a half-full glass pitcher, mysterious and enigmatic. Who is that figure? What does she mean? My favourite was simply a curtain of long dark hair, parted just enough here and there to make out parts of a face: a bit of jaw line, a suggestion of the curve of a cheek. The girl is strange and also familiar. Neither of us knew at the time that these were the photographs that would make his name.

He put the camera back in its case, and smiled at me. 'I need to walk,' he said. 'Alone.' He put his arms around me and we embraced, a long, slow embrace. After these evenings together, there was nothing I wanted more than him.

I slipped on my dress, and mixed the silver chloride crystals with gelatine as Igor had taught me, and began to spread it carefully across the printing paper. He would want to develop these pictures when he came back. The smell of chloride and the resined paper was so sharp it scoured my nostrils when I inhaled, and made my eyes water. As I continued, I thought of Olga, and no matter how hard I tried, I couldn't push her face out of my mind, always with the slightly mocking smile, and her huge eyes, alternately dreamy and sly. Sly, I thought, washing the paper, yes, you're sly. Her image hung in the air with her voice, childlike and musical: 'You should have a lover, Nadezhda Michailovna, at your age it would be good for you. 'I started to wash another sheet of paper. They had to be dry before Uncle Igor could use them. I began to send my thoughts to Olga, talking to her in my mind: *You can't do this, you can do nothing for him, you mean nothing, you can't give what I can, it's me he loves, you fool, it's me.* And so I washed the sheets of paper, ready for Igor, and I talked to Olga in my mind, although her image never lost its sly little smile. When I was finished, I stepped back, blinking the sting out of my eyes, and lit a cigarette. I boiled water for tea and felt hollow with hunger for Igor to come back. I wanted him to look at me the way he looked at me when we were alone. I knew that when he was with Olga he was lying. I believed him, but I wanted other people to know he was lying and I wanted them to believe him; I wanted the world to know and I wanted it to be a secret. *This is madness,* I thought. It was the only reality. Igor had led me into a world with a strange light, a light made within darkness, that gave heat without illumination. *Perhaps,* I thought, *shadows were necessary with love, because otherwise the light would be so bright, the lovers would die in its blaze.*

We had no lemon. I poured the tea into a glass and sat down, crouched over its warmth, wondering why so many emotions pounded in my stomach.

When dawn was starting to silver the sky, Igor came back. He avoided my eyes and said, 'Are they dry?' He picked up a sheet of paper.

'You've been with her haven't you?' I said.

'Nadia, how can you say that?'

'I know you have. I can tell.'

She's necessary. Do you want people to talk about us? Let them talk about her. She's making a fool of herself, let her go ahead. Like you and Alyosha.' His eyes narrowed when he saw my expression. 'Or are you really so fond of him? Do you imagine you're in love with him?'

'No. I'm not.' I said. 'I believe in his ideals that's all.'

'Yes, yes, don't tell me again.' He frowned at me and spoke sternly. 'We need him, too, you know, with his ideals. People gossip, so let them gossip about Olga and Alyosha and not about us.'

'But you run after Olga everywhere. You are with her when I am at Tanya's. Zhenia Arenska talks about it. She lifts a finger and you are there. She's not that beautiful.' I started to cry.

'Oh, Nadia,' he said. 'My Nadyushka. Why can't you understand? We must look after her,' he said. 'We mustn't be cruel. I have to see her. What would she think if I only saw her when I was with you? You must help me in this. If I am not with her she would go back to that place. She has suffered a great deal. You must understand that.'

'We have all suffered,' I said. 'Who hasn't?'

'I know. But she was never a strong person. You know,' he said, 'she lost her child at the beginning of the revolution.'

'How?' I asked in spite of myself.

'Starvation.' He said the word without emotion,

He stroked my hair and picked up the hairbrush. He began to brush my hair in long strokes, gently, and then harder.

'Was it your child?' I asked.

'I don't know.'

He fell into a rhythm with the brush and bent my head forward as he drew the brush down with long, even strokes. 'You know the first time I saw a man draw blood?' he said, and went on without waiting for an answer: 'It was your grandfather. He had been riding and the horse was nervous, the groom was awkward, he did something, I don't know, and the horse shied. Your grandfather lashed at the man with his whip and caught him across the face. It was as if someone had drawn a line across it with a pencil.' He drew the brush down to the ends of my hair. I felt the bristles touch my back. Then he started again at the top, with a light pull and a long, even stroke.

'And then slowly the line changed colour.' He pressed the brush a little harder and I felt the light tug of my hair against my head. 'And the line turned light red, and then darker red,' he went on, as if it was a lullaby, 'as if someone was drawing it from the inside. Then there was one tiny drop of blood and then another drop until there was a row of tiny drops, like little eyes weeping.' He was sweating. 'I used to dream about it all the time – that line of red.'

I closed my eyes. I just wanted to sleep, but I asked, 'Why are you telling me this?'

'I want us to have the same memories.' He said softly.

'What happened to the man?'

'He's probably a commissar, and good luck to him. Nadia,' he brushed my hair back from my temples, more quickly now, 'we're terrible people.'

I felt his heartbeat as he laid me back on the bed and spread my hair around me. 'I don't want to talk about it any more.' He said. 'People have glorious memories of the past as if it was a lost paradise. I don't remember a paradise.'

CHAPTER TWENTY-NINE

JUNE 1924

Alyosha cleared his throat, and smiled nervously at everyone. 'I hope that tonight you will join me in a new group, to be called Young Russia, which will attract the younger Russian émigrés, which will include both new ideas and the Russian tradition.' It was badly put, I thought. He sounded as if he was pleading with them. Where was the glow he usually had when he spoke? A few people eyed each other suspiciously.

There were too many people in the Clamart office, all crammed together in hostile juxtaposition. I wondered what made Alyosha choose these people. There were Monarchists, Social-Revolutionaries, followers of Miliukov, and former Kadets who had refused to follow Miliukov. There were two Masons, one a member of the right wing Grande Loge and the other of the left wing Orient Loge. People overflowed the available seats; they perched on the arms of the sofa, and the sides of the desk. I eyed them all and thought that Alyosha must have chosen them at random.

'It will be a part of the Eurasians,' he added. 'A Young Russian group within the organisation,' he added.

The room was thick with smoke. The two chipped saucers on the worn carpet overflowed with cigarette ends. Siftings of ash had collected around them. The room was cold. The smell of damp mingled with the smoke and Ilya Perkov's hair pomade. I sat hunched in the desk chair over my notebook. Alyosha had told me to 'write everything down so we have a clear record. We must stay organised.' But the meeting had fallen into such disarray, that my notes had turned into a few scrawls and an occasional disconnected word.

'We will return in July 1930. This is a message from the government of the Kurkov District. The peasants expect it,' said Ilya.

'1930?' A woman asked. 'Six years?'

There was a heavy silence.'

I waited for Alyosha's answer, and wondered where Ilya had got his information.

There was a knock at the door. It opened a crack, and Grisha Bobrov sidled in, his whole being crouched in apology.

People looked sidelong at each other in malicious alliance. I could almost hear their thoughts: 'Larissa's lover? Here?' Alyosha stared without expression at his wife's lover, but his face flushed with anger.

'Larissa said it would be a good idea. She thought I ought to come,' Grisha stammered.

'Why?' he asked.

Grisha blushed, looked at the crowded little room, and stammered. 'She said you would need people.' Someone smothered a laugh.

He looked as if he was about to cry. 'She insisted, actually. But I-I-I'll go.' Grisha backed away.

'No.' Alyosha raised his voice. 'Come in then if that's what you were told.'

People watched Grisha with sympathy and a gleam of excitement as he slid down the wall and sat down, leaning against the door. I could imagine how they would gossip later.

I touched the green beads Igor had given me and wondered, *Does everyone feel like me? All these people?* It didn't seem possible that anyone could feel the tumult I felt and still be able to discuss politics. I watched Ilya Perkov blow smoke at the ceiling and wondered if even he had ever been helpless with need. It was impossible. *If everyone felt like me,* I thought, *the world would explode.* I longed to talk to someone about it. I wondered if Mama would ever talk about such a thing. If only she would magically appear, I could tell her and she would understand immediately. I ached for her to be here. The ache sharpened as I knew it was impossible. Kyra would have an opinion, and I didn't want an opinion. I wanted someone to listen to the chaos of emotion within me.

Alyosha coughed and began again, sounding even more uncertain now. I began to push the skin of my index finger with my thumbnail. It had become a habit with me. I had worn away layers of skin and made a hard sunken callus in the finger pad. The pinprick pressure of it was strangely comforting as I wrote down: "unity", "ambition in exile", "contribution", and "Communist link." I underlined the phrase.

'But what is your programme?' a man demanded. 'What are we working toward?'

'You are suggesting we consider an acceptance of Communism!' A woman exclaimed. She stood up and walked out. Grisha had to push himself to one side, away from the door. She stepped over his hand as if it was a lump of coal.

People began to talk at the same time and interrupt each other.

I wrote down more words: "barbarians", "theft", "collapse", and wondered what Igor was doing, where he was and if he was with Olga. After this meeting, I had to go to work. It would be hours until we would be together and the day would begin.

Alyosha struggled to regain control, but he continually looked over at Grisha Bobrov. 'You may be right,' he said to Ilya Perkov. 'It would be something to consider.'

I could see Alyosha's idealism so clearly, his nobility, his honour, and I thought perhaps that's what made him weak, easily won over. Uncle Igor could never be won over. He held life in his own hands and if there was torment in his soul, he bore it and grew stronger.

'The idea is to gather as a group and look objectively at the ideas of Communism and how they develop in practice. We don't have to agree,' said Alyosha. 'Disagreement is democratic.'

'Thank God I am not a democrat,' a woman said.

'We Russians are a violent people,' Ilya drawled, closing his eyes and looking at the ceiling. He reminded me of Oblomov. 'Violent and passive. The Soviets inherit the violent strain. With proper control something could be done.'

A small, thin woman suddenly spoke up. 'Without God, even the violence in the Eurasian inheritance is the work of the devil.'

She launched into a tirade against the Soviets for outlawing churches, folk tales, 'all the beliefs that form the spiritual foundation of Russia'.

'And so we must make a statement on a future union between the Monarchy and the Soviet,' said Ilya. 'You haven't mentioned it. His Majesty will be displeased.'

'Yes,' Alyosha agreed feebly. He nodded several times. 'We will look at it from all sides.'

'His Majesty? Red Cyril? Who wore a red badge on his jacket when Lenin took power?' A woman sneered at Ilya.

Alyosha pressed against the tide of voices. 'But our principal question should be, how has it progressed in Russia today? Without prejudice or ideology.'

'You have said that already,' a man interrupted. 'What is your plan of action?'

'You cannot prove that,' Ilya said to the woman 'And let me tell you, you will regret someday that you said those words. Bitterly regret it.' He stood up. 'The Soviet state can only be controlled by a return of the nobility.'

People were leaving. Ilya Perkov was the first. He had to be at Les Halles to help unload the wagons. The others straggled out.

'Be careful, Alyosha,' said an older woman. 'I know you, but others will say you are turning towards the Left.'

When they had gone, Alyosha slowly picked up one of the overflowing saucers. There were ashes on the carpet.

'It wasn't any good, was it?' he said. He didn't look at me. 'No one was interested.'

'No they weren't,' I agreed. There was no point trying to

cheer him up. 'And now they will only say you have joined the Left.'

'I wonder which of them was the Cheka agent,' he said. 'Someone was.'

'Well, at least it wasn't Ilya Perkov,' I said. I folded *The Latest News* and tried to use it to brush the ashes into a folded copy of *Vorozhdenie*. The meeting had ended early. I would have time go to Igor for a moment on my way to work. I felt my heart literally beat faster at the idea. I brushed a few more ashes onto the paper, and folded it up.

'It might be Ilya Perkov. It's possible.' Alyosha held out the saucer as if he was going to offer it to me. 'These people: everything becomes a quarrel, one faction against another. Will they never stop bickering and plotting against each other?' He emptied the saucer in the wastepaper basket. 'Don't they see that to quarrel amongst themselves is useless?'

'It may be useless,' I said, 'but they won't stop, Alyosha, they will go on quarrelling until you offer a plan of action that will unite everyone. And that is impossible.'

He sat down. 'You're right,' he said. 'And I have a plan. But I wanted to talk to you first.' He took a book off the shelf and opened it. 'Listen to this.' He read: '*Three young maidens sat one night/spinning in the window bright/ If I were the tsar's elected/one of these young maids reflected/ I would spread a festive board/for all the children of the Lord.*' I used to read that with my sisters. It always reminds me of the long summer evenings and the smell of pine trees. My sisters read and I sat at their feet, on the front steps. And Moushka, our dog, would lie with his head on my lap, listening.' He paused and looked at something in the distance. Then he smiled. 'I can hear their voices, and the poetry singing over my head.' He read another line: '*If I were the tsar's elected/her young sister interjected/I'd weave linen cloth to spare/ for all people everywhere.*' He held out the book and I read: '*Had I been the tsar's elected/said the third, I'd have expected/ soon to bear our father tsar/a young hero famed afar.*'

We took it in turns to read the poem down to '*On the morn*

the prince, awaking/And nocturnal visions shaking/marvelled to behold ahead/A prodigious city spread. Walls with crenellated arches/Snowy bastions topped with churches/Dazzling domes to heaven soar/Holy Monasteries galore.' Alyosha read the lines in his warm, beautiful voice. He smiled with pleasure at the words. Then he sighed and put the book down. 'I can't bear to hear more right now,' he said.

'Just before the revolution, I memorised 'The Gypsies',' I said. I began: *Between Moldavian Settlements/ in clamorous throng the gypsies wander...* I remember it better now than I did then,' I said. Encouraged by his interest, I confessed, 'And after we read *Ryssalka* at school I fell in love with Lermontov and I decided to memorise every poem he ever wrote.'

Alyosha laughed. 'And did you manage to do it?'

'No, but I knew more than anyone in my class.' He had drawn me into a half-forgotten memory. 'I thought I go on all my life, just memorising poetry, lots and lots of it.'

'I'll tell you something,' he said. 'When I was a boy, I learned all of "Boris Goudonov." Well, almost. Well, a lot.' His eyes were shining now as he recited stanzas. He spoke them so beautifully, it reminded me that he had once been an actor.

He closed the book and spoke softly. 'Why didn't I refuse to let Grisha Bobrov come in? Because Larissa said so? I looked a fool. He wants to be free of her, she is not ready to let him go, she passes him to me to hold onto for her. It's not the first time. I should stand up to her! I know I they think I'm a weakling, but I'm not, Nadia. I have ideas, I want to make something of my life.' He was trying to light his cigarette. He struck the match unsuccessfully over and over. The tiny scratches of the match against the box sounded like mouse laughter.

'Oh, give me that,' I said. I took the matches from him and struck one. He held out his cigarette, inhaled slowly and blew out the smoke. He looked out the window at the blank grey wall of the house next door. 'I don't know how to say this.'

'What is it?' I asked, half guessing what it was. 'Just say it.'

'I wanted to see what would happen at the meeting today,'

he said. 'And now I know I am doing the right thing. I want you to know, Nadia. I have applied for a Soviet passport.'

I was startled but after the first moment, not surprised. Although I had half suspected it, the words struck me with a sense of doom.

'People will say terrible things about me, but I can't live any longer with this feeling of betrayal.'

'Does this mean you are going back?' I asked.

'My application was refused,' he admitted. 'My army record makes me suspect. But I have applied again. If they refuse, I will apply again. I will apply until they believe I am a patriot.'

'What about Larissa?' I asked. There were so many questions to ask. And I knew they meant nothing. The answers would never affect his decision.

'She refuses to think about it. Larissa has no interest in politics,' he said. 'I can't talk to her.'

We were quiet for a minute. The room felt stale and airless, a place where spring would never come. Outside, there would be cool air and a clear evening sky. 'Alyosha,' I said, 'Are you sure you're not applying because you think you can go back to your memories?' I picked up the book he had left on the table.

'I'm not like that,' he said. 'I look forward. Always.'

It was true. He did. I put the book down.

'I have never wanted to live in the past. These other people,' he made a small gesture which managed to include all of Russian Paris 'they think they can preserve the "real Russia." It's all atrophy. "Human dust." I'm sorry,' he said.

'Don't say you're sorry. Why are you sorry to say what you think?'

'I want you to understand.' He looked directly into my eyes. 'You do understand, don't you? We've talked before. You know how I feel.'

'But does it appeal to you because of its... strength?' I ventured, thinking of what Zhenia and others had said.

'You mean because I'm weak?' he asked. 'I know that's what

people say. I am not weak.' His voice sounded beautiful, with firm, rounded tones. 'I need belief like blood in my veins. It *is* the blood in my veins. When I am no longer ready to shed my blood, then I can't go on. It is impossible. I don't know why they say I'm weak.' He spoke more quickly, with emphasis, as if in his own defence. 'My mother cursed me when I joined Wrangel. But in 1917, it seemed to me the Russia I loved was being destroyed, my family was tearing everything to pieces.' He coughed and stubbed out his cigarette. 'A weak man can be won, or bought. I can't be won or bought, Nadia. I have rethought my past, and I want to have a citizenship in my country. I want to find a way back, to expiate my guilt if you like. I'm sorry.'

'Stop saying sorry!' I said.

He shook his head. 'The Eurasian was one possible way, a way to accept what has happened and find a future. But this isn't the future. His voice grew stronger. He wasn't weak at all. Why did people say he was? They didn't understand him.

'There is only one way to accept the Soviets and that is with one's heart and soul. I am ready. They have to know that.'

'Alyosha,' I began. He shook his head.

'It's no good, Nadia, whatever you say, I have thought of it already. Nadia... may I ask you for something?'

'What is it?' I asked.

'It's about your Igor Fyedorovitch,' he said. 'He has taken photographs of all sorts of people.' He cleared his throat. 'Left and right.' He paused again. 'Groups from all sides.'

What is he getting at? I thought. *Does he know something or has he simply drawn conclusions? Have people talked about Igor?*

'I can't ask Igor Fyedorovitch directly,' Alyosha went on, 'because it will look underhanded. You know, like a bribe. Or begging. But if you would ask him to put in a word, that is, if he could speak for me to the right people, to say that he knows personally that I am a patriot.' He looked at me with his clear, hopeful eyes.

'But Igor is not political,' I said. 'He has no influence over anyone. I don't know what you suspect but it's not true.'

'Suspect? What? I suspect nothing.'

'Really Alyosha, you sometimes sound stupid. How can you want Igor to compromise himself like that?'

'Compromise?' He asked. 'I don't know what you mean.'

'Yes you do! You want Igor to speak for you as your ally, that is to compromise himself. You are unwilling to compromise yourself and yet you want him to do it for you!' I was suddenly furious. 'Why should he swear you are pro-soviet? If he does, whose side will people think he is on? Your honour!' I was hot with rage. 'You think the whole world should help you to redeem yourself? To ease your guilt? You know Igor cannot have any politics.'

'I didn't think. I'm sorry,' he said.

'I told you to stop saying sorry.' The heat had gone. I was only achingly sad. 'I hope you get your passport,' I said.

'Is that all you have to say?'

'What else is there to say, Alyosha? You have thought, you are clear, I know you will always do what you believe to be right, and I hope you will be allowed to do it. But be clear that Igor cannot help you.'

'We are still friends?' he asked.

'I'm sorry,' I said.

Outside, I gulped in the cold air and began to walk away briskly. Then, as I turned the corner, I was stopped by the sight of the grotesque, immobile figure of Isidor, his smashed face caught in the streetlight. After the first moment of recognition, I realised he didn't frighten me any more. Our eyes met, and to my surprise he bowed slightly and his lips twisted into something like a smile. The effort gave it an air of unexpected sweetness. He raised one finger in a small salute, and without thinking, I returned it. Then he vanished into the shadows.

CHAPTER THIRTY

MAY 1924

'The government is in total disarray since Lenin's death,' said Stassov. 'Crumbling. They are losing the support of the army. They are losing the support of the press. Everywhere, in the towns and villages, people have had enough of these Communists. The Trust has supporters throughout Russia. They were completely open with me.' Stassov was a strongly-built man, neatly dressed and he stood very straight and clasped his chauffeur's cap tightly to his chest as he made his report. His military bearing was a light cover for his excitement. 'The Trust believes that with our help, the time is ready for The Return.'

Arensky sat at his desk in the Military Union Headquarters in the Rue Mademoiselle. The house was old, and as shabby as its members. The walls had patches of flaking plaster, the stone steps were worn, and in the small vestibule there were cracks in the walls behind the portraits of Wrangel, Kornilov, Markov and the Imperial Family. There was also a notice-board with announcements of lectures and practice drills. From the small cafe in the basement there drifted a smell of cabbage.

Arensky's desk was bigger than Alyosha's, I noticed, and unlike Alyosha's, it was bare, except for a blotter, an inkwell and an ashtray. Filing cabinets stood behind his chair. Framed photographs of young men in tsarist uniform lined the walls. Behind him, above the filing cabinets, there was a photograph of the emperor and empress on horseback. He had brought in extra chairs for Igor, Gyorgy and me.

Here, in his official role of regimental leader, Mitya was at once more relaxed and more in command. He was not the Mitya who taught me chess and described pre-revolutionary theatre performances with Roschina-Insarova. With one step into this room he had become "General Arensky," no longer an exile. I felt as if he had got physically larger, and I could understand how he had commanded such absolute loyalty from his troops, even when they were huddled in tents during the long freezing winter in Gallipoli. It was more than a return to rank, I thought. It was a return to pride. His pride made me proud of him. At the same time, as Stassov continued his report, with lists of names and places, I felt that this return was a return to a lost world that I barely remembered. I thought, for me, this is a return to an idea. How would it be? Would it be as it was before the revolution? I had a memory of the little boys at the foot of the Lityini Bridge, changing the tram horses. I suddenly remembered their bright-red knitted gloves.

Stassov was still talking about the increasing weakness of the Bolsheviks, their fear of the émigré military unions. 'We are considered the greatest menace to their power. If our united émigré regiments appeared at the border, we would recruit volunteers all the way to Moscow.' He bowed his head. Arensky listened carefully, without moving, while Igor and Gyorgei nodded their interest and agreement. 'Also financial aid will be granted by the powers in the West who are prepared to overthrow Bolshevism and give Russia back to the Russian people.' Stassov added and paused, overcome with emotion.

'The Grand Duke Nicholas and General Kutepov both believe that we abroad cannot decide the future of the Russian people. That must be decided in Russia. Will the people accept the leadership of an émigré army?' General Arensky didn't raise his voice, but there was something in his tone that made me feel that Stassov's words needed more proof. Stassov clearly felt the same.

'It *has* been decided in Russia. The people want deliverance from Communism. You have my word, General,' said Stassov.

'I have met members of The Trust and their agents in key departments of government. Some of them are very close to Lenin himself. I have even taken communion with them in Moscow, openly. I tell you, the Bolsheviks are a spent force.'

He fumbled in his breast pocket. 'I have a letter from Voyetinsky. He's the head of the Foreign Affairs department and also a Trust leader. He asks for a meeting with you to plan a joint strategy for the attack on Moscow.' He gave the letter to Arensky who read it and passed it to Igor.

'If your information is correct and if there is a meeting,' Arensky said, weighing each word, 'it must be in neutral territory and with the strictest security.'

'It goes without saying,' Igor agreed, 'Both parties must be assured of safety. The security arrangements must be in place, we will take care of that.'

'The Trust has agents all over the world.' Stassov said. 'They are ready. I also spoke with the chief of the war office. In fact, we attended mass together. It lifted my heart. He said to me, 'The Red Army are Russians at heart, not Communists.'

'What does the Red Army know of suffering?' Arensky said. He raised his eyes to the photographs on the wall. 'Or sacrifice? They have not had to maintain loyalty in the face of privation, poverty, exile. Our men have suffered patiently, and suffering has given them the strength for this day.' He lowered his gaze as if he had just finished an address to the troops.

'True,' Gyorgei murmured, and Igor nodded agreement. 'Lenin himself said that a defeated army is the most dangerous enemy because of what they have learned,' he quoted. Arensky gave a bitter smile.

I thought of the men I had seen coming out of the Renault factory in Billancourt, with their exhausted, grime-smeared faces. Of people like Grisha's father Count Bobrov, carving wooden boxes, with his sunken cheeks and gait slowed by illness. Of Kyra's father, the doorman at the *Café Cosaque*. They had their old uniforms, their tsarist medals, their shabby coats, mended shoes, their illnesses, their wounds, their poverty. For the first time since Riga, I wondered how such people could rally to fight another battle. Maybe what Arensky said was true, that his own passionate loyalty to the "legitimate" government, could give them enough energy to fight again. After all, they pushed themselves through regular regimental drills at his command. Perhaps, despite outward appearances, they were ready.

Igor and Gyorgei began to talk about neutral meeting places, borders, of ships, of ports. As I listened, something put my mind on edge. Igor's tone was too smooth, too assured, and sat uncomfortably with the twitch of the muscle in his cheek. I recognised the ease with which he used his voice to cover deception and I remembered the way he had spoken about the bare breasted waitress, long before I knew anything about Olga. Gyorgei, too, had flattened his natural ebullience for this occasion, but his solemnity seemed to me to be false, a performance in a second-rate play.

Arensky tapped the letter. 'If this is authentic, today is the most important moment in the history of Russia in exile,' he said. 'Security must be put into place immediately, beginning in this room,' he emphasised, looking at each of us. 'Not one word of this must be spoken outside until I give the order.'

Igor said, 'Gyorgei and I will arrange the meeting: time, place, security. He will arrange the French side. I will make the arrangements with "Moscow."'

Mitya turned to me. 'And Nadia?' he asked.

'Nadia will be with you in Paris.' Igor said.

He smiled. 'As a hostage?' he asked me. Taken by surprise, I shook my head, but his smile held steady.

Igor stood up. 'This is a meeting to be recorded for the future. There are many photographs of Lenin arriving at the Finland station, but there is no record of him boarding the train that took him there. And that moment was also historic. Our return will be recorded from the beginning.'

Mitya looked uneasy. 'A photograph could be dangerous,' he said. 'It could fall into the wrong hands. There must be no photographs.'

'The film will be put in a safe place,' said Igor. 'It won't even be developed until the time is right.' He adjusted the light meter. 'These are for the future.'

'It is for your place in history, General,' said Gyorgei.

'Ah yes, that is important. As an official record. There are no photographs of Lenin, you say?'

Stassov and Arensky sat at the desk, erect and solemn. Igor took several photographs of them separately and together, and then a photograph of them with Gyogy standing behind. 'One more,' he said, and photographed Gyorgei with Mitya. He was unusually careless that time, or perhaps I only imagined that his hand trembled, but if one looks carefully it is possible to see my sleeve in the corner.

* * *

'Arensky has agreed to the meeting,' said Igor a day later. 'He had reservations but I think we have overcome them. And he knows Stassov is incapable of deception. If he still has reservations, you will be here to reassure him.'

I had been waiting for this. I had knelt in front of my icon and looked up at the calm, comforting face as I prayed for success, and then curled up, wrapped in a blanket, trying to concentrate on a book Alyosha had given me, of Mandelstam's poetry. 'Brothers, let's glorify the twilight of freedom,' I read. Our room, as usual, was cold, although a weak sun brightened the small window.

Igor stood over me with his hands in his pockets. I could see the nervous twitch in his cheek. He had the look that told me he was about to make a mysterious request that I could not refuse. From below, an accordion player was wheezing out "Valentina." Played on that instrument, it expressed longing and melancholy. A little dog barked continuously.

'Lewitsky will make the arrangements for a meeting between Arensky and Moscow. We will have roles to play.' Igor sounded business-like.

I pressed my thumbnail into my finger. 'I thought they were finished with us.'

'It seems they are never finished. We have proved ourselves, so now they want us to take the next step. Each step has another step attached,' he said bitterly. Something in his voice struck a chill into me. I desperately wanted him to say no more, but when he was silent, I was suspicious and afraid.

He stretched out beside me. I moved over to make room for him. The mattress was too narrow for both of us. I reached over him and dropped the book on the floor.

Igor took my hand, turned it over and studied the callus on my finger. I had picked at it until it was hard and shiny. He raised my hand to his lips, pressed his lips to the callus, and suddenly pressed his teeth into the edges. I cried out. It felt as if he was going to pull the callus out of my finger with his teeth. He let go. 'You couldn't draw blood from that any more. It's like a little dead fish. Poor little fish.' He spoke to the callus. 'Nadia has killed you and laid you out on her skin.' His face gleamed, his smile made me soften in spite of myself. He gently touched his lips to my finger, then to my palm, to my wrist, to the inside of my elbow. I was wearing an old, faded dressing gown. It had grown very shabby, but I had to save my dress, a last year's model from "Orkho." I had a skirt as well, a gift from Zhenia, and a blouse with a dropped waist and long narrow lapels to wear over it. I had washed it when we returned from the Rue Mademoiselle and it hung in front of the window. It was taking a long time to dry.

'Lewitsky must stay out of it as long as possible.' He looked down at me and paused.

I stared up at the discoloured patch on the ceiling. It looked like a broken top hat.

'He's a good man, considering,' said Igor.

'Considering what?' I suddenly felt like provoking him. I pressed closer and whispered 'Considering what, Igor?'

He smiled and traced my callus round and round with his lips. 'A little Jewish tobacconist in a monarchist organisation! Who would believe that?'

The moment he said it, the chill began to take root and grow.

'Igor,' I asked, 'how was Stassov able to get to Russia and back so easily? He has no passport.'

'It was arranged,' Igor said. 'Remember Pavel in Riga? Nadia, don't think about it.' He gently lifted my eyelids as if to hold me awake. 'He gave a small grin.' Now you look Chinese,' he said.

'He stays out of it, but he sends Isidor,' I said, forcing my eyelids down. 'Isidor is his eyes.'

'Isidor prefers shadows. And if people see him, they are too frightened to ask any questions.'

Now the stain on the ceiling looked a bit like Isidor. Behind the grotesque, misshapen mask I had come to sense the face that should have been there. I was surprised to realise that he didn't frighten or revolt me any more. 'Why does he look like that?' I asked. 'Was he born that way?'

'A pogrom,' said Igor in the same toneless voice he had used when he told me about Olga's child. '1905. The Black Hundreds. The horses galloped over him.' He pressed his face into my shoulder. I stroked his head. He shivered. 'People like me shouldn't take these things to heart,' he said.

I thought about that conversation later. Something uncomfortable rose to the surface, something dark and shapeless. It approached me slowly, coming nearer but always just out of reach.

CHAPTER THIRTY-ONE

I left work very late the next night: The "young ones" as Zenaida Gippius called them, had read poetry: Poplavsky, still in his dark glasses, Remizov, Tsvetayeva, Berberova and Gronsky. It ended in a bitter argument about formalism. Poplavsky denounced Balmont and Gronsky attacked Blok. Names and insults were hurled back and forth. Berberova called Poplavsky an ignoramus and finally Tsvetayeva read poem after poem in an intense but deliberately conversational tone that brought the room to silence. When everyone left, there were teetering piles of small plates and cups and ashtrays to wash. When I finally said goodnight to Tanya, Igor was standing outside with his arms wrapped around his body, as if he expected an attack by the night air. I stopped in my tracks when I caught sight of him. He had never come to meet me before.

'Igor, what is it?' I asked.

He grabbed my arm. 'Come quickly,' he said. 'This is important. We must go to the Rue Bosquet'.

'Now?' I asked. He took my arm. 'Why?'

'She needs us both,' he said, and tightened his grip on my arm.

I noticed the nerve twitch again in Igor's cheek. 'You're afraid to go alone,' I said.

He flicked his eyes away from me as if he had noticed someone across the street. His cheek twitched. Then he looked back down at me. 'I hate doing this. Believe me, I would rather you knew nothing about it. But this is what happens. Whatever side one takes.'

It didn't make sense. Did he mean that if he helped Olga or not, there was trouble?

'Igor,' I said, 'what has taking sides got to do with Olga?'

'I'm not talking about Olga,' he said, and then we were at the Rue Bousquet. He knocked violently and Philippe opened the door.

Olga was a delicate woman, but as an almost dead weight she was unexpectedly heavy. Igor and I both held on to her and slowly, swaying gently like three lovers, we went to Billancourt, to the Rue Jean Jaurès where she had a small room in a dark, rundown hotel. Next door, an abandoned shop had been converted into a small Orthodox church. Icons hung in the window beside notices of a special Russia Day service. Igor and I bowed our heads as we passed, while Olga wept silently. Looking up, I could see the bird cages at her window.

'Olya,' said Igor, 'I'm going to get the Ladinskys to take you to your room.'

The Ladinskys lived across the hall. Olga whimpered in protest and clung to him as he rang the bell. The concierge slowly shuffled to the door, and peered through the crack. Seeing Olga, she opened the door, which released a stench of garlic and elderly dog. Her face was sunk in pillows of disapproval.

'Madame,' Igor said, 'the lady is tired. Will you call one of the Ladinskys please to help her.'

Without a word, the woman turned and plodded up the stairs, as slowly as she dared. I could hear each deliberate footstep, the knock on the door and the murmur of voices.

Olga clutched Igor, pressing herself against him. He put his arms lightly around her and stroked her shoulder. His face was impassive.

'You don't love me,' she wept.

'I do love you,' he said. 'But I don't want to see you so sad.'

'You always come,' she said and smiled vaguely, her eyes unfocussed. Then she caught sight of me. 'But you always bring *her*,' she said, and started to weep again. 'Why is *she* always here.'

'Because she's one of us,' he said. 'You must trust her while I'm away. She will need a friend.'

Olga turned away and continued to weep. I watched her and recognised her tears, her desire for oblivion, and somehow understood her need for the Rue Bosquet. Then I realised what I had just heard Igor say: 'While I'm away.' What did he mean? *When is he going away? He never said anything about going away.* He was telling us at the same time, as if we meant the same to him. I pressed my thumbnail into my finger as Nina Ladinska came down the stairs behind the concierge. The concierge stayed in the tiny hallway, arms crossed. Her fat, ancient dog sniffed at my shoes.

Nina Ladinska took Olga from us, 'Again,' she said, scolding. 'You must not keep doing this, Olga Nikolaevna, it takes all your money and it will ruin your health and your mind.'

Olga laughed. It was her usual laugh, clear and sharp, and it seemed for a shocking moment as if the previous hour had never happened. 'My mind is quite clear, unfortunately,' she said in a voice that made the dog raise its head and attempt to prick up its ears. 'I hate my mind, it's so clear.' Nina began to help her up the stairs.

The concierge stared after us as Igor and I left.

'The French are absurdly suspicious people,' he said. 'Always expecting trouble from foreigners.'

'Why are you so cruel? You didn't tell me you were going away.'

'Cruel? Why am I cruel? I bring her home from that place, I tell her I love her. We're her friends.'

'I'm not her friend,' I said. 'Why didn't you tell me first? Are we all the same to you then, *Uncle Igor*?' I threw the title at him.

'There's no time for that,' he said. 'You know it isn't so. And you *are* her friend.' He looked down at me and I could see his smile, curved like a sabre. 'The women in my life always end up liking each other better than they like me. When I come back, you'll both be united against me.'

'When you come back?' I said. He didn't answer. We were

257

walking back toward the Pont D'Issy. I repeated, louder, 'Why didn't you tell me? You could have told me earlier.'

'I am a coward.' He began to stride out. I caught up with him. I said, 'You were going to leave and not tell me, weren't you?'

'No,' he said. 'I just explained. I'm a coward. I thought this would be the best way to tell you.'

I stared at him. 'This way? You were talking to Olga. What if I hadn't been there? How long have you known this?'

'They told me today. It's the truth. I was going to tell you, but when we were with Olga just now, it seemed easier for everyone to do it like this. Forgive me, Nadia.'

'When are you going? Where are you going? When are you coming back?' I thought, *Say something about this, just for me.*

We had reached the bridge. A solitary man walked his dog. A pair of lovers embraced. A river barge was moored at one side of the bridge and a middle-aged couple were sprawled in sleep on the deck. In the distance I could see the sparkling lights on the Champs Elysées.

'So many questions,' he said. 'I'm going in a few hours. I don't know where. Lewitsky has the instructions.' He took my hand. 'Believe me, I would take you with me, but they said you must stay in Paris.'

'Why?' I asked. *It was supposed to be finished*, I thought. What does *"Moscow" want now?'* Would *"Moscow" direct our lives forever?*

'To stay close to Arensky, reassure him. Or if you like, as a hostage, as Arensky said. Anything you like, but make sure he is at that meeting. Gyorgy will be here in case of trouble.'

'Why should there be trouble?' I asked

He didn't answer.

'When are you coming back?' I asked again.

'I don't know.' he said.

'Well, go then,' I said and pushed him away. I wished that I could push him over the bridge and see the oily waters close over his body. 'Go and don't come back. I'm not going to stay here and wait for you, and I won't spy on my friends.'

His voice was gentle, warm and so close to my ear that the feel of his breath made me shiver. 'It's too late for threats like that, and you know it.'

He brushed my hair back from my temples. 'I'll be here with you all the time.' he said, 'you'll dream of me and I'll dream of you. We'll meet there.'

He's going to invade my dreams, I thought. *He'll come striding into my sleep with his hard body and his narrow smile.* I would be awake and dreaming at the same time. I had no doubt that he could do this. I wanted him and at the same time I wanted to protect my dreams, where my memories were stored.

'Everyone in my dreams is dead,' I said, and leant against the damp stone bridge.

He said, still softly, 'And in mine. Dead people I never knew. So now we can dream together and have our life.'

'Who are those people?'

'I dreamt I was gambling with Trotsky,' Igor said. 'Then I was in a cell with Gumilev and the others from the Taganstev plot. Dostoievsky stood in front of me for a moment and then he went away.' There was a silence. The lovers on the bridge murmured to each other and the woman laughed.

'And I dream of my mother,' Igor went on. 'I almost see her face, but as it's about to appear, there's no one there. Sometimes old Simeon – you remember old Simeon? – tells me my father is coming, but then I wake up.'

'What happened to your mother? Was she Babyshka's friend?' I asked.

'I don't know and I don't know,' he said. 'I don't think about it. Who do you see in dreams?'

I wanted to know more, but his words had shut the door on the subject. I said, 'I dreamt there were bodies hanging from trees in the Neva Park,' I said. Igor and I were murmuring to each other in low voices, like the lovers. The man whistled to his dog. 'There was Papa and Mr Bobrinsky, our neighbour and Mr Baraton the French teacher, and sometimes my school is burning and Natasha cries out for me...' I couldn't go on.

He leant his elbows on the bridge parapet and we stared out together at the black river, the shadowy trees and the lights beyond.

'In my dreams,' he said, so low I could barely hear him, 'I'm always running away because I know something terrible is coming, or I'm running toward something that I know will be terrible. This is a real thing. You understand?'

'What is the terrible thing?' I asked. The lights sparkled against the dark sky. *How beautiful it all is here*, I thought.

'They'll accuse me of unspeakable things.' He looked at me. 'And they are true,' he added.

'What are they?'

'I killed my mother,' he said. 'Unspeakable.'

His face was full of pain. How could he imagine something so terrible?

'But it isn't true,' I said. 'You know that.'

'Do I? Do you think it's true?'

'Of course not.' I started to cry. 'Igor, why are you saying things like that?'

'Don't cry Nadia. It isn't true. I'm mad. Look, you can't cry. You have important work to do.' He looked into the Seine. 'Don't let Arensky change his mind.' He let out a breath, his body sagged and he turned to me.

I held him, puzzled, but also filled with joy that I could give him comfort. *This is why he thinks I'm strong*, I thought. *Maybe I am strong. The one who gives and the one who receives are always one. The one who needs comfort gives strength.*

He drew away and patted my shoulder in a way that reminded me of Olga. Together we walked toward the lights which sparkled like glass music. 'Ah, God, Paris,' he breathed. 'Even if we had never been to Paris, we could still not escape it.' He stood still, looking at it.

'Do you want to walk some more?' I asked.

'No,' he said and his voice silenced all the other sounds in the world. 'I want you.'

* * *

I woke and saw the grey, early-morning mist at the window. I guessed that I had been asleep for about an hour. My eyes felt heavy, my head ached and I felt the deep shame that brought its own kind of pain.

I heard a sound and raised my head. Igor was packing his battered suitcase. I sat up slowly. Silently, I watched him pack the Leica, his pistol and a few clothes. When he turned and saw that I was awake, I averted my eyes. I was more ashamed when he looked at me.

'I dreamed I finally met my father,' he said. 'And when he approached, I saw that he was Isidor.' Before I could answer, he went on: 'The rent has been paid in advance. If Monsieur the bastard asks you for it, tell him so. And take care of Arensky. Remember, behind that beautiful face, you're strong. When you realise your strength, I'm going to be afraid of you,' he added without smiling.

Now I turned my head and we stared at each other.

'Nothing must go wrong,' he said. 'This is what we were sent here for.'

I could only nod. I didn't want to speak to him. I dug my thumbnail hard into my finger and bit my lip. *I mustn't cry*, I thought. *I mustn't.* I smothered my tears and nodded again.

'All right,' he said. He paused for an uncertain moment. Then he was gone, and the room was suddenly empty, except for the line of photographs pinned to the cord, like ghosts, and my blouse, still not dry, which was hanging in the window. I peered around its damp edges and saw him hover for a moment by the front door, hunch his coat a little more tightly around his shoulders, and set off down the street without a backward glance.

I felt as if a layer of skin had been torn from me, leaving me exposed to the open air. Automatically, I turned to my icon.

The face seemed to move slightly and for an instant I had the idea that it was about to speak. Papa and Mama in their frame seemed to hold out their reassurance. *It will be all right,* I thought. *This is a terrible fairy tale.* Igor was under a spell. He would fight back with God's help and emerge the shining protector he had been. We would escape together.

CHAPTER THIRTY-TWO

For a week after Igor left, I sat limp in the chair, or lay motionless on the daybed. I wrapped myself in a much-mended blue shirt he had left behind. I picked at my finger as if I could lift the skin off in one thick slab. After a week, I forced myself to get up. There was not enough money to go to the bath house, so I washed as best I could in the water from our tap, combed my hair, went to the cafe and apologised to Tanya, saying I had been ill.

Now I was late for work, but I felt heavy-eyed and dreamy, as if my head was filled with clouds. I had returned to the Pont d'Issy. A few drops of rain fell in an uneven, accidental way onto the surface of the Seine, where they shone briefly like tiny jewels. I felt the damp through the thin soles of my shoes. I leaned on the parapet, and tried to feel that Igor was beside me, but it was impossible to imagine his presence. His absence was a constant, powerful emptiness that waited for his return. Even familiar streets felt like a new country.

I stared at the outline of Notre Dame, at the broad stone grandeur of it, and felt my insignificance. Igor's green beads lay like fingertips against my collarbone. A few more drops of rain fell, small drops, falling as if they had spilled out of a basket. I touched the beads.

One life held its breath, and in a parallel life, his absence was unremarked, as the days of the week continued to follow each other, as I went to work, served food, washed dishes, went to a debate about formalism at the Green Lamp with Kyra and Alyosha, and typed without comment Alyosha's article on holy fools. The two lives were linked for me by Igor's shirt, which I wrapped tightly around me at night and couldn't bring myself to wash.

Along the Boulevard de la République, old men were sitting quietly on benches in front of the shoddy apartment blocks, waiting for the days to pass. A man lay, drunk or dead, in a doorway. From behind a closed shop came the sound of a harmonica. The oyster-seller's stall was still open on the corner. More people passed. I noticed every face. By the time I reached Tanya's, I realised that I was hoping somehow to see Igor. *I must be mad*, I thought. No one had to look for Igor in a crowd; he stood out immediately.

There were only a few customers in the café as yet. Two young men sat grimly over a chessboard. At a corner table a middle aged woman wrote feverishly in a small notebook, the tip of her tongue protruded in concentration. At a table for two, three elderly women pressed their knees and elbows together, making room. They had been governesses to the children of titled families and had spent most of their lives in Russia. They had named themselves the "former Frenchwomen." Mademoiselle Drogière smiled at me as I passed. She had been the governess of a child called Irina who had played with me in the park when I was small. 'My life in Russia was all a beautiful dream,' Mademoiselle Drogière said to me once. Irina and her family had vanished one night, no one knew where.

An elderly couple sat side by side on one of the banquettes and smoked without speaking. The rest of the tables were ready, covered with paper tablecloths. I wanted to put the Marya Dimitrieva record on the gramophone, but I was afraid if I did, Tanya would notice my lateness. I hurried to the kitchen, preparing an apology and an excuse.

'Nadezhda Mikhailovna.' Tanya, as I expected, was angry. 'Where have you been? Quick, they are waiting for you.'

'Waiting for me? Who?' *Igor*, I thought. *Something has happened to Igor.*

'Arensky of course!'she snapped. 'And the other one. They asked twice. They say it's urgent. First you beg to come back, then you choose to be late!' The bowls of scraped vegetables, blini batter with its little golden buckwheat bubbles, and uncooked chopped meat were crowded together at one end of the table to leave a cleared space where Tanya had laid out a spread of cards. 'Dimitry Sergeevitch wants tea.'

Raissa, a new waitress came in, peered into a saucepan, and poked the contents with a fork. 'More people have arrived and nothing is ready,' she said, and banged down the lid. She was a woman in her mid thirties, with a broad, snub-nosed face and a badly chipped front tooth, who hardly ever smiled.

'Be polite, give them a drink and say there will be a delay.'

'A complimentary drink?' she asked.

'No, of course not. And where is the music? I've told you. Go and be friendly. And put on the music! Loud!'

Raissa tossed her head, sniffed, and carried the bottle of vodka into the other room.

'Really!' Tanya said. 'So stupid. But she is related to my brother-in-law – what can I do?' She cut a large piece of butter and slapped it in the frying pan. She reached for a spoon and noticed me. 'Nadezhda Mikhailovna, I said, take the tea to Dimitri Sergeevitch. They don't listen,' she said into the steam. 'No one listens! They only like to talk, they don't like to listen. Go!'

I hung up my coat, and took my apron off its hook. A bit of food had dried on the front. I picked it off with my nail, putting off the moment. Maybe Lenin's agents had caught Igor. Would they shoot him quickly or would they interrogate him? Was he dead now? This minute? How had Arensky heard so quickly? I felt the wordless suspicion that lay curled in the dark part of my mind.

'No one will notice that little spot,' said Tanya. 'They're waiting.'

The glass stood ready by the samovar, on a saucer with a slice of lemon. I pushed through the curtain that screened off the back room.

The room was smoky and dishevelled. Last night's used glasses and filled ashtrays covered the side table. Russian journals and papers of every persuasion were scattered on the top of the bar. A stained paper table cloth had been wadded up and thrown in a corner. The air smelt of stale food, dregs of wine, late night breath.

The three men sat as if they had been posed for a photograph. Arensky was at the head of the table. The latest edition of *Slova* lay folded in front of him. The other two sat on either side of him: Ladinsky, bald, bearded and portly, in his grey suit and high collar, leant on one hand. Stassov in his shiny blue jacket, with his taxi driver's cap hooked over the back of his chair sat erect, with his gaze rigidly fixed on Arensky. He didn't even look up as I entered.

'Late.' Arensky's voice had its military bark, but his face sagged. Even his moustache drooped listlessly. The room was not cold, but he wore his neatly patched army greatcoat. 'You have been gone for three days. Where have you been?' It was not a question. 'We have something to say to you.' I waited while he watched me.

Finally he spoke. 'I had a dream,' he said.

I breathed again. A dream? A dream could be a dark portent, but for the moment at least, Igor was alive. Unsteady with relief, I put my arm around his shoulders and felt how strong he still was under his heavy coat. He shifted away from me as I squeezed the lemon into the glass the way he liked it, strong and sour.

He sipped the tea, looking at me over the rim. His hand trembled slightly. I saw that Stassov had noticed it as well. Stassov and I both watched Arensky's hand.

In the next room, more people had come in. There was a storm of applause. The gramophone began to play *Akh, Nastasia*. I could hear Tanya and Raissa join in the chorus as the customers clapped in rhythm.

'I saw my brother Yuri. He was very pale, like a corpse, and his eyes were filled with blood. The more I wiped it away, the more blood there was. He has come like that before. It is a sign.' He looked into my eyes. 'What do you think this sign means?'

266

Without thinking I said, 'Death.'

He nodded. 'Death. A warning of death. And not the first warning.' As he spoke his face hardened again. 'Did your people think I would walk into a trap without finding out for myself if it was a trap or not?'

'But you saw for yourself,' I said, looking at Stassov.

'In the Soviet state,' said Stassov, 'it would be extremely difficult to maintain such an organisation. At least to maintain it without the support of the Secret Police. Even the mass,' he said. 'It was all arranged. While I opened my heart, the worshippers around me knew their plan had succeeded. Or so they thought.'

'We know who you are and what you intend.' Arensky's words were like bullets. His voice turned us into strangers.

'Who?' I asked. 'What?' No one answered. I looked at them. Their faces were blank, like the faces of the men who had come in the car that night to take Mama 'for a few questions.'

'Did you really think I would believe people who have lied already?' Arensky's face hardened. 'There is no meeting. The Trust is not planning to overthrow the Soviets. They *are* the Soviets.'

'But Uncle Igor has gone to make the arrangements with "Moscow." It was agreed.'

He spoke a little less sharply. 'I am not as credulous as your people think. And Stassov is not an idiot. Someone here is the eye of "Moscow." I have been informed by certain contacts. They have discovered the true meaning of The Trust.' He looked at Stassov.

'It's a very clever ruse,' Stassov said. 'There is a genuine Trust. It is an anti-Soviet organisation, created in the Kremlin, run from the Kremlin. They have set out to infiltrate and control every counter-revolutionary group in Europe. They use people like you who are concerned for your mother in Russia, or people like Alyosha, who will do anything for a passport. Am I right?'

From the café there came more sounds of music, voices, and the clatter of dishes, muffled by the curtain.

'So I have ordered that these elements must be found and eliminated. These elements in Moscow and their representatives in Paris.' He said calmly.

'Their representatives?' I asked. 'You don't mean Igor? How could he betray you?' But even as I spoke, I could see my suspicions come to the surface and assume a shape.

Arensky picked up the newspaper and shook it as if someone would fall out of the pages. 'You see this paper? On the letters page.' He handed it to me. I scanned it quickly. My hand trembled. There were letters praising someone's house committee, another letter about overtime, accomplishments. Always such good news. I handed it back. 'One of these letters is for me,' he said. 'Never mind which one. And this letter also warns me about this meeting. Can I trust it? Can I trust Igor?' He put the paper down. 'Can I trust you?'

'Don't you trust *me*?'

'You?' he said, almost as if he was amused. 'I have never trusted you. You do what you are told, and your loyalty is to your uncle. If he is your Uncle.'

Ladinsky spoke slowly, like a judge. 'You work with Alexei Mordvinov's Young Russia. They are now known to be a Soviet front.'

'Alyosha is trying to find a future for both sides' I answered.

'I warned you about Alexei Semyonovitch,' said Mitya. He blew on the tea and took a large swallow. 'And you didn't take my advice, so how can I trust you?' He pushed the glass away. 'If you have genuinely believed in The Trust, then you are a fool and a dupe. If you have not believed it and you have lied, then you have betrayed your people. So you are either evil or stupid. But you are not important,' he said. 'There is your Uncle Igor.'

'But you don't suspect Igor…' I began. I stopped. Time itself stopped, while everything, from Riga onwards, formed a picture, like a tale that has been told in chapters, and suddenly comes together to form a complete and terrible story. I didn't want to know, but somewhere I did. 'Your innocence is essential,' Igor had said. My stupidity he meant. That was what was essential. And I had been stupid. I had created my own stupidity.

Arensky smiled slightly, 'I suspect no one in particular, and I suspect everyone in general. Everyone has two faces. Three faces, who knows.' He picked up the tea. "Moscow" has eyes everywhere. I want all the eyes closed,' he said. Although he had not raised his voice, I was chilled by his tone.

I fought back dizziness and nausea as I swallowed the truth. Igor was controlled by "Moscow." The story he had told me about "Moscow" was a pretence. I saw it clearly as soon as Stassov said it. How could I have believed otherwise? Because I loved Igor and I still did. If I still loved him I would have to lie now. If Arensky refused the meeting I knew "Moscow" would blame Igor for the failure. And I knew how they viewed failure: Igor had spoken the truth about that. If Igor and "Moscow" succeeded and I somehow persuaded Arensky that the meeting was a genuine counter-revolutionary plot, then I would have led him into a trap. I knew I could never do that. I longed to betray Igor with every shred of bitterness and anger within me, but I couldn't do it. Not here. I longed to betray him where he could watch me do it, and I could see his remorse, his guilt and his pain.

'Dimitri Sergeevitch,' I began, and then heard myself say, 'Please, please listen to me. I swear to you, you can trust Igor.' Emotion made me sink to my knees at Arensky's feet. A choice had been made. I said, 'I swear, Igor is loyal, he would never betray you. He would never do that. If I thought that, I promise you, I would kill him myself. Please,' I said, my lies clogging my mouth, love, loyalty, anger, clotted together, one on top of the other. 'He believes in you.'

I felt dirty; I wanted to scrub my skin down to the next layer. I wept helplessly as if the tears would wash me clean.

'If you believe what you are saying,' Arensky said, 'you are a fool. And if you don't, you take me for a fool.' He raised his voice in dismissal. 'I have never trusted you. I knew your eyes watched me at the orders of others. And now the others are watching as well.' He stared at me. 'I want all the eyes closed,' he said. 'You are no longer necessary. Go away, Nadezhda Mikhaelovna.'

I stood up, trying to think of something else to say, but fear stopped my mouth. I could only stare at them, as they sat like people in a photograph.

The restaurant was crowded now, full of smoke and noisy arguments. I could hear the familiar words: 'Yudenich', 'Odessa', 'Dennikin', as they fought the battles yet again. I carried plates, cleared tables. The music played. Sometimes people got up and sang. There were occasional bursts of laughter. The evening wore on outside me, while inside I was in a world of pale-faced corpses raining blood, of darkness and threat. *When Igor comes back it will be all right*, I thought, as I piled dirty plates on my tray. When Igor comes back it has to be all right. He has lied to me but surely there is some truth in his story. Such a big lie for such a long time. Some of it must be true. Somehow he will say something that will make it right.

'You don't look well. Eat something,' said Tanya.

'I'm not hungry,' I said. It was my one meal of the day. I was usually ravenous, but tonight I couldn't bear the idea of food. Even the smell of the food I served made me swallow back the vomit that rose in my throat.

'Eat.' Tanya insisted.

'Later,' I said.

'Eat something now,' she said. 'We are busy and I don't want waitresses fainting and falling over. Later there will be nothing but scraps.'

CHAPTER THIRTY-THREE

Headlines screamed from all the émigré journals from *Renaissance* to *Contemporary Notes*: "Soviet Crime!," "Kidnap of General."

"Baseless Suspicions," the French Left wing Press trumpeted in return:

The newspapers on both sides were in agreement on one thing: Dmitri Arensky, last seen on the Rue Emile Zola, in the 15th arrondissment, had vanished.

There were witnesses: it had taken place in the afternoon on a busy street, and there was no shortage of people who came forward to say they had seen a blue car pull over to the kerb, although no one could describe the two men (some said three) who had seized Arensky, wrestled him into the car and driven away before anyone could stop them.

At the café, Tanya seized my arm with her floury hands. 'My friend happened to be in the chemist's at the time,' she whispered. 'She said it looked like an embassy car. She was quite certain of it. The police did nothing. She thinks they were planted.'

Suddenly she embraced me. 'Politics,' she said. 'Politics is not for human beings. But it's human beings who suffer from it.' She tried, ineffectually, to brush the flour off my coat. 'I tell you right now, if this is a Bolshevik plot, no one will ever know the truth.'

Every day, the café was full of noise, shouting, opinion, tears, argument, the latest editions of the papers and whispered rumours. Over and over, I heard the names 'Arensky', 'ROKS', and people remembered the case of Sidney Reilly, mentioned Savinsky and Shulgin. There were stories that the kidnapping had been arranged by Arensky himself, 'and he is now safely in Moscow.'

'It was his own people,' said a man 'They thought he was too cautious. They wanted to replace him. I know that from a reliable source.'

Ladinsky announced, 'I have written to *Le Temps*. I told them: this proves how ill-advised it is for France to recognise the Soviets.'

'There will be a petition,' said Stassov. 'I will circulate it myself.'

Nina Ladinska said in a voice of such assurance everyone paused to listen: 'Mitya has escaped these people before,' she cried. 'In Bulgaria… ah, I could tell you some stories about Bulgaria.' She paused. 'But in Bulgaria he escaped them, and he will escape again, I know it. I feel it.'

'The gendarmes perhaps have the number of the car,' Ladinsky began.

His wife pushed away the pile of newspapers that lay in front of her. 'The gendarmes stood there, watched and did nothing! A Russian émigré has the same rights as a French citizen. Politics are immaterial. But the French police are in league with the Third International.'

Every evening, when I thought they had finished with the newspapers, I unobtrusively cleared them away and read them obsessively, over and over. When I had read enough, I stopped taking in meaning and just stared at the words, which seemed to have a voice of their own.

The émigré journal, *Days*, claimed the kidnappers were Soviet agents, sent from Russia. The French daily, *Le Temps*, insisted they were Germans, in league with French union organisers. Whoever they were, the papers inevitably added "foreigners" and "immigrant intrigues".

Our concierge looked at me darkly as I passed, so did the Frenchman next door: they were both reading *Liberté* which daily featured stories headlined: "Drunken Orgies," and "GPU crimes in France." The Frenchman was an avid reader of

Populaire as well. It ran a story headed "Foreign Plots" quoting the complaints of neighbours about 'mysterious digging' at night in the garden of the "Soviet Lair." in the Rue de Grenelle. The Frenchman gave me a long slow look as I left that evening.

Le Temps warned: "Anti-Soviet hysteria will only react against the émigrés if it succeeds." "Your friends and relatives in Russia will curse you," warned the editor, Leon Blum. 'Remember, Moscow will turn on any citizen with relatives in France."

I prayed constantly for Mitya and also for Zhenia, longing to go to her and comfort her and aching that I could not. This was no time for self-justification and confession. I would only increase her distress. Please let Mitya be found and please bring Igor back soon. I thought, if there is no General Arensky for the meeting, there will be no meeting and Igor will return. And then we would be face to face and I would hurl accusations, one after the other, I would drive him into the truth. As I thought about this, I filled up with the pain of my anger. It blocked out everyone else until everyone seemed to be invisible to me except Igor.

The figures of Gyorgei, Lewitsky and his brother took on grotesque forms in my mind like huge, masked puppets. Even Pavel and Beate from Riga appeared in my thoughts and dreams, like creatures in masks with unknown faces. Only Igor had no mask: the face that shifted and deceived was, I knew, his true face. It was both Uncle Igor and Igor, the face I loved. He deceived me about The Trust, even as we swore our oath in blood. His dishonesty was so much a part of him, I realised, that it was his real self. There was no "real self" behind his betrayals. A gulf of pain opened in my heart, filled with anger, and confusion. I tore at the flesh of my finger and knew I wouldn't be able to go on with this pretence of life unless Igor came back immediately. I had to confront him directly with my knowledge. It was impossible to go on in this incredible web of lies. And at the same time I longed so passionately for him. I wanted to touch him, to feel his familiarity, to see the person I believed him to be. The photographs that were still pinned to their cord, his old shirt, a small sketch he had done for me on my name day, told me that somewhere he had not pretended, somewhere he was my Uncle Igor.

Then there was an announcement in *Le Temps*: a body had been found washed up on a remote part of the Normandy coast. It was identified as the body of Dmitry Sergeevitch Arensky, the White Russian general who had been kidnapped by unknown persons a few days before. The chief of investigations, whose name, incredibly, was M. Faux-Pas-Bidet said that 'no effort would be spared in bringing the culprits to justice.'

I closed my eyes, and saw the Arensky's room with the trunk still packed, Mitya with his small bag of Russian earth.

'Nadezhda Mikhailovna,' said Tanya, 'I am sorry to tell you this, but I have to get a different waitress.' She dropped her eyes. 'I'm so sorry. A relative of mine has a sister Also,' she looked at me sadly, 'there has been some talk. I cannot afford to be associated with any political opinion. I have no choice.' She brightened. 'But you are a clever girl, you speak excellent French, you can type, you will move on. It's better for you to move on anyway. You must make your own life, you understand?' Then she added, 'My cousin's sister wants to start tomorrow.'

She avoided me for the rest of the evening, but when I left, she pressed a large bowl of borsht into my arms. 'It is enough for three days at the least,' she said. Then she added softly, 'S Bogom. God be with you,' and made the sign of the cross over me.

I cradled the borscht as if it was a newborn child as I went back to the Rue des Quatre Cheminées. Tanya had filled it almost to the top and covered it with a white cloth. It was good to be forced to concentrate on the jar and see how little could be spilt. Every spot of red soup on the cloth made me walk more slowly and take greater care. It was imperative for me to believe that holding it steady was the most important thing in the world. It was the only thing I could bear to think about.

When Gyorgei suddenly came out of a hotel and stood in front of me, saying, 'Nadia, thank God,' I was so startled I gave a cry and dropped the bowl, which smashed on the pavement. Broken bits lay in gobbets of grated beetroot.

'Ooh, ooh, noo,' he whimpered as he dabbed hopelessly at the stains on his jacket with his newspaper. 'How can you be so clumsy! Look at this!'

'Go away,' I said. There were red fingers of soup down the front of my coat and on my stockings.

'It's ruined,' he cried, 'ruined! Such good quality. Grand Duke Alexander gave it to me himself, in Nice. I will never be able to replace it. You did it deliberately.' He dabbed at the jacket again. 'How could you?'

'I didn't,' I said. 'But I would have.' I started to leave him, but he shook his head, clamped his hand around my elbow and rushed me across the street, saying breathlessly, 'How could Igor have failed like this? What use is Arensky when he's dead?'

'What makes you think Igor knows anything about this?'

We stood in front of a poster. I was dimly aware of an elaborate design, wild with purples and yellow, green and black. I turned and forced him to look at me directly. 'You don't know,' I said.

I saw now, how under his bright-eyed look, his friendly smile, his mouth was small and mean and the crinkles around his eyes were not from laughter.

'Who else knew?' he demanded. 'Someone organised the murder. Or bungled the abduction. It doesn't matter what happened. It's a disaster for us.'

'It wasn't Igor,' I said. I hated his little fat pursed lips, and his glassy bright blue eyes. 'Someone waited until he left. Who was that?'

'It was such a simple plan,' he said. 'Arensky would have returned from the meeting, everything exactly the same, only he would have been working for us. He would infiltrate his own organisation!' His mouth twisted with rage. 'Now the French police will come into it. The last thing we wanted.'

'It wasn't Igor,' I repeated automatically.

'Who else?' he murmured. He leant against the poster. '"Moscow" doesn't accept failure. They will immediately look for wreckers, Trotskyites… Oh my god, what will happen to all of us? We will be recalled, all of us. Certainly we will be recalled. Unless the murder plot is revealed.'

'Who informed Arensky about The Trust?' I asked. An idea began to unwind like a spool of thread.

'"Moscow" will look at everyone. Even you,' Gyorgei went on. 'Because you must have known something. Or maybe more than something.'

'Gyorgei,' I disengaged myself. 'What are you hinting at?'

His marble eyes rolled back to the side. 'You know.' he said. 'Lewitsky will explain.'

'No. You explain. Are you accusing Igor?' Tell me what you are accusing him of?' I demanded.

'When he comes back, they will find out.'

'When is he coming back?' I felt weak with longing. This shifty little man wouldn't dare make these suggestions in front of Igor.

'I don't know,' he said. 'That's the truth. Only Lewitsky knows.'

I stared at the poster. It was for *Scheherazade*. I stared at it as if I was drugged, not really taking it in. *Who is Igor? What has he done? What did he have to do with this?* All the lies went round like the coloured lines of the poster.

'They say it will be a great spectacle.' Gyorgei's voice hummed against my ear. His breath was slightly perfumed, as if he had been drinking pale lavender. 'Something one must see.' He dabbed again at his jacket and repeated, 'You did this deliberately.'

CHAPTER THIRTY-FOUR

At Lewitsky's shop the windows were boarded up and the grill was locked across the door. A bundle of mouldering newspapers lay on the threshold. A trickle of dirty water ran across the pavement, and some pigeons picked at the ground in a dispirited way. It had an air of abandonment, as if the inhabitants had fled. Gyorgei led me around to the back, down a narrow cobbled alley. He knocked at a low door; after a moment Isidor opened it, stooping to let us in. We felt our way down two uneven stone steps, and followed him to the end of a short dark passage, where he opened a door and ushered us into Lewitsky's office. It was superficially the same, but after a moment I noticed that the radiogram and the maps were missing. *How foolish*, I thought, *'not to replace the maps. Anyone can see the outlines on the wall. They are not so clever after all.* The observation was momentarily reassuring.

One large lamp was on, casting a hard pool of light, which softened and blurred as it was gradually sucked into the surrounding shadows.

Lewitsky was settled back in one of the armchairs looking unnervingly at ease. He spoke as if we were continuing an ongoing conversation.

'So your dear friend Uncle Igor had secrets from everyone. Who were his associates?' he asked abruptly.

He waited while I took in what he had said. A warning voice in my mind said, 'Be careful.' I sensed Isidor shift behind me. The floor creaked slightly, and I knew he was standing in front of the door.

His associates? I looked from Lewitsky to Gyorgei. These were his associates. These were the people he had lied to me about. He had used me in his work for them, told me that it would help Mama.

'Who were his associates, Nadia?' Gyorgei's voice was insistent.

I said aloud. 'He told me nothing. You have always known that, better than I did.' I added, 'You were his associates.'

Lewitsky nodded as if in sympathy. 'Yes. Who were his other associates? Did you work together? It's better that we know now. We will find out eventually.'

My heart was pounding. I hoped he didn't hear it.

'How could she have worked with him?' Gyorgei put in as if Lewitsky had offended him. 'She was only given the cover story. Really, Leonid.'

'Of course, of course... how foolish,' said Lewitsky too smoothly.

He held out the cigarette box. I automatically took one, keeping my eyes on his face. Gyorgei leapt forward to light it.

'This is terrible news about your friend Dmitry Arensky. To lose someone close in that way is a tragedy.' He and Gyorgei exchanged glances.

Gyorgei pursed his lips. 'Unforgivable,' he agreed.

'I never trusted Igor Fyedorovitch,' Lewitsky went on calmly. 'I shall make that very clear to "Moscow."'

Gyorgei nodded vigorously and stood beside Lewitsky so they were both facing me. These people were going to make Igor responsible for Arensky's murder. And they wanted something from me. *Just like Igor*, I thought bitterly.

'It could have been anyone.' I said. 'Read the newspapers. Moscow reads them.' I had kept my voice under control, but something must have pierced Lewitsky's calm, because he abruptly sat forward and pointed his cigarette towards me.

'Moscow will listen to us,' he said. 'The French police are investigating and Moscow will work with them – the murderer will be found. With your help.'

'What help do you want from me?' I asked, my suspicions immediately aroused.

'A small thing. Meet the train from Geneva at the Gare de Lyon tomorrow. Igor Fyedorovitch will be on it. Be natural, behave exactly as usual, lull any suspicions he might have. You know nothing about Arensky. This conversation never took place. You will want to meet the train, I'm sure.'

'Oh yes,' I said, caught off guard. 'Yes.' I thought, *He's coming back, coming back, coming back.* The words repeated themselves over and over like the sound of the train itself. Then my suspicions returned. How could Igor's return help them? He could prove he was not involved.

He sat back again. 'I'd like to know your version of the events around Arensky, Nadia.'

I carefully worked through each event. 'Igor left to arrange the meeting as he had been told. By you.' I began. 'Two weeks later, Dmitry Arensky discovered the real nature of The Trust and refused to go to the meeting.' The two men exchanged a quick glance.

'How do you know it was two weeks?'

'After Igor left, I was away from work for a week. General Arensky told me about this the evening I returned to the restaurant. He had not been there for two weeks himself according to Tanya. '

'Did he tell anyone else? Did you report his decision to your Igor Fyedorovitch?'

'No! I didn't know where Igor went or where the meeting was to be held. Therefore Arensky told someone else!' I said.

'Possibly your uncle's associate,' Gyorgei began, but Lewitsky interrupted: 'Let her finish. Go on, Nadia. What else do you know?'

I took a deep breath. 'Five days later General Arensky was abducted on the Rue Emile Zola. After that...' I couldn't say it, couldn't bear to think about the body lying on a deserted Normandy beach. I thought of the indifferent waves, the tides washing in and out. 'The Trust might have arranged the killing themselves.' I kept my face still and my voice even and expressionless, like Igor. 'It might have been organised from

Moscow.' I paused for a moment. 'Or even from Paris. And who informed Arensky about The Trust?' I asked. 'And why?' I was unwrapping the lies that surrounded me. It made me feel lightheaded.

Lewitsky pointed his cigarette at me and this time he raised his voice. 'That is very clear to everyone. Your friend Uncle Igor almost certainly informed Arensky. He or his associates. Who were these associates?'

Their net tightened. 'If he informed Arensky,' I reasoned, 'then why abduct him when he refused the meeting? What associates?' I raised my voice for the first time.

'That's what we want you to tell us,' Gyorgei said.

Lewitsky put out his cigarette. 'You are wrong on several points, Nadezhda Mikhailovna. I will show you the true facts.' He began to use his singsong storyteller's lilt. 'Why would The Trust have Arensky taken like that on the street? Why would they want the French police involved? These things have to be handled carefully and smoothly, with no mistakes. So. Who would plan to inform Arensky, let him refuse to go, and then create a disaster which could destroy our work?' He raised his head at his climax, 'The traitor eliminates Arensky *and* The Trust.' Lewitsky lowered his voice. 'Clearly the work of Trotskyites. Undercover espionage agents. And who could they be? The murder of your friend has made your thinking unclear. I can understand that.' Now he grew confidential. 'I always thought your Uncle might present a problem. Some of his emotions were...' he gestured, 'uncontrolled.'

'The way he behaved in Riga for instance,' said Gyorgei.

I remembered the patches of snow on the pavement, the early morning, the comfort of Igor's voice, telling me I was part of a great plan.

Lewitsky lit another cigarette and blew out a stream of smoke. 'Murder? Scandal? Articles in the French press? No, Nadia. This is a terrible thing. With Arensky's help we would have infiltrated the largest émigré organisation in Europe, and directed its activities from "Moscow."

I kept my voice as polite as his. 'Why did they kidnap him?'

Gyorgei said, 'If he refused to go, it was the only way.'

'The only way,' I repeated. 'But whoever kidnapped him also murdered him.'

'You are still very young,' Lewitsky said.

I almost laughed. Did they think I was so frozen in youthful ignorance I couldn't think for myself? Yes, they did. Like the marks of the maps, it told me that they didn't think of everything.

'Yes, I am very young,' I agreed, 'so you must explain everything. How did Arensky learn the real nature of The Trust?'

'It seems Igor Fyedorovitch must have informed him.'

'Igor informed him, and then when he refused to go, arranged for him to be kidnapped and murdered?' I asked. 'You will have to explain.'

'I don't have to explain anything to you.' Lewitsky suddenly became severe.

'Not to me,' I said. 'To "Moscow."'

'After Riga,' said Lewitsky, 'I do not have to explain to Moscow. They suspected then that he might prove unreliable.'

Again I saw the street, and Igor's hand as we mixed our blood. 'Riga.' I said. I knew these people were capable of anything. But as I stared at them, I knew something else. They are afraid. More frightened than I am. They have blundered over Arensky. Moscow will call them to account and Igor will pay. The room stank of fear.

'What happened in Riga?' I asked.

'He was told to give you our counter-revolutionary cover story and he refused,' Gyorgei said. 'He had no right to question Party orders.'

Lewitsky's voice soothed. I thought how it would have calmed the little girl in Riga. 'Think of it: a young girl, frightened, confused, also passionate and idealistic. She clings to her Uncle Igor...' He nodded to himself. Then he looked at me again. 'And he to you, incidentally. His affection for you was more important to him than his work for the Party.'

'Peculiar,' said Gyorgei. 'Considering.' He turned away to light another cigarette as Lewitsky continued: 'Our cover story let you believe you were helping your mother. So you were willing to go with Igor Fyedorovitch.' He spread his palms, presenting me with the gift. 'An ideal. Something to believe in. You should be grateful to us.'

Gyorgei turned back to me sharply and flipped his used match toward the ashtray. He missed. Isidor picked it off the carpet, threw it into the grate and returned to his position in front of the door. 'He objected. Talked about "having truth between you…" he quoted Igor and I could imagine how Igor had said it, 'and about his honour and your trust,' Gyorgei finished.

Lewitsky said, 'I reminded him that these were Party orders. His loyalty to us must come first. He saw reason very quickly.'

Gyorgei said, 'He told you the truth in fact.' He paused. 'With one omission. That it was a cover story.' Again that short, nervous giggle.

'He tried to tell me the truth,' I said, remembering the moment, how we sat in the snow and swore our oath. 'I made up the story he told. It was me.'

'And he did not disagree or contradict you,' said Gyorgy, still smiling, 'You were his accomplice from the beginning whether you knew it or not.'

I had loved him so honestly. His smile, the curve of his lips, even his darkness. Did the darkness come from his lie? *Oh Igor, have I lost something that might never have existed?*

'Mama,' I said. 'It was for her. He told me. Where is she?'

No one answered. I heard the floorboard behind me creak again as Isidor shifted position.

Lewitsky said. 'She is alive. We know that. But after that…' He let the words drop.

I repeated the one thing I could hold on to. 'Igor wanted to tell me the truth.'

'Possibly. At least that's what he thought,' said Lewitsky. 'But he was easily persuaded to betray your faith in him. Here

282

and in Riga. You mustn't protect him now, Nadia, or you too will be implicated.'

'Isn't that right?' I pressed. 'He wanted me to know the truth. He lied to me because of you, didn't he?'

'In the event,' said Lewitsky, 'he was loyal to the Party.' He held out the cigarette box.

Without thinking, I took one, craving the obliterating taste of nicotine and the feel of holding something in my hand. I put it to my lips and thought, *a man has been murdered, Igor is in danger from these people and I am smoking with them.*

'This is not a way to live!' I cried.

'No,' Lewitsky agreed. 'It's more important than that.' He held out a handkerchief. 'I know what it means to mourn a friend like Arensky,' he said. 'Believe me, I have grieved for friends many times over.'

The handkerchief was immaculate. I wondered if he had brought it here especially, thinking he might need to offer it. I blew my nose. I thought they are working so hard to persuade me to do... what? I handed back the handkerchief, but he waved it away.

'In Paris, he was ashamed to confess the truth to you,' Lewitsky's voice was filled with contempt. 'He managed to continue to seduce you with the lie.'

'He was very seductive,' Gyorgei murmured.

The word "seductive" and the way he said it, struck me like a blow. I felt my body grow hot and I held back the tears which stung my eyes.

'He wanted you to think well of him. If you knew he had lied, he was afraid you would leave him. Riga is one thing, but in Paris I disapproved. Igor Fyedorovitvh played dangerous games with you, Nadia. I said to Isidor, "How could he have any real feeling for the girl?"'

Igor never trusted me, I thought. *Even when he said he loved me, he didn't trust me.* I couldn't bear to think that I still wanted to love him.

Gyorgei seemed unable to keep still. Now he was standing by my shoulder, too close. I could smell his pale lavender breath. I shifted away from him in the chair.

Lewitsky was still speaking. He sat forward, and became more confidential. 'Consider your uncle's behaviour with Olga Nikolayevna. It was not that of an honourable man. People noticed. And some people were starting to ask questions. One thing leads to another. He was not supposed to attract questions.'

'Understandable,' said Gyorgei again. 'His attitude. After all, his mother's suicide…'

Suicide. Igor had said, '*I killed my mother.*'

'Suicide?' I interrupted. 'What do you mean?'

Gyorgei shrugged. 'You must know. She took poison a few days after his birth. No one was ever allowed to mention her. Your grandfather refused to speak her name.'

Lewitsky spoke as if making a report. 'No one knows the father, but there are rumours.' Gyorgei smirked. 'She was the governess. They sent her packing of course. Afterwards, the old man took the child in. Guilt, charity, who knows? But unsuccessful. The boy was a bastard, and the old man couldn't bear the sight of him.'

'I recruited him,' Gyorgei said. 'I found out everything. It's wasn't difficult. A word here, a whisper there. Someone's friend has a friend. If one wants information, there are many ways of getting it. There was no need to tell him. It was felt that he would be more useful if he didn't know. '

I remembered something else. 'Was his mother's name Sonia?' I asked.

Gyorgy nodded. 'Sonia Ivanovna Marmedova. No one would speak her name, so he was never told, but you see, no secret can be kept completely.'

No, I thought. *Some things are too huge to hold.* 'He told me her name,' I said aloud. 'It's a beautiful name.'

Lewitsky said, 'We are telling you these things so that you will be clear about your loyalties, Nadia.' He went to the desk, and took out two typewritten pages. 'Before you welcome Igor Fyedorovitch's return, you need only sign a statement, a report on his undercover Trotskyite sympathies, his friends among the émigré wreckers: all of it. Everything he told you about the plans for Arensky's murder. Everything that will prove he is an enemy of the State.'

I looked at him in horror.

He held out the pages. 'We have it written already,' he reassured me. 'You only need to sign it. When his train arrives from Geneva tomorrow, you forget all this and behave as usual for a day or two. It won't be longer than that.'

'You want me to be your accomplice,' I said.

'Ally,' Lewitsky corrected.

'How can you ask me to do this?'

'Oh you will do it, Nadia, because otherwise you will be implicated.'

'Let me be implicated then,' I shouted. I stood up. I would go now, go anywhere. Let them do what they liked, I would not do this thing.

Isidor barred the way. Gyorgei took my arm and forced me around and back to the chair.

'Sign this, Nadia. You can sign it now or hours from now. We have time. But you will sign it in the end. You are too intelligent to sacrifice yourself for a man who corrupted you,' said Lewitsky.

'We know about that as well,' said Gyorgei.

'I won't tell these lies about Igor,' I said.

Lewitsky put the pages on the arm of my chair. 'You have no choice, Nadia. Think how he has used you and betrayed you. If you have loyalty, it is to us.'

Lewitsky held out a pen. I didn't take it.

'And if I refuse to sign it,' I said. 'If I choose not to.'

'You have no choice,' he said again. 'If you don't sign it, "Moscow" will hold you responsible as well.'

'Particularly after hearing the rumours about the two of you. If you sign this, you protect yourself,' Gyorgei put in.

Lewitsky continued to hold out the pen. 'He corrupted you, didn't he? Didn't he seduce you?'

'We know all about that. I mentioned it to Olga Nikolayevna,' said Gyorgei. 'She confirmed it. I think she understood what I was saying,' he added.

"Moscow" has already heard about it. Very soon other people will know.' Lewitsky held the pen near my hand. 'He trapped you,' he said. 'When he is arrested, you will be free of him.'

Free? How could I ever be free? I had a choice of traps. I remembered how Igor brushed my hair, with those long careful strokes, over and over.. *I am like you, Igor, I am a coward.* Then the memory of shame, lies, fear and deceit obliterated everything else. *Igor brought me to this place..*

Slowly, slowly, I took the pen. *I am sorry, so, so sorry. Forgive me, please, forgive me.* Slowly, slowly I signed the statement. *The French police will also question me and I can tell them the truth.*

'Everyone sees reason,' said Gyorgei.

'I always admired your uncle's photographs.' Lewitsky said, folding the papers. He might have made a name for himself.' He smiled. 'When I was young I wanted to be a painter, but ... well...'

Isidor held the door open.

Who could forgive this? I thought as I left. I tried to find my feelings of passion, love, loyalty, even anger. But suddenly I could feel nothing for anyone.

CHAPTER THIRTY- THREE

Igor wasn't on the train. Not the first train, which came in at six thirty, or the second train, two hours later. I waited on the platform, watching passengers collect their bags and leave: an Italian family, a businessman in a hurry, a woman with a small dog, four nuns. After what Lewitsky had told me, I knew he wouldn't come and as the hours passed I knew it with a cold certainty. He had told too many lies, he is too frightened. I could see him clearly now: not the protector, the comforter, the passionate, frightening Uncle Igor, but the abandoned illegitimate child of a suicide, an unwanted, unloved outsider, a man who had been so angry he had joined a movement committed to the destruction of his own people. His love was the love of a shadow. For all his power, he was only a shadow of what he might have been. I knew that I was not a shadow, but I had followed a shadow and lived as a shadow for his sake. I felt a wrench of anger and pity. Mama said when you make a promise you must keep it. I made a promise with my whole heart and I had broken it. I had to face him with this, he had to face me, we had to have truth between us no matter what it was.. Clear all the lies away. I would not follow Lewitsky's orders and say nothing. And when I confessed what I had done, perhaps there would still be a way out. I would wait until the very last train from Geneva.

Another train arrived. It was the most crowded train yet, but he wasn't on it. I let myself cry, silently, my tears in mourning for Papa, for Mama, for home and for Uncle Igor, for the true Igor who was mine, for everything that could have been between us that had gone bad and rotten, for the loss of my own innocence. I wept into a mist of memory and left my tears as a remembrance and tribute to the past, as if they were flowers on a grave.

'Mademoiselle are you all right? Do you need anything?' It was a young porter, looking at me with concern.

'No,' I said. 'Thank you, I need nothing.' *What does he want?* I wondered.

Time passed, trains arrived and departed, and I drifted into a hazy state, where I seemed to be half awake, half asleep, in a strange yet familiar place: I was in a car with Mama. Papa was driving. Mama held my hand but she didn't speak. 'Take care of the photographs,' said Igor. My green beads rolled along the pavements. 'I love you,' said Igor. The car drove faster and faster. 'Be careful!' I shouted, but Papa couldn't answer because he was dead. I ran along deserted streets, chasing the beads, but they rolled away from me. 'I can't find Mama,' I said. Then one green bead rolled slowly past me. I stretched out my hand and just as I touched it, I felt a hand on my shoulder and I opened my eyes.

'Mademoiselle,' said a man's voice, 'You should eat something.' It was the young porter again. He held out a baguette filled with ham. 'I thought you might be hungry,' he said.

I took the roll, feeling absurdly grateful, as if he had offered me a kind of salvation. 'Thank you.'

The last train pulled in. A few passengers got out. They didn't linger. It was after two o'clock and I was alone on the platform. The young porter had left. An elderly woman slowly pushed a mop up and down and around. I got up, easing the stiffness in my legs. I had nothing but the rest of my life, but at least it belonged to me. I was alone but I would be able to live without shadows. Again something snapped shut inside me and the only feeling I could reach was the urgent need to plan what had to be done next.

I went into the cloakroom, and splashed cold water on my face. In the mirror, I looked drawn and old. I can type, I thought, I can speak French, I can wait on tables. Wash dishes. I can make my way. I caught sight of the green beads Igor had given me. I have the photographs, I thought. The beads are worthless, but the photographs are not. Long ago, Mama said, 'keep something for hope.'

I prepared to leave the station.

The photographs are my hope. They are the best parts of him and the best of our love. He had been forced to suppress them, to work only for "Moscow" but I had not agreed to anything. The truth of Igor is our photographs, I thought and somehow I will make sure everyone knows it. But first I must find a cheaper place to live.

BIBLIOGRAPHY

The following books were especially helpful to me during the writing of this book:

Nina Berberova: *курсив мой* Russica Publishers Inc. New York 1983

Brassai: *The Secret Paris of the 30's.* Translated from the French by Richard Miller. Thames and Hudson 1976

Ivan Bunin: *Russian Requiem 1885-1920* Translated by Thomas Gaiton Marullo Ivan R. Dee. Chicago -1995

Ivan Bunin: *From The Other Shore 1920-1933.* Translated by Thomas Gaiton Marullo Ivan R. Dee. Chicago -1995

Ilya Ehrenburg: *Мой Париж* Edition 7 Paris 2005

Orlando Figes: *A People's Tragedy* Jonathan Cape 1996

Natasha's Dance Penguin Books 2003

W.Chapin Huntington: *The Homesick Million Russia-out-of-Russia* The Stratford Company publishers 1933

Linda J.Ivanits: *Russian Folk Belief* ME Sharpe, Inc 1992

Robert H. Johnston: *New Mecca New Babylon – Paris and the Russian Exiles 1920-1945.* McGill-Queens University Press 1988

Irma Kudrova: *Death of a Poet The Last Days of Marina Tsvetaeva.* Translated by Mary Ann Szporluk, Overlook Duckworth 1995

Konstantin Paustovsky: *Years of Hope* Harvill Press 1968

Nicholas Rzhevsky,ed:*The Cambridge Companion to Modern Russian Culture*

Viktoria Schweitzer: *Tsvetaeva* translated from the Russian by Robert Chandler and H.T. Willetts. Edited and annoted by Angela Livingston. Harvill 1992

Andrei Sinyavsky: *Ivan the Fool. Russian Folk Belief, a Cultural History* Glas 2007

GS Smith: *D.S.Mirsky A Russian English Life 1890-1939 by* Oxford University Press 2000

Anatoli Vichnevski : *Lettres Interceptees: Boris, Dina, Kot et leur Monde, de 1917 a nos Jours.* Traduit de Russe par Marina Vichnevskaia. Gallimard 2001

Nadine Wonlar-Larsky: *The Russia That I Loved* Pavlovsk Press 1937

* * *

I am grateful to the following people for their help and support along the way:

Roger Jones, Sarah Bower, Nikita Struve, Dmitri Antonov and Ebonie Allard. 'Thanks also to Gerry Beswick, Elizabeth Rutherford-Johnson, Sarah Tyrer, Fiona Bell Currie, Linda Leatherbarrow, Laurence French, John Hay and Sue Booth-Forbes of the Anam Cara Writers and Artists Retreat Centre where much of this book was written. Particular thanks to my daughter Kefi Chadwick, whose enthusiasm for the project never flagged.

£1 from each sale of this book will be donated to St. Gregory's Foundation for aid to families in Russia and the former Soviet Union.